All I Need

Rebecca Carrigan

All I Need

Rebecca Carrigan

Carrigan Publishing
Cambridge, Ontario
Canada

To contact the author or to order additional copies of this book:

E-mail: allineednovel@hotmail.com

http://www.allineednovel.com

Visit the Facebook page: http://www.facebook.com/pages/All-I-Need/123350957744653

Printed in the United States of America

For Worldwide Distribution

ISBN 978-0-9878132-0-6

Dedicated to Vivian Carrigan,
my loving grandmother.
I miss you and love you with all my heart.
Thank you for believing in me,
and my dreams when no one else did.
It's just how you said,
"Everything happens for a reason."
I wish you could have seen
how the real story ended . . .

"Most of us never allow ourselves
to want what we truly want,
because we can't see
how it's going to manifest."

Jack Canfield, *The Power of Focus*

1

Nate

Most of us believe that after we die, we go on to a better place—a place called Heaven and for some of us, hell. But what if it didn't exactly work like that?

What if we got one last chance to make things right before we were sent to our "so-called" destinies—almost like a middle gate that we had to pass through before getting to the main ones.

What if there was unfinished business or tasks that we must pass before we completely disappeared? Could we do it? Would we care enough to finish our lives doing the right thing? Or would we give up and perish?

For Nate, he was going through the motions carelessly and numbly. He was undecided if he cared where he ended up. But on the other hand, he couldn't stop himself from trying. His life to him was sad and full of disappointment. His family had died when he was young, leaving him to move from foster home to foster home. When Nate died, no one attended his funeral. Except for her.

Nate attended very few of his classes in high school. Actually, he didn't show up for any of them except one, English class. It was the same when he went to college. English was the only class he would attend. For some reason, he always managed to show up for this class on time and took his regular seat in the back of the room.

Beside him sat a girl who never wore her hair in a ponytail. It always hung long and beautifully over her shoulders. Her skin was soft looking. She was naturally beautiful, not one of those girls who had to wear a lot of makeup or wear flashy clothes to show off. They never spoke, but always exchanged smiles when entering the classroom.

Until one morning . . .

"Hey, it's Nathan, right?" the girl whispered.

"Um, ya. Nate actually," Nate answered, completely thrown off guard.

"Cool, I'm Serena. Listen, sorry to bug you, but can I borrow a pen?" She smiled, while tucking her long blonde hair behind her ear.

Nathan checked his pockets and pulled out a pen.

"Here." He smiled back.

"Thanks!" She grabbed the pen from him happily.

When class was over, Serena rushed to gather her things to catch up to Nate who was already out the door and heading down the hallway. Serena raced down the hallway, bumping into people the entire way. Nate had almost reached the front doors when Serena called out to him.

"Hey! Nathan, Nate!" she said, as she corrected herself.

Nathan waited, as she caught up to him.

"What are you doing?" he said with a smirk.

Serena stumbled over her words "Well, I, just wanted to give you your pen back."

"You chased me down the hall like a lunatic, just to give me back my pen?" he said, laughing.

"Just thought, well, you might need it," she answered nervously.

"Keep it. I have tons."

"Are you sure?"

"Ya, seriously, it's just a pen. I'm sure I'll survive." He smiled at her and then turned to head out the door.

"Where are you going?" Serena yelled after him.

"I'm leaving."

"But school isn't over yet! That was only the first class! Do you have a spare or something?"

"Nope."

"What do you mean? I don't get it? Do you only come to school for like one class?"

"Pretty much," he joked.

"Why?"

2

"Well, for one, it's the only class I like. And now I have you in it, so it's much more entertaining. Plus, it's not like I'm going to get anything out of school anyway. I mean, I'm not going to accomplish much in my life. I'm not meant to."

He shrugged, and then headed to a car that was waiting for him in the parking lot. There were three guys his age in it waiting for him, staring Serena down. Serena's heart dropped, as she thought about the words he said so carelessly.

"See ya tomorrow, Serena!" he yelled, jumping into the car.

"Wait!" she half yelled, as she tried to process what she had just heard.

The beaten up car sped off and just like that, he was out of sight. For the rest of the day, Serena pondered over what Nate meant. What had happened in his life to make him think that he would never accomplish anything or be anyone? Who had hurt him so badly that he would decide to give up on life?

The next day, as usual, they greeted each other in the back of the room with smiles. Nate was always writing in this black journal-type book—if you could call it that—and it looked like it was about to fall apart. Serena always wondered what he was writing about.

"Hey, Nate," she whispered over to him.

He glanced up from his book. At that moment, Serena noticed how beautiful his eyes were. They were so kind looking, hidden partially behind his dark brown hair that wisped over his eyes. It made her sad for a moment, thinking about what he had said the day before. This beautiful boy, how could anyone not notice him? How could he not be anything but something fantastic? She knew there was more to him, something special.

"Serena . . . " Nate whispered back.

She forgot for a moment why she had whispered to him.

"Uh, ya, can I borrow a pen?" she snapped, as she brought herself back into the conversation. He paused for a moment, smiling, and then reached for a pen in his pocket.

"Geeze, there must be a shortage of pens at your place," he teased.

She smiled awkwardly, as she took the pen from him.

"Keep it," he said with a laugh.

"Thanks." Serena blushed, feeling like an idiot for using such lame excuses to talk to him. She turned to face the front, so Nate would not see her red face.

This went on for days. Every morning, she would smile at him and ask to borrow a pen. He would tell her to keep it, she would say "Thanks," and that would be it for their conversation.

One bright and sunny morning, it all changed. Nate and Serena spoke their normal words to each other, until the teacher came around and paired students up for a project. The two of them were to write an essay together on both of their views of a book they were assigned to read. At the end of class, they both gathered their things and headed for the door.

"So, how do you want to do this? Do you want me to come to your house after school?" Serena stuttered.

"No, um . . . I mean, how about I just come to yours," he suggested.

"Okay, sure," she said, smiling.

"I won't be able to come until after dinner sometime, though. I've got something to do," he mumbled. "Where do you live?"

"Ya, that's fine, um, I live over off of St. Andrews. 756 Concession Rd. Do you need directions?"

"Na, I'm good. I know where that is. I'll see you later, then." Nate quickly turned and headed down the hallway.

"Ya, see ya later," Serena mumbled to herself.

She couldn't figure out where he was always going. What could he be doing every day after class? As she turned and headed to her next class, she thought about how great of a chance this would be to hang with Nate. Her feelings were growing for this boy she barely knew. There was something about him.

She wanted to know more and tonight would be the perfect chance for her. It would be the first time that she and Nate would be together in a room for more then forty-five minutes, and would actually have a real conversation. Tonight would be her chance to get to know him better and to learn what was going on in that beautiful boy's head.

That evening, Serena finished her dinner and tidied her room, so they could study. Her parents were constantly gone on business trips, so most of the time, Serena fended for herself and lived alone.

Around eight o'clock, Serena decided to start reading the book alone. It did not look like Nate was going to show up. At nine-thirty, she got up from the couch and cleaned up the kitchen. She emptied the garbage, tied it up, and dragged it to the front door. It upset her that he had not come. Why couldn't he at least call? She opened the door and dragged the garbage down her sidewalk to the edge of the driveway.

"Here, let me help you," a voice said quietly. Serena jumped, tripping over her feet, and stumbled to the ground.

"Oh, geeze . . . take it easy there." Nate laughed, as he held his hand out for Serena.

"Nate?" She trembled. "Oh my god! Didn't anyone ever tell you to not sneak up on people? Especially a girl in the dark?" She took his hand, and he helped her to her feet. He picked up the garbage and put it on the corner for the morning.

"Sorry, Serena. I didn't mean to scare you. Are you okay?"

After catching her breath, she looked at him more closely, noticing a dark bruise around his right eye. It was partially covered by his hair, but looked to be fresh. It was bleeding at the corner.

"Nate! What happened to you? Are you okay? You're bleeding!" she said, slowly reaching her hand up to the side of his face. He pulled back quickly.

"Oh, ya, this? I'm good. Just messing around with some friends."

She didn't believe his lie.

"Look, I'm sorry I'm so late. Can we still work on our project? If not, I understand."

Her heart stopped for a moment, as she looked into those beautiful eyes. Even bruised and bleeding, she still got lost in them.

"Come on. First, let's get you cleaned up, okay? Then we'll study." She smiled, as she turned toward the house. She led Nate into the kitchen.

"Great place," he said, looking around.

"Thanks. It's my parents'. It gets pretty quiet around here. Lonely at times, so, sometimes, it's not so great," she sighed.

"What do you mean? Where are your parents?"

"They work out of town, constantly traveling. So, most of the time, I'm here alone. It's been like this since I was thirteen." She got some ice cubes out of the freezer and wrapped them in a towel.

"Harsh, ya, I can see how that can be lonely." Nathan reached out for the towel, but Serena pushed it down and gently placed it on his eye.

"Are you mad at them?" he asked, looking her in the eyes.

"Mad at them for what?" she asked, smiling.

"For abandoning you." He now had a serious look on his face.

"Um, no and yes. I mean, I don't know. It's their job. It would be selfish of me to ask them to stay here when they are providing a place for me and paying for everything."

"But there's more to being a parent than just providing, Serena. If I had kids, I wouldn't abandon them. I'd be there every step of the way. I mean, its bullshit that parents take their kids for granted." Nate's voice quickly trailed off.

"I guess. I mean, I guess it's the life I've been given, so I have to deal with it." Serena looked more closely at his bruised eye. Their faces were close, and she loved every minute of taking care of him.

He seemed to have a gentle soul under this rough exterior, acting like he didn't care about his life. They looked at each other for a moment, as if to connect to each other's life for that split second.

"Nate? Can I ask you something?" She paused. "Where are your parents?"

He slowly took the towel of ice from her hand.

"They both died when I was five."

"I'm so sorry, Nate." She took a step back to lean against the counter. "So, who took care of you?"

"I went into foster home after foster home. I don't really have any relatives, since both of my parents were an only child. Not even my grandparents are alive. Well, my father's mother is, but she wanted nothing to do with me." He walked over to the sink and dumped the ice.

"Anyway, I kind of got sick of moving from home to home, so I left. Ran away, I guess you could say. I've been on my own since I was thirteen."

He folded the towel and placed it neatly on the counter.

"I can take care of myself. It's not so awkward anymore. Now I don't have some strangers pretending to love me." He turned to face her. "I have friends I stay with here and there. I had a place, but it got harder to work while school is in. So, I lost it."

"Is that why you don't stay at school for any classes other than first period? Because you have to leave to go to work somewhere?"

"In the beginning, yes. I didn't want to miss English class, because I love writing and reading books. I like learning about what goes on in someone's life and what makes them write the tales they do. The mind is a powerful thing. I believe that improving the mind is the best thing you can do in life." He smiled and stopped his thought.

"But . . . "

"But what?" Serena urged.

"There's only so much a person can take." His smile faded away.

"I'm sure if you just hang in there . . . " Serena pleaded.

"I mean, I was working my ass off for everything and for what? Where did it get me? I still have nowhere to live, no family or loved ones, and I'm definitely not getting an education, which will never get me a great job. There's nothing for me here. I wasn't meant for anything."

He slammed his fist down on the counter. "I'm just passing time. Sometimes, I just wish things would hurry up."

Serena's eyes teared up. "Why would you say that? That's horrible."

Nate looked up to see her eyes fill with tears. Feeling bad and slightly embarrassed, he smiled, and then lightly grabbed her by the shoulders.

"Serena? Why are you crying? You don't even know me," he asked, laughing.

"Don't be like that. Why do you have to act like no one will ever care for you?"

His smile faded, as he saw how serious she was.

"You should never doubt yourself." She choked back.

"You crazy, silly girl. I didn't come here to spread my life story out to you and make you cry. Come on, let's get to our assignment, so you don't fail!" He patted her on the shoulder.

"Don't worry about me, but thank you for your craziness … I think." He laughed and turned to walk away. Serena stood there in awe, shocked for a moment. Then, she ran to him.

Nate turned just as she reached him, and she fell tightly into his chest. She hugged him like no one had hugged him before. He stood awkwardly and then slowly wrapped his arms around her, too.

"Thank you, Serena."

"You got it all, Nate, you do. Trust me, I'm your friend now and I care about you. If you ever need something, please don't be scared to come to me," she begged, looking up at him.

"All right, okay." He laughed, trying to lighten the mood.

"Please, can you be serious for just one second." The tears fell slowly down her face. He lifted his hand gently to her face and wiped them away.

"Okay, I promise," he whispered.

She stepped away from him awkwardly, amazed at her reaction to all this and how she threw herself thoughtlessly into his life. Did he think she was prying? Was it overwhelming? What if he never wanted to see her again after this? Had she overstepped her boundary as a new friend? She stood there processing it all, as he stared at her, confused.

"Serena? I think we should get to work now."

"Sorry, I mean I'm sorry for making you talk about all this." She looked away.

"It's okay. It was nice having someone interested in my boring life."

She turned to head toward the stairs.

"Is it all right if we work upstairs? That's where all my stuff is."

"Uh . . . ya, I guess," Nate answered nervously. Though Nate always played it cool, he was nervous to be in a room alone with Serena—especially her bedroom. His feelings for her were getting harder to hide the more time he spent with her.

He had noticed her from day one and it was amazing to him to be there in that moment with her. If she hadn't made the first move to speak with him, who knows if he would have had the guts to talk to her.

They walked up the round staircase and down to the end of the hall. Serena opened the door to a huge lit-up room. It was very neat and girly, but a comfortable bedroom. Nate stood in the doorway.

"Wow, this is one big room," he said, as he looked around.

The walls were dark purple—almost blue—with white trim everywhere. "Very nice . . . I like." He laughed.

"Thank you. I designed it myself," she said proudly.

Everything was decorated with white fluffy pillows and plushy rugs. On the walls were portraits of a Japanese girl.

"Who's the girl in the pictures?" he asked, pointing to one in particular. It was of a girl standing under cherry blossom trees.

"She beautiful, right?" Serena asked, walking toward the picture.

"Yes."

"Her name is Ayumi. She's famous in Japan." She smiled, looking at the picture.

"You know the Japanese are wonderful people. Their whole culture is based on respect and beauty. They believe in harmony and true love. I love everything about that country." Nate looked down at Serena, noticing how her face lit up when talking about the subject.

"Do you know you wear your heart on your sleeve?" he asked with a smile.

She glanced back at him. "I know. It's a habit I haven't been able to break yet. It's only one of my many flaws," she joked.

"I don't think it's a flaw," he said, heading to the other side of the room, but then stopped and looked at the foot of her bed. On the floor was a lounging area built by many big fluffy, white pillows.

"Do you mind if we sit here to read?" he asked.

"Sure, wherever is fine. This is where I usually sit and read."

They sat down on the plushy pillows, leaning against the foot of her bed. They picked up their books and began to read. He tried hard to concentrate, but he couldn't help but glance over at her every few seconds. It was surreal to be sitting beside her and hanging out. She seemed perfect to him with her delicate hands and long blonde hair. He noticed a green bracelet on her left wrist with cherry blossoms on it.

"Hey, Nate?" Serena said without taking her eyes off the book.

"Yea?" he said, not sure if she had noticed him staring.

"It's been good getting to know you more," she said softly, still not making eye contact.

He smiled and then continued to read. They read in silence for at least an hour.

Before they knew it, they had both dozed off. They slept against each other, safe and not on their own for this one night.

2

Sunrise

Morning came and the sun shined through the big bay window. It was warm on their faces. Nathan slowly opened his eyes, looking around the room. He shifted a bit to sit up when he noticed Serena sleeping soundly on his shoulder. He sat there for a moment, wondering about this girl. Why was she so interested in his life? She was so eager to talk to him and hear his story.

Serena was beautiful, smart, and she was going places. She definitely shouldn't be bothering with someone like him, who would only slow her down. All he knew at that moment was that he was not going to let her be late for school. This girl deserved nothing but the best. He would work hard on their project, and she would ace it.

"Crazy girl . . . " he whispered quietly.

He slowly sat up more and lifted her gently to sit her up.

"Serena? Wake up."

She mumbled a bit, bobbing her head. He laughed, thinking how she was clearly not a morning person. She lifted her head and opened her eyes.

"Nathan? What happened? Where are we?" she asked, rubbing her stiff neck.

"We fell asleep reading last night. Come on, we have to get up and get ready for school." He pulled, lifting her to her feet.

"Are we late? Oh my god, what day is it? I must look like crap. Sorry . . . ugh . . . This is just so . . . " she said, as she stumbled around the room.

"Serena!" He grabbed her, as she tripped over the pillows.

"Relax, we're up on time. It's only 7:00 a.m. It's also Thursday, and our project isn't due until Friday. You're fine." He laughed.

She stopped and shook herself back into reality. "Sorry, I'm not a morning person," she said with a giggle.

"Really? I couldn't tell. For someone who's so put together, wow! I definitely didn't expect to see this side of you," he teased. They gathered their things quickly.

"Help yourself to the kitchen. Make whatever you want. I'm gonna have a shower and pull myself together before I embarrass myself anymore." She laughed, walking into the bathroom.

Nate headed down the stairwell to the kitchen. The cupboards were full of anything and everything a person would need to have a full and healthy meal three times a day.

He smiled. "Nice." Then, he had an idea.

He quickly grabbed some bacon, eggs, and a couple of pieces of bread that he chucked into the toaster. On the counter was some fresh fruit. He grabbed some bowls and cut up a few bananas. Then, he took the melon from the fridge and sliced it up, too.

By the time Serena had finished getting ready for school, Nate had finished his surprise. When she entered the kitchen, Nate was sitting at the table with a beautifully prepared breakfast.

"Wow, this is amazing, Nate." She walked over to join him at the table.

"Well, it's kind of an apology for last night. You know, being late and all. Plus, I wanted to show off my mad skills," he joked.

"Apology accepted. I wish I could eat like this everyday. I usually don't eat breakfast at all." They exchanged smiles, and then ate in silence.

After they finished breakfast, Serena cleared the table and left the dishes in the sink for later.

They grabbed their stuff and headed out the door to school.

On the way to school, Serena carefully asked more questions about Nate's life. In exchange, she told him more about hers. By the time they reached school, they felt like old friends, finding out that they had more in common than they thought.

Nate listened, as Serena told him about everything from her family to things she was passionate about. He loved how her face lit up with excitement when she talked about Japan and the music she loved. He tried not to laugh, as he found some things silly, but he would listen to her talk about anything.

He laughed at the idea of the exchange journals. They were books that were shared between a couple in Japan. They would take turns writing in it and pass it back and forth to each other, so they always knew what the other was thinking or feeling. They would write about their hopes and dreams, about their day, and most importantly, about how much they loved each other.

She even told him about Para Para dancing, which was one thing he could not help but laugh at. But her favorite thing was the Japanese Cherry Blossom tree. She even had a bracelet with them on it that she never left home without. One day she hoped to visit Japan and see them in real life. She told Nate of how beautiful it would be to walk through them, because when they fall, it looks like pink snow.

And when he spoke about himself, she listened attentively, giving him a smile here and there that warmed his heart. Suddenly, the world seemed like such a perfect place.

He felt good around her. No one had made him feel this way ever, and even though he did not share the same beliefs in their future, he loved hearing about what she hoped for hers.

How could all this have happened in such a short time? She was a friend whom he had only read about in books. She was his now a great friend and hopefully something more if things went his way.

They entered their class, taking their regular seats in the back. Most of the time was spent reading their novels and talking about the project.

When class was over, Serena walked Nate to the front doors.

"So, we'll finish our project tonight, then? I promise not to be late this time." He smiled, turning to head out the door.

"Hey, Nate?" she called.

He stopped and turned. "Ya?"

"I was just thinking, if you're not doing anything, why don't you just come over after school, like at four?" She paused, "I mean, maybe you could show off some more of those mad skills again and cook us something to eat for dinner," she suggested.

"Uh . . . I can't. There's something I have to do."

"Nate, I know you said before that you always left school because you went to a job or something, but what about now? What exactly do you do when you leave school?"

She was nervous about asking him this—for one, not to pry, and for another, not to cross the line and break his trust.

"Nothing, I'm just helping out a friend. What are you? My mother?" They stood there in an awkward silence.

"I'm sorry. I didn't mean to . . . but are they the same friends who pick you up each day? The ones you got that bruise from?" she trailed off.

"Look, Serena, don't worry about it. I'll be there around 7:00 p.m., all right?" He shook his head, frustrated, and he slammed out the door.

"Nate . . . I'm sorry . . . " she called out, but he was already in the parking lot, getting into his friend's car.

Serena didn't understand why he couldn't tell her. It was upsetting to her that he had snapped at her like that. She never meant to be rude. It worried her that he had this secret side to him. She hoped it wasn't anything bad. She had definitely crossed the line this time, and she knew she would have to take it easy with Nate.

This was all so new to him. She could tell that he was a good person. He just needed to realize that he is so much more than he thinks he is. She was willing to wait as long as it took for her to show this to him. He was worth it, and she was certain of it.

After school, Serena headed home and put her stuff away. She walked into the living room and sat on the couch in front of the window to watch for Nate. She hoped he would change his mind and come early. Around seven-thirty, she got up and headed to the kitchen to clean up the dishes from the morning. She took her time cleaning, wondering where he was, and hoping he was okay She thought of the wonderful breakfast he had made for her. It seemed so long ago.

She must have really upset him. Maybe he wasn't even going to show up. Just as she put the last dish away, the doorbell rang.

"Nate!" she said, as she ran to the door and flung it open.

But it wasn't Nate at the door. It was someone else. She closed the door a bit, just enough so that she could peek her head around it.

"Hello, beautiful," he said with a smirk.

"Can I help you?" she said nervously.

"I'm looking for your friend Nate."

"Nathan isn't here."

"Really? Are you sure?" he said, trying to peer into the house.

"Can I pass something on to him for you if I see him," she asked, trying to end the conversation quickly.

"Well, I guess. You see, his boss was supposed to pay me tonight, but the last few weeks he's been missing payments and I'm really getting tired of it. Your friend, or is he your boyfriend?" He glared at her. "No matter, he was supposed to show up this afternoon with the money. I haven't seen or heard anything from him all day." He looked her up and down.

"You know, darling, I've seen you two together at school. I saw him come here last night, too. I can only assume he's your boyfriend."

"He's not my boyfriend. Look, I'm sorry he's not here, but I'll pass on the message if he shows up." She slowly started to shut the door, but the man quickly shoved his foot in the door, stopping it.

"I think I'd rather stay here and wait for him. I do need my payment tonight, or at least something in return." He smiled. This sent a chill up Serena's spine, and she tried hard to quickly slam the door shut.

"Now, now, you don't have to be rude!" He pushed the door open, throwing Serena to the ground.

"This could've been a lot easier, but you had to go and be a little bitch, didn't you?" He walked toward Serena, as she scrambled to get to her feet.

The man grabbed her by the wrists and pulled her up. Serena struggled, trying to break free.

"Please, you're hurting me," she cried. Then, he pushed her toward the stairwell.

"Help! Somebody, please, help me!" Serena screamed at the top of her lungs.

"Close your mouth, girl, or I swear I'll hurt you." But Serena continued to scream.

With one hard blow, he hit her across the face, knocking her down onto the stairs. Serena lifted her hand to her mouth. It was bleeding really badly and it felt numb.

Tears were streaming down her face, as the man continued to hit her. She could barely move—it hurt all over.

"Please" she begged.

"I'm not leaving here until I get some sort of payment, so this can be easy or we can do this the hard way." He ran his hands under her shirt. Serena tried to move, but her body was so numb. He continued to run his hands up her skirt, pushing his body against hers. Serena cried in fear, fighting back as much as she could.

Down the street, Nate walked slowly, unaware of what was happening. He turned the corner onto the street where Serena lived. He stopped when he noticed the familiar car parked in front of her house.

"Serena . . . " he gasped, as he started to run to her house. The man in the car got out to greet Nate, as he reached her house.

"Nate, buddy. You should've shown up today," he said with a smirk on his face.

"I didn't show up because I couldn't find my boss. What are you doing here?" Nate screamed in his face.

The man grabbed Nate by the arm. "He'll be finished soon. Someone had to pay, Nate."

"What? Serena has nothing to do with this! This is between you and my boss." He broke free, running into the house. He slammed through the door to find Serena lying on the stairs helplessly. He ran to her, furious, grabbed the man by his shirt and threw him against the wall. Punch after punch, he violently hit the man's face until he fell to the floor.

Nate turned to Serena and his heart sank. He rushed over to her and lifted her head. The man scrambled to his feet and hurried out the door. Figuring someone had to have heard the commotion, he jumped into his car.

"I'll be back, Nate. You still owe me!" the man yelled, as they sped away.

Nate wasn't pay attention to him or anything he had said. His eyes were on Serena.

"Serena," he whispered. "Oh my god, you're gonna be all right? Do you hear me?" He brushed her hair from her face.

"Nate . . . " Serena's voice broke.

"It's okay. I'm going to help you. I'm here, okay?" He looked over her beaten body. Choking back his tears, he lifted her carefully into his arms and stood up. He carried her up the stairs and into the bathroom.

"Don't worry. I'm not gonna let anything else happen to you. I'll protect you. You're gonna be fine," he said, trying to reassure himself.

"I'm going to get you cleaned up, okay? Do you trust me?" he asked, making sure she was comfortable with him.

"Yes," she managed to get out.

"I'm gonna run a bath." He set her down carefully and started running the water until it was warm. Then, he walked back over to Serena.

"I'm going to remove your clothes, okay? I promise I won't look," he whispered.

Nate gently lifted her shirt over her head, keeping his eyes on hers. On her left hand was the green bracelet she always wore with cherry blossoms on it. He slid it off her wrist and placed it on the sink. When he was finished, he gently lifted her up and carried her over to the tub, placing her slowly into it. He sat on the side to hold her up.

With a soft towel, he gently wiped the blood from her face and rinsed her hair. They sat there for about an hour. He hoped it would help soak away some of what had just happened. Knowing it wouldn't, Nate sat there, hating himself for letting anything happen to her. How could he have been so stupid to let her get involved?

This once passionate and full-of-life beautiful girl now sat there lifelessly. It killed him to see her like this. She didn't deserve this. He knew he couldn't call the cops. How could he explain this without getting himself taken away? He wanted to be here, to take care of her, and to protect her. It was selfish of him to think like that, but he couldn't bear the thought of walking away from her, not now, not ever again.

This girl, this one girl, had meant more to him than anyone and anything in his entire life. He realized this now and to deny it would be cruel to her and to himself. He loved her.

"Serena?" he whispered with his hand on her cheek.

"I'm so sorry. I never meant for any of this to happen. I never meant . . . "

She reached her hand up to touch his. "Nate . . . "

He closed his eyes, picturing her before all this. A single tear fell from his eye.

"I . . . " he started to say, as Serena's hand slipped down. He reached over for the towel beside him. Carefully he lifted her from the tub and wrapped the towel quickly around her. She hung lifelessly in his arms, as he carried her into the bedroom and placed her on the bed. Her eyes opened slightly, as she tried to regain consciousness.

"Serena? Can you sit up on your own, while I find you something to put on?" he asked.

"Yes," she answered, as he stepped away, watching to make sure she could.

He scrambled around the room, trying to find her clothes.

"Top drawer, right side," Serena mumbled.

He followed her instructions and opened the drawer. He pulled out a shirt and flannel pants. Slowly he pulled the shirt over her head and the pants up from under the towel. He leaned over and pulled the covers back.

"My hair," she said, as she touched his arm softly. He smiled, as he grabbed the comb from the night table. He ran it through her long hair, and then helped her slide under the covers, pulling them up around her. Nathan sat there for a second, staring at her, as she started to doze off. He turned to get up when he felt her hand take his.

"Nathan, please don't leave," she whispered.

"I'm not going anywhere. I'm just going to lock up. I'll be right back. I promise."

Nate headed downstairs to lock the front door and clean up a bit. He wasn't sure what to do about his situation. He knew the right thing would be to call the police. The men would for sure be back and he couldn't afford for anything else to happen to Serena. He decided that in the morning, he would make the call, but for now, Serena needed him.

He quickly headed back up the stairs with some pills and a glass of water. This would be okay for now, but she would have to see a real doctor the next day. It would all be over in the morning. Things would change drastically for the both of them. But tonight, he would stay by her side.

Heading back into her room, he turned off the lights as he went, and then stopped by the bathroom to grab her bracelet he had left on the sink. He turned the lamp on her nightstand on low, and then sat down beside her on the bed.

"Take this," he said, lifting her head, so she could swallow the pain pill and water.

"Thank you," she said, closing her eyes again.

"Lay down, Nate," she said softly. He lay down beside her on top of the covers, brushing her hair behind her ears. He held out his hand for hers, and then carefully slid her bracelet down to her wrist. She smiled at the touch of his hand.

"Nathan, under the covers. I trust you."

Her eyes were sad looking. The fear was still there behind them, as she tried to act brave. He lifted the covers to get under them. She put her arms around him, moving closer into his chest.

"Serena, I know you're scared. It was petrifying what you just went through. I promise I'm here, and nothing will touch you again, believe me." He hugged her.

"I know, Nate." Her voice broke and she silently started crying into his chest.

"It was horrible. I tried, I tried so hard to get away, but he was too strong." She cried harder, tightening her grip on him.

"I should've been here. I'm so sorry." He let her cry for a while until she softly spoke through her tears.

"Nate, you were here. You came just in time. He didn't get to me fully, but he was so close. He would've if you hadn't pulled him off." She lifted her head to look him in the eyes.

"Serena, he still touched you. He should've never been able to get that close. Your body, it's so bruised. It kills me to look at you. All I can think about is what could've happened." Nathan's eyes closed, as he tried not to cry. The anger in him was building, and she could feel his heartbeat race against her.

"Nathan, you saved me."

Her bracelet on her left hand brushed across his face, as she ran her fingers through his hair. "Thank you."

This broke him. Small tears ran down his cheek against her hand. He held her close, never wanting to let her go.

"Nathan? I love you," she whispered into his ear.

He pulled back just a bit to look her in the eyes. "I love you, too."

He meant it with everything in his heart. He had never wanted to say it before, to anyone and truly never believed that he would find someone to say it to. She slowly leaned up and kissed him on the lips.

3

Tragic Nights

The next morning, the sun didn't shine quite as brightly through her windows. The room was quiet and a feeling of change was in the air. Nate was already up, since he couldn't sleep. He awoke early to finish their project. He wanted to bring things back to normal as soon as possible for Serena.

He glanced over to see Serena rustling around. He packed up his things and set them by the door, and then he headed back to bed and got in beside her. He kissed her softly on the forehead.

"Are you going somewhere?" she whispered with her eyes still closed.

"Good morning," he said, holding her hands. Serena opened her eyes to look at him.

"I'm going to head over to the school to hand in our project. You need to stay here, though, and rest, okay? I'll tell them you're sick, and I'll bring any homework back for you." He ran his fingers through her hair.

"Then, I'm going to the police, Serena." He glanced away from her eyes.

"What? Nate, you know they're going to take you in, because you were a part of this in some way." She started to panic. "I mean, you were obviously doing something illegal, and who knows what kind of person your boss really is. You could get put away just for being associated with him. And . . . Nate, you can't. You can't . . . " Her eyes started to tear up.

"I know, Serena, but someone has to get these guys and make them pay for what they did. It was my mistake and I need to take responsibility for it. This is the only way I can protect you, because they'll come back, Serena. Do you understand that?"

"Nate, please. I'm okay. I promise and you can protect me. Please, I don't want to lose you. It took us so long to get here, to get you. I need you. Please," she cried.

"Serena, I've never had someone who was important to me in my life. The way I feel about you, I've never felt ever. It scares me. I can't imagine hurting you again. It would kill me. Please let me do this," he pleaded with her. "Let me protect you."

He kissed her over and over again. "Who knows, maybe it'll be okay. Right?"

"Nathan . . . " she said, as she hugged him tightly. "Promise me you'll come here after school before you go to the cops?"

"I promise. I'll call them from here." He smiled. "I'm gonna go. I'll be back in two hours."

She pulled him in for one last kiss. "I love you, Nate."

"I know and I will never love someone as much as I love you," he whispered back to her.

Nate headed down the stairs, taking her key with him, so he could lock up behind him.

He managed to reach school minutes before class and handed in the project. By the end of class, he was eager to get back to Serena. The teacher had marked the projects during class and handed them back on their way out the door.

An "A" was written in red at the top of the paper with the remarks, "What a marvelous duo you two have become, straight from the heart. Very good!"

Nate smiled, as he headed to the front doors. He quickly ran across the parking lot and down the street. Every second he spent away from her, he felt colder. As he turned the corner onto the street where Serena lived, a smile began to grow on his face from thoughts of her. He stopped to catch his breath and walked up the sidewalk to her front door.

He checked through his pockets to find the key he had borrowed that morning. Just as he found it, a car screeched around the corner, and a man yelled out from it.

"I told you I'd be back, Nate. Maybe in your next life, you'll do your job right." Nathan turned in fear to see the car driving by and the man hanging out the window with a gun. One single shot and it was over.

20

The car screeched off down the street. Neighbors screamed, as they watched Nate's body drop on the front steps. Serena heard the shot from her bedroom and hurried down the stairs. She flung open the door to see Nate lying there on the ground.

"No! Nathan . . . " she cried, dropping to the ground. She cradled his head in her lap.

"Nate, come on, Nathan, please! You're gonna be okay. You can't die," she yelled.

People surrounded her, keeping their distance out of fear.

"Please, someone, help him!" Serena screamed in horror. His eyes fought hard to stay open, as the life rushed out of him.

"You promised me. You're not supposed to leave me here alone. Nathan . . . you promised." She lifted him more into her arms.

"Stay with me, you hear? We didn't have enough time together. It's not fair." Her tears fell softly onto his face, but he didn't move.

"Nathan . . . I can't live my life without you," she whispered, hugging him.

The crowd of strangers stood silently, watching Serena hold Nate for his last few breaths. The cold morning air rustled through the leaves on the trees. Then, everything went still. For Serena, there was nothing left.

Nate's funeral was held a few days later. Serena took care of everything. She was the only one at the funeral. His casket was decorated with orchids, and on top was a journal Serena had secretly written in since the first day she had seen him.

She pulled a piece of paper from her pocket that she had copied from the journal to read to him.

"You're perfect. You always sit so quietly beside me in the back of the room. I love it that we share a smile in the mornings. I love it that I borrow a pen from you and our hands touch slightly in the exchange. You're so kind, but you hide your true self from people.

"I don't know why you don't care about your life. Whatever it is, whoever hurt you, leave it in the past. Tomorrow is a new day. Don't give up, because I believe in you." She wiped away a tear.

"You're the best friend I've found. You needed me and I needed you. I love getting to know you more, because you make me smile. I hope you'll rely on me. I love how you make breakfast, because I'll never starve while you're around." She giggled and continued to read.

"Every step I made felt lost without direction, but I kept on trying, and it brought me to you. We have a lot in common and understand each other. We were meant for each other, but you just don't know it yet. I knew from the beginning that there was something special about you and I was going to show it to you."

"You know Nate . . . I swore to myself that I'd never let you fall, but I did. And I'm so sorry that I couldn't have helped you sooner. But know this. You weren't alone in life." She stopped to watch, as the men piled the dirt on top of the coffin. When finished, they picked up their stuff and walked away.

"I wanted for so long to be able to talk to you, Nate, so I'm thankful for the time we had together."

Serena walked up to the grave and sat beside it.

"You still got me, Nathan. I'm still here."

"What am I going to do without you? I wish you could've read my journal. I hope you understand that you were loved. I will never love someone as much as I loved you. You were my one. You're still my one. My heart and soul are with you always. I love you, Nathan." Serena sat there, watching the sunset until darkness fell. Then, she slowly got up from the grave.

"Remember, you aren't alone. I'll be with you again someday. Good-bye, Nate," she said, as she walked away into the lonely night.

4

Sophie

It was after midnight when Sophie opened her eyes and looked around the room. The summer air blew in from the window. It rustled through the curtains and across her dream catcher, hanging over her bed. The feathers lifted into the air, and then floated back down to the wall. It was another night of endless nightmares.

Sophie's nightmares visited her every night. Some would be fantasy-like. Others were very real. She had gone through a lot in her short life so far. It was hard at times and some days she wanted to give up, but every morning she would wake up and start a new day with a smile on her face.

She lay there with tears in her eyes that night, as she reflected on the memory that began her nightmares. It had been two years since high school had finished. She had graduated with amazing grades and hope in her heart.

Sophie had a big group of friends in school and a boyfriend who was her best friend. The group was close-knit and did everything together. Her very best friend was Catie. She had been a friend of hers since kindergarten. They had gone to different schools growing up, but when it came time for high school, Sophie transferred, so they could be together.

There wasn't a person in the entire world who knew her as well as Catie did. She couldn't imagine her life without her. In grade ten, Sophie met a boy named Dean. He was perfect. He enjoyed all the same things she did and was very social like her. Dean was a musician and she was completely in love with him. She was sure that he was the one, and he believed it, too—until one day when it all came to an end.

It was the year of graduation. Prom was over and there were only a few weeks of school left. Catie had planned one last party at her house and everyone came. They usually were up until the late hours of the morning, so everyone would just stay over to make things easier on their parents.

In the middle of the night, Sophie woke up expecting to see Dean beside her, but he was nowhere in sight. She assumed that he had gone to the bathroom or something, so she went back to sleep. The next morning, Dean was back sleeping soundly beside Sophie. They woke up, went about their day, and everything was normal.

That night, Sophie's other good friend, Marissa, called her and asked if she could come over. She wanted to speak to Sophie and it had to be now. When Marissa arrived at the door, Sophie opened it for her and smiled. Marissa didn't smile back.

"What's up? You look upset?" she asked.

"Look Sophie, I just wanna say this, and then I wanna leave, okay?" Marissa followed Sophie to the couch. "This is really hard for me to tell you, Sophie, but if it were reversed, I would want you to tell me."

"What is it?" Sophie looked at Marissa nervously.

"Last night, Catie and Dean slept together. She told me this morning and asked me not to say anything, but I just can't. It's not right. I'm so sorry, Soph." She choked over the words.

Sophie sat there in silence, not knowing what to say. She knew Marissa would never lie to her.

"Sophie, I'm sorry, I didn't wanna hear anything like this either, and it put me in a very awkward position, too. I hope you're not mad at me for telling you . . . " She trailed off.

"No, I'm not," Sophie whispered. "I just can't believe it."

Marissa stood up and pulled Sophie to her feet. She hugged her tightly, and then turned to leave. Sophie followed her to the door.

"Thank you, Marissa, for telling me," she said, as Marissa headed for her car in the driveway.

Was this really happening? Why would Catie do something like this? Why would she do this to her, of all people?

That was the last time Sophie saw Marissa. She didn't understand that, either. Why would Marissa just leave her to deal with this on her own? She had been friends with her for five years. They shared family vacations together and more. She was almost as close, if not closer, than

Catie was. Why did she just leave like that? Did she not want to deal with this? Was it too weird?

After Sophie confronted Catie and Dean, her worst fears were revealed. It was true, and when she asked Catie why she did it, all she said was, "Well, if you weren't always bitching about your parents and their divorce . . . " and that was it.

It was like she didn't have an answer and this excuse was the best thing she could come up with at that moment.

It was true that Sophie's parents were going through a divorce and it was really bad. She had confided in her friends and Dean for help through this, as her parents pulled from both sides, leaving Sophie in the middle of it all. Was that a reason to do this? She knew Catie was just spitting out words. It was confusing to see her best friend deceive her so badly.

Dean had nothing to say, except, "Sorry." Even though he said it over and over again, it didn't seem real. What was even more difficult was that Catie didn't say, "I'm sorry" even once. Wouldn't she be feeling horrible right now? Didn't this tear her apart like it did to Sophie's heart?

She found out about a week later that Catie and Dean had been together more than that one time. In fact, there had been many times in the summer, while Sophie was away with Marissa on her family vacation. To lose her very best friend in the entire world broke her heart more than anything had before. All she could say to herself was, "Here's to fifteen years of friendship. Here's to everything that ended up being nothing."

Their friendship would never be the same. It just didn't exist at all any more. It was like it had just evaporated into thin air, and it was the same with Dean. As much as he begged her to stay with him, Sophie couldn't bring herself to trust him again, so she walked away.

Their group of friends was no more. Everyone went his or her own way and never spoke again. It killed Sophie to lose all of her friends in that one act of stupidity. It was lonely in her world now. She had to start fresh, with no one by her side, divorced and bitter parents, and a broken heart. She didn't know if she could go on.

Every night, she dreamed of her friends, and as much as they had hurt her, she missed them so much. It was hard to have people in your life who meant so much to you, for so long, and then, in one instant, lose them all. How do you begin your life again? All of those memories were worth nothing now. Would she ever feel normal again? Would she ever meet someone whom she could trust again with her life, and hope that he was exactly who he claimed to be?

Sophie cried for many nights and still does to this day, when she remembers back to the memories growing up, and then the tragic end that came to her friendships.

When the nightmares began, they were just scattered dreams. Sometimes, there were too many at once, and some were just flashes in the night. The one thing she knew about her dreams was that no matter how bad they were, no matter what the situation was, he would always save her in the end. She relied on him every night.

This boy was always there. In every dream, without fail, he would show up to save her. Sophie had no idea who this boy was or how she even began to think of him. He was just there. She figured it was just her mind, looking for someone to rely on, so she had made up this imaginary guy.

He would always talk her out of bad thoughts and pull her out of terrible situations. She could talk to him about anything, like she always knew him. He was perfect, with dark brown hair and warm eyes.

"Why can't you be real?" Sophie whispered to herself, staring at the ceiling.

"You can't be real, because you're too good to be true," she mumbled, as she turned over and went back to sleep.

The next morning, Sophie awoke to a sunny new day. It had been weeks since she had done anything with herself. She needed to find a better job and do something with her life. She was staying with her father at the moment, and he suggested that she try a job on the cruise lines. He had mentioned that it paid well and the fact that she would get to see the world would be a bonus!

She hesitated at the idea. The thought of living completely alone in the middle of the sea and making new friends definitely scared her. She knew it would be a challenge, but maybe this would be exactly what she needed. Maybe you have to do things once in a while that scare you, to make you stronger.

So, that day, she sent off her resumes to three different cruise lines. Later that week, she was asked by Limitless Cruise Lines to fly to Montreal for an interview. Her father pushed her to go and bought her a ticket. It was comforting that he joined her, for she had never been to Montreal or travelled alone before.

The interviews were held in a school, and people were called into the room in pairs. She thought it was very awkward to be interviewing with another stranger beside her, in line for the same job. The interviews were fast and Sophie was offered a position instantly.

Sophie was to leave in two weeks to a Caribbean destination. She felt pleased with herself after leaving the interview. She was going to be a youth counselor on the ship, running fun activities, sporting events, contests, hosting the parties, dances, and more! This was looking better by the moment. Her father was pleased, and she had something to look forward to.

The weeks passed quickly, and finally it was the night before she was to leave. She lay in her bed, pondering what she had gotten herself into. She hoped she was taking the right path in life, but then again, who knows the right path? Eventually, Sophie dozed off.

Her dream was bright that night, and she could feel the warm sun-rays raining on her skin. In front of her was a beautiful turquoise sea. It was relaxing and quiet—too quiet. She looked around and noticed that she was the only one on the ship. A sudden panic feeling came over her, as she stumbled around the ship's patio, trying to find someone.

"Hello? Is anyone there?" she yelled, but no one answered.

Suddenly, the sky became dark and the boat was crashing against the waves. She dropped to her knees and crawled to the side of the boat to try to hang on. The waves lifted the boat to one side. Sophie slammed her head against the side, gripping the post in fear, and closed her eyes. A voice whistled through the air. She recognized it, but she couldn't see him.

"Sophie, let go. It's all right," the voice said calmly. "You're fine."

Sophie looked around frantically, but didn't let go of the post. Warm hands touched hers softly and she released her grip.

He was there. He looked her in the eyes and held her hands tightly.

"Everything's fine, Sophie. You're just scared of this new path. You're doing the right thing." He smiled at her.

She looked into his kind eyes, relaxing a bit.

"How do you know? I won't know anyone, and what if something happens?" she asked, as she started to tear up.

"Sometimes, you need to take a chance in life, even if you can't see how it's going to work out. Trust me," he said calmly.

"Trust you? I don't even know you. Where did you come from? Who are you?" she said, not expecting an answer.

The last few times she had attempted this conversation with him, he would just smile and fade away into the night.

It was much different this time. He lifted her to her feet.

"Think of me as a guardian angel, as silly as that sounds."

"A guardian angel? How did I get you?" she asked.

"I chose you," he said back, brushing a strand of hair from her face.

"Why?"

"Because you're a good person, Sophie, and you're swaying away from your destiny's path. I'm going to help you stay on it. So, you need to trust me, all right? Look." He pointed out to the sea.

The sun had returned and the sea was calm. It was amazing looking. The sounds of the ocean filled the air along with the crowd behind her. She could hear sounds of children playing and families laughing. She couldn't believe how quickly it changed. She turned back to him quickly with a smile on her face, but he was gone.

The next morning, she woke up very early. She packed the last bit of her stuff into her suitcase and closed it tightly.

Sophie sat on her bed for a just a moment, trying to prepare herself.

"If you truly are my guardian angel, you better be right about this. Please don't let me down." With a deep breath, she gathered her things and headed for the door, looking at her bedroom one last time.

"Oh my gosh, Barkley!" She ran back in and grabbed the stuffed dog off the end of the bed, tucked him under her arm, and then headed downstairs. Her father waited at the door.

"Seriously, Sophie? You're twenty-one years old. You don't need to take that ragged old doll with you," he said with a laugh.

"I've had Barkley since I was five, and he reminds me of home." She smiled, looking at the old fluffy dog. He had been the only thing consistent in her life. She felt silly for taking him, but it calmed her soul.

"Whatever, Sophie, get in the car." He lifted her suitcase and took it over to the trunk of the car. Her father's little dog came running over and jumped up on Sophie. He was a Maltese, a chubby, old, little white thing.

"See ya, Falcor!" she said, rubbing his head gently.

She jumped in and watched her house fade away down the street, as they drove off to the airport.

At the airport, she said good-bye to her father and walked down the hallway to the terminal. She choked back tears, trying to stay strong.

Boarding the plane was quick, and before she knew it, she was in the air. She pulled Barkley from her backpack and leaned against the window. The smell of Barkley's hair reminded her of everyone and everything she had left behind at home. She closed her eyes and tried to sleep.

"You see? So far so good, eh?" a familiar voice said.

She opened her eyes, and to her left was that boy again.

"You!" she yelled.

"Shhhh. No need to yell. People will think you're crazy. No one else can see me, just you. So, I wouldn't make too big of a scene." He laughed.

"Oh, sorry," she whispered.

"Hey, it's cool with me. I'm not the crazy one."

"What are you doing here?"

"Just checking in on you. That's all."

"Okay." Then, the flight attendant interrupted her.

"Would you like a drink or some crackers?" she asked politely.

"Umm." Sophie looked at the boy, and then back at the flight attendant.

"Are you all right, dear?" she asked Sophie with concern.

"Ya, oh ya, I'm fine. Water and crackers, please." The flight attendant handed her a bottle of water and a bag of crackers, and then slowly walked away.

"Wow, way to look weird." The boy laughed. "Can I have a cracker?" He said putting his hand out.

"Can you even eat? I mean, if you're not really there? I mean, ugh. I don't know what I mean. I'm so confused." She put her face in her hands.

"What are you confused about?"

Sophie peaked out between her fingers. "You!"

She opened the crackers, pulled one out, slowly handing it to him.

"Thank you," he said, taking the cracker from her hands. His hands were cool against hers. She watched him eat it just as normal as could be.

"What? You've never seen someone eat a cracker before?" he said, taking the water bottle from her hands, opening it, and taking a sip.

"How can you? If you're not real, how can you be touching me and eating things and . . . "

"Because I am real. I'm real for you. To everyone else, I'm not real, so they can't see me. It's a guardian angel thing." He smiled. "Sophie, relax. Sometimes, you won't understand everything in your life, so just go with it, all right?"

"How do I know I can trust you? I know nothing about you and you claim to be my angel that's guiding me on the right path in life. Do you know how crazy that sounds?"

"Well, what do you want to know?" he asked, turning more toward her.

She thought for a moment, "Okay, for one, what is your name?"

"Nathan, Nate. Either one works."

"Nathan . . . all right. How old are you, Nathan?"

"When I died, I was twenty-four, but that was years ago." His smile left his face.

"When you died?" she said sadly.

"It's a long story, not important right now," he said, changing the subject. "Are you ready for this job?"

She could see that he wasn't comfortable with where that was going, so she went along with his question.

"I think so."

"I know so. You're a fun person. This job is going to be amazing for you, and just what you need to change your outlook."

"Why? What's wrong with my outlook?"

"Nothing. It's just that you're getting too isolated from people and things. It's not good for you. You need to get out there and become more independent. This will be a good experience, if anything."

She looked at him, confused. "What do you mean if anything? Is this not the right choice now? What the hell, Nathan?"

Sophie sat up in her chair and started to panic again.

"Sophie, you're gonna give yourself a heart attack. Relax, crazy girl," he joked.

"It's fine. You're supposed to do this. I'm gonna be here the entire time if you need me. I won't exactly be in sight all the time, because people will really think you're crazy if you're always talking to me, but you get the idea."

This whole thing confused her, so she gave up on the questions for the time being.

"You know, ever since you first appeared in my dreams, I've felt comfortable around you. It's like I've always known you. Maybe we knew each other in another life, right?" She smiled at him.

"Maybe" he said, smiling back. "You do remind me of someone I used to know, so that's why I chose you."

Sophie placed her hand on his and looked him in the eyes.

"It's been good getting to know you better. Don't let me down, okay?"

A moment from his past flashed in his mind, as he stared at her in silence for a moment.

"I won't. I promise."

They exchanged smiles, and then he was gone.

It was a quick flight to Florida, and Sophie was feeling a bit more confident about the idea after Nathan's talk. She stepped off the plane into the warm air, taking a second to breathe it all in. Then, she followed the crowd to the baggage claim.

Written on her itinerary was an information desk she was to visit. They would place her on the right bus that would head to her ship's port. It was crowded and hectic at the info desk.

She asked one of the agents which bus she should head to. The lady in blue directed her to one of the buses out front and quickly disappeared. She handed her bag to the driver to put underneath.

"Excuse me? Is this the bus heading for Port Canaveral? I'm working on the Limitless Cruise Lines."

"Yes, yes, miss, get on," the driver insisted. Feeling fairly confident, though rushed, she boarded the bus and took her seat.

The bus ride was about three hours. People were beginning to make conversation with each other to pass time.

"So, what ship are you working on?" Sophie asked the woman beside her.

"I'm working on the World's Vacay as a server. What about you?"

"I'll be working on the Limitless Ship as a youth counselor."

"The Limitless?" the woman questioned.

"Ya, why?"

"Sweetie, this bus is heading to Tampa Bay to the World's Vacay only," she said with concern.

"What? Are you sure? I asked the bus driver and the woman inside, and they both said this was the bus!" Sophie began to freak out.

As the bus came to a stop, all the passengers piled out to grab their bags. The bus driver urged her to get off the bus. She picked up her bag and headed to the big ship in front of her. There was a line for the crew and a separate one for guests. As she reached the front of the line, she asked the boarding agent if this was the Limitless Ship.

"The Limitless? No, missy, this is the World's Vacay. Is this the ship you're supposed to be on?" He checked the papers in Sophie's hand. "I'm sorry, love, but this isn't your ship."

"What?" Sophie felt a lump in her throat.

This was not starting off so well, and now she was in the wrong city, at the wrong boat, and now officially scared.

"What should I do? You have to help me, please. I have no idea where I am." She began to tear up again. The man asked her to wait there, as he went to speak to the Youth Staff Manager, and then he quickly returned, asking her to follow him to the ship.

At the entrance to the ship, she met Rose, the Manager of the Youth Staff. She was a wonderful person and very helpful. They had contacted the Limitless and let them know that one of their staff had gotten on the wrong bus and would have to meet up with them, because the ship had already left port.

"Sophie is it?" Rose asked politely. "Sweetie, your gonna have to stay in a hotel tonight and get on a flight to the Bahamas to catch up with your ship tomorrow, okay?"

This scared Sophie even more. Now, she had to stay in a strange city alone, fly again, and travel alone in a car in the Bahamas to her ship. Tears began to fill her eyes, and she just wanted to leave and go home. She was certain this had to be a sign. This is the wrong road for sure!

Following Rose' instructions, Sophie got in a taxi and headed to the hotel that the company had arranged for her. It was an older hotel, and kind of scary with nothing around it. Down the street, there was a diner and a gas station. She hurried inside to check in.

The inside of the hotel was clean, but not very modern. It had an uncomfortable feeling. At the front desk, there was a large, dark woman. "Can I help you?"

"Yes, I have a room on hold for me. The name is Sophie Reid."

The woman looked through her records and found the reservation.

"Here it is. One bed or two? Are you here alone?" the woman asked.

It made Sophie nervous to say that she was by herself.

"One bed, please, and can you tell me a cab number, so that I can get a ride in the morning to the airport."

"We'll make the arrangements for the cab. You just tell us what time you need to be there."

"My flight leaves at 8:00 a.m., so I would like to be there by 6:30 a.m., please." The woman nodded and notified her that a cab would be waiting out front for her at 6:00 a.m.

"So, how will you be paying for this?" the woman asked.

"What do you mean? The company isn't paying for my room?" Sophie choked.

"No, mam. They only make the reservations, but they informed us that they booked your flight, and we have your itinerary here for you." She handed it over to Sophie, waiting for her answer.

" I, I don't have any money with me. I'll have to call my dad."

The woman handed her the phone.

"Normally, we wouldn't take credit cards over the phone, but because this is a rare situation, we'll help you out."

Sophie finally got a hold of her father and asked him to pay for her room. After completing all the plans and confirming payment, she headed outside toward the back of the hotel to her room. It was bare in the parking lot except for one or two guests. It felt uneasy.

This hotel wasn't in a highly populated area, and there were no businesses around except for that diner and gas station. People could definitely go missing here and no one would see anything. She was sure of it.

It looked like one of those hotels where the staff is in on the killing and stuff. Sophie gave her head a shake before she frightened herself too much. She quickly walked around the building to the back and up the metal staircase to her room on the second floor. She went inside and locked the door behind her.

"Seriously? There's no one in this friggen hotel! Why did I get a room all the way at the back?" She threw her bags on the bed and flopped down on top. She was not very hungry, but daylight was fading fast, so she decided she had better go get something to eat.

She took her cell phone and grabbed a small pair of scissors from her makeup case. She thought this would be her only weapon, if needed. She opened the door and peered out. No one was around. She quickly shut the door and headed down the stairs and across the parking lot. So far so good, she thought.

She hurried down the street and into the diner. She quickly noticed that she was the only white person around. Normally, this wouldn't bother her, but this time, it did. She got her food and left immediately. A group of guys outside the restaurant whistled and called to her, as she passed them on the way out.

She began to run down the street, not looking back. She didn't stop until she had reached her room. She quickly went inside and locked the door.

The bed was hard, but she sat on it and flicked on the television. Eating her dinner, she pondered over maybe heading home the next day.

"Yuk! Tastes like it's been sitting for a while!" she said, as she choked the food back. Thoughts filled her head. She knew she would have to ask her father again for money if she wanted to go home. He had just flown her all the way out there, and then paid for a hotel. She knew he would be disappointed if she gave up. Sophie didn't have the guts to ask him anyway, so she would have to hang in there and see this through.

It was around seven o'clock when Sophie decided to call her grandmother. The phone rang a few times before her grandmother picked up.

"Hello?" her gram said.

"Gram? Hi! It's me." Her eyes started to tear up.

"Hi. Hun! How are things? Are you there?" Sophie sat in silence for a moment. Her grandmother could tell by her voice that something was wrong.

"Sophie? What's wrong?" she asked. Sophie began to tell her the entire story. When she was finished, her grandmother took a moment to let it sink in, as she listened to her granddaughter cry.

"Honey, you're fine. I understand this is scary, but you're a strong, smart girl. You'll get through this. It's just one night." She listened for a moment, as Sophie sniffled in the background.

"Sophie. You've been through a lot in the last few years, and I think you need this. It'll make you stronger. I promise."

Sophie cleared her throat. "Then, why does it feel like I'm being shipped out? If people cared so much for me, why would they want to send me away?"

"No one's sending you away. Your father was just trying to get you back on your feet, dear."

"Seems a little harsh. I miss you, though," Sophie whispered to Gram.

"I miss you, too. I promise you'll be fine, Sophie. Just keep trying."

"Fine," she said, wiping her eyes. "Well, I better get to bed, since I have an early flight tomorrow. I love you."

"I love you, too, and remember this, Sophie—I'm always on your side, all right? Don't forget that ever. Everything happens for a reason. Have a good sleep."

"Thanks, Gram, goodnight." She hung up the phone and took a deep breath.

She got up from her bed and decided that a hot shower would help her relax. She grabbed her pajamas from her suitcase and headed to the bathroom. She stood in the shower for a good forty minutes before the water started to get cold, so she stepped out and dried off.

On the counter were her pajamas. She shivered, as she put them on. The refection in the mirror was foggy, so she wiped it off with her towel. The girl staring back at her was a stranger to her. She couldn't feel the soul that belonged in her body. What was she doing with herself?

After she was dressed, she opened the door and let the steam float out into the room. As she walked around the corner, she squeezed the water from the ends of her hair. She headed for her suitcase beside her bed and knelt down beside it. She opened the side pocket and pulled out her comb.

Suddenly, she felt a hand placed down gently on her shoulder. Startled, Sophie fell back onto the ground, kicking and swinging her comb in the air, as she screamed in fear.

"Hey, hey! Sophie, stop! I surrender!" A voice laughed, as he fell back onto the bed.

Sophie opened her eyes to see Nathan. She sat there with tears in her eyes.

"Sophie?" Nathan said, kneeling down beside her. She quickly covered her face.

"Sophie, I'm sorry. I didn't mean to scare you," he said softly. "Look at me."

She slowly lifted her face from her hands.

"Nathan," she cried, as she fell into his arms.

He wrapped his arms around her and hugged her tightly. They sat there for a moment in silence.

"Hey, Soph, come on. Look at me." Nathan rubbed her back, trying to comfort her.

"I'm sorry, I just I don't know what to say" she said, as she stumbled over her words.

"Come on, crazy girl, let's get you into bed." He helped her up and pulled back the sheets on the bed. She climbed in, still gripping her comb. Nathan sat on the bed beside her.

"Here, give me that thing before you hurt someone," he said, taking the comb from her hand. "Move up a bit."

Sophie scooted herself forward a bit on the bed, as Nate moved in behind her on the bed.

He began to comb through Sophie's wet hair.

With his legs wrapped around Sophie's body, she rested her arms on his knees.

Nathan was a lot taller than Sophie, and his body was fit and always smelt so good. Something about him all together totally relaxed her. She felt safe with him around. When he finished, he placed the comb on her nightstand, and slipped out from behind her to sit by her side.

"Thank you, Nathan," she whispered. He got up and turned off the television.

"You should get to bed."

"Wait, Nate, please don't go," she pleaded with him. He paused as this sentence burned a hole in his heart. He walked back over to the bed and sat beside her.

"Will you stay with me tonight, please? This place scares me. Please, I need you."

"I don't think I'm allowed to, Sophie."

"Nathan, please. Just this once." She stared at him with puffy eyes from crying.

"You're going to get me into trouble. This is against our rules, you know," he said, joining her under the covers.

They lay there facing each other. Nathan brushed a hair hanging over Sophie's eye.

"What's going on in that crazy mind of yours?" he asked, smiling.

"Nothing, I mean, I don't know. I feel like, I have no idea what I'm doing. I can't even think straight. There are so many thoughts in my head. It's frustrating. Like I'm lost."

"I know, but it's part of life, Soph. It sucks and it's scary not knowing things, but everything will work out, and you just have to trust that your life will be amazing."

"Did you when you were alive? Was it everything you wanted it to be?" she asked.

"No. It wasn't," he said sadly. "I gave up on my life too early, I had no one to care for me, and no one I had to worry about. I didn't try for anything. I just gave up. Until one day . . . " he trailed off.

"What? Until one day . . . What happened?" she begged him.

"I met someone, and she believed in me. She saw things in me that I'd never seen before. She actually loved me." He paused for a moment, remembering.

"She was kind and made me feel like no one had before. I didn't understand why I would deserve her. She was the only person I let my guard down with. I knew I could be myself around her. It was so easy with her." He paused.

"She deserved better. I should have been better for her." He looked away from Sophie's eyes.

"Did you love her?" Sophie asked.

Nathan didn't look at her. She could see the corner of his eye begin to water, but he quickly blinked it away.

"Yes," he whispered. Sophie turned his face back to hers.

"Nathan," she said sadly.

He wiped his eyes again and cleared his throat.

"It was years ago. It doesn't matter now. I've missed my chance. But you, Sophie, this is your chance. Don't waste your life. Get out there and try things and meet people. I know what you've been through. I've been watching you for the last eight years. You have such a love for life, or you used to. But it seems fake now, Soph."

She didn't say anything.

"I know you feel like you're alone, but you're not. You know, I didn't have someone to watch over me and guide me, but you do.

"You know, I'm breaking a lot of rules for you. I'm only supposed to stop in and give you words of wisdom and be gone. I'm supposed to watch from above, not by your side." He laughed.

"Why has everything been so sad, Nate? What did I do to deserve losing all my friends? I lost my best friend and my boyfriend, and even my family fell apart. I'm a good person, Nate. I never do anything to hurt anybody. I just don't get it. Now, I have to do all this searching to find myself again?" she said, as she squeezed her pillow in frustration.

"I know, Soph, it isn't fair. You don't deserve that in my opinion, but this is what fate has brought you and it has a good reason if you'll just hang in there. You'll meet more friends and they'll be better, I swear. As for the guy . . . He was an idiot to cheat on you. Any guy would be happy to be with you, Sophie. You're beautiful, smart, and you have one of the best hearts I've seen in a long time. Promise me you'll keep trying, Soph."

"Why? It doesn't seem worthwhile, Nate," she sighed.

"Why? Just because you can't see how things are going to manifest? It doesn't mean they can't. I didn't believe in my life, and by the time someone had reached me, it was too late. If I'd trusted her words, I would've had a long and happy life, Sophie. I could've loved someone who loved me in return."

She took Nathan's hand in hers and held it close to her heart.

"I'm sorry, Nate."

"I just want you to have everything you want in life."

"I'll try, but you have to promise me something."

"What?" Nathan asked confused.

"You have to promise me that you'll be happy, too, from now on. You can still have a happy life, or whatever you're living. You deserve it, too."

"Soph, my life is over, but thank you. You're sweet"

"Promise me, Nate." She squeezed his hand.

"Fine, Sophie," he said, as he pulled his hand away. "Now go to sleep, crazy girl. You have to get up early."

"Don't leave, you promised, Nate," she said, taking his hand again.

"I know. I'm not going anywhere."

Sophie closed her eyes, as Nathan lay there, watching her doze off.

He leaned over once she was asleep and gently kissed her forehead.

"Good night, Sophie."

5

The Limitless Ship

The next morning, Sophie awoke to her alarm on her phone. She slowly sat up, looking around for Nate, but he was nowhere in sight. She got up and dressed for another day of traveling. After packing her things away, she headed out the door to the front entrance to check out. There were muffins and juice in the lobby. Sophie looked over them, as her stomach growled, and picked out a chocolate muffin and an apple juice, and then sat on the patio to wait for her cab.

The drive to the airport was short. She then boarded a very small plane. It had to be the smallest plane in the world, with one seat on each side! Luckily, the plane ride was only an hour. As the plane landed, she looked out the window to the bright landscape of the Caribbean. Stepping off the plane, she was pounded by the heat of the sun. She followed the crowd inside to the baggage claim.

After going through some crazy security and guys holding guns, she went outside and got in a cab to head to her ship's port in Nassau, the Bahamas. Sophie gripped the sides of the van, as the drivers there drove like they were in a high-speed chase! The vans only went about sixty, but they were all over the road, if you could call it a road. They finally arrived at the port an hour later.

She slowly walked up to the ship, and looking at its massive size, her heart calmed finally. A weight lifted from her shoulders, as a feeling that she was safe and sound filled her body in place of fear. The Manager of the Youth Staff greeted her at the entrance.

"Hello there! You must be Sophie. You poor thing, you finally made it." She laughed. "I'm Jan, your boss."

"Yea, it was so crazy this whole adventure." Sophie smiled.

"Well, you're here now and that's all that matters. I'll take you to your room, so you can meet your roommate, and then I'll show you around the ship. Sound good?"

Sophie nodded, as she followed Jan through security and down the hall. Jan was a very short woman, from England. She had bleach blonde short hair and was kind of stocky.

Sophie thought it was funny that this little thing was her boss, but then again, sometimes you can't judge people. She looked like she could pack a punch. She spoke very tough and bossy-like, as she led Sophie down a small hallway to a room.

"Here's where you'll stay," she said, knocking on the door. A young girl opened the door. She was tall, blonde, and very excited.

"Hey, Jan! Is this my roommate?" Before Jan could answer her, she grabbed the bag from Sophie's hand and took it inside.

"Hi! I'm Chelsea! Where are you from? I know it's Canada, but whereabouts?" she asked with a smile.

"Cambridge, Ontario," Sophie answered. She thought it was great that her roommate was so welcoming.

"Cambridge? No way! I'm from Kitchener! Shut up, this is awesome!" she yelled.

"I assume that's near you?" Jan asked Chelsea.

"Yea! It's like fifteen minutes from me, so weird! Oh my god, do you like Britney?" She laughed, holding up a C.D.

"Ya, she's my favorite!" Sophie giggled, as Chelsea's face lit up.

"It's a friggen sign, I swear! We're going to be best friends, Sophie. This is hilarious!"

Jan's face was awkward. She looked at the two of them like they were demented or something.

"I'm gonna go, I'll let you two best friends get to know each other. Chelsea, will you take her to the boat drill with you today? Then, I'll take her afterward to explain the job more."

"Ya, for sure! See ya there!" Chelsea slammed the door behind Jan and ran back to Sophie.

Although Chelsea was very outgoing and seemed a little wild, she was kind and fun—the type of person you could have a good time with. And it was nice to have something in common with a new friend. Sophie was feeling better about this job already, thanks to Chelsea.

"Thank god I got an awesome roommate. I was scared to get someone I wouldn't get along with, ya know?"

"Ya, that would suck, eh?" Sophie laughed.

They chatted all afternoon, while Sophie put away her things. The bedroom was small with bunk beds on one side. Sophie took the bottom bunk. The room had one cabinet and each girl had a side to put her clothes on. There was a small table with a mini television on it and a mirror on the wall.

The bathroom was on your left, as you walked into the room. Sophie actually thought it was a closet until she opened it. It had a small toilet and sink, with a shower that was very, very small. The bathroom was big enough to slip in, do your thing, and get out. It also didn't have a fan, so you had to be quick, so you wouldn't overheat.

That evening, after the guests had boarded the ship, the staff and crew held a boat drill. This was done every time they docked to receive new guests. It was basically a demonstration for the guests, so they would know what to do in case of an emergency.

Sophie watched, as they showed the guests how to put on their life jackets and where they would load into safety boats if needed. They also showed the parents where the children would be brought to by the youth staff in case of an emergency. This entire presentation made Sophie nervous for some reason.

After the boat drill, the staff and crew were asked to stay behind to go through their demonstration on how to blow up the staff lifeboats. They assigned people to do certain jobs, and that would be their personal job if needed.

The captain was a tall Russian man, giving orders. But what freaked Sophie out was the fact that the orders were being given to Mexican men who didn't speak English at all.

Sophie watched as the men giggled, trying to blow up the boats. They were clearly not doing so well.

"Is this a joke?" Sophie asked Chelsea.

"I know, ridiculous, right?" Chelsea laughed.

"Ya, those guys don't even understand the directions they're being given! We're definitely all going to die if we have to depend on these guys coming through for us. What the hell?" Sophie complained.

Chelsea laughed. "Yup, pretty much."

The presentation ended and Sophie followed Chelsea to the welcome party where she could meet up with Jan to learn more about her job.

The rest of the day was spent with Jan, as she taught Sophie about the schedule and how hers would work. She would randomly get a day off here and there to rest or explore the islands when they docked.

Hours were not a set time. You could be working four hours in the morning, and then not work until eight o'clock later that night. Sometimes, you may not work at all until the evening, or have a two-hour shift, and then be off.

Other days, you could be working an entire day! What was great was that everybody got paid the same at the end of each week, no matter what hours you worked. You were paid in cash with no tax taken out.

Sophie began to love her job. Sometimes, she would have a group of teenagers, and other times, she would be with five to six year olds. It would be a different age group every four days! The ship sailed from Port Canaveral, Florida to Nassau, the Bahamas, and then onto Freeport, the Bahamas, and back again. The guests were on a four-day cruise, so they constantly got new kids to meet all the time.

As the days went on, Sophie learned more about the job and the crew she worked with. She connected instantly with two of the most random characters.

There was a kind and beautiful young girl named Nova. She had a gentle heart and always thought of others before herself. She also loved to dance like Sophie did. On the nights they had off together, they would go to the dance club on the ship, or get off in a group and go to the local bars!

That's where the two of them met a DJ named Joe! He was really outgoing and super entertaining—the kind of guy everyone wanted to hang with. The three of them became very close. Sometimes, if they were not working, they would spend the day in Nassau at a resort!

There was this one special resort they would always visit, it was the most beautiful resort Sophie had ever seen. It was filled with pools, aquariums, shows, clubs, casinos, and a beautiful landscape along the beach. They had waterslides that went through tunnels of sharks, dolphin encounters, and more. Seeing the sea horses was definitely Sophie's favorite part. She had always wanted to see them in real life!

It was just about six months in when things started to change and Sophie began to think differently of her work. She found out fast that the lifestyle on a ship was more than she expected. The staff went out every night they could, and they drank until they couldn't walk.

People hooked up together, and then rumors spread like fire around the ship the next day. It was like high school all over again, except worse, if possible. This was stuff you watched on reality shows or something.

The staff and crew were constantly pressuring Sophie to drink and hook up with guys. She didn't like where this was going at all. Sophie slowly started to back out of their nights out and tried hard to keep her distance. She was all about having fun with some drinks, but hooking up with random guys was not her style.

The guys on the ship were suddenly rude to her, because she wouldn't join in on their fun. Sophie started to feel like an outcast when she didn't join the group for outings, even to the crew bar on the ship. This was the way of life on the ship, sad to say.

On Canada day, the team had decided to go to the crew bar for drinks and celebrate with the Canadians on board. They harassed Sophie until she agreed to join them. Chelsea dragged Sophie back to their room to get ready after their shift.

Chelsea was different than the rest. She didn't mess around with a bunch of guys. She actually liked this one boy who was a waiter on board. She had been in a really bad relationship before joining and she was on the rebound. So, every night she would get drunk and then go after this boy.

Sophie felt badly for her, because she knew Chelsea was only looking for someone to love her, but she was going about it the wrong way. Chelsea still had strong feelings for her ex-boyfriend.

Sophie knew Chelsea would ditch her before the night was over, so after she got ready, she headed down the hallway and knocked on Nova's door. Nova was not a drinker, and she seemed to always be working when everyone went out. Jan always conveniently scheduled her that way. The door opened quickly.

"Hey, Sophie!" Nova smiled. "Come in, please!"

"Hey, Nova. I was wondering if you're going to the bar tonight?"

"Sorry, friend, I'm working the babysitting shift."

"Ugh, that sucks! I was hoping you were going, so I wouldn't have to go alone. I'm not sure I wanna go, but I don't wanna be rude and not try to get along with them." Sophie flopped on the bed.

"Soph, I know they're embarrassing sometimes and they have no pride in my opinion, but maybe you could just go for a bit, and then slip out when they're hammered." She laughed.

"True." Sophie giggled. "I guess tonight I will, but this will be my last time. I'm getting sick of this. I'm starting to realize that you, Chelsea, and Joe are my only true friends on this ship. The others I just have to put up with while I'm here." Sophie got up from the bed and headed for the door.

"You're my best friend here, too, miss Sophie," Nova giggled, as she gave Sophie a hug. "Hang in there, you only have one more month."

"Thanks, Nova," Sophie said, heading out the door.

As Sophie walked back to her room, she opened the door to a bunch of people partying.

"Come on, Sophie, you need to catch up to us!" a guy yelled, throwing Sophie a drink.

"Uh, right, thanks." She opened the beer and took a sip.

The group headed out the door and toward the crew bar.

This bar was only for the staff and crew of the ship, and it was packed and loud as always. People were hammered and yelling across the room. Many languages were being spoken, and many drinks were dropping on the floor. Jan bought everyone two rounds.

It wasn't casual drinking, but it was pounding drink after drink. Sophie took her time and drank only what she wanted to. They hassled her to hurry up, passing her more drinks. Finally, she got up.

"Where you going?" Jan yelled, grabbing her.

"Just to the bathroom. I'll be right back." Sophie pulled her arm away.

It was so weird. Isn't your supervisor supposed to be someone you can go to in case you don't feel comfortable or in case of an emergency? How could Sophie go to her if she was completely trashed?

"Some boss," she huffed.

On her way back from the bathroom, a young man was sitting in her seat.

"Excuse me," Sophie said politely.

"Hello to you, too. I'm Sergio, and you are?" Sophie looked at the tall Russian man.

"I'm Sophie."

"I'm in your seat, am I? I kept it warm for you and got you a new drink." He smiled at her.

"Um, thanks," she said, taking a sip of her beer. She felt uncomfortable around him. He wouldn't leave, no matter how many hints she gave him that she was not interested.

The thought of finding someone that she would date here on this ship was a joke. You definitely couldn't trust the motives of people here in this atmosphere.

Some of them have lived this life for a long time and this was all they knew, but they were happy with it. As the night dragged on, Sophie started to feel sluggish, but how, she wondered? She had only had two drinks, maybe three.

Suddenly, her body began to feel very heavy, and her hands and lips went numb. Her eyes became blurry. She blinked to try to regain focus.

"Looks like someone had too much to drink, eh, Canada?" Sergio said to her.

"No. I'm fine . . . " Sophie slowly answered, knocking her drink over, as she was trying to get up.

"Ahh, yes, you did. I'll help you to my room and take care of you, okay? We go, I swear you'll be fine." He grabbed Sophie and dragged her to her feet, laughing.

"Ha ha. Sophie finally got smashed!" Jan yelled to their team.

They laughed and watched, as Sergio helped her to the door. Sophie stopped for a moment, trying to regain energy to handle her body. It was so heavy and numb. What was happening? Sergio stopped outside of the bar and pushed Sophie against the wall, and began to kiss her. Sophie tried to speak, but she couldn't form words, and she had no energy to fight back. She was scared and didn't know what to do.

"Sophie, fight back!" a familiar voice suddenly yelled.

"Sophie! Listen to me now!" the voice screamed into her ears.

Sophie stood there helpless. Suddenly, Sergio was thrown against the wall and Sophie fell to the ground.

"I . . . Can't . . . I . . . " Sophie slurred her words quietly. Sergio got up and came at her again. He lifted her to her feet and headed toward the staff dorm hallway.

"Man, what happen back there. Did you really push me? It's okay. I forgive you. You can make it up to me, Sophie," he said, dragging her down the hallway. As they turned the corner to the men's hall, Nova ran into them.

"Sophie? Oh my god, what happen to you?" Nova said, noticing what state Sophie was in.

"She is fine, she is coming with me," Sergio said, shoving past her.

"I don't think so, my friend. That girl is not okay. Give her to me!" she insisted, pulling Sophie from him.

"No, I said she was fine. Go away and mind your own business, girlie," he said loudly, pulling Sophie back.

Nova was not impressed and immediately pushed herself in between the two of them, as Sophie fell to the ground.

"I'm telling you to leave her alone. Not only will I get you fired, but you'll be begging me for mercy when you see how hard I can crush these!" she said, squeezing his privates.

"I know guys like you and I know where this is going! Now go to your room before this gets messy." She stood her ground, gripping him tightly, as he screamed in pain.

She was tiny, but she packed a punch, and he quickly retreated down the hall. Nova bent down to Sophie on the ground.

"Sophie? Are you okay? Can you hear me?" she asked, shaking her softly.

"Nova?" Sophie whispered. "Help me."

Nova lifted her friend as best as she could, putting Sophie's arm around her neck. As she dragged Sophie down the hallway, they ran into a familiar face—it was Joe.

"Nova? What's going on? Is that Sophie!" he asked, helping her hold Sophie up.

"Ya, I just saved her from some Russian dude, trying to sneak her into his room, while she was clearly out of it. I've never seen her like this. It isn't like her at all," Nova said nervously.

"Ya, really! Here, let me take her." He lifted Sophie into his arms and carried her down the hall to her room

"Thanks, Joe, I appreciate it," Nova said, opening the door for him. He set Sophie down, facing her toward him. He lifted her face to take a good look at her.

"Sophie? Are you okay? Did he hurt you?" he said calmly to her. Sophie bobbed her head, trying to lift it. She could barely sit up.

"I . . . can't . . . " Sophie mumbled.

"I think she's going to be sick!" Nova yelled, opening the bathroom door. Joe lifted her inside toward the toilet. Sophie rested her hands on the seat with her face in the bowl.

"There's something wrong here, Joe. Sophie wouldn't have gotten smashed like this. I know her," she said, turning away from Sophie.

"Nova, this isn't normal drunkenness. She can't form a sentence. Drunken people mumble words and create some kind of sentence, but Sophie can't move her lips to make them. I used to work in a lot of clubs before I came here. I've seen girls like this before, and it's not drunkenness. Nova, I think she got slipped something."

"What? Like some sort of date rape drug?"

"Exactly."

Just then, Sophie dropped from the toilet to the floor, smashing her head against the cement.

"Soph!" Joe yelled, as he lifted her up. There was blood coming from the side of her head. He lifted her up and carried her to her bed. Nova quickly pulled back the covers, and then ran to get a wet towel to wipe her head. That night, Sophie didn't dream—there was nothing at all. The entire night was a blackout until later on in the early hours of the morning.

"Sophie, wake up," a gentle voice said. "Come on, Sophie, wake up."

"Nathan . . . ?" Sophie slowly opened her eyes and looked around her dark room.

There was someone in her bed beside her.

"Nova? What are you doing?" Sophie mumbled. Nova opened her eyes and sat up quickly.

"Sophie? Are you okay? I was so worried."

"Um, ya. I guess. I feel kind of sluggish or hung over like. I didn't think I drank that much. What happened? The last thing I remember was that I came back from the bathroom to find a guy sitting in my seat." She rubbed her head where she had hit it.

"Soph, did that guy give you a drink?" Nova asked.

"Um, ya. He was so creepy." Sophie felt the cut on her head—it was still sore. "What's this? What happened?"

"Sophie, I think that guy drugged you. He must have slipped something in your drink. I caught him in the hallway, trying to bring you back to his room. Joe and I brought you here, and we thought you were going to be sick, so we put you in the bathroom.

"You collapsed to the ground, hitting your head on the floor. It was so scary, Soph. It was like you couldn't control your body at all. I can't even imagine what would've happened if we hadn't found you."

Sophie lay there, taking it all in. "Thank you so much. I don't know how to repay you."

"I'm just glad you're okay, friend." Nova smiled.

"This is it! That is the last straw. I'm done with going out here. These people are crazy. I don't know how you do it, Nova—how you put up with them. I just wanted to make new friends and be social again, but not at this expense, when you can't even trust the people you're with."

"I only put up with it because I need the money. I try to keep my head straight to get through it, because I need this experience to get to where I want to be in life. So, unfortunately, I have to stay just a while more."

Just then, there was a knock at the door. It was Joe.

"Hey, Soph! I'm glad to see you're okay. I was worried about you." He smiled. In his hands, he held chocolate milk and some toast that he had snuck from the kitchen—Sophie's favorite.

"Joe, thank you so much for helping me last night. I owe you two my life." She sat up on the edge of the bed, as he handed her the drink and toast.

"I thought you may need something good in your system.

49

"Thank you, this is perfect."

"Sophie, you understand what happened last night don't you?" he asked politely.

"I heard, and it scares me to death," she said, swallowing her food. "You two are truly good friends. Thank you."

"I want you to understand something, Sophie. You only have one life. Everything we choose to do will affect our lives. I do this job because I love being a DJ. I love the crowds and the music, but I know how to handle myself with what comes with the job. Plus, I'm a guy. I don't really have to worry about people drugging me or crap like that.

"But you girls need to be careful, because there are people here from all over the world. Some don't have the same values as you and me, and some of them, you just can't trust at all. Not everybody, but most, so you need to stay alert. Use your head. Sometimes, you need to see the red flag and change your direction. You have to do what's best for you," Joe said kindly.

"I hate worrying about you two. You're my good friends, but you have to face it. You're beautiful girls who guys wanna get at, and you have to be smart about this."

"He's right," Nova said, rubbing Sophie's back.

"I know. It's so weird that when you first get here, they make it seem like it's the best place in the world to be. Then, after you get into it, their true faces show. It's too bad, because this is a great job and the places you get to see are amazing," Sophie said, rubbing her head again.

"I just don't think I can look at the faces of my teammates and trust them anymore. I don't want to work in an atmosphere like this. Most of them come drunk to work and they talk shit about everyone. It's ridiculous! I won't be part of this, it's just not fun anymore." Sophie finished her milk and placed it on the table.

"You know, if you're thinking of quitting the job, you're not allowed to come back to any ship. You know that, right? Just make sure this is what you really want. We support you either way. We'll be friends no matter what or where we are in life. I promise," Nova said, looking back and forth at Sophie and Joe.

"It doesn't matter to me if I get to come back or not," Sophie said sadly.

"I think it's a good choice, Soph. There's lots more you could do with your life. I'm gonna miss you, though." Joe sat beside her on the bed and hugged his two friends.

"Ahhh, group hug! I love you guys!" Nova giggled, hugging the two of them back.

"I love you guys, too!" Sophie laughed, as she was squished between them. "We'll have to hangout once more before I go."

Joe and Nova left Sophie to rest. She didn't work until late that night, which was perfect, because she could regain her energy. She planned to talk to Jan before her shift. It was good timing, too, because when you quit on a ship, they immediately escort you off the boat at the nearest dock.

It was brutal, but they were at sea for the day on their way back to Port Canaveral, Florida. She wouldn't have to leave until the next afternoon. At least, she could get off in Florida. She decided that she would get a plane ticket when she arrived at the airport, maybe catching a last minute deal. Until then, she would rest.

6
Farewell to the Sea

Around five o'clock, Sophie woke up and showered for work. She didn't feel her best, but it was good enough. After getting ready, she started to pack her things. Just as she zipped the last bag, Chelsea came in.

"Sophie?" she asked, confused. "What's going on? Are you leaving?"

"Ya, I think it's best. This isn't really my kind of thing."

"What are you talking about? You can't leave. Are you serious?" Chelsea said, sitting on the edge of the bed.

"I'm going to talk to Jan before my shift. I'll probably have to get off the ship tomorrow when we dock."

"Ahhh, Soph, I'm gonna miss you!"

"I'll miss you too, Chelsea, but listen to me. Be safe, okay? You deserve a great guy. Don't settle ever. Promise?" Sophie said, hugging her.

"I promise, but who will listen to Britney with me? What if I get a roommate who hates Britney?" she said, laughing.

"Well, you'll have to convert her." They giggled about the thought of Chelsea making someone listen to the CD over and over again.

"I gotta head to work. I'll see you a bit later, okay?" Sophie got up and headed out the door.

It was a quiet day in the Youth Staff room. Jan was in her office, working on schedules. Sophie knocked, as she entered the office.

"Hey, Jan, can I talk to you for a moment?"

"Oh my god, she's alive!" Jan joked. It made Sophie mad that Jan

52

didn't think of her safety the night before. She really didn't care. A feeling of snapping and wanting to shake some sense into the woman burned through Sophie's veins.

"Ya, about that. Last night was out of control. I was in trouble and you guys didn't think anything of it. I don't understand how you can go out and not keep an eye on your friends. You guys get so smashed you wouldn't have noticed if someone fell off the boat. I'm not trying to be rude, but this isn't my style, and I don't feel comfortable here anymore." She watched as Jan's quirky smile left her face.

"Look, Sophie, we can't all watch out for you drinking. You just had too many and that's how the cookie crumbles. This is the life on board here. If you don't like it, then maybe this isn't the job for you. We aren't your babysitter, so you can join in the fun and get along with us or be a loner like Nova." She stood her ground, staring at Sophie.

"So, basically you're saying deal or go, right? That's ridiculous, you're not being very professional, Jan, seriously." Sophie stared back at her.

"Don't give me attitude about your sloppy night and the poor you speech. This is how it is." She turned, continuing to do her schedule.

"Fine, then, I'm giving my notice today. I'm ready to leave tomorrow when we dock. You know I was really excited about this job, and I thought it was going to be fantastic. But working with people like you in this atmosphere was hell on earth. I don't know how any normal person would subject herself to this. I wish it didn't have to end like this. Thank you for the opportunity, though. I'll finish my shift tonight and leave quietly tomorrow." Sophie headed for the door.

"All right, it's your choice. I'll get your papers together," Jan said, keeping her eyes on the schedule.

This made Sophie feel more confident about her choice to leave. That was it. She had quit. She finished her shift that night—it was a short one—and then she headed back to her room. On her way back to her room, she ran into Joe.

"Hey, Soph! Come with me. Hurry." He grabbed her hand and ran down the hallway. They headed upstairs to the main deck and outside onto the patio. It was a calm and perfect evening. Sitting on a bench were Chelsea and Nova. They both had little presents for her wrapped in gift bags from the gift shop on board.

"Guys! You didn't have to do this. You're so sweet. I'm so gonna miss you all."

"We're gonna miss you, too, Soph!" Nova said, walking over to hug her.

"We have gifts for you!" Chelsea said, handing Sophie a card. It was beautiful and signed by her friends—they each had written a personal note in it for her. At the bottom of the card were all of their emails and mailing addresses, so they could keep in touch. Sophie's eyes teared up.

"Thank you, this is so wonderful. I promise to write." She hugged each one of them. After opening the gifts, Joe brought out some desert he had gotten from the kitchen. They sat on the deck visiting. It was a fantastic ending to her crazy adventure.

That night, a familiar feeling came over Sophie again, while she lay in bed. The boat was rocking back and forth a lot that night. It almost made her sick to her stomach.

"Nate?" she whispered. "Nathan, are you there?"

"Ya, Soph, what's up?" he answered, appearing by her bedside.

"Hey, there you are. I haven't heard from you in a while. Where have you been?" She turned to face him.

"I've been busy helping others, but I've been watching, don't worry," he said, smiling at her.

"Helping others? You mean I'm not the only person you watch over? I thought I had you all to myself," she joked sadly.

"Soph, it's what I do, crazy girl. Don't worry, though, I've been here when you needed me. But I got in a little trouble from the archangels. After I threw that Sergio guy against the wall when he tried to kiss you, I was banned for a bit."

"You threw Sergio against the wall? Did anyone see you? Oh, wait I guess not. He must have thought I did it."

"Ya, physical contact is a big no-no up there. I just couldn't watch and do nothing. It killed me to see you being used like that. It made me so angry."

"Thank you, Nate," she said, touching his hand softly.

"That includes you, too, Sophie. I can't have any physical contact with you, either."

He pulled his hand away from hers. "Sorry," he said quietly.

"Really?" Sophie's smile faded, as Chelsea leaned over the bed.

"Sophie, who are you talking to? Are you talking in your sleep again? Lie down and go to sleep."

Chelsea knew that Sophie talked in her sleep, so it wasn't a surprise to hear her talking. Sophie looked at Nathan and he smiled back at her. "Good night, Sophie."

She lay down and went to sleep. That night, Nathan appeared in her dreams—they were sitting on a dock by the water, drinking slushies and saying nothing at all. It was nice.

The next morning, she woke up early, excited to leave, but not excited to say good-bye to her friends. The announcement that they had docked came across the speakers.

Sophie grabbed her suitcase and threw her backpack over her shoulder. Chelsea awoke and jumped down from the top bed.

"Don't forget your bag of gifts!" She handed the bag to Sophie, hugging her tightly.

"See ya, Chelsea, get a hold of me when you're back in town, okay?"

"Cool! I'll see ya, then." She watched as Sophie headed down the hallway to the gangplank. As Sophie reached security, she noticed Nova and Joe waiting to say good-bye.

"Bye, friend!" Nova yelled, as she ran to Sophie.

"Bye, Nova! I'm gonna miss you so much." She found it funny that Nova always said 'friend' when she referred to Sophie. It was so cute.

"See ya, Soph, keep in contact," Joe said, giving her a huge hug.

Nova quickly joined them. "Our last group hug. Awh . . . my friends." They laughed, squeezing each other tightly.

Sophie stepped away and headed down the plank to land. When she reached the ground, she stopped and turned. "Bye, friends, I'll miss you!" she yelled, as Joe and Nova waved good-bye to her. She followed the crowd out to the transportation area. As she waved down a cab, she felt a little sad, but relieved.

"Now what?" she thought to herself, as she got in the cab and headed for the airport. Looking out the window, she watched the sea get further and further away as they drove. The Florida sun was shining brightly and it glowed on her tanned skin.

It reminded her of the trips they used to take as a family when she was young. Her family used to pile in their blue station wagon and drive to Florida for a week's vacation every summer.

Then, she began to think of the world she was returning to back in Ontario. With all of the fighting between her parents and her friends, why was she going back to that? Would anything ever work out for her? She thought about maybe trying to fix something this time going home. Maybe she would try living with her mother and try to build their relationship stronger. She would ask when she got home.

She only hoped that her father would not be angry with her for quitting. She knew he wouldn't understand the lifestyle of living on ship—no one would. You had to be there and experience it to understand it all.

So, she decided to tell everyone that she got seasick. That was the best she could come up with. It's all she had. The flight was long going home, so Sophie relaxed her mind from everything that had happened. She would deal with what was to come when she got home.

After returning home, Sophie took some time to think about what she would do next. She had many late-night conversations with Nathan that went on for hours. He tried to convince her of all the talents she had. She just had to decide which talent she loved the most, and take a chance on that dream.

He pointed out her piano skills. She had played for eighteen years and was really good. She had a passion for music. She could play it, sing it, and write it. He also talked about her drawings. Years back, she used to draw all the time—she was amazing with her attention to detail. She also had a love for animals, so perhaps working with them might interest her.

She was great at so many things and so artistic in many ways. She also had great people skills, like the way she used to host those welcome aboard parties on the ship.

Handling a group of two to five hundred people at a time demanded attention and a great personality. There was so much she could do, but as usual, Sophie denied all of this, as Nate tried to drill it into her head.

"Soph, I think there's something else going on here other than you not believing in yourself. Tell me what's going on," Nathan said seriously.

"It's dumb, you'll think it's stupid," she said, pulling her pillow up against the head of the bed to sit up.

"I think you're crazy anyway, so what do you have to lose?" he joked. "Seriously though, Sophie, it's me you're talking to, so spill it." She took a breath to relax, and then gave in.

"It's just that when I was growing up, my parents supported things I did, like when I played baseball or took piano. Then, as I got older, they kind of . . . I don't really know. It's like they gave up on me. It didn't matter while I was in high school, because I had my friends to talk to. It was after their divorce and the whole thing with Catie and Dean, that I noticed how alone I was." She took another deep breath and continued.

"They didn't pay much attention to me. They didn't even talk to me about the whole breakup. They just went on like nothing had happened, like I shouldn't be so upset. I know that they had just gone through the divorce, but I still needed them. The divorce was hard for me, too, and losing all my friends didn't help. I didn't know where to turn or whom I could talk to.

Now that I'm back, I'm already hearing negative things from my other extended family members, saying things like how I abandoned and betrayed my mother to live with my dad. They don't even know the whole story, like the fact that I didn't even see my dad that much during high school, because he took a job in another province. I missed him and wanted to spend time with him.

No matter what has happened between them, they're both still my parents. I mean, who do they think they are? It makes me hate my aunts, uncles, and cousins for saying crap like that. I don't wanna hear any of it."

"I just thought that my dad would be happier that I came to live with him, but instead, he shipped me off. It's just really hard to get motivated to do something with your life when no one cares and no one is there for you. You should know that, of all people, Nate, from all that you went through!"

Nate sat up beside her and took a moment before answering.

"I do understand, but, Sophie, that job was a good experience, and you learned a lot from it."

"I know, Nate, but it didn't work out, did it? And now, I feel like a failure," she said, staring at him.

"Hey, you gotta stop this negative thinking. It's going to be hard at times, like I said, but you're . . . " Nathan was cut off by Sophie rolling her eyes.

"I know I'm on the right path," she said sarcastically. "It's just that I'm on this path with no family behind me and no friends to support me. It's just really lonely, that's all," Sophie said sadly.

"I know." He smiled at her, feeling her pain.

"Like, what do I have to do to get someone to care about me?" Her voice cracked, as she spoke those embarrassing words.

"Sophie . . ." Nathan said, as he was about to take her hand, but then, he stopped, remembering those stupid rules.

"See, you can't even care about me." Small tears fell from her eyes.

"I care about you, Sophie, or I wouldn't be here," Nathan said softy.

"Ya, but it's your job. You help lots of people. I'm not any more special than anyone else." She pulled the pillow back down to lay flat.

"Look, I just wanna go to sleep, okay? Good night."

Nathan watched, as she closed her eyes.

"Okay, Sophie, sorry. I'll leave." He got up from the bed. "Remember I'm not going anywhere. I'll see you later."

The next morning, Sophie lay in bed until noon. She finally leaned over to grab her cell phone off of the nightstand to give her mom a call about her idea. The phone rang twice before her mother picked up.

"Hello?"

"Hey, Mom, how's it going?" she said nervously.

For some reason, she was scared to ask her mom about moving in. What if what her aunts and uncles had said were true. Did her mother also believe that she had abandoned her after the divorce?

"Hi, Sophie, you're back, eh? Well, that didn't go so well, huh?" She laughed.

"Ya, it didn't really turn out how I wanted it to. I didn't realize how sick I would get living on a boat."

"Now what, Soph? What are your plans now?" she asked.

"Well, I was thinking of coming back to Ontario, getting a job, and taking it from there." She waited for her mother's response.

"Oh, ya?" her mother answered.

"Ya, I was thinking maybe I could live with you. Would that be okay?" she asked quietly.

"I was actually thinking of selling the house. I don't need it anymore. It's just me living here, but you're welcome to stay until then. After that, we'll have to figure things out." Sophie took a deep breath, trying to be mature about the situation. She couldn't tell if her mom was mad or not.

"Thanks, Mom, I was thinking of driving home maybe this weekend. Would that be okay?"

"Ya, that's fine, so I'll see you this weekend."

"All right, then. I'll talk to you later. See ya." Sophie waited for her mom to answer.

"See ya soon, bye." Her mother hung up the phone.

It was an awkward conversation, but it was finished.

The rest of the week, Sophie spent packing her things from her father's house and loading her car for her drive home.

Her father seemed to be fine with her leaving, but it was hard at times when he threw out a few mean words like:

"I still don't know why you would want to live with your mother. What has she ever done for you?"

That was the difference between her father and mother. Sophie's dad would make comments out loud and her mother wouldn't say anything at all. You would have to find out later that she was mad, usually after a big silent treatment.

Either way, it was horrible to be between them. It wasn't like she could pick a side or anything. She only wished that maybe someday her parents could just be civil. Until then, this would be what she had to deal with.

The weekend had finally arrived, and she was ready for her drive home. As she loaded the last few things into her car, she thought about Nate for a moment. She hadn't heard from him in a week or so, and she wondered if he was mad at her. Maybe she had been too rude the last time they spoke, or maybe he had given up on her. She hoped not.

Her father came out to say good-bye, as she got into her car.

"Be safe, Soph, and pull over if you get tired." He gave her a hug, and then stepped back as she closed the door.

"Yes, I know, and I will." She waved to her father, as she pulled away. The drive was only sixteen hours, but it gave her a lot of time to think about her life and what she should do next. Surprisingly, she enjoyed the quietness of the drive. She even pulled out some of her favorite music and sang at the top of her lungs, as the warm summer air blew through her hair. It was exactly what she needed, for now.

7

A New Road

The first week at her mother's house, things were pretty normal. Her mom went to work and Sophie arranged to get her old job back until she knew what she was doing. Her mother went on with the plans to put the house on the market. Sophie did her best to stay out of her way.

She wanted to have a good talk with her mom, but every time she tried to bring up the subject, a foul mood filled the room. So, she decided to keep her mouth shut and plan her life alone. Maybe her mother and she would just move on, no talk needed.

She applied for some full-time jobs and finally landed one as a receptionist. She would be working 8:00 a.m. to 5:00 p.m. After that, she would go to her part-time job until midnight, four nights a week. It was tiring, but she was saving money to go to school as soon as she decided where.

Her parents hassled her about finding a real career. She found it annoying that they didn't notice how hard she was working. Many times she wanted to scream at them, but instead, she walked away and cried in her room. She was mentally and physically exhausted! She knew she had to make a plan now and get herself out of there! After a while, Sophie got used to the nonstop work schedule. She kept a positive frame of mind, knowing that it would all pay off eventually, she hoped.

One night, she got a phone call from one of her friends. It was Lisa. They would see each other every summer when their families went on vacation. That was where they had met and become close friends, but the only problem was that Lisa lived far away. Since her parents had divorced, they hadn't seen each other too much.

"Hey, Sophie!" Lisa screamed.

"Lisa, how are you?" Sophie asked, excited to hear a friendly voice.

"I'm great! I have some exciting news!!!" She giggled.

"Really, what?"

"I'm moving to Cambridge!"

"No way! Seriously? I'm so excited." Sophie felt her heart stop for a moment. She was so excited to hear that she would have a good friend around again. Lisa had no idea what that did for her.

"I know, right? Yay! We'll be close and we can hang out all the time!" Lisa yelled through the phone hysterically.

"This is amazing! When are you coming?" Sophie asked.

"Well, we actually already found something, while you were away. We move in next week! I was wondering, though, if maybe you could pick up the keys for us in Cambridge there? We won't get in until late, and the office will be closed, so could you meet us at the house? Do you think you can do it?" Lisa asked.

"Yes, definitely! I'm so excited you're coming!" Sophie took down the information needed and wished her luck in the move. Then, she dropped down on her bed and lay there smiling to herself, almost relieved from the news. Maybe this year wouldn't be so bad. Maybe Lisa could help her decide what to do next in life.

That night, Sophie lay in bed, staring at the ceiling as usual. Where was Nate? Why hadn't he come back yet? She fell asleep, feeling happy and sad all at the same time. She dreamed of many things that night, dreams of her going places and traveling, and dreams of how fun her life would be now that Lisa was there. She also dreamed of Nate.

This wasn't the normal Nate dream that night. He wasn't saving her this time. He was just there, in her life, a friend or possible boyfriend by her side. The dream was slow and detailed, with Nate and her walking hand and hand, talking. She couldn't hear the words they were saying, but she could feel it—a feeling of safety, calm, and love.

He knew just how to make her feel happy. She wondered if there was a guy out there who could do just that. Slowly, they walked through the park and over to an old dock by the river. As she continued to dream, she heard herself say, "Nate?"

She could feel his hand in hers, as she watched herself move closer to him. He hugged her tightly. She breathed deeply and leaned back to look him in the eyes, and he smiled at her. Their faces were close, breathing in each other's breath. Nathan leaned down toward her lips . . .

"Sophie? Sophie, wake up," a voice whispered to her. She opened her eyes with a frown on her face.

"What's that look for? I thought you might be happy to see me." Nathan laughed.

"Nathan? What the? Why did you wake me up?" Sophie groaned, sitting up slightly. He sat down on the side of her bed.

"Wow, must have been some dream? What was it about? Or should I just look for myself?" he joked.

"What? No! You can do that?" Sophie screamed.

"Shhhh! You're gonna wake your mom up. Yes, I can do things like that. Quiet, geeze. I won't look. Can you at least tell me what it was about?" he asked.

"No!"

"Why not?"

"Because, it's personal!" she snapped at him.

"Okay, relax, crazy girl." He laughed. "So how are things going?"

Sophie lifted her elbow up on the pillow, leaning her head on her hand.

"Um, good, I guess. My friend Lisa is moving here, so that's exciting, but other than that, nothing else is new. Where have you been lately?" she asked.

"I've been here. Have you decided yet where you want to go to school?"

"Well, I was thinking of acting school. I talked to my parents about it. They think it's ridiculous, a waste of money. Then, my mom suggested that maybe I could take a night class to see if I like acting or not. I don't know what the point of that is, though, because I've been acting throughout high school and I've been performing since I was four. Anyway, I agreed, and I start this week—Wednesday nights."

Nate pushed Sophie over on the bed and lay down beside her.

"There, that's something! Negotiating with the parents is always a step toward what you want. You have to make them believe you're making an adult decision."

"Ya, I know. I secretly applied to school in a few places without telling them, though. I've been saving and I almost have enough. I got accepted into a school in Los Angeles, but when I told my dad, he freaked out at the thought of that and convinced me to stay in Canada. So, I think I'm going to go with an acting school in Vancouver."

"That's great, Sophie! Now you're talking. Are you excited?"

"Well, I'd be more excited if someone else was excited with me. I'm stoked for myself and proud that I'm doing all this, but it sucks that the people in my life have nothing positive to say about it." Sophie sighed.

"Hey! I'm excited, seriously!" Nate said with a straight face.

"Thanks, I know," she said, smiling at him.

"Hey, why do you always say I know? Do you actually know? Do you really believe me or are you just agreeing with me?" he said, staring her in the eyes.

"No, I do believe you. I promise." She smiled back. "It's good to see you again. I hate it when you're gone so long."

"I know." He smiled back.

"Well, I guess I should let you get back to your dream. Are you sure you don't want to tell me about it?" he pushed.

"No, Nate!" Sophie laughed. "Do you really have to go? Can't you just stay a little while longer and talk with me?"

"Sophie, you're gonna get me in trouble again . . . " he paused, looking at her. Her eyes glanced away from him sadly.

"Fine," he said, pulling the pillow up higher behind his back.

"What do you want to talk about?"

"Let's see. Tell me more about you. Who was this girl who you loved? Is she still alive? Have you seen her?"

"So, that's what you want to talk about? It's not really a motivating topic, Soph."

"Please, Nathan, I really wanna know you more," she begged.

Nathan paused, as he thought to himself.

"Her name was Serena. She was kind, smart, beautiful, and had the best heart a person could have. She was always making conversation with me, asking me questions about my life, like she was really interested. I guess she really was, though, because she wouldn't leave me alone about it." He laughed, remembering how persistent she was.

"She kept telling me how great my life was going to be, and that she would make sure of it. I used to love listening to her talk about the stuff she dreamed of and hoped for in her life. Serena had her share of ups and downs, don't get me wrong. Her parents were never there, but she continued to try to find the positive things in life."

He sat there for a moment, thinking of her. Sophie stared at him, infatuated with his story.

"Have you seen her lately?" she asked.

Nathan was silent for a moment. Then, he answered, "Yes."

"Where is she?" she asked nervously.

"I visited her grave the other day," he whispered.

"Nathan, I'm sorry."

"I assume she lived a happy life, something I couldn't give her." His face became tense. "Soph, I'm not the good person you think I am. I got what I deserved. If I had been different, maybe Serena and I would've been together."

"Nathan, you are a good person. Why would you say that? What happened with you guys?" she said nervously.

"I was so stupid. I was in college and I used to cut class to go work for a guy. He sold illegal stuff, and I guess I never asked. I only delivered the products or took the money to the head guy, but my boss wasn't very trusted by his clients."

"He got himself into some trouble, and these guys who we were dealing with just wanted their stuff—no excuses or someone pays. You don't mess with these guys and their money." Nathan sat there, getting angrier at every word he said.

"Serena, we were just getting to know each other. Hanging out to work on a project, it was the best excuse ever to get to know her. It was just bad timing. I didn't mean to get her involved."

Sophie's face looked worried, as she waited for Nathan to continue.

"My boss owed a lot of money, so he cut town, and I was left to answer for him. I guess these guys had been following me to see if they could catch my boss. When they saw me going to Serena's house, they must have thought she was my girlfriend. Basically, if they couldn't hurt my boss, they were going to hurt me in the deepest way.

"They showed up at her house and broke open the door. By the time I got there, he was all over her, touching her. It still kills me—the thought of his disgusting hands touching Serena's innocent body. I grabbed him and ripped him off her. I wanted to kill him! The guy ran off, and I was left there with Serena.

"She was so bruised and bloody, but she wasn't even mad at me. She just wanted me there by her side. I couldn't believe she could still care for me after that. I stayed with her all night. I promised to never leave her side again. But I did and it was the last time."

"What do you mean the last time?" Sophie choked.

"I went to school the next morning to hand in a project that Serena and I had worked on together. She was so good in school, and it was so important for her to keep her grades up, so I was only going to hand it in and come back right away. She asked me to stay, but I didn't listen. I thought it would make her happy. I wanted to change my life for her, do anything she wanted me to do.

"On the way back to her house from school, that same guy was waiting. He pulled up to her house, just as I reached the door and shot me from behind." Nathan closed his eyes, remembering those last moments. "I died on her doorstep. I remember hearing Serena's voice and the scent of her holding me in her arms. She was . . . " Nathan stopped.

"I never wanted her to feel like that. I didn't mean to do this to her. We should have been together—I promised her." His voice cracked, as he tried to stop himself from crying.

"Nathan," Sophie whispered, not knowing what to say.

She quickly leaned over and hugged him tightly. She didn't care about the stupid rules. She knew Nathan needed this. After a few seconds, he pulled Sophie's arms from around him.

"I didn't get the chance to change my life. I didn't try soon enough. Sophie, this is why you can't just give up. No matter what the situation is or how bad it gets, you can't give up, because you never know when your last day will arrive. Life is short, and people don't appreciate life until it's taken from them."

"Nate, I . . . " She stopped, as Nathan slowly got up from the bed.

"Are you leaving?" she asked sadly.

"Yea, I think that's enough talking for tonight. You should get some sleep," he said, without looking at her.

"Nathan, I didn't mean to upset you, I swear. I just wanted to understand you more. I like you and you're my only friend right now," she said, waiting for him to turn around.

"I know, Soph, I like you, too. But I can't like . . . it's just that you remind me of her." He turned to face her.

"Sophie, you have the same spirit as her, and you're beautiful. You remind me so much of her when you talk to me. It's so hard to ignore. When I picked you, I didn't realize how hard this would be. I thought it would help me deal, because you were so much like her, but it's just confusing me more!"

Sophie stared at Nate, wondering what he meant by that.

"I confuse you? Do you think you made a wrong choice in picking me? Is that what you're saying, Nathan?" Her eyes teared up.

"No, Sophie, definitely not. Don't ever think that. You're so special to me," he said, walking back over to the side of the bed.

"It's not that. It's not like you remind me of her so much that I confuse you with her or anything like that. It's because some of the things about you, were the same things about her that I . . . " he paused, looking at her.

"That you what? What, Nate?" Sophie's voice raised, and he could see the hurt in her eyes.

"That I fell in love with!" he yelled back at her.

Sophie's face dropped. She was caught off guard. She didn't expect him to say that.

"Are you saying that you're falling in love with me?" she asked quietly.

Her faced blushed, as she spoke to him. Suddenly, in an instant, things were different between them.

"No, well . . . But it doesn't matter, because it can never happen and it's against the rules. My time is over. I'm here to help you in your life," he said nervously.

Sophie sat there silently.

"Sophie? I didn't mean to make you feel weird. This doesn't change anything. I promise I'm still going to be here for you. Forget that we had this conversation, all right?" he said, about to grab her hands, but then stopped. Sophie still didn't answer.

"Soph, what are you thinking? I'm sorry. I know I have no right to throw this on you. Forgive me."

"Forgive you? Why? For expressing your feelings?" she said, looking up at him.

"Nate, I'm not mad. Why would I be? An amazing guy just said that he thinks he might be in love with me."

"But it doesn't matter, because I'm dead and you're still alive. We can never be. You need a great guy who will take care of you and love you with all his heart—a guy who can be by your side everyday, actually be here, Soph," he said sadly.

"Nathan, I have thought of you. You're always there. Maybe there is a way that we can . . . " She thought this would be a great time to express her hidden feelings for him, but he cut her off too soon.

"No, Sophie, I'm sorry. It will never be. You will have better, I promise. I'll make sure of it. This discussion is over, because it will go nowhere," he said firmly.

"You deserve happiness, too, Nathan."

"I'll be happy when you're happy, crazy girl," he said, trying to lighten the mood.

"How do you know that you aren't the one to make me happy?"

"Trust me. I'm not. Now, go to sleep." He got up from her bed. She looked at him in silence and decided to give up for the night. He had completely stolen her heart. Nathan leaned against the doorway, looking at her with a soft expression in his eyes, as she tried hard to fight sleep. But it eventually took her over, as Nate watched her slowly close her eyes and begin to dream.

"I wish I were the one for you, Sophie. Believe me," he whispered to himself, and then disappeared into the night.

8

An Old Friend

The day had finally come for Lisa to move to Cambridge. Sophie woke up early that morning and jumped in the shower. She was so excited for her friend to move to her town. She plugged her cell phone into the speakers and turned the music up. Sophie was a closet performer. On days she was down or even in a good mood, she would blast her music and dance like there was no tomorrow.

Sophie secretly always wanted to be a singer—not just any singer, but a great artist! The only problem was she was terrified to sing in front of people. Thank god no one ever walked in on her lip sync performances, as she would never be able to live it down.

Her younger brother was away at college, studying recording, music, and more. He had picked up the talent on his own. Sometimes, when he was home, he would do some recording, and Sophie would help out on the piano, but she longed to sing and make an album of her own.

Her older brother shared the same love for music, but with turntables. She never saw much of him anymore, because he had moved far away after getting married. Sophie just hoped that someday she could overcome the nerves and get out there on stage. Until then, she was the lip sync queen!

It was almost 5:00 p.m. Sophie had sat around the entire day watching television and impatiently waiting for her time to leave. Finally, she jumped up, grabbed her keys, and ran out the door.

"Ah! I forgot the address!" Sophie screamed to herself, as she ran back into the house to get the address of the real estate office off the counter. Quickly she jumped into her car and drove off. She reached the office just in time, and the sales agent was waiting at the door for her with Lisa's keys.

"You must be Sophie?" he said.

"Yes, I'm here to pick up my friend's house keys."

"Great, I have everything here for them." He held the door for her, as she entered the office.

The man walked over to his desk, grabbed a big brown envelope, and handed it to Sophie.

"In this envelope are their keys and the house documents. If they have any questions, they can call me. My business card is in here, too."

"Thank you," Sophie said, shaking his hand.

"They have a great day to move in, eh?" the agent said sarcastically, as he walked her to the front door. It had been raining all day, but to be honest, Sophie hadn't really noticed, as she was too excited.

"Ya, I guess it is pretty crappy out, huh?" she said, laughing.

"Good luck" he said to Sophie, as he headed out the door.

She waved back, as she got into her car. It was rush hour, so it took a half hour to get down the main road. She finally reached Lisa's new house and pulled in the driveway. They weren't there yet, so Sophie went down the street to the coffee shop. She ordered a hot chocolate and sat in the parking lot, listening to music.

"Exciting day, eh, Sophie?" The voice startled her. It was Nathan.

"You gotta stop doing that. It scares the crap out of me," she said, even though she was so glad to see him.

"Sorry" he said politely.

"Ya, I'm super excited. They should be here soon," she said, taking a sip of her hot chocolate.

"It's going to be so nice to have someone to hang out with and Lisa really knows me. I feel like I can confide in her about anything." She smiled.

"That's good, Soph. She's exactly what you need right now," Nathan said, taking the cup from her hand and taking a sip.

"Hey," she said, laughing. "But she isn't replacing you, Nate, just so you know."

"Maybe she will and that's not a bad thing," he said, handing the cup back to her.

"Yes it is. No one could ever replace you."

They sat there silently, and it became awkward.

"Well, good luck. I'll let you get back to her house. This is a good thing, Sophie."

"Yes, it is," she said, as he disappeared into thin air.

She finished her drink and drove off to Lisa's house.

By the time she arrived, Lisa was waiting in the driveway. Sophie pulled in beside her to see Lisa's face smiling. She waved hysterically at her friend. Lisa jumped out of the car and ran over to Sophie.

Just as Sophie closed her door, Lisa ran up to her with a huge hug.

"Hi!" Lisa said, laughing and almost hugging Sophie to death.

"Hi, my friend, I missed you!" Sophie giggled.

"We have so much to catch up on and now we can! Let's go inside. I want to show you our place!"

Sophie handed her the envelope as Lisa's mom came around the car.

"Hi, Sophie, how are you? Thank you so much for getting our keys today."

"Oh, no problem, I'm excited you guys are here!" Sophie said, giving her a hug.

Lisa's mom was a lot older. She was a quiet lady and kind. Lisa almost didn't seem like she could be her daughter, because the two of them were so different.

They led Sophie inside to show her around. The home was beautiful and cozy. It was a bungalow style and just the right size for both of them. The rest of the night was spent unloading their boxes and suitcases. They ordered a pizza and turned on some music to keep their energy going. It was eleven o'clock when Lisa's mom suggested they stop for the night.

The two girls sat up for another hour, catching up, while Lisa's mom went to bed.

Sophie told her about the cruise lines and how she was feeling lately. Lisa already knew about her parents and the whole Dean and Catie thing.

"Why does this crazy shit always happen to you, Sophie?"

"I know! It's insane, right? I'm hoping life is going to give me a break soon," she said with a laugh.

"Well, I think it's great that you applied to school again. Even though you're leaving me after I just got here, I do hope you get in," Lisa teased.

"Ya, me, too. I just sent the audition tape out yesterday. I'm thinking this is really what I want to do and it will really help build my self-esteem. And it may give me a thicker skin in life . . . I don't know."

"Going to acting school is perfect for you, Sophie. You're so fun, but I hear some of these schools really tear you apart—like mentally." Lisa laughed.

"I guess that's the point, right? Acting is all mental work, isn't it? I have enough crap in my mind all the time, so this may be the best way to release it." Sophie sighed.

"Well, just get famous fast, so we can travel and party in L.A. Then, I can live off of you for the rest of our lives." Lisa giggled, as she stood up to stretch.

"Will do. I guess I better get going, so you can get some sleep."

"Thanks again, Soph, for helping out today," she said, hugging her goodbye.

"No problem at all."

The rain had stopped and the night air was crisp with the smell of spring. Sophie waved to Lisa and got in her car.

As she drove home, she felt like a weight had lifted off her shoulders after her talk with Lisa. She didn't think about her troubles even once, while hanging out with her. It was fantastic! Life was really looking better by the moment, but she was worried about one thing—Nathan. What if he thought she was fine now and didn't need him anymore? Would he leave?

She had to make sure that he wasn't going anywhere. She wasn't ready for that, yet. She had to speak to Nate before anything happened.

That night she dreamt of him. The two of them were walking through a park again. It was sunny and they had a little dog with them. He was black and shaggy looking. They stopped at a bench and sat down. Nathan had his arm around her, and the little dog sat quietly at their feet. They laughed as they watched the dog sit there with the wind blowing against his face, lifting his ears up into the air.

"Come here, Bruce, you goof!" Nathan said, lifting the little dog onto his lap. That was the first time Sophie heard the conversations in her dreams.

Sophie watched herself, as she rested her head on Nathan's shoulder.

"I love you," Nathan whispered into her ear.

Sophie quickly awoke from her dream. "He loves me," she said out loud to herself.

The room was dark. She looked around to see if Nathan was there.

"Nathan?" she whispered.

He didn't answer and he didn't appear. Sophie lay back down, thinking of her dream.

She pulled Barkley tight against her chest. "Why can't we be together? There has to be a way."

She thought of Nathan and then thought of Serena. What had happened was so sad. But maybe she could be the one to make him happy. The thoughts flooded her mind the entire night until she finally fell asleep.

The next morning, Sophie woke up to the sun shining through her window. She stretched out in her bed, breathing in the air that blew through her window.

"What should I do today?" she mumbled to herself.

After showering, she went downstairs to have a bowl of cereal and sit in front of the television. Just then, her cell phone rang, and she reached into her pocket to answer it.

"Hello?"

"Hi!" Lisa screamed into the phone.

"Oh my god, you're so loud." Sophie laughed.

"Sorry, but what are you doing today? Wanna hang out?"

"Ya okay. Sounds good. What do you wanna do?"

"Anything, it's so nice out! Let's meet at the park and we'll go for lunch or something."

They met up and went for lunch at a close-by diner. Afterward, they got some ice cream and walked around the park, chatting all afternoon.

This began to be something they did every weekend, and in the evenings, they would hit the clubs. The odd days in the week were spent watching movies and going shopping, when Sophie wasn't at her part-time job. Both of them were having as much fun as possible while they were together.

As summer went on, the weekend outings became more fun! There were foam parties, beach parties, and lots of boys to meet. One night, Lisa and Sophie hit up one of their regular bars, and even some of Lisa's friends came along from her hometown.

The girls were doing shots and mingling with the crowd. Lisa and Sophie together were hilarious! It was a side to Sophie that she had missed dearly. Sophie was quick to make up a story to chat about with boys. The girls loved to dance, and they were on the floor 80 percent of the time.

What was great was that the girls all watched out for one another, something they could always rely on. It was a whole new set of friends to hang with. Later in the night, Lisa exchanged numbers with a guy she danced with on her way out of the club. Sophie waved down a cab, as she stumbled to keep her balance on the curb. She may have had a little too much fun.

"Bye, Lisa! See ya, everyone!" she said, turning and tripping into the cab.

"Bye, Sophie!" the group yelled to her. Sophie giggled, as she sat herself up, slammed the door, and buckled her seat belt.

"Okay, Mr. cab driver, take me home!" she slurred, giving the cab driver her address.

The cab pulled away and headed to Cambridge. Sophie's head bobbed back and forth, sometimes banging off of the window on the door.

"Hey, don't throw up in here, missy, or you'll be paying for it," the cab driver said strictly.

"No, I won't. I never throw up, never!" Sophie mumbled back to him.

"I'm the best, 'cause I can never throw up in the car. Except when I was little, I used to get car sick," she said, laughing.

"I'm just gonna make . . . sure . . . " Sophie's words kept cutting off, as the cab driver watched her in the rearview mirror.

She rolled down the window and stuck her head out. "If . . . If I breathe deeply, I won't throw up. Don't worry. I know what I'm doing, so you don't have to call the cops," she blabbered on. "I am the cops . . . I'm . . . I'll take you in if I throw up."

The cab driver rolled his eyes, as he listened to her ramble on until they finally reached Sophie's house.

"That'll be thirty-five dollars, please."

Sophie scrambled around her pockets and pulled out two twenties and gave them to him.

"Here, keep it." She got out of the car and stumbled to the side door. Suddenly, she lost her balance and fell into the bushes.

"Crap," she said, lying there helplessly, and then started to doze off.

"Sophie. Sophie, come on. Get up," a voice said.

"God? Is that you?" Sophie mumbled, staring up and trying to get a steady visual. "Hey, I have a question for you, God . . . it's very important . . . Do you know? Do you know . . . cause I don't . . . where my shoe is?"

"No, Soph, it's me, Nate. Come on, crazy girl, get up. Your mom will freak if she has to pull you out of her garden in the morning."

"I'm just resting. I'll just be a second." Sophie closed her eyes again.

"No, come on, Sophie. Get up. I can't have any physical contact with you, so you're gonna have to do it on your own," Nathan urged.

"No, physical contact . . . that's so . . . dumb." Sophie giggled, reaching around and feeling around for her shoe that was clearly still on her foot.

"I mean seriously . . . I hate you for that. I hate you. I hate . . . you 'cause I love you and you . . . you are so mean."

"Sophie." Nathan paused for a moment, staring at her. He quickly reached down and lifted her out from the bushes.

"Whoa . . . too fast!" Sophie said, gripping Nathan's shirt. "You smell good. I just wanna . . . no, you don't want me."

"Come on, Soph, let's get you to bed." He lifted her into his arms and carried her inside and up to her bedroom.

He carefully placed her down onto her bed, got her a glass of water, and took her shoes off for her.

"Nate, why won't you fight for me?" she whispered.

"Sophie, let's not talk about this now, okay? You're drunk and it's just not the time, all right?"

"You make me so sad, Nate. I . . . I think the world of you and you have . . . I just don't get it." A tear fell from the corner of her eye. He sat down on the bed next to her and brushed the hair away from her face.

"Sophie, if I were alive and here, I would want to be with you, all right? This is my job. I have to make sure you have the life you're supposed to have. It just wasn't meant to be, sweetie."

"Nate, please." She breathed deeply. "Can you just kiss me?"

Her eyes opened slightly, as he stared at her sadly. "Sophie, you know I can't," he said sadly. "Just go to sleep, and we'll talk in the morning."

She stared at him, as another tear fell from her eye. It hurt Nate to see her like this, so he stayed by her side until she fell asleep. Then, he leaned down and kissed her forehead to say goodnight.

The next morning, Sophie woke up with a killer headache. She pulled the covers over her head, so the sun wouldn't shine in her eyes.

"Never again . . . ugh," she mumbled to herself, feeling sick to her stomach.

"Sophie! Come on, it's time to get up," her mother yelled to her from the kitchen.

Slowly Sophie rolled out of bed, as tiny pieces of bushes fell from her sheets.

"What the hell?" she said, plucking out a few in her hair as well. Suddenly, she felt even worse and ran to the bathroom.

After throwing up what felt like her entire body, she brushed her teeth and headed down stairs. Hopefully, she thought, her mom wouldn't notice too much.

"Late night, eh, Sophie?" her mom said, setting a plate of waffles in front of her.

"Ya, it was fun." She smiled back, trying to act normal.

"You were really talking in your sleep last night—talking to some guy named Nate. Is this someone you know? It sounds like you like him a lot," she asked, setting a glass of grapefruit juice in front of her.

"Nate? Oh, um . . . kind of. He's just some guy, but there's nothing happening between us."

Sophie ate her breakfast quickly to end the conversation.

"Anyway, you wouldn't believe what happened to my garden last night. It must have been raccoons. I'm gonna have to do something about them. I can't have them playing in my plants and ruining everything," her mother said, tossing her plate in the sink.

Sophie's eyes got wide in embarrassment. With the evidence in her room, she had an idea of what had really happened.

After breakfast, Sophie went outside to help her mom with the garden. It was hell and hard to keep herself awake in the bright sun. She felt like a thousand pounds, and all she wanted to do was go back to bed. When they finished, she quickly ran upstairs and jumped back into bed. She slept for the rest of the day, right on until the next morning. It was definitely needed.

9

Goodbye to You

The weeks went on as Lisa and Sophie began to hang out more and more with the guy Lisa met from the club. Lisa and Tom had become official as a couple and they were perfect for each other. The group got along great with one another, but something was lacking. Sophie was beginning to see less and less of Lisa. Only on their group outings would she see her, and even those became less often.

Sophie understood, though. Usually, when you meet a person you're infatuated with, you become obsessed with that person in the beginning, because it's all new and fun. So, Sophie didn't take it to heart when Lisa didn't call her as much.

By the beginning of August, Sophie received her letter of acceptance to the acting school in Vancouver. She called Lisa and invited her and Tom out to celebrate. They had drinks and danced until the early hours of the morning.

After that, the weeks went by quickly. Sophie tried to spend some time with Lisa, but it became harder to get together with her. It got to the point where Sophie would ask her to do something and Lisa would say, "Let me check to see if Tom's free, and if he's not, I totally am."

That was the final straw. She begged Lisa to hang out, but Lisa stuck to her guns about checking with Tom. Finally, Sophie gave up, and she figured she would just go on packing for school and see Lisa when she called her.

It was Sophie's last week home before Lisa finally called. They met for dinner that night. When Lisa entered the restaurant, she ran up to Sophie like nothing was wrong and hugged her tightly.

"Hi! How excited are you to be going to Vancouver?" she asked.

"I'm very excited. I actually found out that a friend of mine from high school got accepted, too. Well, she's not really a friend, but an acquaintance. I had told her about the school when I ran into her, and I guess she applied. So, at least I'll know someone, right?" Sophie tried to ignore the fact that she was mad at her.

A hostess greeted them and led them to their table. Looking at her menu, Sophie couldn't shake the awkwardness out of her. There was unfinished business to talk about.

Lisa went on and on about how great Tom was and the stuff they had planned to do that year. Sophie finally interrupted her when she couldn't take anymore.

"Lisa, can I talk to you about something?" she asked.

"Sure, what's up?"

"It's just, you've been very distant lately. I mean, I'm happy that you're with Tom, but it's like you don't even care about your friends anymore. I feel like I'm nowhere near on the top of your priority list and it really hurts my feelings."

"I'm sorry, I didn't think I was doing anything wrong. I spend lots of time with you, Sophie. You know I'm always here."

"I know, but it's just that I'm leaving this weekend and you can be alone with Tom as much as you want from now on, but you couldn't spare a moment for me in three weeks." Sophie's voice rose.

"I am spending time with you. I'm here now," Lisa said defensively.

"Ya, now, but I just don't want us to lose touch when I go away. I know I won't, but I'm afraid you will. I mean, you can't even stay in touch with me, and I live fifteen minutes from you!" Sophie started to get really mad, but she tried hard to keep her cool. Lisa just wasn't seeing it at all. She was absolutely oblivious to everything!

"I won't. I promise. We've been friends for so long. Why would I let that happen? Trust me." Lisa smiled, trying to lighten the mood.

"I'm sorry. I'm not trying to be a bitch. It's just that you're a really good friend and I don't want us to change."

"We won't, so stop worrying, silly girl! Now, let's order something. I'm starving!" Lisa picked up the menu to decide what to eat. Sophie looked at her, not fully convinced, and then picked up her menu, too. The conversation was over.

The dinner continued to have awkwardness to their conversation, at least to Sophie it did. The girls visited and said their goodbyes for the night. Lisa had agreed to come over the day before Sophie left to help her pack and stay over for the night. But Sophie never heard from her that day.

She packed up her things and got ready for bed. It was about 11:00 p.m. when Sophie received a text message from Lisa. It read:

"SORRY I COULDN'T MAKE IT. I WAS BUSY. GOOD LUCK TOMORROW!"

Sophie shut off her phone and threw it on her nightstand. This pissed her off completely. She couldn't believe that Lisa would have the guts to do this. She obviously didn't care about their friendship. Sophie decided to not let this affect her new path in life and to move on with a positive attitude. She hit the lights and went to sleep.

The next morning, Sophie woke up bright and early. What Lisa had pulled the night before was still bothering her. She needed her to show up, something to confirm that maybe she was over reacting about the whole abandoning thing. Now, it only confirmed her feelings. She also wondered where Nate was. She could use him to talk with right about now.

"Sophie, are you up and moving?" her mom called.

"Yea, I'm just getting in the shower now," she yelled, gathering her clean clothes to put on afterward. She didn't have to dress up that much, because she would only be on a plane. Sophie hurried to get ready, as her mother loaded her things into the car.

The friend Sophie spoke about, who had gotten into the school with her, was to meet her at the airport. They would be on the same flight heading to Vancouver. Sophie's mother had breakfast ready for her by the time she came downstairs—just in time to eat and go.

"Are you nervous?" Sophie's mom asked her.

"Kind of. I mean it's a whole new city. I'm very excited, too, though." She smiled.

"I'm nervous for you," her mother said.

"I'll be fine, Mom, no worries. Plus, my friend who's coming, her aunt lives there, so if we have a problem, we can call her, okay? So, there's nothing to worry about." Sophie finished her breakfast and put her dishes in the sink.

Everything was already loaded into the car. Sophie jumped in the passenger seat and they were off to the airport. It seemed like no one was on the road that Sunday morning. Glancing out the window, sadness filled Sophie's heart with the feeling of unfinished business and loss.

She hated this whole friend thing, the more she thought about it. You put so much faith in someone and they become such a big part in your life for what? Just to lose them in the end?

As of this point right now, she didn't have a best friend. The hole in her heart hurt so badly that she had to constantly change her thinking, because if she thought too much on the topic, it would make her cry. She gave herself a shake and tried to stay positive.

As they reached the airport, Sophie began to get excited and very nervous at the same time. They parked the car and entered the airport to check in. Sophie glanced around for her friend.

"Sophie!" a voice called out to her. She turned to see her friend.

"Hey, Natalie!" Sophie said, running up to her.

The girls said their good-byes to their families and headed to the counter to check in.

They chatted a little about their lives, catching up, but mainly spoke about what they expected in Vancouver. It was nice to talk about something new, Sophie thought. It would be a new beginning and hopefully new friends, she thought to herself once again.

The plane ride was about three hours. When they landed, their home-stay family was there to pick them up. Natalie and Sophie had gotten their apartment through home-stay, which Natalie's family had checked out for them before agreeing to rent it. Home-stay is when a family rents out rooms to students, usually a basement apartment. The family had their names written on a sign, for the girls to know who they were looking for.

The drive from the airport was exciting, because Vancouver was so green and fresh looking. They arrived at their house and the family helped the girls with their luggage. The basement apartment was a perfect size for them—with a built-in kitchen and two bedrooms. The girls also had a living room with a television and a fireplace. It was exactly what they were looking for.

That night, the girls settled in, unpacking and relaxing by watching some television until it was time for bed. They knew they couldn't stay up too late, because they were to head to their school the next morning for registration. They had to make sure they could figure out their way around town with the transportation and be on time! Sophie was sure it was going to be fantastic.

10

Vancouver

After showering the next morning and eating her breakfast, Sophie got ready for school. Natalie slowly moved from her room, dragging her feet, covered in pink fluffy slippers that slapped across the floor. She was just getting into the shower. Sophie looked at the time and rolled her eyes.

"Hey, Natalie, you better hurry up. We have to leave soon."

Natalie yawned and closed the bathroom door without saying a word.

"Okay, fantastic, this is great. Nothing like being late on your first day," she thought to herself.

Sophie continued to pack up her stuff, and then laid her bag at the front door. She flopped on the couch, looking at her city map. The shower continued to run for what seemed like forever.

Finally, Natalie came out, walked into her room, and closed the door. Sophie looked at her watch, knowing that they had to leave in ten minutes! She dropped her head back and closed her eyes with frustration.

"Hey, if you stay tense like that, you'll get wrinkles. I swear."

Sophie opened her eyes and looked to her left.

"Nathan!"

"Shhhh, your friend will hear." He laughed.

"How are you?" she whispered back, smiling.

"I'm good, how are you doing? This is exciting, eh? Vancouver is such a fantastic city." He stood up and walked over to the window.

"Really? Well, good, that's just what I need. I'm nervous, but anxious for today." She followed him to the window.

The sun began to shine through the blinds that were partially open. His eyes lit up from the warm light.

"Just wait until the cherry blossoms bloom. They're beautiful, especially when they begin to fall and it looks like pink snow."

Sophie stood there, staring at him. "Have you been here before?"

"No. But I remember Serena telling me about the cherry blossoms, so I want to see them, you know, see what she was so obsessed about. I felt Japan would be too far to go." He smiled.

"So, how are you and this whole Lisa thing?" he said, changing the subject.

"It hurts. I feel like I always lose people who are close to me. Even you are starting to show up less and less."

"Sophie, I told you that I'm not going anywhere. There are just some things I have to let you experience on your own." He turned to look at her.

"But you're the only friend I have now." She sighed.

"You have Natalie. You're not alone, Soph. Anyway, I'm not even alive, so how can I be your friend? I'm your guardian angel, remember? That's all," he said sadly.

"Nathan, you're a friend to me. At least I think of you as one, and more than that . . . " she trailed off.

"Thank you, Soph. That's nice of you. But you need some real friends, not one that people will think you're crazy for having." He looked back out the window. "That's all you need—people knowing you as the girl with the imaginary friend."

"You're real to me," Sophie said confidently, as she raised her hand to touch Nathan on the arm.

He quickly stepped away. "Sophie, you can't."

"It's so stupid," she mumbled.

"Come on, Soph, don't be like that. It's the rules and I can't do anything about it."

"Why don't you just do what you want?" she said, as she raised her voice a bit.

"Don't you think I would if I could? What kind of person do you think I am? I can't do anything about it, so just drop it."

"Let's not fight, okay, Sophie, please?" His face softened, as he tried to comfort her with his smile.

"Sorry, you're right," she whispered. "Look, you better go, Natalie should be about ready now and we have to leave."

"Sophie, don't be mad at me." He stepped in front of her, as she tried to walk away.

"I'm not mad, Nate. I'm just frustrated. I'm not mad at you, I swear." She tried to smile, but it just looked awkward, because she didn't really mean it.

"Wow, that's a crazy looking smile. Don't use that at school, okay?" he joked.

"I'll talk to you later, then?" she asked, looking back at him.

"I promise. I'll talk with you this week. Good luck and have fun." Then, he was gone.

It was perfect timing, because Natalie had just finished getting dressed and was coming out of her room.

"I'm ready!" she announced with a smile.

It was like she was a whole different person. Who knows who that person was who came out of the room earlier.

"Good morning. I grabbed you an apple and a granola bar to eat on the way. I figured you didn't have time to eat," Sophie said, picking up her bag.

"Thanks, buddy." Natalie smiled, stuffing them in her pocket.

They headed out the door and down the street to the bus stop. The bus took about ten minutes to the sky train, and then the sky train was another fifteen-minute ride to the stadium exit. The sky train was a great way to see the city. It went across the ground and above the ground to many destinations. The view was fantastic and it was a fast way to get from one place to another.

The school was only three blocks from the sky train. It was an old stone building, a little rundown looking. As they entered the building, the doors slammed behind them and the floors creaked, as they walked up the stairs to the third floor. It was cold and the floorboard heaters made funny sounds throughout the building.

The door at the top of the stairs was open and flagged with colorful ribbon and a big sign that said, "Acting for Film & Television."

The girls entered the room. Very few people were there yet. A tall man came up to them and introduced himself.

"I'm Patrick. I run this place and I'll be your lead acting coach," he said, shaking their hands.

"I'm Sophie and this is Natalie." The girls smiled.

"Ahh, yes, you're the girls from Ontario, right?" He laughed.

"Hey, what's wrong with Ontario?" Natalie said defensively.

"Oh nothing, it's just that we never get anyone from there. We've always thought it was because they think they're too good for us. Well, have a seat while we wait for the rest to arrive."

"He was interesting." Sophie laughed. Natalie was still pondering the whole Ontario thing. Sophie headed over to the row of chairs.

There was a girl with beautiful long curly hair, who turned toward Sophie, as she sat down beside her.

"Hi! I'm Elaina," she said happily.

"Hey, I'm Sophie. Where are you from?"

"I'm actually from here, well, more like Victoria. Is this your first acting class?"

"Yes," Sophie admitted.

"Don't worry. A lot of people will have no experience as well. You'll be great. I did some theatre for my university last year, but I've never acted for film before."

Something about Elaina was so relaxing.

"These guys behind us are Brandon, Josh, and Chris," she said, pointed to each guy.

"Hi, guys," Sophie said, shaking their hands.

Josh had a skinnier boyish kind of look to him. He had dark brown hair and braces. You could tell he was one of those guys who would be the show-off of the class, but not in a bad way.

Brandon had a kind face, but was a total goof. And then, there was Chris. He was much older and taller, with the build of a boxer, and was kind of creepy. As more students walked in, everyone introduced himself, and they tried to get to know each other as best they could.

There was a girl with bright, fire-engine red hair named Adel. She was definitely an exciting person and very blunt! Another boy, who walked in, acting very shy, looked to be the youngest. His name was Mark and he was about nineteen years old.

Just then, a young girl sat beside Sophie. She had platinum blonde hair and was very fair-skinned with bright blue eyes.

"Hi, I'm Julie." She smiled.

"Hey, I'm Sophie."

"Wow, there are a lot of people here, eh? We must have like twenty students in our class," Julie said, looking around.

"Ya, actually I was expecting a small class. This is kind of intimidating." Sophie giggled.

The orientation began with Patrick introducing all of the teachers.

There was a different coach for each class. All of them seemed to be really nice and very outgoing. Patrick told the class about what they expected from them and what they should expect from their coaches. The classes included learning to act for film and television, improv classes, voice lessons, auditioning skills, breaking apart a script, and more.

They had arranged for agents and casting directors to join the class throughout the year for the students to practice auditioning. It was also a great way to get your name out there! At the end of the year, the class would do a showcase for a room full of agents and casting directors in hopes of being signed or noticed. It was also open for friends and family to come see what they had learned throughout the year.

The orientation ran about three hours, because the graduating students from the class before had their ceremony. It was nice because afterward, they spoke with the new students, answering a lot of their questions. When everything was said and done, Patrick invited everyone out to a local pub for dinner and drinks.

As the night went on, they were all enjoying themselves and became more comfortable with each other. One of the graduates came over to Sophie and tapped her on the shoulder. She turned around to see a young man standing there.

"Hey, I'm Jake." He smiled.

"Sophie," she answered, blushing.

"So, we're short some people. Do you wanna play some pool?"

"Um, sure. I'm not that great."

"No worries, lucky for you I'm fantastic." He laughed.

"I see, well then, lucky me," she said, getting up from her chair to join him.

"Can I play?" Natalie called from the table.

"Sure, we need one more player," Jake hollered back.

Natalie jumped from her seat and ran to the table. There was another guy at the table, waiting for them.

"This is my friend, Kevin."

"Hi, I'm Natalie and this is Sophie! Whose team am I on?" Natalie said eagerly.

"You're with me, girly," Kevin said, throwing his arm around her shoulder. He was tall and handsome. Natalie was totally smitten with him.

When Natalie was interested in someone, no one should get in her way. She was persistent and knew no fear! It wouldn't matter if that guy's girlfriend were standing there. She would still pursue him. Natalie enjoyed a challenge and thrived on it. Sophie admired her confidence, but was sometimes embarrassed by how forward her friend was. She really had no shame in doing whatever it took to get a guy.

"You guys break," Kevin said, handing the white ball to Jake.

"Thanks, man." He turned to Sophie and held it out for her to take.

"Oh, no! You go right ahead. If I do, there will be balls all over the floor!" she said seriously.

"Balls all over the floor, eh?" Jake laughed.

"I mean, it's just, oh god, fine. Give it to me," she said, with a bright red face, while grabbing the ball.

"That's the way to take hold of the situation, Soph. Show those balls who's boss!" Kevin joked.

Natalie giggled, slapping him on the arm. "Kevin, you're so funny!" She laughed ridiculously.

Sophie rolled her eyes and aimed her cue stick at the white ball. "You asked for it."

With one loud crack, the white ball skipped across the table, slamming into the balls and throwing them everywhere.

"Holy geeze!" Kevin said, ducking, as a blue ball flew past his head, followed by a striped ball that hit Natalie on the hand.

"You weren't kidding!" Jake laughed.

"My hand!" Natalie complained. It barely touched her, and more like grazed across the top of her hand.

Sophie walked over to her. "I'm sorry, Nat, I didn't mean to. You know how bad I am at this game," Sophie said, checking her hand. She knew Natalie was only doing this for attention, but she went with it.

"Ahh, Natalie, let me see." Kevin lifted her hand, and then kissed it softly. "There, you're all good now." He smiled.

"Ah, thanks." She smiled back, hugging him.

Sophie thought this was so dumb, but this was Natalie. She was definitely going to make a good actress someday.

Kevin stepped up and took his shot, knocking in a lot of their balls. It was now Jake's turn.

"Come here, Sophie," he said, pulling her near. "Let me show you how to shoot the right way."

Sophie smiled nervously, as he touched her. He leaned over her with his hands on hers, controlling the shot. Softly, he shot the ball into the hole.

"And that's how it's done," he whispered in her ear.

"I see," she said, standing up, with his hand still on her lower back.

He was so cute, she thought. Sophie admired him more and more as the night went on.

The four of them played many games and chatted, getting to know more about each other. They had even made plans to get together one weekend and go clubbing. Finally, around 1:30 a.m., Sophie yawned.

"I think we should head out, Natalie," she said, grabbing her jacket off the stool. Natalie sighed.

"Do you guys want a ride home? It's kind of late for girls to be walking alone," Jake said.

"That would be great. It makes me nervous walking at night," Sophie said.

"Well, Kevin has to drop me off, so we'll drive you two home. Let's go," he said, helping Sophie with her jacket.

The four of them headed out the door and down the street to Kevin's car. They were all pretty tired on the ride home. By the time they reached their house, Natalie was out cold, sleeping in the front seat. Kevin woke her gently and helped her out of the car.

"I'll take her from here. Thanks again, guys. Let us know when we can hit the clubs, okay?" Sophie said, dragging Natalie up their sidewalk to the door.

"I'll call ya for sure. Good night," Jake yelled from the car.

Sophie struggled, as she helped Natalie inside and to her bed.

"See you in the morning, Nat," Sophie said, turning off her lights.

It was 2:30 a.m. by the time Sophie got into her bed. She lay there looking at the ceiling. Jake was pretty cool, she thought. He was the boy next door with an edgier rocker look. She couldn't help but think of him that night. Would he really call her? She would have to wait and find out.

The next few weeks were filled with outgoing and exciting classes. Sophie got to know her classmates a lot better and even texted with Jake throughout the day. She found herself becoming more confident and speaking her mind a lot more. After school, she would hang out with Julie and Natalie. The three of them went shopping, saw movies, and went clubbing.

Once a week, the class would go to their usual pub and have appetizers and drinks. Some of the grads from the previous class would join them at times, including Jake and Kevin. The more Sophie and Jake hung out, the more she liked him. They never spoke much, but the conversations they did have were simple and almost shy.

Julie would tease Sophie about him, telling her to go for him! Sometimes, the two of them would sit up all night, talking about boys. Natalie usually fell asleep somewhere in the middle of the conversation. She was a heavy sleeper and a good one at that. Sophie joked how they could probably throw a party while Natalie slept, and she wouldn't even flinch an eyelash.

One night, Jake texted Sophie, asking her to come out clubbing with him, Kevin, and a few friends. She then texted Julie, asking her if she wanted to come. Julie answered back instantly. She was always up for a good time!

"Hey, Natalie!" Sophie yelled into the other room.

"Ya?" Natalie answered.

"Wanna go out to the club tonight with Kevin and some friends?"

"Hell ya!" Natalie yelled, running out. She was in her pajamas and it was only 6:00 p.m. That girl lived for sleeping. Sophie only saw her at school in normal clothes. It was so weird.

Sophie texted Jake back and agreed to meet them at the club.

"Do you need to shower, Natalie?" Sophie asked.

"No, I'm good. I did earlier today." She smiled.

"Thank god," Sophie whispered to herself. The thought of waiting for Natalie to shower and get ready was frustrating, because of the amount of time it took. Sophie jumped up and ran into the bathroom before Natalie changed her mind. About an hour later, Julie arrived at their door. She had brought her stuff to stay over night.

"Yay, fun night out!" she said, jumping onto Sophie's bed. Sophie shook her head. She loved how crazy Julie was all the time. Julie ran to the bathroom to touch up her makeup alongside Sophie.

"Looking good, Soph! Any reason for that?" she teased.

"Ha ha, very funny, yes I kind of like Jake. But I look the same every time we go out. Just today I curled my hair, just trying something new," Sophie explained.

"Whatever, Soph." Julie laughed. "Hey, where's Nat?"

"She's in her room getting ready."

"Oh god, I hope she started early."

"She did and I also helped by telling her an earlier time than when we're going, so we won't be late." Sophie giggled.

"Nicely played, my friend." The two of them smirked at each other.

Sophie stood back from the mirror to look at herself. She had on a cute jean skirt and a tube top, with her long hair hanging down in curls over her shoulders. Julie was dressed in a cute little black dress with heels. Sophie ran into her room to grab her tall black boots from the closet. She slid them on.

"How do they look?" Sophie asked.

"Sexy, very sexy, Sophie," Julie said with a smile.

"Shut up." Sophie laughed.

"I'm ready!" Natalie yelled, as she ran into the room.

She quickly looked over Julie, "You're wearing that?"

"Yes, why?" Julie said, looking at her rudely.

"Oh, no, it looks good. It just was surprising that you chose that dress, since you're so pale," Natalie said, turning toward the mirror to check herself out.

"Julie, you look great, so don't worry about it," Sophie said, trying to turn her attention from Natalie.

"Thanks, Soph," she said, staring Natalie down.

"All right, let's get going. We have to catch the sky train," Sophie said, grabbing her purse off the bed. They grabbed their jackets and headed out the door. Natalie ran closely behind, locking the door behind her.

11

The Dragon's Club

The sky train was filled with people heading into the city for the night. Vancouver was always so lively and there was always something happening. The tension between Julie and Natalie hadn't passed, but at least Julie was speaking to her.

Sophie reached into her purse and pulled out her phone. She was hoping for a text from Jake, but there was nothing there.

"Are you hoping he'll text?" Julie teased.

"No, I was just checking the time . . . " Sophie responded quickly.

"Ya, right. Don't worry. He'll show."

"I'm not worried. I have you girls to entertain me for the night!" She giggled.

"Of course, we'll have a blast no matter what."

"Hell, ya!" Natalie jumped in.

The sky train slowed, as it pulled up to their stop. "Granville Station," the voice said over the monitor. The girls hopped off the sky train and headed up the escalader to the street. It was so weird that it was called a sky train, since there were times when it would come from the sky down to the underground like a subway.

The streets were filled with lights with lively people, heading out for a good time. Sophie had fallen in love with everything Vancouver had to offer. They stopped at the corner of Robson and Granville, waiting to cross the street.

"I hope there are some hotties there tonight!" Natalie giggled.

"I'm sure you'll find them," Sophie teased.

"Or are you going for Kevin?" Julie asked. That made Natalie all flustered and their conversation blew up. Sophie laughed and shook her head.

"You look pretty, Soph." The voice startled her. To her left was Nate.

"Nate!" she whispered surprisingly. She quickly glanced over at the girls, but they hadn't noticed, because they were still gabbing.

"What are you doing here?" she asked.

"I wanted to say hi, that's all." He smiled. "You going to meet that guy?"

Sophie blushed and didn't know what to say. "Well, ya, but he's just a friend. I mean, we're all going out as friends," she stuttered.

"Sophie, it's cool. I'm just asking. I'm happy for you."

For some reason, Sophie felt so awkward talking to Nate about another guy, especially one she could possibly like. Sophie looked at the ground, not knowing what to say.

"Well, Soph, I'll see you later. Have a good night. You really do look pretty." The crossing light flashed for the girls to cross.

"Nate!" Sophie yelled, but he was gone. She looked around for him, but Julie soon grabbed her arm and pulled her along the way.

"Who's Nate?" Julie asked.

"Oh, um, I just thought I saw someone I knew."

"All right, friend, then let's go." She laughed. The three of them hustled down the street to the nightclub. Out front were Kevin, Jake, and Josh waiting to go in. Sophie blushed, as she walked up and saw Jake smiling at her.

"Hey," he said.

"Hey, hope you guys weren't waiting too long," Natalie said excitedly.

"Na, we just got here. Everyone else is inside already. So, let's hurry and head in," Kevin said, pulling the girls into the line up. Once inside, they took their jackets off for coat check.

"Here, I'll put yours with mine," Jake insisted to Sophie.

"Oh, sure. Thanks," she said, handing her jacket to him. She rubbed her arms, as the doorway was chilly with the air blowing in.

"You'll warm up soon," he said, walking up behind her, rubbing her arms. Sophie blushed at the touch of his hand.

"You look nice," he said, as they walked into the club.

Sophie instantly thought of Nate. She wasn't sure why, but her mind was trailing off from her short awkward visit with him.

"Ya, she does! She's a hottie!" Julie yelled, running up beside them.

"Thank you, Julie!" Sophie laughed, hugging her.

"Let's get some drinks!" Kevin yelled over the music.

They headed over to the main bar. Waiting there was the rest of the class. Sophie always loved how everyone came out together.

"Hey, Soph!" Adel yelled.

"Hey! You look great, girl!" Sophie said, hugging her.

"Thanks, I think so, too. Get a damn drink. You gotta catch up to us!" Adel said, waving the bartender down for more drinks.

"Soph, what you drinking?" Jake leaned over and asked.

"I think I'll go with Vodka Ice tonight! Thanks."

They all grabbed their drinks and headed to the dance floor. The music in the club blasted with some of the top hits on the radio with a perfect mix of old school. Everyone was drinking and having fun. Sophie looked around, as she danced. It was awesome to have a big group of friends with her.

She thought, "This is a good life." At that moment, she was happy with her life and who was in it. But if this was working out so perfectly, would Nate then decide that she didn't need him anymore? She gave herself a shake and shut her mind off. It was time to have fun, not worry.

Natalie pulled Sophie over to her and Kevin dancing. That was one thing that she and Natalie had in common—they both loved to dance. Jake moved in behind Sophie and started to dance with her. She turned to face him, as they danced closer. He smelt good, and slowly, they started to pull away from their group into their own area.

It made Sophie nervous, but she went with it. Their faces moved closer together and soon their bodies were touching. He stared at Sophie in the eyes and she smiled at him. Just then, Natalie ran over and grabbed Sophie's hand.

"Soph! Come dance with me. Kevin is back at the bar." She pulled at Sophie.

Jake looked at her a little disappointed for destroying their moment.

"Um, Nat! Where is Julie?" Sophie asked, looking back at Jake.

"She's up on the stage, dancing with some guys." She pointed.

"Nice! We should go join her!" Sophie said, figuring she could move them all up there, and hopefully, Natalie would find a guy to dance with. They joined Julie on the stage. Natalie pulled Sophie in to dance with her. Sophie decided she had to make a move now.

She turned and pulled Jake close to dance. But Natalie was not pleased with having no one to dance with.

When they went out to clubs and Natalie had no guy to dance with, she needed the girls. If she did, it was like the girls didn't exist. You could definitely say she craved the attention. Natalie turned to dance toward Julie, but she was caught up in the guy she was with. Suddenly, Julie ran over to Sophie.

"I'm running to the bathroom. You wanna come?"

"No, I'm good," Sophie said.

"I know you are," Julie teased, and then hurried off the stage. Jake pulled Sophie's waist in to him.

"Hey, you," he whispered in her ear. He was drawing her attention back to him.

Sophie smiled at him. "Hey." Their faces drew close again.

The music pumped and they danced closer every second. Just then, she heard Julie's voice yell, "What the hell?"

Sophie looked over Jake's shoulder to see Julie standing behind him. Sophie stepped away from Jake to see what she was looking at. Natalie was dancing close with the guy Julie was just with. Julie stormed over and pulled him back, as Natalie gave a look of death to her.

The guy was quick to join Julie, and it seemed like he would take whatever he could, because he didn't care whom he was dancing with. He also looked smashed.

Sophie took another sip of the drink she was carrying, thinking it was about to get messy, and she was definitely not drunk enough to handle it.

"This looks bad," Jake joked.

Natalie started dancing again and close to Julie. Then, she reached over, took the boy's hand from Julie's waist, and pulled him over. Julie pulled him back. It wasn't even about the guy; it was more about not letting the other win. Natalie finally pulled him back once again and pressed him close to her. Julie's face was flaming! Natalie then leaned up and kissed him.

"Bitch!" Julie screamed. She reached over and grabbed a chunk of Natalie's hair and ripped it out, and then stormed off the stage. Natalie had the look of accomplishment in her eyes. Sophie shook her head back at Natalie. "Not cool, Nat."

"Well, I can't help it if I attract guys," she yelled back.

Sophie grabbed Jake's hand and headed off the stage. They looked for Julie and finally found her at the bar. "Are you okay?" Sophie asked.

"No, she's such a skank. Everything is a competition with her. She can't stand it if she's the only one not getting attention."

"I know. It was a really shitty move," Sophie said, hugging her friend.

"Come on, girls, let's have a drink and brush it off. You're a hottie, Jules. You can do better than that guy and better than Natalie any day. So, don't sweat it," Jake said, ordering the girls some shots. Julie smiled and tried to forget it.

"Come on, buddy, let's party!" Sophie said, lifting her shot to cheers. Soon everyone joined them and the entire class was drinking shot after shot. Finally, Natalie showed her face.

"I want in on this!" she yelled, as if nothing had happened.

"Walk away, just walk away." Julie pointed toward the door.

Once again, this was about to get messy. Everyone had a bunch of drinks in them now and it was getting late. Jake pulled Sophie over and whispered in her ear.

"Let them work it out."

Sophie looked at Nat, as Kevin and Josh quickly joined her. At least she was occupied for the moment.

Jake lifted his hand up to Sophie's face, tucking her hair behind her ear.

He leaned in again. "So, I just want to let you know, I don't have a girlfriend."

"Oh, really?" Sophie said, blushing again.

"Ya, and I kind of really like you," he said, squeezing her hand.

Sophie didn't know what to say. He pulled her face in toward his. Suddenly, Sophie was shoved from behind into Jake. He caught her quickly. It was Julie. Natalie pushed her and the two of them were going at it. They were screaming and pulling at each other, when the guys jumped in to separate them.

"You okay?" Jake said, helping Sophie to her feet.

"Ya, I'm good." She got her balance for a moment and realized the alcohol was kicking in. Then, she grabbed Julie and pulled her toward the front door.

"I swear to god, I'm gonna smack the shit out of that girl!" Julie said, fuming.

"Okay, well, for now, walk with me. I need you. I drank too much," Sophie said, hoping to take her mind off of Natalie. But she also needed her because she really was drunk.

They headed to the coat check. Jake ran up to them and handed the coat ticket to the lady. "Can you believe her? Like really? She better keep her distance tonight or I'll ... "

"You'll what?" Natalie interrupted, walking toward her.

"You really are a stupid girl, aren't you?" Julie laughed, pushing through Jake and Sophie.

"Whoa, hold on, guys. Let's not do this!" Jake said, holding Julie back.

"Oh my god," Sophie said, giggling to herself. She shook her head, thinking of what the rest of the night was going to be like once they got home. Sophie slipped her jacket on and grabbed Julie's arm.

"Come on, let's go," she said, leading her out the door.

Everyone said their good-byes until the only ones left were Kevin, Jake, and the three girls.

"Want a ride home, Nat?" Kevin said. He had someone coming to pick them up in his car. "Ya, that'd be cool," Nat replied, smiling at him.

"Here's my car now. Get in girls," he said, opening the door.

Nat got in the front with Kevin. His car held three people in the front and back.

Julie slid in the back and Sophie followed.

"Oh, crap!" Sophie yelled, as she slipped off the curb and fell to the ground. Then, she started laughing hysterically.

"Oh, man, are you okay, Soph? A little too much for you tonight, eh?" Jake laughed, lifting her up into the car. Julie pulled her friend from the inside.

"Oh my god, are you okay? That friggen made my night. You are so funny." Julie laughed.

"Oh, ya. I'm sooo good, Nate." Sophie giggled, slurring her words.

"Nate?" Julie said.

"No . . . not Nate," Sophie said, laughing.

It was awkward for only a moment. The group was all too drunk for anyone to really concentrate on what Sophie was talking about.

Jake leaned against the window, falling asleep slowly. Sophie laid her head down on Julie's shoulder. "Hello, friend. I'm going to use you as my pillow if you don't mind."

"No worries" she said, resting her head on top of Sophie's.

The ride home was kind of brutal, due to the amount of alcohol in everyone.

Natalie and Kevin were singing at the top of their lungs the entire way. Jake fell asleep, and Julie and Sophie tried to contain their dizziness as the car shook. Suddenly, they heard Kevin yelling.

"Nat! Oh. man, that's so disgusting!"

He was freaking out. Sophie flew up, looking over Kevin's shoulder. Natalie had thrown up all over the front seat and floor.

"Oh my god, I'm gonna throw up!" Sophie said, sitting back quickly. "I can't look!!" she said, covering her mouth.

"Don't you dare!" Kevin said, turning around to see if she was serious.

They were only a block from the girls' place, but it felt like forever. The car pulled up, and Kevin pushed his friend out quickly and followed behind. He flew around the car and opened Natalie's door.

"Come on you, out of the car before you make a bigger mess," he said, carefully lifting her from the vehicle.

Julie and Sophie got out and stumbled together to the door. Jake was fast asleep, so Sophie couldn't say good-bye. Kevin carried Natalie to the door. Sophie tried to get the door unlocked as quickly as possible, but she was having a hard time seeing the keyhole.

Finally, they got in. Julie threw on the lights and led Kevin to Natalie's room, so he could place her on the bed.

"My car is a mess. Do you have anything I could do a quick clean with, Soph?" he said disgustingly.

"Ya, there's some paper towel on the counter. Ohhh! But we should get the water to clean with . . . and Nat's towel," Sophie said confused.

"What?" Julie laughed. Sophie ran off and grabbed one of Nat's towels and wet it with water to scrub with.

"Oh, Nat's gonna be so pissed when she finds out you used her towel, Soph," Julie said with a smile on her face.

"Whatever . . . she made the mess." Sophie laughed, heading toward the door to go help Kevin clean his car. She ran down the steps toward the street, and crossed the road, not even looking for cars.

"Sophie!" a voice yelled, grabbing her by the hand. She was quickly pulled toward the curb, where she fell onto the grass, as a car raced by.

"What the hell?" Sophie laughed, lying there. She hadn't noticed what happened or who grabbed her. Kevin stepped out of his car.

"Soph, what are you doing on the grass?" He laughed, helping her up.

"Oh, you know, just checking, checking the stuff grass does," she said, brushing herself off.

"Awesome. Can I have that towel while you do so?" he said, taking the towel from her hands. She stood there, waiting for Kevin to finish.

"Okay. I think that's as good as it's getting tonight. I'll have to take it to the car wash tomorrow and get it scrubbed out. Tell Nat I'll send her the bill," he said seriously.

"Will do," Sophie said, saluting him.

"Oh, Sophie, you need to get some rest there, solider." He laughed, giving her a hug good-bye. "Too bad Jake isn't awake. He'd want to say goodnight."

"No worries—let him sleep. I'll talk to ya later," Sophie said, waving goodbye, as he got in his car and took off. Sophie took a deep breath. Her head was still spinning.

"Sophie, look before you cross, all right? Look at me for a second."

Sophie blinked her eyes a few times before her sight adjusted to the person in front of her. "Nate?" she said softly.

"Ya, it's me, what are you doing? You almost got yourself killed!" he said, holding her face and looking her over for any bruises.

"I'm fine! It's fine, Nate, geeze," she said, moving his hands from her face.

She started to cross the road. Nate followed her closely, and then grabbed her hand, as she started to stray from the straight line she was walking.

"What are you doing? I'm fine," she yelled at him.

"No, you're not. Let me help you," he yelled back. He led her to the door, still trying to look her over for any scratches.

"Nate, just leave me alone, okay? If you're gonna be here, actually be here, all right?" she said, pulling her hand from his one last time. Suddenly, the door flew open and Nate was gone.

"Get in here, girl." Julie laughed, pulling Sophie inside.

"What a crazy night, eh? Did Kevin get his car cleaned?"

"Well, for what it could be for now. It's still really disgusting in there."

"Man, Natalie better pay for it. That lazy cow."

"Oh, I don't think Nate would let her off without paying," Sophie said, grabbing a glass from the kitchen cupboard to get some water.

"Nate? You mean Kevin. Who is this Nate you keep talking about, Sophie?"

"I said Kevin."

"No, you didn't." The girls stood there awkwardly, as Sophie pondered what to say.

"Anyway, where is Nat? Asleep? Wow, are things gonna be weird in the morning."

Sophie grabbed a pot from the cupboard and filled it with water. She then placed it on the stove.

"What are you doing, Soph?"

"I'm making crap dinner, duh. Want some?"

"Ohhh, yum, yes, definitely," Julie said, pulling up a chair at the table. They tried hard to stay awake while the water was boiling. A creaking sound came from Nat's door, sounding like it was opening. Natalie slowly stumbled from her room.

"What are you guys doing?" she said, smiling.

"Nothing, go back to bed," Julie said, brushing her off.

"Oh, get over yourself, Julie," Nat said, staring her down.

"You get over yourself, Natalie," Julie said, getting up to face her. "I've never seen someone so full of herself! I can't even believe what you pulled tonight. Were you that threatened by me?"

"Please, I don't need to ever worry about you," Nat said, walking up to the stove.

"Hey, guys, let's not fight anymore. We can eat crap dinner and just chill, okay? Sound like a plan?" Sophie said, pouring the pasta into the pot.

"Shut up for a minute, Soph. This is between Julie and me." Sophie shut her mouth, giving Nat a dirty look and continued to stir.

"Don't yell at her. She didn't do anything," Julie said, getting in Natalie's face.

"Guys, its cool, come on," Sophie said, waving her wooden spoon in between the girls.

Natalie ripped the spoon from her hand and threw it on the counter.

"Hey, my spoon! Now you get no crap dinner!" Sophie teased. She was not taking any of this seriously.

"Get out of my face, Nat, cause I could take you down in a second!" Julie threatened.

"I dare you to!" Natalie screamed back.

"Oh, shit, it's going down now!" Sophie laughed, jumping up on the counter for a better view.

"Soph!" Julie laughed. "Get down or you'll fall."

"Sophie! You're burning the crap dinner!" Julie yelled, pulling it off the burner. It was pretty black. Sophie had not put enough water in the pot and it had evaporated, causing the noodles to stick to the sides and burn.

"Ewww . . . I'm so not eating that!" Sophie laughed, slipping down from the counter.

"Let's just leave it in the sink for tonight. I think you should go to bed, Soph." Julie turned her interest toward helping Sophie to bed.

Natalie stood there smiling, thinking she had won this one.

"Oh, and you and me? We're not finished yet," Julie said quietly.

"Oh, I know," Natalie answered, watching Julie lead Sophie to her room. Finally, she gave in and headed to bed herself.

"I'm good, Jules, thanks. I Promise." Sophie smiled to her friend, releasing Julie's grip from her arms.

"You sure?"

"Yes, I swear."

"All right, girl, have a good night. I'm gonna crash on your couch. See you in the morning," Julie said, closing the door behind her. Sophie stumbled over to the bed and plopped down. Her body lay half on and half off the bed. She breathed slowly, trying to stop the dizziness. Then, she slowly slipped off the bed and crashed to the floor.

"Ouch." She giggled to herself.

She felt a hand on the back of her neck.

"Come on, slowly." It was Nate carefully helping her up back onto the bed.

"I don't need you, Nate. I said I was fine," she moaned.

He didn't say anything and continued to help her. He pulled back her covers, as Sophie stood up again and started to undress.

"Soph, just leave your clothes on and get into bed, all right?" he said, turning away from her. She pulled at her shirt, as it got caught on her bra strap.

"Ahh! Help me. I'm stuck."

"Soph, you don't make this easy," he said, turning toward her to help.

"Then, don't help me," she said, as he pulled the shirt off over her head.

"Don't be like that, Sophie. Why is it every time you get drunk, you're angry with me? Is there something you want to say to me? Have I upset you or something? I really don't get it," he said, guiding her to her bed.

She sat down and started to pull her jean skirt off. Nate looked away as she did. Sophie climbed under the covers and didn't answer him.

"All right, Sophie," he said, stepping away from her bed.

"Because you make me mad, Nate," she blurted out.

"Why?" he said, sitting down on the side of her bed.

"You know why," she said, opening her eyes to look at him.

Her eyes began to water, and she looked away, pulling the covers up tight to her face.

"Sophie," Nate said, putting his hand on her. He didn't want to talk about what he knew she was getting at. She continued to cry silently.

"Why can't you for one night just care, Nate?" she said, turning over, so she didn't have to face him.

"Sophie, I care about you more than you know. More than I'm allowed to."

"No, you don't."

"What do you want me to do, Soph? Don't be mad at me."

She didn't answer, and just moved over a bit to the edge of the bed.

"Come lie here for a bit."

"Sophie. I can't," he said, hesitating.

"Fine. Good night, Nate," she said, closing her eyes. Nate looked at her, knowing this was definitely against the rules, but he couldn't stand her being like this. He slowly pulled the covers down and got in the bed beside her.

She opened her eyes and turned back over to see Nate, lying across from her. He smiled at her.

"I'm sorry, Soph," he whispered, grabbing her hand and holding it close to him. She moved closer to him until their faces were almost touching.

Nate felt uneasy with this, not because he didn't want it, but because he knew this was going too far. But, at the same time, he couldn't stop himself. They lay there, staring at each other. He watched, as Sophie's eyes slowly started to close.

"Don't leave me, Nate," she said quietly. She squeezed his hand close to her heart.

He brushed a strand of hair from her face, as she shifted in closer against his chest.

Nate sighed. He couldn't help himself. He pulled her waist in close, holding her for the night, as she slept.

"Sophie, you're gonna get me in so much trouble, crazy girl." He smiled, closing his eyes. It was the deepest, calmest sleep Sophie had had since moving to Vancouver.

Morning came and the sun shone through the windows, lighting up the room. Sophie opened her eyes to see Nathan fast asleep. She smiled, as she watched him breathe softly. He was so beautiful, even as he slept.

Waking up beside him felt nice, like this was the way things should be. His left arm was around her waist, holding her tightly, and his other hand held hers. There was something about him. She didn't want to let him go.

Even if he weren't real, he was what she needed. There had to be a way she could keep him in her life. She just couldn't believe that he was just there to guide her. How could he be there to show her the right things when he was the right thing himself? Sophie was sure of it.

But was she sure that he felt the same way? He definitely didn't like to talk about it. If he were only there to do a job, how was she to ignore the perfectness right in front of her? Maybe she did have to learn to control her feelings. Suddenly, Nate's eyes shifted and started to open.

"Morning," Sophie said softly.

He smiled back. "Good morning." He pulled his arm from around her and from her hand to stretch. "Oh, man, this is the smallest bed I've ever slept in."

"Ya, sorry about that. And sorry about last night, Nate. I'm not sure what all I said to you but, thanks for helping me" she said, embarrassed.

"Sophie, it's fine. But you have to understand something. There are rules to what I do and I have to follow them carefully. Or I won't be able to help you at all."

"You seem to think I don't care about you, but I do very much. But whatever I do or say is what's good for you, okay? Please don't make me feel bad anymore for doing my job. I push the limits for you every day, because I feel that you need it, even if I get in trouble for it. So, help me out here, Soph," he said, smiling at her.

"I know. I'm sorry. It's just that things are better when you're around and I . . . "

"I know, Soph, I know," he said, cutting her off. She knew he didn't want to hear anymore.

They lay there in silence with an understanding.

"So, what do you want to do today?" Nate asked.

"What? What do you mean?" she said, confused by what he meant. It sounded like he was asking her to hang out.

"Well, I figure you need a fun day. Those two have some stuff to work out, so you should let them, and I'll help you have some fun!" he said, smiling.

"Really?" She couldn't believe what she was hearing—a day with Nate?

"Ya Soph, really…"

"Um, ya, definitely. Let me just jump in the shower and clean up. But what do I say if the girls ask what I'm doing?"

"Just say that you're out with that Jake kid, like you're on a date. Then, they won't want to come."

"A date?" The thought of this was exciting to her, but a date with Nate would be different, really different.

"Okay, then, go get ready and, Soph? Please don't strip in front of me again. That was awkward last night. We haven't even gone on our first date," he joked.

"Oh my god, I did that? This is definitely embarrassing. I'm gonna go now." She grabbed her towel, a change of clothes, and ran to the bathroom.

Nate stretched out again on the tiny bed. He was taller than Sophie, so it was pretty amazing that the two of them fit into that single bed. He laughed to himself, thinking how everything and every moment with Sophie was a challenge.

She was so different from the others he had helped. There was a connection here and he couldn't figure out why this one was so special and why she was the most difficult to be a guardian for. He pushed the boundaries for her constantly.

Then, he really began to think. What would happen when it came time to leave her? The thought of not having her in his life was hard to believe, and would she accept it, too? She had to; it's how things were meant to be. He'd have to do this strategically, so she would believe that she didn't need him to make it through life. He had to put her on the right path and let her go.

Suddenly, he heard the water from the shower turn off, and a few seconds later, Sophie entered the room. She was dressed with her wet hair tied up in a towel.

It was so weird having Nate there for such a long time. It was almost like he was real. She quickly did her makeup and blow-dried her hair.

"I'm ready," she said, grabbing her purse.

Nate got up from the bed and headed toward the door. He quickly stopped and turned to Sophie. "Are you really ready? Because I'm not too sure if you can handle me. I'm a lot of fun... Seriously.." He smirked.

"Oh, I think I can," Sophie joked back, and then shoved him aside, walking out the door. Julie and Natalie were still asleep. She wrote a note for Julie and left it on the coffee table beside her. Then, they quietly slipped out the front door.

12

A Dream Day

The sun was bright that day as Sophie and Nate headed down the street to the sky train. The cherry blossoms were just in bloom and when they fell, it looked like pink snow. Nate stopped for a moment, standing in the middle of them. "She was right, wasn't she?"

"They're really beautiful," Sophie answered.

"They are. I'm glad I got to see them for myself. It would've made her happy." Nathan smiled, remembering Serena's words.

"Here, I'll take a picture, so you remember it always." Sophie pulled her camera from her purse and took a shot of him standing in the pink snow.

"Soph, you goof, I'm not gonna show up in pictures." He laughed.

"Really? Crap, that sucks. Ah well, at least the picture will remind you of where you were."

She checked the screen, no Nate. But she didn't care, as she knew what it was. They continued to walk down the street, chatting the whole way to the station. The sky train wasn't too busy that day, so they found seats right away. Sophie pointed things out along the way to Nate, explaining what they were and if she had been there yet.

The people beside her looked at her, and they definitely thought she was crazy, talking to herself and laughing. But she didn't care.

One lady even leaned over the seat to her. "Hun, are you okay?" she asked.

"Oh, um, ya. I'm fine. Just practicing what I'll say, um, when I lead my tour group next week." Sophie giggled. That was the only thing she could come up with.

The lady leaned back and looked at her strangely, but took it as an answer.

Nathan smiled at Sophie. "Crazy girl," he teased.

"It's your fault!" She pushed him back.

The train pulled up to the Chinatown stop. Nathan and Sophie ran off the train and up the escalader to street level. Chinatown was full of little shops and treats. They walked through them all and tried many Asian snacks along the way.

"Oh, man, ugh, what is this?" Nathan took a bite of a roll that had some sort of bean or meat filling.

"I have no idea. You picked them out!" Sophie laughed.

"Try it," he said, shoving it toward her mouth.

"No way, your face said enough," she said, blocking it.

"Try it, come on, we're in this together. Do it, Sophie, please!" he insisted, pulling her hands down from her mouth.

"Fine!!" she said, giving in. She took a bite of the roll. It had a dry spongy taste.

"Ugh, so nasty!" she said, spitting it out. Nathan quickly took a photo of her.

"Mean!" she said, pulling the camera from his hands.

"You're mean for making me eat nasty Asian food!" he teased, throwing the rest of the roll at her and running away.

"Get back here! You're such a jerk!" She laughed, chasing after him down the street. After two blocks, Nathan came to a stop.

"Okay, okay, truce! I can't run anymore," Nathan said, catching his breath.

Sophie caught up to him and pushed him to the ground. He lay there in the grass for a moment, resting.

She held out her hands to help him up.

"Ahh, I'm injured. Injured by a crazy girl."

"You're fine." She laughed, pulling him to his feet. "Come on, let's go get a drink."

After getting slushies at the corner store, they walked to a local park to sit in the sun and relax.

"Man, this is a lot better than listening to Natalie and Julie fight," Sophie said, taking a sip of her slushie.

"For sure, man, those two go at it, eh?" he said, taking the slushie from Sophie's hand and handing his to her.

"Ya, I have no idea why things are that way between them, They're both beautiful girls and yet they insist on competing with each other all the time. Julie isn't as bad though. She only gets like that when Natalie starts it. I can understand because sometimes that girl can really drive you crazy," Sophie said, handing the slushie back to Nate and taking hers back.

"Well, don't worry too much about it. Things will work out. Just do your own thing, and try not to choose sides."

"Nate, are you saying this because you know what's going to happen? Tell me if you do and save me the worrying," she said, taking his slushie back and keeping them both to herself.

"Sophie, you know I can't say anything, and holding my slushie hostage isn't going to win you points with me," he teased, grabbing the drink back.

She sighed dramatically, "I know." Nate sipped his drink and smiled at her.

She decided this would be a perfect moment to ask Nate a few things she had been wondering about.

"So, Nate, about this guardian angel thing . . . " She hesitated, not wanting him to get upset.

"Is this something you'll be doing for the rest of your life, or whatever? Like, is this what you do, forever, or do you pass on or something?"

"Well, not forever. But I'll have to do it a bit longer. I mean I like doing it and it makes me feel like I'm using myself well for whatever life I'm living." He laughed. "But yes, we pass on after a certain amount of time."

"But is that it? Is there anything like a choice of reincarnation or something? Is that stuff real?" she asked.

"Do you mean, will I get to come back after doing all this?"

"Well, ya."

"I've heard there are some instances where angels have gotten to come back, like a second chance. But it's really hard to do, really hard. There's something that has to happen, but they won't tell me what. I asked once after hearing about it, but they said we couldn't talk about it."

"Really? Nate, we have to figure that out. You could have a second chance!" Sophie pulled the drink from his mouth. "This is great, I mean, you have to try for it!" she said excitedly.

"Whoa, Sophie. Didn't you hear me? It's really rare. Almost everyone who's like me has failed to do it. There's only like two or three that have succeeded. And again, we don't even know what it is we have to do, because no one can talk about it."

"I know, but maybe. At least try, Nate."

"Okay, Sophie, I'll try." He laughed.

"Nathan, be serious, okay? I know you're just saying that to shut me up. Promise me that you'll try. I'll help you."

"All right, Sophie, I promise. But listen to me, okay? This isn't something that you can just ask someone how to do it. No one speaks of it and no one asks about it. It's the rules. That's the point of it. The person who does whatever needs to be done, will deserve it, but it must come from that person's choices only—by him doing what he chooses to do."

"I see. Maybe it's only for the angels that have done something spectacular in their guidance. You've said you've helped lots of people and you enjoy it, so maybe you're on the right path." Sophie's eyes lit up.

"I don't know, maybe." They sat there for a moment, thinking to themselves.

"But for now, can we get back to our fun day?" Nate said, getting up.

"All right. Where to next?" she said, getting up from the grass.

Nathan grabbed Sophie's hand and headed down the street.

The rest of their day was spent wandering around the city of Vancouver, through the gardens, and taking pictures along the way, even if Nathan couldn't be seen in any of them.

They stopped at a bookstore, because Nathan had told Sophie about a book he loved to read, and he wanted her to read it. Sophie wasn't a big reader, but for him, she would do anything. He scanned through the fantasy section and pulled a small book from the shelf.

He handed it to her.

"The Hero and the Crown?" Sophie said uncertainly.

"Ya, it's great. You'll like it. It's about a girl who's strong minded and beautiful, and it even has adventure, fighting, and a love story in it."

"Okay, I'll give it a try." She laughed.

"I love to read. I think it's because I love to write. It's something I've always done. You can say so much—all the things that you don't want to say out loud." He smiled, as he looked through the shelves of books.

"Nathan, I didn't know that you wrote. Can I read something that you've done?"

"Someday, I promise. I'm working on something now. Well, I've been working on something for a while now."

"Come on, Nate, I really want see your work," she begged.

"You will. I promise. When it's finished, you'll be the first to read it. I swear."

"Good," she said, tucking the book under her arm. "Now let's get out of here."

"Wait. I just want to get one more thing." He headed over to the travel area and pulled out a book about Japan.

"Cool! Can I see? Now, this is something I love to read about," she said, leaning over his shoulder. Sophie longed to travel and see the world, so this book was a definite interest to her.

""I don't really know that much about Japan, but I'm interested."

"Who knows, maybe someday, right?" Sophie said, encouraging him and hopefully making him think about that reincarnation thing.

"Ya, someday. Listen, will you buy this for me? Please. I know it sounds crazy, but it would be weird having a book float up to the register," Nathan asked.

"Nate, I got it." Sophie laughed. "Give it here, of course I'll get it for you. It's the least I can do, since you've shown me a great day."

"Thanks, Sophie. I'll pay you back."

"No, you won't and you can't, plus, I wouldn't let you even if you could." She turned and walked toward the checkout counter.

Sophie paid for the books and they left the store to continue their day.

Just then, Sophie received a text message. It was from Jake. It read:

"HEY, SOPH, SORRY I DIDN'T GET TO SAY GOODBYE THE OTHER NIGHT. I HAD A GOOD TIME, THOUGH. WANNA MEET FOR DINNER?"

Sophie blushed, as she read the message.

"Is that Jake?" Nathan asked.

"Um, ya. He asked me if I want to go for dinner."

"You should go," Nathan responded quickly.

"No, I'm spending the day with you."

"Sophie, it's fine. Go."

"I don't want to. I'd rather spend it with you."

"Soph, he's real and I'm just here passing time. You need to go."

"Nathan. Why are you being so persistent with this? It makes me feel like you don't want to be here with me."

"Of course, I do!" Nathan paused in shock at how quickly he had snapped at Sophie. "Nate, what's the matter?"

"Nothing, can you just go?" he said, starting to lead them home. She hurried to catch up to him.

"Nathan, stop!" Sophie cried.

"What?" He turned. "What don't you understand? He's who you're interested in, so just go live your life and do what you're supposed to do, Sophie."

"Nathan . . . " Sophie was surprised by how he was talking to her. He had yelled at her before, but he was never this mean. There was a different tone in his voice. He normally didn't react like this—ever. Nathan was always so calm. She stood there, staring at him. She felt that he was hiding something behind those dark brown eyes.

"Don't ruin our day, Nate," Sophie said softly.

His expression softened, as he took a deep breath, ashamed of how he was acting.

"I'm sorry." He stepped closer and wrapped his arms around her. "I'm so sorry, Soph. I didn't mean to talk to you like that."

"It's fine," she said.

"This really has been a great day. I haven't ruined it, have I?"

"No, it's all good," she said, forgiving him instantly.

"I really should get you home. I mean it. You should go out with him. You have to remember that he's what's happening in your life, so you need to put all that first before me. Okay, Soph?"

"I understand what you're saying, Nate. It's just that I'm having such a good time with you."

"I know. I did tell you I was a fun person, didn't I?" he joked.

"Very true," she said with a laugh. "But I still wish I could stay here with you. Don't you wish that, too?"

"Of course I do, Sophie. I can stay around, as long as you remember to keep your real life a priority, always. Promise?" He looked at her seriously.

This time, she didn't argue with him. "Promise."

"All right then, let's get going." Nate grabbed Sophie's hand and headed toward the sky train station.

When they got back to the house, no one was home.

"Hmm, Julie must have left? And where is Natalie?" Sophie looked around for a note.

Nathan followed her into the house. On her bedroom door was a note from Natalie. It read: "Went out for the evening. See you in the morning."

"Thank god," Sophie said, ripping the note down from the door and heading into her bedroom.

"At least, you missed the fighting, and that's a good thing. That Natalie scares me," Nathan teased.

"Me, too," Sophie said, throwing her purse on the bed along with the books they had bought. "I should probably shoot Jake a text back and get changed."

"Ya, do you mind if I stay here and read through my book?" Nathan asked.

"Sure, um, do you mind stepping out for a sec, while I change?"

"Not a problem." Nate stepped out and closed the door behind him.

Sophie looked around her closet for something to wear. She was excited to go out, but still felt bad about ditching Nate. But she couldn't change his mind, and she knew that if she didn't follow his rules, she could lose him. It wasn't a bad thing, though.

She did like Jake a lot. But she couldn't get rid of the feelings she was developing for Nate. She kept thinking about him getting that second chance. What was the key to getting it? She pondered, while she got dressed. Maybe it depended on what kind of person you were, and if you were kindhearted. Nate definitely was. He had helped so many. That boy didn't have a cruel bone in his body.

Or maybe he had to make a difference in the world or something. What could it be? It must be something huge, since only two or three of them had achieved it. She finished getting dressed and opened the door.

"Nathan?" she said, but he was nowhere in sight.

"I'm still here," he answered from behind her. He was lying on her bed with his book.

"Nate! How'd you? Never mind," she said, shaking her head. "Very tricky."

"Yes, I am." He smiled back. "You look good, Soph," he said, standing up and walking over to her.

"But your, um, strap. It's caught on your shirt. Turn around." He lifted her long hair and laid it over her left shoulder. Slowly, he ran his fingers down her back to where her bra strap was caught on the tank top. He unhooked it carefully. His fingers were like a cool breeze across her bare back.

"Um, thank you," she said, turning to face him, as his hands slowly rubbed her arms.

"Do you need a sweater? You might be cold."

"Ya, that's probably a good idea," she said, but she didn't move and neither did he. He stood there close, as she placed her hands against his chest and stepped a little closer.

"Sophie ... " he whispered.

Her heart was beating faster. What was happening? Was Nate doing this all because of Jake? Was he having second thoughts about her going out with him? He brushed his hand through her hair, looking down into her eyes. Sophie had waited for a moment like this with Nathan, but what would it mean and what would happen between them? She closed her eyes, as he leaned down toward her.

Suddenly, her phone went off. She opened her eyes and Nathan was gone.

She looked around. He was nowhere in sight. "Nate . . . " she whispered quietly to herself. The phone call had ruined her moment! She pulled it out from inside her purse. Julie's name lit up, and with a sigh, she answered it, flopping down on the bed.

"Hey, Julie."

"Hey, yourself, geeze you don't sound so happy to hear from me. What's wrong?" she asked.

"Nothing, no I'm good. I just, um, I'm just nervous about having dinner with Jake tonight."

"Dinner with him? Didn't you say on your note you left me that you went out with him today on a date?"

"Ya, I did, I mean I just came back to change for dinner, and I'm meeting up with him again," Sophie said, nervously trying to cover it up.

"Ahhh, can't get enough, eh?" Julie teased.

"I guess not. It was really a good day, so why stop now, right? So, when did you leave today?" Sophie asked, trying to change the subject.

"Um, I left around noon. I heard Natalie getting in the shower, so I thought it would be best if I slipped out then. I still can't believe what happened last night, can you?"

"I know it was a little out of control, Julie. I don't want it to be like that every time we go out. I can only remember parts of it, but I know it was messy."

"Hey, it wasn't my fault. She started it!"

"I know. Natalie is totally to blame for this. But we can't let her get to us, okay?"

"I know. I'm sorry. It's just that someone has got to stand up to her."

Sophie knew she wasn't going to get anywhere with this conversation, so she took Nate's suggestion and didn't choose a side. Quickly, she changed the topic.

"So, what are you up to today?" Sophie asked with a little more positivity in her voice.

"I'm actually getting ready to head to set. I got a call from my agent for some work on a TV show today," she said excitedly. Julie was the only one out of the students who had an agent. She had arrived in Vancouver a year before taking the class to try her luck in the acting world.

"Wow, that's exciting! So cool! Well, good luck! I wanna hear about it afterward, okay?"

"Ya, I'll tell you everything in class on Monday."

"Sounds good. See you then." Sophie hung up the phone and threw it in her purse.

She thought that was so exciting for Julie to be on set. Their class had been able to do some extra work for companies filming around Vancouver. Her favorite was when they did a day of voice-over at a local studio. Sophie had fallen in love with voice-over work. Since she was always nervous about her looks on set, it was way easier to stand in a booth and only worry about her voice.

It was the same reason she was always scared to sing in front of people. She was never comfortable with herself, but wanted to sing so badly. Her acting classes had given her a little more confidence, but she still had a long way to go.

She sat down on her bed for a moment to think. There were only another few months of school left. What was she going to do when she was finished? Could she succeed in acting? She started to feel that nervousness in her stomach again.

She got up from the bed. She knew that there was no point getting all worked up about something that hadn't happening yet. She finished getting ready and grabbed her jacket. Just then, she heard her phone go off with another text message from Jake. It read:

"HEY, I'LL BE THERE IN TEN MINUTES. SEE YOU SOON."

She closed her bedroom door and went to sit in the living room to wait for Jake. As she sat down on the couch, Nate came to her mind instantly. She began to replay in her mind what had happened in her room before Julie called.

Would he have really kissed her if they hadn't been interrupted? She thought he had rules. What made him act like that? Not that she minded, but it just surprised her. It was further than he had ever gone with her. It felt different, like he wanted her this time. Was all this because of Jake? Was Nate jealous? She thought about him holding her arms, and how close he stood to her. His face was so close that it was like he couldn't control himself.

She also wondered what it would be like to kiss Nate. He looked like he had really soft lips and was probably a really good kisser. Sophie giggled to herself, picturing how stupid she must look, sitting there daydreaming. If Nate had listened in on this thought, she would just die of embarrassment. He was so perfect and kind and . . .

She stopped herself and thought about what he had said to her. She had to put her real life first. Jake was going to be there any moment. So, she shook Nate from her mind and concentrated on what was happening right then. If she didn't, Nate would know.

She did wonder what Nate was thinking after their heated moment that afternoon. He vanished so quickly; it made things kind of awkward. What would she say when she saw him next? She started to get nervous again.

"Okay, stop Sophie," she said to herself. "Enough of Nate. Think about right now." She got up from the couch and looked out the window. Jake's car was just pulling up. She grabbed her purse and headed out the front door, locking it behind her. Jake jumped out of the car to greet her.

"Hey, you," he said, opening the door for her.

"Hi," she said, as she got into the car. He quickly ran around to the other side and got into the driver's seat. Sophie looked at her house, as he got into the car. There was a shadow in the window, peering through the white drapes. As the drapes drew back slightly, she saw Nate in the window. She lifted her hand to wave to him slightly, but he was gone.

"Who you waving to?" Jake asked.

"Oh, um, no one, just my landlord," she said. "So, where are we going for dinner?"

He smiled at her and said, "It's a surprise." They pulled away from the curb, as Sophie took one last glimpse at the window. No Nate.

They drove through the city of Vancouver with the sun just setting and the city full of lights. The car headed down toward the harbor. There where large boats everywhere, lit up with sparkling lights. Jake pulled into a small parking lot and turned off the car.

"Come on. You're gonna like this. I know it." He jumped out of the car and went around to open the door for Sophie.

"Thank you, but where are we going? Are we having dinner down by the docks?"

"No, not by the docks, on a boat!" he said, guiding her down the ramps to the boats. "It's a dinner ferry—dinner, dancing, and sightseeing all in one."

"Oh, um . . . " Sophie thought about her last experience on a boat and how it actually made her sick. The motion really made her lightheaded.

Of course, it was a huge cruise ship, but a smaller boat couldn't be any better, could it?

"What? Don't you like it?" he asked, stopping to judge her body language.

"No, no, it's fine. I just have never been on a boat like this. I'm good," she said, trying to convince herself.

Jake grabbed her hand. "Come on, we'll be late."

He led her down to one of the smaller boats, pulled two tickets out of his jacket, and handed them to the staff at the loading gate. Then, they walked up the ramp onto the boat.

It was actually really nice; the dining room was lit up with candles and there was a side bar with cocktails. They walked up to the second floor and saw a DJ set up for dancing. The boat rumbled, as the motor started up, and everything vibrated around them. It slowly turned around in the harbor and headed out for their night at sea.

"Let's head down and get something to eat, okay?" Jake suggested.

"Sounds good," Sophie said, trying not to concentrate on the motion of the boat.

They headed back downstairs to the dining room. The host led them to their table by the window overlooking the sea. Sophie gazed at the menu, trying to decide what to eat and what wouldn't add to her sickness if the boat did bother her.

"Sophie? You all right?"

"Ya, I'm fine, sorry, I just can't decide. But I think I'll have the chicken linguine tetrazzini," she said, closing the menu and setting it down.

"Good choice. I'm ready, too." He motioned for the waiter to come over and they ordered.

"So, the other night, that was pretty crazy, eh? Kevin woke me up when they arrived at my place to drop me off. I can't believe Natalie threw up in his car!" he laughed.

"Oh, I know. It was so disgusting. I feel so bad for Kevin. I hope he got it out."

She covered her face in embarrassment for her friend.

"I wish I'd gotten to say goodnight to you. You should have waked me up."

"You looked so comfortable. Plus, I was really drunk, so it might have been messy."

"Messy in what way?" he asked, with a grin on his face.

She blushed. "I mean, I may have, well . . . It just wouldn't have been how I . . . Never mind."

"No, no, I wanna hear this. What did you imagine? Come on, spill it." He looked her straight in the eyes. "Sophie, you know I really like you. But I'm not sure how you feel about me."

She looked up at him nervously, not knowing what to say. She knew she liked him, but she wasn't sure if she wanted to say it out loud, yet. Maybe it was because in the back of her mind was Nate. But she wasn't supposed to be thinking about Nate.

Jake was great and all, a really nice guy, and good looking, but something stalled her. As they sat there in silence, a waiter came over and placed their food in front of them. She smiled at the waiter, almost in relief for interrupting their moment.

"All right, Sophie, I'll let you off the hook for now," Jake said, picking up his fork to eat the meal in front of him.

"Jake, it's not that I don't. I mean, I do," she stuttered.

"So, you do like me?"

"Of course, I've liked you since the first day we met," she said softly.

"Good," he said, taking a bite of his dinner.

They ate in silence, passing a glance now and then toward each other. When they were finished, the waiter cleared their plates and brought them some champagne.

"I didn't order any," Sophie began to say, but Jake cut her off.

"It's included with the dinner, Soph."

"Oh, okay. Thank you," she said to the waiter. "This is really nice. Thank you, Jake."

"You're welcome," he said, giving her soft cheers with their glasses.

The music played softly from upstairs. Jake looked at her and motioned with his eyes. "Would you like to dance?"

"Sure," she said. As she slowly stood up, she felt the ground move a little. But it wasn't the ground. Her balance was off, and she quickly gripped the table to stable herself.

"You all right?" he said, grabbing her by the waist.

"Yes, sorry, I just . . . sometimes, I get unbalanced by the motion of the boat, but I'm fine."

"Good, let's go." He held her hand and led her up the stairs to the dance floor. The music was soft, nothing like what was on the radio. It was strictly instrumental—dining room or ballroom music, I guess you could say. Jake pulled Sophie in closely, his hand wrapped around her waist. Then, he slid one hand down her arm to lift up her hand.

He held her tightly, looking into her eyes. He really was good looking, and it made her nervous being so close to him. Her body trembled a bit with the feel of his against hers. He leaned in closer, their cheeks touching softly.

"You look beautiful, Sophie," he whispered in her ear.

She smiled at his words. She could feel his soft breath blowing on her neck. He smelt of sweet cologne, as the wind blew through the windows of the boat. Every part of them was touching, and her nerves were kicking in. She began to get weak in the knees.

"Don't worry, I have you," he said, noticing her quivering.

"Jake, I don't feel that good," she said, squeezing her eyes together, trying to regain her focus. The motion was really getting to her now.

"You're just nervous, I can tell. Just relax, Soph."

Sophie started to lean more onto Jake, relying on him to keep her up.

He turned his face toward hers. Slowly, he ran his fingers down her face. Their noses touched, and she could feel his lips close. Her eyes closed and everything went black.

Minutes later, Sophie woke up to the crashing of the waves and the mist from the water blowing against her face. She looked around. She was lying on a bench and her head was on Jake's lap. She sat up quickly.

"What happened?" She asked, as blood rushed through her body. She was still dizzy.

"You should lie back down. You're fine," Jake said, putting his arm around her.

"No, I'm okay," she lied.

"You passed out on the dance floor. Guess I made you too nervous, trying to kiss you," he teased.

"I did? I'm so sorry. I'm really not that good with boats. I used to work on one, and it never hit me until half way through my contract, and ever since, I just can't take it."

"It's cool." He laughed.

"Wait, did you say when you tried to kiss me?" She looked at him, and he was smiling.

"Ya, I tried, but no success."

She held her head, as the scenery spun around them, but she tried to ignore it. She didn't want to ruin her night with him. She leaned against him, laying her head on his shoulder.

"So," he stalled. "Are you going to give me a second chance to try to kiss you?"

He lifted her head to look at him. She didn't say anything, but her heart started to race.

He slowly leaned in and kissed her. He pressed firmly against her lips, holding the back of her neck. What seemed like an eternity only lasted a few seconds. She opened her eyes, as he pulled away.

She looked away nervously and smiled. She instantly thought of stepping away from him for some reason. She slowly stood up from the bench, but her knees buckled underneath her.

"Sophie!" Jake yelled, catching her.

"Jake, I mean it. I really don't feel well." She breathed deeply.

"Sorry, I have that effect on girls," he joked, trying to lighten the mood. "Okay. Sorry, bad joke. It's okay. We're pulling up to the harbor now. I'll get you home."

He lifted her into his arms and carried her down the stairs to wait at the gates, as the boat pulled up to dock. People were staring and whispers were being passed amongst the crowd.

"She's fine, just a little seasick that's all," Jake said to them.

Sophie felt embarrassed by this whole situation—what a way to spend a first date. Jake carried her off the boat and headed toward his car. He placed Sophie in the passenger seat and headed back to his side of the car. As he started up the car, he turned to Sophie.

"Sophie, I'm really sorry. This was a bad choice for a first date. I hope I didn't ruin anything. I should have . . . " Sophie cut him off.

"No, Jake, it's all my fault. This was so sweet and I ruined it."

"Okay, we are both guilty, then." He laughed. "I hope you'll let me make it up to you? Listen, next weekend, a couple of us from the school are going to Chris' cottage. You should come, and bring Julie if you want, but just come, please?" He held Sophie's hand tightly.

"Sure, Jules will definitely come with me. It'll be fun."

"Then, I'll really get to spend some time with you. And we'll be on stable ground," he teased, as he pulled out of the parking lot.

It was a quiet ride home, more on Sophie's part. Jake tried to make conversation, but Sophie felt so ill that all she could get out were one-word answers.

"Are you going to be all right? Do you want me to come in with you?" he asked, undoing her seat belt.

"No, I'll be okay," she answered, grabbing her purse from the floor. She was lying, but she really didn't want Jake to see her so uncoordinated and sick. He leaned over and kissed her on the forehead. "Good night, Sophie" he said, staring into her eyes.

"Good night, thank you, and I'm sorry for everything. But I'll see you next weekend, okay?" she said, getting out of the car. She was very careful to step as planned. Her balance was still off and her ears were heating up. It felt like her head weighed a thousand pounds. Her body started to ache all over. She waved, as Jake drove away, and then she hurried inside.

Natalie's light was on in her room. Sophie passed it quickly and headed for the bathroom. Nausea kicked in and she felt as if she may throw up. She closed the bathroom door and locked it. Throwing herself over the toilet, she banged her elbows on the sink on the way down.

"Ouch, damn it!" she yelled.

Natalie heard the sound and came over to the bathroom door.

"Sophie? You okay in there?" she asked politely.

"Yes, I'm fine. I just banged my elbow on the sink." Her voice echoed from the toilet bowl.

"Okay, well, I hope you had a good night. I'm heading to bed. See you in the morning for school, okay?"

"Okay, Nat, see you in the morning!" Sophie said, trying to get rid of her. She just wanted to be left alone to deal with this.

How long would it take to get rid of this horrible feeling, she wondered. Finally, she managed to throw up, but it didn't help. Her head was still spinning and her ears really began to ache. She tried to stand up, so that she could head for her bedroom, but she couldn't stable herself.

Her eyes rolled back into her head, as she dropped to the ground. But she didn't hit anything; it felt as if she was floating. She could smell something familiar and there was warmth against her body.

It was Nathan. He had caught her, lifted her into his arms, and carried her into her room. She wrapped her arms around his neck, squeezing him to stabilize herself.

"Nate, I feel so . . . "

"It's okay. I've got you." He carefully set her down on the bed, laying her back and lifting her legs up. He tucked her under the blanket, and then brushed her hair from her face. Sophie lay there, trying to relax.

Nathan then reappeared with a glass of water and some medicine. "Here, take this." He lifted her head and put the pill in her mouth. "Now, drink." She was able to take a few sips, and then he laid her back down.

"Nathan . . . " she whispered.

"Ya, Soph?" he answered, running his hand over her head to check her temperature.

"I'm sorry about . . . "

"Sophie, not now. It's fine. I know what you're going to say."

"No, you don't." She opened her eyes to look at him.

"It doesn't matter whatever it is," he said, trying to calm her.

"I kissed him. I kissed Jake."

Nathan looked at her and took a deep breath. "I know, it's fine." He smiled at her.

She could tell he was lying. She lifted her arms up to him and pulled him down quickly. She hugged him tightly. His brown hair brushed across her face. He pulled up slowly, lifting her arms back down and under the covers.

"Go to sleep, crazy girl," he said softly. Her eyes were very heavy, and eventually, she gave in to sleep.

13

Not So Perfect

The next morning, Sophie woke to the sound of her alarm on her phone. She rubbed her eyes and lifted the phone from beside her pillow to check the time. It read 6:30 a.m.

She wondered who had set her alarm, because she sure hadn't. It had to have been Nathan, since he was the last one there. The sun was shining through the windows, and it looked like a nice day out. She was feeling a lot better. The gravel must have really helped. She got up out of bed and headed to the shower to clean up. After getting dressed and ready for school, she headed to the kitchen to have a bowl of cereal.

Natalie came out of her bedroom, her slippers slapping across the floor all the way into the bathroom. Once again, Natalie was late. It was 7:10 a.m. and they were to leave at 7:30. Around 7:25, she emerged out of the shower and walked back into her room.

"Good morning," she said, smiling at Sophie on the way by.

"Morning," Sophie said with a mouth full of cereal. "Better hurry. We have to leave soon, okay?"

"Okay," Natalie yelled from her room. Sophie finished her cereal and gathered her things for school. She once again grabbed some granola bars for Natalie to eat on the way to school. Finally, at 7:45 a.m., Natalie came out of her room.

"Ready!" she said, grabbing her jacket off the bedroom door.

"Here, for breakfast." Sophie handed Natalie the granola bar.

"Thank you, you're so sweet," she said, hugging Sophie.

There were times that Natalie just weirded Sophie out. It was how she spoke and acted. Everything about her seemed fake. She knew Nat

125

from high school, but she had never really hung with her. The few times she did, she always just thought that Natalie was trying too hard to please people. But as she got to know her here in Vancouver, there was definitely something else to it.

She couldn't put her finger on it, but she knew that Natalie could surprise her at any time. Natalie was always much slower than Sophie, which made their walk to school take so much longer.

"So, Nat. Can I ask you something?" Sophie said, trying to get her to hurry and catch up.

"What's up?" Natalie asked, running to Sophie's side.

"So, what's happening between you and Julie? Did I miss something, like as per why you two don't get along?"

"Well, I feel like she's always thinking that she's better than me."

"Did she say that to you?" Sophie asked.

"No, but it's how she acts. There's something about her that I just don't like."

"Okay." Sophie thought to herself. "So what can we do about this situation, because I don't want to have to choose between you two? And it's really embarrassing to go out and have your friends fight. It really ruins the night, ya know?"

"It wasn't my fault, though, Sophie. She started it. I honestly have no idea, because I'm not doing anything wrong," Natalie said, getting defensive.

"I didn't say you were, Nat. I just want to fix whatever is going on, so we can move on."

"Well, I'm going to be nice to her until she's a bitch to me. I'll be the bigger person for now obviously, but I can't promise anything."

Sophie rolled her eyes. She knew that it would be Julie who would have to be the bigger person. She knew Natalie would start something if anything were going to be started.

Did Natalie really believe that she did nothing wrong? That girl was either oblivious to everything or just plain mean. Sophie decided to ignore it and not push the subject.

"Okay, well, that's good enough. All I want is for you to try, Nat. It'll be so much more fun if we can all get along."

Sophie pondered telling Natalie about Chris' cottage. Should she invite her, too? Natalie was bound to find out even if she didn't invite her, and that would definitely start a fight.

"So, when I was out with Jake last night, he invited us all to Chris' cottage this weekend. Do you want to go?"

"Ya! That sounds like fun. I'm definitely in!"

"Great, well, I just have to ask Julie, and then we can plan out how we're getting there."

"Julie's coming?" Nat asked.

"Yes, Nat, remember the bigger person thing?" Sophie warned her.

"I know. It's all good," she lied.

Sophie shook her head and continued walking. The girls arrived at school just in time.

Everyone was already in class, and their teacher Rob was setting up a set on stage.

"All right, everyone, sit down. Let's get started," he said, walking centre stage.

Sophie walked over and sat down next to Julie. Natalie sat behind them next to Adel.

"Hey," Julie whispered.

"Hey you!" Sophie smiled back.

Natalie gave a smirk to Julie and then faced the front.

"What a bitch," Julie whispered to Sophie.

"All right, guys, today I have some new plans for our showcase at graduation, so listen up," Rob said, grabbing a paper off the side desk.

At the end of the year, the class was to hold a showcase night where local agents, casting directors, and people from the industry could come watch, in hopes of breaking the students into the industry. Everyone was nervous for this big event.

Vancouver was very well known for its entertainment industry. Sophie was excited for her chance to be in front of real agents. She had already gotten to do some voice-over, and they even filmed an audition reel for each of the students to send to agents with their headshots.

"I'm going to read off partners. These people will be working together for their final showcase performance. I've already chosen scripts for you, so practice them hard and we will go through them in class for the next two weeks, so you can sharpen them up for your final performance." He lifted the paper up and began to read off names.

"Natalie and Josh, Chris and Elaina, Sophie and Julie, and let's see who else . . . " He continued to read and hand out scripts as he went.

"Yes!" Julie said, high fiving Sophie.

Sophie was relieved to be partnered with her. The two of them worked well together, so they could probably come up with a good plan of attack on this script. After the teacher finished assigning all the scripts, he continued with class. Today, they were working on auditioning skills for casting agents.

The classes were always tiring, mentally tiring. By the time you were finished, your emotions were all over the place. It was hard to stay awake in class sometimes. When you sat there, watching the others do their scenes and how much time it took for the teacher to work with each person, you found yourself at moments dozing off.

Sophie always found the classes really interesting, but she just couldn't help but slouch in the chair and lean her head back.

Her head bobbed at times and she had to concentrate really hard to keep her eyes open.

She sat up a bit and looked around the room, trying to stay awake. As she turned to her left, she was startled by Nathan, who appeared right beside her.

"You okay?" Julie laughed quietly, wondering what Sophie was doing.

"Ya, I, uh, just got a shiver," Sophie lied.

She looked at Julie, and then back at Nate.

"Scared you didn't I?" Nathan laughed.

"Yes," Sophie whispered softly.

"What are you doing here?" She said as quietly as she could.

"Just checking up on you. These classes are really intense, eh?"

"You're telling me." She laughed.

"So, are you going to Chris' cottage this weekend?" Nate asked, staring down at Sophie's bare shoulder. She was wearing a tank top that day and jeans. Her hair lay loosely over her right shoulder.

"How did you know about . . . ?" Then, she stopped herself. She knew how. Nate could listen in at anytime and to any thought in her head.

"Um, ya, I think we're all going," she said, looking at him. She noticed him gazing over her. "What? What are you looking at?" she asked uncomfortably.

"Nothing, Sophie, you look nice. Geeze."

She smiled embarrassingly, and then changed the subject, hoping to get an answer from Nate about the awkward moment they had had.

"So, I was wondering, about last time? I mean, not when you helped me last night, but the moment we had in my room before my phone rang?" She stuttered over her words, pondering how to go about this.

Nate's smile slowly faded. He knew what she was talking about. She was talking about their almost kiss that was interrupted.

"Were you about to . . . "

"Sophie! Are you listening to what's happening here?" Rob yelled to her.

"Yesss . . . Uh. Ya," she answered back quickly. The class stared at her.

She looked back over to where Nate was sitting, but he was gone. She turned her attention back to the stage and suffered through the rest of class. She would have to finish her conversation with Nate another time.

After class, Julie walked with Sophie to the station. They were going over some ideas on what to do with their script. Natalie walked behind them, joining in the conversation here and there. Sophie told Julie of Chris' cottage, which she was definitely in on.

They had planned on taking Julie's car for the weekend. Natalie mentioned that she might be going with Chris himself that night. Sophie knew it was because she didn't want to ride with Julie and also the fact that she could flirt with the boys the entire way. That didn't bother the girls, though. It would be way more fun without her.

The week went by quickly and Sophie didn't see Nate at all—not since that day in class. She wondered what he was up to. She really wanted to talk to him about what was happening between them, or almost happened.

It was Friday afternoon around 4:00 p.m. and the girls were loading up their car for their weekend at the cottage. Natalie had left straight from school that day with the boys. Julie shut the trunk of her car and jumped in the front seat. She rolled the window down and yelled to Sophie, who was locking the front door.

"Come on, friend!!"

Sophie giggled to herself. Every time she heard "friend," it made her think of Nova on the ship. She wondered what Nova and Joe were up to lately. Every once in a while, she would get an email from them and she would return one, just so they could keep up on what was going on in each other's lives.

Sophie ran down the sidewalk and hopped in the passenger seat.

"Are you excited to spend a weekend with Jake?" Julie teased.

"Very funny, Jules, but yes," Sophie said, slapping Julie's arm.

"I bet you are! Okay, I've made us a great CD to listen to on our drive." She popped the CD into the player and pulled away from the curb.

The two of them always had so much fun together. They sang at the top of their lungs to the music and danced in their seat. It was about an hour's drive to Chris' cottage, so the girls had lots of time to chat.

"All right, girly, spill it! I wanna hear about this date with Mr. Jake," Julie said, turning down the music.

"Well, it was good except for a few things." Sophie sighed at the thought of their tragic date. As she pulled down the mirror to check her hair, she noticed a figure in the back seat.

"Ahh!" she screamed. It was Nate. She looked at him, wondering what he was doing there.

"What the hell? What is it?" Julie asked, freaking out.

"Oh, uh . . . my hair looks like crap!" Sophie responded quickly.

"Oh my god, it's fine. You're avoiding the subject! Tell me!" Julie begged.

"Okay, no, ya, I will." She was nervous now that Nate was sitting in the back seat, listening to her every word.

She wondered how much to say. It wasn't like Nate didn't know what happened, but still it was awkward talking about another guy when the other guy she liked was sitting right there. She thought over her words for a moment, and then responded.

"Well, he took me to the docks for a ferry boat dinner cruise. It had music and dancing, and it was really quite sweet."

"Really? Nice! So you had dinner. Did you dance?"

"Um, ya, we ate and then he asked me to dance. But I started to not feel that well. Remember me telling you about the cruise lines?"

"Oh, ya! You get seasick! Damn! How was it?"

"Not so good. I started to feel weak in the knees. He was basically holding me up, so you couldn't even call it dancing."

"Oooooh, did he hold you close?" Julie teased.

Sophie looked in the mirror again. Nate was looking away from her and his eyes were disturbed.

"He did, and he actually insisted on us dancing."

"Did you kiss him?" Julie looked at Sophie with excitement in her eyes.

"Well, he kissed me. Then, I fainted." Nathan looked at her through the mirror, but he wasn't smiling.

"Yay!!" Julie yelled, shaking Sophie's arm.

"Jules, calm down. It wasn't anything great. I mean, I blacked out and he carried me outside to a bench to get some air. That's where I woke up."

"How sweet and romantic!"

"What? How is that sweet? I was the worst date ever."

"Then, what happened?" Julie urged Sophie to go on.

"Well, I woke up, lying on his lap. I was really sick. Then, he told me that he had tried to kiss me."

"So, did he try again?"

Sophie looked at Nathan before responding; he stared at her and smiled slightly.

"Yes," Sophie said softly.

"Oh my god, so awesome! You must be so excited! Now you're going to spend a weekend with him. This is really going great. He could be the guy for you, Sophie!"

"Calm down." Sophie laughed.

"Well, you like him a lot, don't you?"

"Yes, but . . . "

"But what? You're just scared. Go for him! He's so cute and nice."

"Julie . . . " Sophie tried to stop the conversation. It was so awkward with Nate right there. Why was he there? She couldn't even ask him.

"Hey, you never know what could happen this weekend, right?" Julie nudged Sophie's arm.

"Stop it, geeze!" Sophie looked in the mirror once more and saw Nate's face, and he wasn't impressed.

"It's definitely not going that far. I don't know him that well!" She checked the mirror again, but Nate was gone. She really wanted to know why he was there. What could he have wanted? Or was he just there to hear the details? The girls pulled down the winding roads full of trees until they came to their turnoff.

"I think we're almost there. This road should lead right to his place," Julie said, flicking on her headlights. It was starting to get dark.

Sophie began to get nervous; she was excited to spend the weekend with Jake, but also scared. Would Nathan be there, watching in the background? She hoped not.

Suddenly, Sophie's cell went off.

"Hello?"

"Hey girl! Are you almost here?" Natalie asked.

"Yup, I think, just coming up the path."

"Hurry up and get here," another voice said in the background. It was Jake.

"All right, we'll see you in a sec," she said, hanging up the phone.

"This is it!" Julie said, pointing out the window to the little house in front of them. It was older, but nice and it wasn't far from the water. Not that they were going swimming in this weather, as it was too cold. Julie pulled the car up next to Chris'.

"Let's do this!" she said, hopping out and popping the trunk. The girls grabbed their stuff and headed toward the house.

The music was blasting through the windows. Chris greeted the girls at the door.

"Ladies," he said, holding the door open for them.

"Thank you!" Julie said, dancing her way into the house.

"Sophie," Chris said with a smirk on his face.

For some reason, Chris always gave Sophie the creeps. He was nice and all, but there was something off about him. Sophie smiled at him and entered the house.

Natalie was dancing in the middle of the room with Josh. Adel, Brandon, Kevin, and Elaina were playing cards at the table. There were also few other people there whom Sophie didn't know. They must have been friends with Chris or one of the others. Sophie felt someone behind her.

"Hey, you," Jake said quietly.

Sophie turned and smiled at him.

"Feeling better?"

"Yes, a lot better, thanks. I'm so sorry about that. I should have said something earlier."

"Don't worry about it, no worries." He hugged her gently but quickly and headed over to the table to pick up his beer.

"Want me to get you a drink?" he asked, walking into the kitchen.

"Sure," Sophie said uncertainly.

There was something wrong with this picture. He wasn't being as cozy to her as he normally acted. Was he mad at her? Maybe he had decided that he wasn't that into her. Sophie started to worry. She didn't want to ruin anything with him, especially over something so stupid. Jake returned quickly with two drinks.

"Here, it's for you and Julie." He handed her the drinks and went to join Kevin and the others at the table to play cards.

Sophie stood there. She couldn't figure out what was happening.

"Hey, is that for me?" Julie said, taking a drink from Sophie's hand.

"Um, ya. There's something's different here," Sophie said, turning her back to the table and facing Julie.

"What? With Jake?" she asked.

"Ya, it feels like he's not really that excited that I'm here. He just said "Hi" and got us the drinks, and then sat down to play cards."

"Maybe he was in the middle of a game?"

"Maybe." Sophie looked over her shoulder at him.

Natalie ran up to Sophie and wrapped her arms around her. "Soph!! You made it!"

"Hey, Nat." Sophie laughed, as she hugged her back.

"Come on, we're going to play some drinking games!" Natalie dragged Sophie over to the table, and Julie followed behind. They all sat around the table. Jake sat across the table from Sophie and smiled slightly at her.

"All right, kiddies. Listen up. If you get any pairs of kings, queens, or jacks, you must chug your drink. If you get a run on someone else's cards, they drink. I'll explain more as we go. There are also truth and dare cards here, so if you get an ace, you must pick up a card and choose truth or dare, okay?" Chris shuffled up the cards and started to deal them out one at a time to each person at the table.

"What they hell kind of game is this?" Julie laughed.

"It's a secret," Chris smirked from behind his cards.

One by one, people laid their cards down and the game began. People were drinking more quickly than normal. Sophie didn't really care for games like this—what was the point to hurry up and get drunk? That just ends your night sooner and you feel like crap the next day. Natalie was dared to kiss Josh, which she happily accepted. Brandon had to run down to the water and jump in it with only his underwear on.

The dares became more challenging and ridiculous, as the game went on. Some of the truths that were coming out of people were so surprising. Sophie continued to watch Jake, but his eyes never connected with hers. He was avoiding eye contact. She looked around the room. It was filled with people dancing and drinking.

Outside, there was a campfire going. People had marshmallows on sticks over the fire, and a guy was playing music on an acoustic guitar. Everyone seemed to be having so much fun. What was so wrong with this picture that Sophie couldn't figure out?

Just then, a girl came over to the table with a drink in her hand. She stood by Chris.

"Who's winning?" she asked.

"No one. You can't win at this no matter how hard you try," he said with a laugh.

"No winners? Jake, you don't like those odds, do you?" she asked, walking over to his side. He didn't answer and he didn't look up. The girl lifted his arm off the table, so she could slide down and sit on his lap. Sophie's heart stopped. She watched as this girl leaned against him and he didn't seem to mind at all. Julie looked over at Sophie. Her face was blank.

"Hey, you okay?" she said quietly.

Sophie didn't answer. It felt like there was something in her throat, choking her from speaking. How could he? How could he? She kept thinking over and over again. Her eyes started to become blurry. The girl kissed Jake on the cheek and wrapped her arms around him. Finally, he looked up to see Sophie's expression. She was barely holding it together.

Sophie got up from the table and ran into the kitchen. She didn't want anyone to see her. Julie followed after her.

"Oh my god, Sophie. Did you know he had a girlfriend? No, of course you didn't! What a jerk. I'll kill him! What the hell? Like seriously?" Julie stopped to see Sophie bent over the counter. She still hadn't said anything.

"Sophie, I'm so sorry. This isn't cool." She walked up and hugged her friend from behind.

"What happened?" Sophie whispered. "Who has the guts to do that to someone? Why would you even pursue someone if you already had someone? I don't get it," she said, wiping her eyes.

"I know. Some people just don't care," Julie said, rubbing Sophie's arms. "Just don't let it bother you, okay? He's not worth it. We can still have a good time, all right?"

"I don't know, Jules."

"Please, let's just try to have a good time. It's only two nights and there are so many other people here to hang with. It won't be so bad. I promise. I'm here with you," Julie insisted. Sophie wiped the last bit of her tears to see Chris standing behind them.

"You okay?" he asked Sophie.

"Who is that girl?"

"The girl on Jake's lap? His girlfriend. She's visiting this weekend. She comes every other weekend to visit him. You didn't know?" he said, half smiling.

"Of course she didn't. Don't be so dumb!" Julie snapped.

"Did you know she was coming all along, Chris? Did Kevin know about her?" Sophie asked.

"Ya, everyone did."

"What?" Sophie's heart dropped again. "Everyone knew he had a girl-friend and no one told me?"

She couldn't believe what she was hearing. It wasn't like Sophie promoted that she liked Jake, but it had to be obvious to everyone when they were out, didn't it? He was all over her and no one thought to say anything? Weren't these people supposed to be her friends?

"Sorry," Chris said.

It didn't seem like he meant it. In fact, it seemed like he wanted Sophie to find out this way. He of all people was closest with Jake and Kevin. Wouldn't they talk? What about her date with Jake? Why would he do all that if he had a girlfriend? Nothing made sense!

Sophie couldn't think about it anymore. It made her so angry with everyone and with herself. She pushed past Chris into the other room where everyone was partying. She stopped in the middle of the room and looked at Jake with that girl on his lap, and then she noticed Natalie dancing again. She quickly joined her. She was determined to have some sort of fun if she came all this way. Natalie passed her a drink and Sophie pushed it down her throat.

"Sophie, stop it," a voice whispered in her ear. She knew who it was.

"Shut up, Nate." She continued to dance and drink. Nate knew this was going to happen! Why would he let her go through this humiliation?

Julie came out and joined the girls, and for that night, the three of them got along.

The night became early into the morning, and slowly people started to crash and fall asleep anywhere they could. Sophie and Julie managed to grab a bed. The beds were kind of old and not too impressive. They were almost scary, like they had been found in some old abandoned house. The last they saw of Natalie, she had gone off with Josh into another room.

Sophie lay there thinking, while Julie fell right to sleep the moment she hit the bed. Sophie's head was racing; she definitely drank way too much. She got up and ran to the bathroom. She flung herself over the toilet just in time. She lay there for a moment, making sure she was really finished being sick, when a voice called her name through the door.

"Sophie?" Jake said.

"Go away," she mumbled from the toilet seat.

"Can I please talk to you?" he said quietly.

"No."

Jake slowly opened the door. "Hey," he said, closing it behind him.

"Jake, I can't even look at you. You make me sick," Sophie said, turning away from him.

"Is that literally speaking?" he joked. She didn't answer him.

"Okay, look, I know you must be mad. But hear me out. I had a girlfriend, but I wasn't sure if it was going to work or not. It was kind of a break for us. When I met you, things changed. I wasn't cheating or anything, Sophie. She surprised me by showing up this weekend."

"That's exactly what you were doing, Jake! When you're in a relationship and you take someone else out on a date and say you like her and kiss her, that's cheating!" she yelled at him.

"Shh!" he said, making sure no one heard her.

"You're not the person I thought you were. Just leave me alone. I'm sorry I ever met you!"

"Sophie, you don't mean that. I would've broken it off eventually if things hadn't worked out with her." He kneeled down beside her.

"Get away from me, you jerk." Her eyes started to water.

"Sophie, I'm so sorry, I never meant to . . . " He attempted to hug her, but she pushed him back against the wall.

"I'm serious, Jake. Go away!" The sickness suddenly came back, as Sophie put her head in the toilet bowl again.

"At least let me help you, so you don't die or anything," he teased, trying to relax the mood.

"I'd rather die than let you help me. Please go."

He stood up slowly, not sure what else to say, then finally left the room.

"I really would rather die than live through this crap anymore," Sophie mumbled to herself. She pulled away from the toilet and lay down on the bathroom floor. This was just like in high school. Everyone knew that her guy was cheating and no one cared enough to tell her. Was she about to go through this again? Lose her friends and a guy? She couldn't handle it.

"I must deserve better than this, don't I?" she whispered.

Then, she wondered about Nate. Maybe people like her got guardian angels, because so much bad stuff happened in their lives that they needed someone to pull them through it all. How much more could she handle? Sophie lay there breathing slowly. Maybe she didn't want Nate anymore if this was the stuff she had to keep living through.

She looked up at the bathtub, and on the edge of the tub was a razor. She reached up and grabbed it. She thought about it for a moment. How bad could it really hurt? How long would it last?

"Sophie, what are you doing, crazy girl?" Nathan's voice said softly.

She didn't answer, as she held the razor close to her wrists.

"Soph, knock it off. I mean it." Nate's voice was stern this time. Sophie once again ignored him. Nathan reached down and lifted her up from the floor, put the toilet seat down, and set her on top. She was still gripping the razor tightly.

"Sophie, look at me," he said, holding her face gently. She looked up into his beautiful eyes. Her face was flushed, but she wasn't even crying. She was just in a blank state.

"You don't want to do this. Not over someone like him." He ran his hands down her shoulders and over her arms to her hands.

"Give it to me, Sophie."

"It's not just him. I'm sick of having shitty people in my life. Why do they always find me?"

"It's because you're too kind, Soph. You trust people instantly, and others thrive on using people like you. It's not a bad thing though, Soph. You just have to be more aware of it."

"That's bullshit," she said, looking down to her hands.

"Sophie, please just trust me. Give me the razor. Everything's going to be fine. You can't leave me, okay?" His hands were still on hers.

"Nate, you knew. You knew and you didn't tell me."

He looked at her sadly. "I know and I'm sorry."

Her eyes started to water and her breathing became deeper. Slowly, he pulled the razor from her hands, as her grip loosened. He tossed it into the tub.

"Sophie . . . " he said, wrapping his arms around her and hugging her closely.

At first, her arms hung down lifelessly, as her chin rested on his shoulder, and then she slowly lifted them up, gripping the back of his shirt tightly.

"Nate," she said quietly, and then her heart started to race. Her breath shortened and she went into panic mode.

"I can't breathe," she said, squeezing him.

"Yes, you can, calm down," he said, holding her.

She wasn't sure what had happened or why she acted the way she did, but all Sophie knew was that at that moment, she couldn't let go of him.

"Sophie," he said, trying to lean back from her, but she just gripped more tightly.

"You're okay, sweetie. Let go. I'm not going anywhere. I promise."

Finally, she loosened her grip and leaned back to face him.

She swallowed a lump of nerves in her throat and choked back her tears. Nate examined her carefully.

"Hey, you're back." He smiled at her, holding the side of her face. He wiped the tears from her eyes. She didn't answer him yet, as she was still processing what had happened. The thing about Nate was that he never needed explanations. He just knew what you were thinking and needing and that was all.

He stared her in the eyes, studying every thought in her head. The kind expression on his face calmed Sophie instantly. He held her hands in his, making sure not to lose eye contact with her. It was almost like he was calming her from the inside out without saying a word. Her eyes lost connection with his, as she gazed away toward the tub, and then to the ground. Then, it went black.

Sophie woke up the next morning back in bed beside Julie, who was still fast asleep. Sophie rubbed her head, as the pain from her hangover pounded inside of her.

She turned to look out the window, wondering if what happened the night before was real. Did Nate put her back in bed? He had saved her once again, but she wasn't too sure if she would've actually done it or not. But it was a good thing that Nate was there just in case.

Today felt different. Today, Sophie didn't want to get out of bed. She wished she were at home in her own bed where no one could bother her.

Instead, she was here in this house with a whole bunch of people and a guy she used to like. Julie moved around beside her, stretching out, as she woke up.

"Soph? You awake?" she whispered.

Sophie turned over to face her. "Ya."

"How you feeling?"

"I don't really feel anything. I just want to go home."

"Home? Why? I promise we'll have fun today. It's the last night. Can't you hang in there a little longer?"

"Jules, this is really awkward. I don't want to be here with him."

"Please, Soph," she insisted.

Sophie sighed at the thought of being there any longer.

"Okay, but if it gets too weird, I really want to go, okay? Understand?" Sophie said, as she sat up.

"Promise. Let's get up and head down the street to that little diner for some grub, okay?" Julie lifted the covers, jumped out of bed, and ran off to the kitchen.

Sophie got up slowly and dressed. They were able to sneak out without anyone knowing. Most people were sitting around in the living room, eating breakfast, and Chris was up to something in the kitchen, so even he didn't notice. The girls drove down the road to the diner. It was nice to get out for a while, as the house had begun to feel a bit suffocating with the number of people there.

They ordered breakfast and took their time eating. No one spoke a word. After breakfast, Julie tried to liven things up by taking Sophie over to the little shops. She had hoped that some shopping would cheer her up. Sophie dragged her feet, not showing any interest in anything they were looking at.

"Soph, you okay?" Julie hesitated, knowing Sophie was clearly not okay.

"I don't know if I can go back. It's so embarrassing," Sophie said, covering her face.

"Why is it embarrassing? He should be the one embarrassed. He screwed up, not you!" Julie yelled back.

"Listen to me. This is crazy. Why would I want to be in that house with him and his girlfriend? I look like an idiot being there."

"No, you don't. Stop thinking that way, please, you promised!"

"Why do you want to be there so badly? Don't you care about me at all?" Sophie said, storming away from her.

Julie ran after her and grabbed her arm. "Of course I do, silly. I just don't want you to let him win, Soph!"

"Well, he did," Sophie said, pulling her arm away.

"No, you're wrong. Don't walk away. You have nothing to be embarrassed about. Please, just finish the night and we'll leave first thing in the morning. I swear!"

Sophie continued to walk toward Julie's car, got inside, and put her seatbelt on. Julie followed closely behind, getting into the driver's seat.

"First thing, Jules, I wanna leave first thing," Sophie said, looking out the window.

"Thank you," Julie said, starting up the car.

They headed out toward Chris' place for one last night. As they pulled up to the house, Chris was peering through the window. Then, he quickly disappeared, as the girls walked closer to the house.

"He's so weird," Sophie said, walking up to the door. As they stepped inside, they noticed that the house was unusually quiet. They passed the kitchen and entered into the living room.

"Surprise!! Happy Birthday!" Everyone yelled.

Sophie stood there in shock. How did everyone know it was her birthday? She had only told Julie. Of course, Julie. That's why she didn't want to leave.

"Surprise, buddy!" Julie yelled, hugging her. "You see why I didn't want you to go?" she whispered in her ear.

Sophie stood there, not knowing what to say. "Thank you, everyone," she managed to squeeze out. But she didn't mean it—how could she? All these people knew about Jake and let her walk right into it. She knew Julie meant well by this, so she would go with it for now. Everyone came up to her and hugged her. Jake eventually came up slowly.

"Happy Birthday, Soph." He leaned in and hugged her.

She didn't hug him back. In fact, it really upset her. It was hard to swallow and she started to feel sick. Julie grabbed her hand and led her over to the table where a big ice cream cake was waiting there for her. There was a smudged picture of Britney on top.

"Sorry, it kind of melted in the back of my truck." Chris laughed.

"No, it's fine. Thank you, guys." Sophie put on her fake smile, as Chris cut the cake for everyone. Sophie took small bites from it. Everything felt more awkward than before. What kind of face was everyone putting on here? She was finding it more difficult to stay there by the moment. Jake moved over beside her.

"Nice surprise, eh?" he said, smiling at her.

"What are you doing?" she said without making eye contact with him.

"What? I'm just trying to be nice."

"Then, go away," she insisted. This time he didn't argue and just got up. Sophie placed her plate down on the table and got up. She headed for her room and grabbed her stuff. Julie ran after her.

"Where you going?" she said, grabbing the bag from Sophie.

"I'm leaving, now. I'll find someone to drive me home, or grab a cab. Don't worry. You can stay here." Sophie grabbed her bag back.

"Soph, come on."

"Julie, you just don't get it. Thank you so much for thinking of me on my birthday, but it's just bad timing, okay? I don't want to be here. It's so hard. Don't you understand?" Sophie started to tear up. "I can't do it. I just can't."

Julie walked over and hugged her friend.

"I'm sorry. Okay, we'll go. We'll just tell everyone you're sick, all right?" She grabbed her things, as Sophie headed out to the car. Julie explained to everyone the situation and met Sophie back in the car.

She took one glance at Sophie wiping the tears from her eyes and said nothing the whole way home. She knew she had pushed her too far, making her stay there. The drive home was quiet. When Julie reached Sophie's place, she watched as Sophie got out of the car without saying a word and went inside her house.

14

In the Cold

There was only a week left of school and it flew by. Julie and Sophie practiced their scene almost every night after school. Once in a while, Julie tried to talk to Sophie about the whole Jake situation, but Sophie just brushed it off. She didn't want to talk to anyone about it ever again.

On Wednesday night, after practicing, Sophie cleaned her school stuff up and went into her bedroom. She was getting ready for bed when Natalie came and knocked on the door.

"Sophie?" she said, slowly opening the door. "Hey, are you sleeping?"

"No," Sophie said, getting into bed.

"You're upset, right? I'm sorry you went through that, Soph."

"Whatever, it's done with."

"No, it's not whatever. You really liked him. Everyone could tell."

"Everyone could tell? Then, why didn't everyone tell me that I was wasting my time?" Sophie snapped back at her.

"Well, we didn't know how to tell you. It's a hard situation to be in," Natalie said, sitting on the bed next to her.

"A hard situation? How hard is it to say, 'Hey, Sophie, I think he has a girlfriend?' That's such bullshit, Nat! If I knew, I would tell you immediately." Sophie sat up and leaned against the head of her bed.

"Don't get mad at me. It's not my fault. Look, I didn't come in here to fight with you. Actually, I came in here to talk to you about Julie," Natalie said, getting defensive.

"What? What about her?"

"Well, today she was a total snot to me. All I did was suggest to her some things that would help her lose weight, and she freaked on me. I can't stand her, and I don't want her over here anymore."

"Nat. She has to come over. We have to work on our scene. Plus, she's still my friend and you can't tell me who can and can't come over to my own place. The two of you are being ridiculous. Both of you need to stop being so immature and grow up." Sophie lay back down and pulled the covers over her head.

"Oh, really? Well, thanks for being a friend and backing me up. I thought you were on my side." Natalie got up and headed for the door.

"I'm not on anyone's side, Nat. This is between you two. Stop dragging me into it. I'm your friend, but a real friend wouldn't make me ditch another friend."

"Whatever, Soph, just lay there and depress yourself some more over a guy who never liked you in the first place. Who's being immature now?" Natalie said, slamming the door.

Sophie couldn't believe what Nat had just said. Her words burned in the back of her mind.

"No, I'm not letting that little creep get to me," Sophie said to herself.

But she continued to lay there with Natalie's words still running through her mind. Her stomach grumbled. She hadn't eaten too much that week other then a random bowl of cereal here and there. She just didn't feel like eating. Basically, she went to school and acted normal, came home, practiced with Julie, and then went to bed. She glanced over to her nightstand.

On it was the picture she had taken of Nathan in the cheery blossoms. Well, it was actually just the cherry blossoms, because you couldn't see him. She smiled, remembering that day. She wished every day would be that relaxing.

Their showcase was on Friday, and then school would be over. She felt good about their scene, but was still stressed. There was so much running through her mind.

What had just happened between her and Jake fed nicely into her mood of the scene, though. It was about two girls. One had a really mean boyfriend who mistreated her. And the best friend, who happened to be Sophie, had to convince her friend to leave him and stop her from doing harm to herself. Sophie was sure she could sell this. She would do better than what any of her so-called friends did for her.

Earlier that week, she had called her family to see if any of them would be coming out for her graduation, but no one was. Her mom had said she would try, but Sophie felt like it was only because she had complained about no one coming. She still felt like her family didn't support anything she chose to do. It was constantly Sophie doing and making decisions on her own, and she always felt so alone.

The only person she talked to was her grandmother. Sophie kept in touch with her every week, filling her in on what was happening. She told her everything, even the embarrassing parts, because she knew that she would at least listen and give Sophie an honest opinion.

The great thing about Gram was the fact that she would listen to Sophie's side and try to understand it before saying her own opinion. Gram wanted so badly to come to her showcase, but couldn't afford to come. Plus, her walking was getting worse, so it might be too difficult.

She hadn't told Gram yet about what had happened with Jake. She knew of him and how much Sophie liked him, but not about what happened the past weekend—how he had totally humiliated her. She also hadn't spoken to Nathan too much. He showed up a few times late at night, but Sophie ignored him and turned away in her bed.

She hated that Nathan let her go through this. He knew her past and what she had gone through, and if he cared as much as he said he did, then he would have warned her. She was just another person to him, another poor soul to help through a crappy life. She wondered if her life was going to get any better, because it seemed to keep getting more complicated.

She still felt like she didn't have any close friends, she had no guy who truly cared about her, and her family still didn't support her. Julie was a good friend, but she had no idea what Sophie was going through. All she had was her grandmother, who was super far away and not doing so well healthwise.

So, sometimes, Sophie felt badly about pouring her heart out to her gram and not being there to help her in return. All they could do was talk. She missed her gram so much. She decided that the next day after school, she would call her and tell her everything she had to get off her chest.

It was hard leaving the whole Nathan thing out of the subject, because he played a big part in what was happening in her life. But there was no way anyone would believe her, even if she tried. They would definitely think she was crazy.

It was late that night, around 11:00 p.m. when Sophie received a text from Julie. It read:

"HEY, FRIEND. I'M REALLY SORRY ABOUT LAST WEEK-END. I SHOULDN'T HAVE MADE YOU STAY. I PROMISE I GOT YOUR BACK FROM NOW ON. I WAS JUST SO EXCITED TO SURPRISE YOU FOR YOUR BIRTHDAY. I KNOW YOU DON'T WANT TO TALK ABOUT IT, BUT I'M HERE IF YOU CHANGE YOUR MIND."

She was right about that. Sophie had no intentions of talking about what had happened the past weekend. She shut her phone off and leaned over to turn off the lamp on her side table. There was nothing to say. She couldn't get over how people had the guts to betray a friend like that. Didn't anyone know the meaning behind friendship anymore? She lay there for a moment, and then she grabbed the phone back off her night table and turned it back on to text Julie back.

"THANKS, I'M SORRY ABOUT BEING THIS WAY. I APPRE-CIATE WHAT YOU WERE TRYING TO DO FOR MY BIRTH-DAY. I JUST WANT TO MOVE ON FROM THIS WHOLE THING, SO LET'S DO THAT. I'LL BE FINE. I'LL SEE YOU IN CLASS TOMORROW."

She felt guilty about not speaking to Julie on the issue, but it was just too hard. She hated being mad at her friends, but some of them deserved it, didn't they? Her feelings on the subject were all over the place. It was nice, though, that Julie acknowledged her birthday. Usually, her birthday went unnoticed, so she never made a fuss over it and tried not to tell anyone.

The only reason Julie knew was because she had asked in a "get to know each other" game in acting class. She must have made a mental note. Sophie had actually almost completely forgotten until they yelled, "Surprise." She hoped that maybe one year she could have a nice birthday, with close friends and family who cared for her. Hopefully, that day would come sooner than later, because she was running out of mental steam for her life.

She looked at her phone, pondering over setting an alarm for the morning, but then turned it off and placed it back on the nightstand. She pulled the covers up close to her face. Why did this stuff always happen to her? What was she doing that was so wrong to deserve all this?

"If your phone is off, you won't have an alarm to wake up to, Soph," Nathan said, as he appeared on the side of her bed.

"I don't care."

"Yes you do, come on."

"I'm not planning on going to school tomorrow, I just want to sleep, okay? Why don't you go help one of your other poor victims and leave me alone? I'll be just fine on my own."

Nathan looked at her, clearly upset with her words.

"Sophie, don't say that or you'll become my unfinished business."

"Unfinished business? Of course, that's all that I am to you. Better hurry and help me, so you can move on. Well, I'm officially telling you that you have no more business here."

"Knock it off, Soph, I mean it. I get that you're upset and I'm sorry that it happened to you, but you know I'm not allowed to tell you things about your future. You will be my unfinished business for the rest of my life if I choose, because I'm not going anywhere until I can help you. I don't care if you hate me or yell at me. I'm not going anywhere, understand? I decide when I leave, all right?"

"Why? Why do you want to stay when I clearly don't want you here," she said, sitting up in the bed.

"You do want me here, but you're just too stubborn to say it right now. I can read your thoughts, Soph. I know how you feel about me. And as much as you don't believe me, I care about you so much and I want to help you."

She crossed her arms and looked away from him.

"Why are you so angry with me all the time, Soph? Can you please talk to me?" He said, sliding himself up beside her and leaning his back against the headboard.

"I don't know, Nate," she said, continuing to look away from him. "I'm so confused."

"Confused about what, Sweetie?"

"About everything, especially you!" She turned back to him, and there were tears in her eyes.

"So, you know how I feel about you? Then, you should know how much it hurts me to have everything I want and need in a guy right in front of me, but he tells me it will never happen."

"I know, Soph. I know what you think. But I'm not all that, you just feel that way because I'm always here. I never let you down, and you can take everything out on me and know that in the back of your mind, I'll still be here the next day. Of course, it's attracting."

"Nate, why do you always do that? You always say that you're not all that. Why can't you just see that you could possibly be an amazing guy? There's more to you than you know, and you just won't admit it, and it drives me crazy!"

He smiled at the words she said, as they reminded him of Serena.

She took a breath to calm down, and then asked what she had been wondering about for the past few nights.

"Can I ask you something, Nate? Without you disappearing on me?"

"Sure."

"What happened between us in my room the day you almost kissed me? You were about to kiss me, weren't you?"

He paused for a moment, deciding if this was the time to put everything on the table for discussion. He couldn't keep avoiding the subject. It might as well be now.

"Yes," he said quietly.

"I knew it. Things were so different between us that day. It didn't feel the same, Nate. It felt as if you were my . . . boyfriend or something," she said shyly.

"Boyfriend? That's cute, Soph, I wish. I don't know what happened that day. I wanted to hang out with you and cheer you up, but as the day went on, my feelings took over. I'm not allowed to act like that, and I got in a lot of trouble from the archangels for it. Thank god I didn't kiss you or I would be finished."

"Thank god? Didn't you want to?" Sophie asked sadly.

"Of course, Sophie, I want to kiss you everyday I see you. But I can't. They will take me away from you if I cross the line."

"Take you away? What do you mean?"

"They'll remove me as your guardian. Then, you won't have one at all. You only get one, Soph, and it's really important that you have me, okay?"

"But you wanted to kiss me? What are your feelings for me, Nate? Be honest, please." She looked at him nervously.

"I didn't lie the day I told you I may be in love with you. I am, Soph. It's just as hard for me as it is for you. I know nothing can ever happen between us, and I have to stand here and push you toward these horrible things that happen and the stupid guys who don't deserve you at all. I hate watching it, but if I can't have you, I want to at least make sure that you end up with a great life and someone who cares for you."

He turned toward her and placed his hand gently on the side of her face. "Sophie, if I hadn't been there when you were in the bathroom that night at the cottage, you would've . . . " He paused with that horrific thought.

"I have to protect you. I need to, Sophie. Please understand how this thing works. If I can't have you, let me do what I can for you while I'm here, all right?"

"Is that why you were in the back seat that day? Were you thinking of telling me? You looked upset."

"I knew what was going to happen and my jealousy took over. I hated hearing you talk about him so positively, knowing what he was really like. I wished it were me you were talking about, but I also wanted you to hate him. I'm sorry. I'm so sorry I couldn't tell you. I have to follow the rules, Sophie. I don't want to lose you."

"I know that sometimes I walk a very close line. I have to be more smart, because the angels are watching me more closely now."

"Nate." She leaned over and hugged him tightly.

"I'm sorry that I make your life more complicated. I don't mean to," he said, wrapping his arms around her.

"You don't, and I'm sorry, too. I want you in my life any way I can. But I can't just shut off my feelings for you, so you'll have to be patient with me, okay?" she said, leaning back to look at him.

"I know. But we need to erase this "us" topic out of our heads, okay? You need to live your life and I need to help you without getting my feelings involved. At least, then we can be part of each other's lives for however long we can. Deal?" He waited, as she thought through things in her head. He could tell she was thinking of ways to beat this.

"Okay, but you're still going to try to get that second chance, right? We can still work together and try to figure it out, can't we?"

"If it doesn't interfere with your life, I'll continue to try."

"Good, thank you," she said, smiling back at him. She wasn't too pleased about the ending of the "us" topic, but she would have to keep it to herself. If she could find a way to help Nathan get that second chance, then they could possibly be together. But for now, she would go along with him. She was happier now that she understood his feelings and he knew about hers, and she wondered if this would make things easier or harder.

Nathan got up from the bed, as Sophie lay back down.

"So, I guess we'll never know about that kiss, will we?" Sophie said, taking a chance on the topic one last time.

Nathan slowly sat back down on the bed. He looked at her and began to smile slightly. She swallowed nervously, as he leaned down to her. She didn't know if she was ready for this or not, and she closed her eyes. Was he really going to do it?

Nathan gently kissed her on the forehead. His breath was warm and soft against her face.

"I guess not," he whispered. Then, he was gone.

Sophie opened her eyes, her body energized from the soft kiss from Nate. She wanted him so badly, but she didn't want to lose him. They would both have to be strong and get though this until they found a way to get that second chance.

The next morning, Sophie awoke to the sound of the shower running across the hall. Could Natalie really be up before her and almost ready? She leaned over to look at her phone. That's when she realized that she never turned it back on the night before, even after Nathan had warned her. She jumped out of bed and decided that she really should go to school.

"What to wear?" she said, scrambling through her clothes in the closet. Finally, she grabbed a pair of jeans and threw on a hoody. It would have to do for today, as it was only rehearsals for the next day's graduation performance. She couldn't believe it was almost over! After Natalie got out of the shower, Sophie ran in to quickly wash her face and brush her teeth. Then, she hurried back into her room to throw on some makeup and grab her backpack. For the first time ever, Natalie waited at the front door.

"Come on, Sophie, hurry up!" Natalie complained.

"I'm almost ready. I just want to grab a granola bar to eat on the way."

As Sophie ran to the door, she noticed that Natalie had just left and started to walk down the street. She locked the door and ran to catch up with Natalie.

"Hey, slow down." She couldn't believe what she was saying. It was kind of funny to think that Sophie was asking Natalie to slow down.

"Can't, I'm late," Natalie said, brushing her off.

"Nat, come on. You're not honestly mad at me, are you?"

Natalie didn't answer.

"I just don't want to choose between you two. Don't you get that? This thing has to be worked out between you guys, not me. I don't get why you have to compete with each other. This whole thing is so silly, don't you think?" Sophie asked, grabbing her arm to stop her for a moment.

"Sophie, no I don't think it is. Sometimes, people need to be shut down and shown reality. Julie thinks she can do whatever she wants, and she's always trying to be the centre of attention everywhere we go."

"She is not, Nat. If she is the centre of attention, it's not because she's trying to be. It's because she's really fun and outgoing. People like her and they enjoy having her around. That's all, and you're like that, too. I don't know why you have to be better or have more attention than her. Can't you just be happy with being somewhere with your friends having fun, and leave it at that?"

"You don't get it, Sophie!" Natalie said, turning to walk away again. She looked like a little kid pouting, as she walked away. This whole conversation was so frustrating. How was Sophie going to get through to either of them? She was never going to pick between them.

"Wow, it's begun, eh?" Nate said, appearing beside Sophie, as she walked slowly behind Natalie.

"What am I going to do with these two?" Sophie laughed.

"Well, I'm thinking we should tie them up in a room and let them work it out. It always works in the movies!"

"Good idea, Nate. I'm sure I have a cellar room available and some rope, and I could even tape their mouths shut!"

"No, no, you have to leave their mouths open, so they can talk. Geeze, you really don't know how to hold someone hostage," he sighed. "So much to teach you."

"Sorry, my kidnapping skills could use some work. I'll be more prepared next time."

"I know you got it in you, crazy girl," he teased. "So anyway, graduation is tomorrow, eh?"

"Yes. I'm really excited, but kind of sad it's all over. It seems like I just got here."

"Have you decided what you want to do afterward?"

Sophie paused for a moment, as she boarded the sky train, looking for Natalie. She had sat far away from the entrance, clearly hiding away from Sophie.

"Oh my god, really?" Sophie laughed. "This girl can really hold a grudge," she said, taking a seat near the doors where no one else was.

Nate slid into the seat beside her.

"I told you not to pick sides and to try to stay out of it."

"I am. But I've been thinking that I'll stay in Vancouver. I really like this city."

"Good choice. It's perfect for you! Plus, you have a lot friends here."

"Friends, right," Sophie said, thinking to herself about the whole Jake situation.

"Listen, I know you're upset with your friends for not telling you about Jake. But here's the thing, Soph. Some people really just don't have common sense, and they actually have a fear of confrontation and taking control of situations. Not everyone is like you.

They won't give an arm and leg for a friend in need. And it's not that they don't care. They just don't think they have to go out of their way for anyone but themselves. People are so weird these days. Their values are so different than what they used to be, ya know?"

"I know, but it's just hard to understand. I didn't think it was that big a deal to come tell me. I guess I just miss that whole best-friend-who-knows-you-inside-out-and-will-stick-by-your-side feeling."

"I know, but you may never experience it again. It's really rare, Sweetie."

She took a breath, knowing what Nathan said was true.

"Well, this is my stop," Sophie said, getting up from the seat. "Will I see you later?"

"For sure," he said, and then he was gone.

She hurried off the sky train when it stopped and ran up the steps to street level. Natalie was already half way down the street. Sophie couldn't believe that Natalie was moving this fast. It was a miracle! When she reached school, everyone was already seated. She was the last to arrive. Julie motioned to her, as she had saved her a seat.

"Hurry up, Sophie, sit down," Patrick said, waiting at the front of the class.

"Sorry," she said, hurrying to her seat.

"All right, today is the last day, everyone! The graduation ceremony will be tomorrow after our showcase, so hope you're all ready. Make sure you get a good sleep tonight, so you'll be full of energy tomorrow." He pulled up a stool to sit down in front of the class.

"Tomorrow is a very important day. This is your chance to show off what you have to people in the industry. Hopefully, agents will approach some of you afterward, but if not, don't worry about it. All of you should have your headshots and demo reels together in a package ready to take to agencies when school is finished anyway. The more you get yourself out there, the better. It's all about promoting yourselves."

As Patrick continued, Sophie began to think about her plans. She definitely wanted to be part of the voice-over field, but perhaps she should take a private lesson to get herself more prepared.

Then, she thought about her living situation. Was she going to stay with Natalie in that basement apartment if they weren't getting along? Could she afford to live on her own out here?

"Whatcha thinking, friend?" Julie whispered, leaning over.

"About what I'm going to do—career-wise and living-wise stuff."

"About that, I was wondering something. Would you be interested in moving in with me? We could look for a cute two bedroom apartment together."

153

The thought of that sounded really appealing, but she wasn't sure if she could just ditch Natalie.

"What? You don't want to?"

"No, I do, Jules, definitely. I'm just wondering about Nat. I just don't want to leave her on the side of the road, ya know?"

"But didn't you say that she has an aunt out here? If she ends up with no place to go, then she can just move in there for a bit. Her family will take care of her, so don't worry."

"You're right. That's true. Okay. I'll do it! But let me tell Natalie. I want her to have enough notice, so she can plan. I owe her that."

"No problem. I don't want to speak to that creep anyway."

Sophie rolled her eyes and brushed her remark off.

"Yay, this is so exciting! We're going to have so much fun as roommates, Soph!"

"I know. We better start looking, because my lease is up this month."

"We'll start this weekend, then!" Julie's face lit up with excitement.

Well, that took care of that problem, Sophie thought. She had a place to stay where she would be happy . . . now onto the job front!

After class, everyone headed straight home to work on the final touches to their scenes for the following night. Julie and Sophie got home before Natalie. She was still at school, working on her scene with Josh. They took this chance to work on their scene one last time. Once they felt confident about it, they stopped for the night. Julie grabbed Sophie's laptop and jumped on the couch.

"Come here. Let's look at places now!"

"Good idea," Sophie said, grabbing two sodas from the fridge and joining her on the couch. They looked through many rental ads, but the prices were all over the place. Most of the two bedroom apartments ranged between $850 and $1,600 a month. It would be tight, but they were sure they could do it. Some of the apartments were in sketchy areas.

They wanted to be close to the sky train, but some of the cheaper apartments were too far from any transportation. Sophie wondered about bringing her car back from Ontario, since she just may need it. After writing down a few addresses to look at that weekend, they turned off the computer for the night.

"All right, buddy, I'm gonna head home. I gotta get my beauty sleep for tomorrow."

"Sounds good, Jules. I'll meet you at noon at the Broadway Station and we'll go together to the theatre."

"Great, I'm so excited, Soph. I know we'll be awesome!"

"Of course, we will." Sophie laughed, giving her friend a hug good-bye. She then remembered to call her gram, so she quickly grabbed her cell phone and dialed her gram's number.

"Hello?" Gram's voice said weakly.

"Hey, Gram! How are you?"

"Sophie? Hi, Hun. I'm fine. How's everything out there?"

"It's going. Tomorrow is my showcase and graduation. Julie and I have our scene down pat and are feeling pretty good about it."

"That's great, Soph. You do your thing and get signed by a fancy agent, you hear?"

Sophie laughed. Her grandmother always loved the entertainment industry, and she was always going on about how glamorous it was.

"I will, Gram, thanks."

"I wanna see you on TV real soon. I know you can do it! So, what else is new out there in the lovely city of Van . . . " Her voice cut off, as she started coughing.

"You okay, Gram?" Sophie asked nervously.

"Ya, I'm all right. I just have some fluid in my lungs. They think I may have pneumonia again. That's all. I wanna hear about you, so never mind me."

"Gram, wait a sec. Are you getting it looked after okay?"

"Oh, yes, don't worry about me. Now go on."

It was hard to not notice the recent change in her gram's condition. She was always in and out of the hospital with pneumonia. Her immune system was not holding up too well, and her walking was getting worse, from what she heard from the family.

"Well, you remember me telling you about Jake?" Sophie began.

"Oh, yes! That cute boy."

"Well, he didn't exactly turn out to be what I thought he was." Sophie went on with her story, telling Gram everything, except for the part about Nate and the bathroom incident. She knew Gram wouldn't want to hear that, and she had no intentions of worrying her.

"Oh, Sophie, I'm so sorry."

"Me, too I really thought he was different. Guess he fooled me, huh?"

"Don't you worry about him, all right? There are plenty more guys out there and the right one will find you. I promise. But you have to go through a bunch of duds before you find the one."

Sophie thought instantly of Nate. He had already found her, but she couldn't have him. Not yet, at least, but she still had hope.

Sophie continued to tell her gram about Natalie and Julie and their silly fight. Gram actually found it quite entertaining, but thought that Sophie was doing the right thing by moving out with Julie. Everything seemed less horrible after talking with her, as she always brought so much insight to everything Sophie was thinking.

"I really wish you could be here tomorrow, Gram," Sophie said sadly.

"Me, too, Hun, more than anything. Is anyone else coming?"

"No, I thought my mom might make it, but she bailed."

"Sophie, you don't worry about them, all right? You know I'm there in spirit, cheering you on! Don't let their negativity bring you down. You have so many talents and you should use them all. Don't ever be ashamed of what you love to do, because you only get one life and you should live it how you choose, not how someone else tells you. You're such a kind person, always worrying about others and helping everyone out, but this is your time. Think of yourself, my love."

"I know, Gram. I just wish my family shared my passion or at least understood it enough to support me. I always want to tell them the exciting things that I've done here, but it's like they don't want to hear it or I'm boring them with my silly life."

"Then, don't waste your breath on them. That's why you have me. I'm always excited to hear your stories. I want you to be happy, so do what you love and know that I'm always here any time always."

Sophie felt a lump in her throat from her gram's words. She missed her so much, and it was so nice to hear that someone was in her corner 100 percent of the way.

"Now, listen to me. I want you to go out there and give it everything you've got, all right? Do it for me and do it for yourself, because you deserve it. Then, I want you to call me the next day and tell me everything!"

"I will, I swear. Thank you. Thank you for always being here. I wish I could be there to help you out more. I'm slacking in the granddaughter department by being out here."

"Don't be silly, I'm fine. I'm tough as a rock, so you just worry about you right now. I enjoy our talks and look forward to them. That's good enough for me."

"I know you are, Gram, but you worry me, and I want to be there to help you."

"You are, by keeping in touch, Sweetie. You never forget about me, no matter where you are. I mean, you even kept in touch on a moving boat around the world with lovely letters. That's all a grandmother could ask for. I love you very much, and don't you forget it."

"I love you, too," Sophie said sadly.

"Now cheer up. You have a big day tomorrow. I'll be praying for you!"

"Thanks, Gram, I'll do my best. Talk to you Saturday, all right?"

"I'm looking forward to it! Good night, honey."

"Good night, Gram." Sophie hung up the phone with tears in her eyes. She really needed to hear those inspiring words, especially then.

Just then, Natalie walked in the front door.

"Hey, Nat, how was your practice?"

"Fine," she answered, walking right past Sophie and into her room.

"Okay," Sophie said, shaking her head. She couldn't believe this was how it was going to be. Natalie was being so immature, but she wasn't going to let it bother her, not tonight. Tomorrow was a big day and she needed a clear mind, at least for that one day.

15

Graduation

Morning came and Sophie was up bright and early getting ready for her big day. She had showered, packed her stuff, and even had a good size breakfast.

The bathroom was a mess. There was makeup everywhere, hairbrushes on the counter, and some sort of glue-like gel on the sink from Natalie. She was always trying out new hair products, and it always left everything sticky.

Sophie refused to use hardly any product in her hair, except once in a while, she would use some oil, but that's all. There were only a few minutes left before she had to leave to meet Julie, so she hurried to finish her hair and brush her teeth.

As she walked back into her room Natalie coasted by, slapping her pink fluffy slippers on the floor all the way to the bathroom and slammed the door shut.

"Thank god, I'd finished in there," Sophie said to herself with a laugh.

"Seriously, you may have lost a hand in the door if you tried to push back" Nathan added.

"Nate! Oh my god, you scared me."

"Sorry. You look good as always, Soph. I just wanted to wish you luck before you go."

"Awh, thanks, Nate. That's sweet." She walked over to hug him, but he stepped away.

"Right. The rules, sorry. I just feel like we're a lot closer now, but I'll try harder to think before I act."

"Thanks, Soph," he said, smiling at her.

"I just want to let you know that you'll have someone in the audience tonight cheering you on."

"I will? Who?" Sophie asked confused.

"Me. I'll be there. I want you to know that you have someone there, actually there for you. So, do well, or I won't clap."

"Nate . . . " She laughed. "Thank you, that means a lot."

She stared at him for a moment. It was like they were thinking the same thing. She wanted so badly to hug him, but knew she couldn't break the rules, not now. Instead, she grabbed her purse off the bed and smiled at him with a big grin from ear to ear.

"Well, I'm off! See you there?"

"I'll be there," he said, grinning back at her, and then he was gone.

She was feeling pretty good about today. The only part that bothered her was the fact that Jake was going to be there, as well. Whenever there's a showcase, it's open to all alumni from the school to enter. It makes things more interesting for the crowd to see a variety of newcomers along with the more experienced ones. She wasn't sure how she was going to handle him, yet. It would just have to play out.

Natalie was just finishing up when Sophie was heading out the door to the sky train. She thought about saying good-bye, but then she decided not to because she wasn't worth it. The sun was out and the air was just warm enough for a light cardigan. Summer was on its way soon.

Vancouver was always blessed with such amazing weather. They had light winters that weren't as cold as Ontario, and then a beautiful spring full of cherry blossoms and a summer that was nice, with warm days with an ocean breeze to fill the air.

Of course, the city was known for its rain, but it was still better than hail or blizzard weather any day. The sky train was packed with people going to work on Friday, so Sophie was forced to stand in the entrance and hold onto a rail.

It zipped through the city with perfect timing. When she reached Broadway Station, she saw Julie through the windows, as the train pulled up. It jerked to a stop and the doors slid open.

"Hi!" Julie yelled over the crowd.

"Oh my gosh, I just started to get nervous the moment I saw you."

"Nervous? For what? Today?" Julie laughed.

"Ya."

"Well, I was nervous all night, so we're in the same boat now."

"Let's get going, as we have to catch the bus that crosses over to Granville Island in five minutes." Sophie grabbed Julie's hand and pulled her through the crowd. They made it to the bus stop outside the station, just as it pulled up. They jumped on and found a seat in the back. They had time to relax now, because it was a twenty-minute ride to the theatre.

"Soph? You know that Jake's going to be there today, don't you?" Julie asked timidly.

"Ya, I know."

"What if he tries to talk to you?"

"I don't think he will. I made it pretty clear last time we spoke that I wanted nothing to do with him and he should just leave me alone."

"Really? When was this? How did I miss this?"

"It was after you went to sleep, and I went to the bathroom and he stopped me to talk." That wasn't entirely true, but it would do for now. Julie didn't need the exact details.

"What did you say?"

"Basically, that he made me sick."

"What?" Julie laughed.

"Then, I threw up."

"That's awesome! What did he say to that?"

"He tried to joke about it, and then I got really upset, cause he wouldn't leave. He actually made me cry a little, so I guess he thought he could fix it with a hug, but I pushed him back against the wall. That was it for us, I guess."

"Wow! Good for you. He deserves it."

"I just can't get over him trying to convince me that he didn't cheat. He actually said to me that he would've broken it off eventually for me if it didn't work out with her. So, basically, he wanted to date us both and see which one worked out. How dumb is that?"

"Seriously? You can do so much better, Soph, so just forget about him."

"I plan on it. It still hurts a little, though, because I did like him."

"I know. He really fooled us all with his charm. But there are better guys out there, believe me."

Sophie sat there, thinking about what Julie said. She knew who that better guy was.

"So, I want to ask you something that's been bothering me a little."

"What's that, Jules?"

"Well, I happen to notice—I don't know how, but when we are drunk, you always talk about a guy named Nate. Who is he?"

Sophie was shocked by his name coming into the conversation and wasn't sure how to respond to it.

"Nate?" she stalled.

"Ya, Nathan. You've said his name a few times and even called Jake it that night after the club. Where did you meet that guy and why don't I know about him?"

"Oh, Nate. Right. Well . . . " she thought for a moment, making up something in her head. "I met him back in my hometown years ago. I guess he's a family friend. We're pretty close, but we don't see each other that much anymore. Maybe I'm just rambling when I talk about him."

"Maybe. Do you have a picture of him? Is he cute? Single?" she teased.

"Julie, nothing's happening between us. I just miss him, that's all."

"Well, is he coming out here to visit you anytime soon? I want to meet him."

Just then, the bus pulled up to their stop and Sophie jumped up from her seat.

"Come on, Jules, we're here." This was perfect, the perfect distraction from their conversation and just what Sophie needed. They headed off the bus and down the street. The theatre was only a couple blocks down from the bus stop. Outside the theatre, there was a sign that read:

"VANCOUVER ACTORS' SHOWCASE TONIGHT ONLY"

Sophie stopped to take a picture with her phone.

"I want to remember this," she said, heading into the front door. It was 2:00 p.m. when the girls arrived. There were actors everywhere, running around, getting dressed, practicing their scenes, and warming up. Julie led them over to their teacher, and he directed them to the back rooms to get ready. Everyone had many emotions going on at that moment—excitement, fear, nervousness, and more. Kevin plowed through the people over to Julie and Sophie.

"Hey, girls!" he said, giving each of them a hug.

Sophie still felt embarrassed around everyone about the Jake thing, but decided to try to ignore it for the day. She had to eventually get over this, so why not try now.

"Hey, Kev, who are you doing your scene with?" Julie asked.

"Oh, Jake and I have a hilarious scene. I'm stoked for it."

"That's great, buddy. Well, good luck," Sophie said, smiling at him. He paused to look at her.

"I'm sorry, Soph, don't be mad at me," he said, throwing his arms around her tightly and hugging her.

"About what?" she said, acting dumb, hoping he would take the hint to end this conversation, but he didn't.

"About the whole Jake thing. I should've told you I wasn't sure what was happening. But whatever, I'm sorry, anyway. Okay? Forgive me, because I didn't mean to hurt you."

"It's fine, Kevin. I'm fine. I don't hate you," she said, stepping away from him. "Let's just forget about it, deal?"

"Deal," he said, shaking her hand.

"All right. Well, I have to go find Jake and get ready, since we're on first tonight."

"Good luck," Sophie said, as he ran off.

"Well, that went well," Julie said.

"Ya, it actually was nice," Sophie said, feeling a little more confident.

"Okay, let's get dressed and go over our lines."

"Good idea." Sophie set her things down in a corner and grabbed the clothes for her scene. She headed to the bathroom to get dressed. That was when a guy appeared right in front of her, nearly knocking her down.

A boy with brown hair and a great smile said, "Hey, sorry about that. I wasn't looking where I was going. Are you okay?"

She stared at him. He was good looking. That was the only word she could think of to describe him. He had dark brown hair, dark eyes, and a perfectly built body.

"Hello? You okay?" he asked again, touching Sophie on the arm.

His hand was warm.

"Uh, ya, I'm good," she said nervously.

"She speaks finally!" He laughed.

"Sorry, I'm just, uh, running lines through my head. Are you all right?"

"Oh, I'm fine. I'm Devon. You are?"

"Sophie. Are you acting tonight?"

"Ya, I have a solo performance. It's actually the first monologue I've ever done. I thought, why not now? Take a chance, ya know?"

"Wow, that's cool. I couldn't be on stage alone, well not yet."

"Oh, ya? So I can assume you're not doing a monologue, so you must be in a partner scene, right? I'm sure you'll do fine." He smiled.

"Thanks."

"Cool. Well, I'll let you get ready, and maybe I'll see you later at the after party?"

"After party?" Sophie asked.

"Ya, every time there's a showcase, someone holds a party afterward to celebrate. You should go."

"Sure, my friend and I will."

"Great. Just ask people afterward. Someone will have decided where we're going. I'll see you there then."

"Okay, cool. Good luck," she said, as she watched him walk away. He waved to her, flashing a smile from his perfect face.

Sophie hurried into the bathroom to get changed. Seconds later, Julie walked in. They were finishing up with their makeup when Natalie flew through the door, went into a stall, and slammed the door.

"Hey, Nat," Sophie said, trying to cool the air.

But Natalie didn't respond.

"Brat," Julie said softly.

"You're a brat!" Natalie yelled back.

"Okay, children, that's enough. Come on, Julie, let's go before this gets out of hand," Sophie said, dragging her out of the bathroom.

"What? What did I do?" Julie laughed.

"Julie, I gotta tell you something. You will not believe the guy I just met," Sophie said, changing the subject.

"What? Who?"

"His name is Devon. Do you know him? He's doing a monologue in tonight's performance."

"Hmm . . . I don't think so. Maybe he was a student from a few years ago. Is he cute?"

"Yes, definitely!" She smiled. "He said that everyone is going to a party after the performance and we should go."

"Then, we should go. You have to talk to him again. Where's the party?"

Sophie knew Julie would like this idea. One, because she loved parties, and, two because she was trying so hard to get Sophie to forget about the whole Jake thing, and a new guy would do just that!

"I'm not sure yet. They hadn't decided where it would be. We'll just ask around afterward."

"Ya, for sure! Now, let's finish getting ready. The doors are about to open."

They dropped off their stuff back in the corner, and then headed to side stage. Patrick was there, waiting for everyone, so he could make his speech.

"All right, is everyone here? Good." He motioned for everyone to sit. "This is it, people. It's now or never. Take your time and let it all sink in, but most of all, have fun out there. Be true to your characters and give it everything you've got. The doors are now open and the audience will be seated within ten minutes.

"Remember that the agents, casting directors, and the rest of the industry people will be in the first two rows. They have a clear view of you all, so remember where they are. I'm going to raise the lights on the stage and introduce the first act, so please remember to keep it quiet back here, while the others are performing. Good luck to you all and I'll see you afterward."

The sounds of people whispering among themselves filled the theatre, and within ten minutes, like Patrick had said, the stage lights were raised to shine on the first scene that had been set up. Patrick walked out on centre stage and welcomed everyone.

Patrick was good with the crowd and introduced the school in an appealing way. He also spoke of the students and how hard they had worked. After a few minutes, he finally introduced the first act, and the night began.

Sophie stood side stage, watching Patrick walk off the other side. The lights went down.

"Wish me luck," a voice said beside her.

"Jake," she said quietly.

"You aren't still be mad at me, are you?" he whispered.

"Of course, I am. What you did was a shitty thing."

"Soph, I'm really sorry. I really was into you. It was just bad timing."

"Look, Jake, now's not the time to talk about this. Just go out there and do your scene, you're on."

"Not 'til you forgive me," he said, standing there. Kevin had already walked on stage and was waiting for him.

"Jake, go!" She shoved him forward, but he pushed back.

"Say you forgive me and I'll go. Otherwise, you'll mess up our scene."

"Fine, whatever, I forgive you. Now go!" Sophie said, walking away from him.

"Thanks, Soph, see you afterward," he whispered back, heading out on stage.

Sophie turned to see him meet Kevin on stage. The lights came up and their scene began. Of course, Sophie didn't really mean it when she said that she forgave him, but she had to get rid of him. The performances went flawlessly one after another until it came time for Sophie and Julie's.

Patrick walked back on stage after a ten-minute intermission and introduced their scene. When the lights went down, Sophie felt sick to her stomach. Julie grabbed her arm and whispered to her.

"We got this, friend. Let's just have fun. Good luck."

Sophie smiled at her words and suddenly felt better. She really did love doing this and she had to eventually let her nerves go. She took a deep breath and walked on stage. The audience was quiet, as her character walked into the scene.

She took a quick glance at the audience to see it completely filled. And just as he said, Nathan sat front and center in the audience. He seemed to stand out from the rest.

He was there in a white v-neck t-shirt and jeans. Sophie's eyes connected with his for a quick moment before returning to her character's scene. Then, Julie entered the scene in full character. They worked smoothly together, knowing every point to hit and how to react to each other. It was perfect.

Sophie felt herself getting lost in the character and the lives they lived. Her feelings on the situation played out nicely into the scene, and Julie was amazing. They were meant for this. After their last line, the lights went down and the crowd cheered. Their scene was the darkest of all of them that day, but the crowd seemed to love it.

The rest of the performances flowed nicely into the night, and soon it was all over. The current students were brought back on stage one by one to give them their certificate for completion of the Dramatic Arts Program. After thanking everyone for coming, all the performers were brought back on stage for meet n' greets with the industry people.

There were professionals, families, and performers everywhere. Sophie felt a little sad that she didn't have anyone there. She thought of her gram for a moment before a warm hand touched her shoulder from behind.

"You were amazing, Soph. Congrats."

She turned to see Nathan. "Hey. Thank you. Thank you for being here for me, Nate."

"I promised you, didn't I? I wouldn't miss this for the world." He smiled. "Don't I get a hug? "What? But people will see me. It'll look weird, Nate. You're not really here."

"What are you talking about? I am here."

Sophie stared at him confusingly. She thought about his warm hand touching her shoulder.

"I don't understand. What do you mean you're here?"

"I told you I would be here for you, that you needed someone actually here for you, so I am."

"You mean people can see you?" she said nervously.

"Just for a few minutes, yes." He smiled at her.

"But what about your rules? Won't you get in trouble?"

"Don't worry about that right now. I'm doing what I think is best, so go with it, Soph." He laughed.

She was nervous for the first time to touch him. Maybe it was the fact that everyone could see. Maybe it was because this was real and everything she wanted. She stepped toward him, and he wrapped his arms around her.

She slowly lifted her hands up around his back. He was warm to her for the first time. She could hear his breathing, and it was slow and calm. He tightened his hold around her.

"Nathan . . . " She whispered. She wanted this so badly, all of this—to really have him here in her life. It was like a glimpse into the future she couldn't have, almost like a dream.

"I don't understand how you're really here."

"Well, I'm kind of breaking the rules again, but you needed it."

"What? Nate, I don't want you to get in trouble. You said that they could take you . . . "Hey, Soph! Who's this?" Julie said, interrupting them.

Sophie couldn't believe that Julie could see Nate, and she didn't know what to say.

"Hey, it's Julie, right? I'm Nate," he said, dropping his arms from around Sophie and shaking Julie's hand.

"Nate? Oh, Nathan! Yes, I've heard of you," she said excitedly. "Sophie, you never told me he was coming tonight!"

"Uh . . . Well." Sophie was lost for words.

"I surprised her. She didn't know," Nathan said to cover up.

Julie pulled Sophie her way. "Sophie! He's totally cute! No wonder you think about him all the time!"

"Julie!" Sophie pulled away, because she knew that Nathan could hear everything, even if they whispered. He walked over and put his arm around her shoulders. "You guys should be really proud of yourselves. You did great."

"Thanks!" Julie said.

Sophie had no idea what to say. This whole thing was so unreal!

"Hey, Nate, we're going to this after party. You should totally come," Julie said, nudging Sophie's arm.

"Oh, ya? Sounds fun, but sorry, I can't tonight. I only had a few moments of spare time, and I just wanted to stop in and see Sophie here."

"Awh . . . That's too bad, eh, Soph?" Julie said sadly.

"Ya, maybe next time, then," Sophie said awkwardly.

"But Sophie said you were an old friend from home . . . so what are you doing here in Vancouver?" Julie asked.

"Oh, well, I'm here on business. Just happened to be good timing, I guess."

"Okay . . . Well, I'll leave you two to talk. I'm gonna go ask were this party is happening, so I'll be back in a sec, all right?" Julie said, leaving Nate and Sophie to say good-bye.

Sophie turned to look at Nate. "I can't believe you're actually here. This is so weird."

"I know. Feels nice though, eh?" he said, sliding his hands down the side of her arms.

"It does, almost too perfect. Nate, it makes me sad," she said quietly.

"Why? I thought you'd be happy," he said, lifting her chin to look at him.

"I am, but I'm sad, too, because it only shows me what I can't have. I don't know if I want to see what that's like, yet. I mean, you're here talking to my friends, and people can see you hugging me, and I'll probably have to answer questions now on who you are. And I just can't."

"I'm sorry. I'll go," he said, stepping back from her. ~~His face was disappointed.~~

"Nathan, no it's just . . . " But he was gone.

She looked around, and no one seemed to notice him disappear. "Nathan, I'm sorry."

Her stomach started to turn. She felt sick for turning him away like that. Isn't that what she always wanted? Why did she say that to him?

168

Just then, a lady approached her, ~~saying,~~ "Excuse me. Are you Sophie Reid?" *She asked.*

"Yes," Sophie said, caught off guard.

"I'm Audrey Patell. I'm an agent with Vancouver Coast Talent."

"Oh, hi, it's nice to meet you."

"You girls did an amazing job. It was a hard scene to do, especially when the rest of them are so much lighter, eh?"

"Ya, it was a lot different than the rest, but Julie and I were up for it."

"That's good. It shows you like a challenge. Listen, I was wondering if you would be interested in meeting with me later this week?"

"Uh, ya, I mean, yes, I would love to," Sophie said nervously

"Great, then. Here is my card. Give a call to the office and they'll book you an appointment. We'd like to see about maybe signing you on with us. We're very interested in you."

"Wow, yes, that would be great. I'll call first thing Monday morning. Thank you."

"Good, then I'll see you next week. Don't forget your headshots and resume. I look forward to speaking with you, Sophie." Audrey waved, as she walked away.

"Me, too, thank you again," Sophie said with a big smile on her face.

Sophie ran through the crowd to find Julie.

"Sophie!" Julie yelled from straight ahead. *Just happened.*

"Hey, Jules, you'll never guess what? That Audrey Patell from Vancouver Coast Talent gave me her card! She wants to meet with me next week! She might sign me!"

"Really! That's awesome, Soph! Congrats! Now, we really have a reason to party," Julie said, ~~hugging her.~~ *giving her a hug.*

"It's too bad that Nathan can't make it. Man, was he cute! Sophie, you need to keep tabs on that one. What a nice guy, too."

"Ya, he is." Sophie smiled.

"But anyway, where's this other guy you met? The one who told you about the party— Devon, is it?"

"Um, I'm not sure. But he'll be there tonight. We should go home and get ready. Did you find out where the party is happening?"

"Ya, it's going to be at this guy Steve's house. He's a past student from the school, Everyone's going. So, it should be a blast!"

"Cool, do you have the address?"

"Yup, we're gold! Let's hurry home and get ready. We only have about two hours," Julie said, flashing a piece of paper with the address on it in front of Sophie.

They gathered their things and headed to the sky train. It took them about thirty minutes to get home. They each showered and cleaned up. Sophie gave Julie a new shirt to wear with her jeans.

"I'm gonna crash here tonight, okay? So, I'll just leave all my stuff here in your room, cool?" Julie asked.

"Ya, that's fine," Sophie said. She knew Natalie would freak out, but she didn't care.

"We have to look at our apartments tomorrow, anyway, so my staying over works!"

"Oh, ya! I forgot!" Sophie laughed. Now she really didn't care. Julie had to stay over and they would be gone before Natalie woke up, hopefully.

The girls headed out the door, ready for a night of celebration.

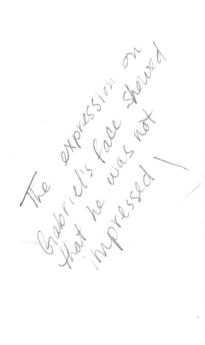

The expression on Gabriel's face showed that he was not impressed

16
The Wrong Mix

Nate thought for sure that he was doing the right thing. Did she really not want him there? Perhaps he did do it for himself, or maybe he was just giving her something to hold onto. Nathan pondered over his recent actions. It felt so nice to be part of her world, even if it was just for a moment.

"What do you think your doing, Nathan?" a man's voice said.

"Gabriel," Nathan said, turning to see the archangel behind him.

"You have been pushing the limits with that girl a lot lately," he warned.

"I know, I apologize. It's just that she's different and I can't treat her the same as the rest of them. She needs a different type of help."

"The kind that involves you physically being there? No one gets that kind of help from guardians, ever—no matter who they are."

"I know, I know. But this is different, and I ask for you to trust me," Nathan said confidently.

"The rest of the archangels, including myself, believe that this is getting out of your hands, Nathan. You've done so well over the years, helping people and your services are almost complete with us. So, don't let yourself get too attached before you pass on."

"I know, thank you. But . . . "

Gabriel raised his hand, cutting Nathan off. "You're leading this girl on. She will not understand when you have to leave, and it will destroy her."

"No, it won't!" he snapped back.

Gabriel's face was not impressed, so Nate quickly recovered his words.

"I'm sorry. I mean she will make it through this. She understands how this all works. It's just that we have such a close connection. It looks like she can't live without me, but she can and she will. I promise you."

Gabriel stared at Nathan while studying him. There was something about his words that saved him in that moment.

"Don't make us step in, Nathan. Choose your actions wisely." Then, he was gone.

Nathan wasn't sure if he actually believed the words he had said, but it had bought him some time.

Sophie and Julie arrived at the party just in time. The apartment was filled with people having a good time. The music was blasting and everyone was mingling, trying to get to know one another.

That was the great thing about actors. They were always so outgoing. Nobody was shy and everyone acted as if they had known each other for years. There were also people there who were friends and family of some of the actors, so it was a nice mix.

"Hey, you guys made it!" Kevin yelled from down the hallway in front of them.

"Hey, Kev, how's it going?" Sophie said, trying to show him that she was cool with everything. He ran up and hugged them. She really was trying to feel better about everything. Kevin was a nice guy and he really didn't mean to hurt her. The only person she should really be mad at was Jake. She wasn't sure if she could ever really forgive him.

"You did so good in your scene, Kevin, congrats!" Julie said encouragingly.

"Awh, thanks, girlie, you guys, too! I mean, you had the only dark and depressing scene, and that's mad hard to carry in any show." He laughed. "Now, come on, let's celebrate. Come with me to the kitchen. I'll get you both a drink!"

They walked through the crowd of people into the kitchen. Adel was there mixing drinks with Elaina and Mark.

"We need to get these girls some drinks!" Kevin yelled.

"Hey, Sophie!" Mark said, throwing his arms around her, nearly knocking her over.

"Oh my gosh, Mark, are you drunk?" She laughed.

"He's just feeling good." Adel laughed.

"Jules!! Julie Julie Julie . . . you look so pretty tonight," Mark said, holding his arm out for Julie to join the two of them hugging.

"Hey, Mark, you're feeling good, eh?" She laughed, hugging him. "I keep forgetting you're the youngest of us. Welcome to our party world. We'll have to keep an eye on you," she teased.

"Sophie, come here," Adel said, pulling her from Mark's arms.

"What do you want to drink? I can pretty much make anything."

"How about a whisky sour?" Sophie asked.

"Hmmm . . . Not that. Anything else?"

"Well, I'm good with just a Vodka Ice if you have one."

"That we do . . . check the fridge."

Sophie started to head over to the fridge when Adel grabbed her, pulling her back.

"Listen, Soph. I'm sorry about the Jake thing. Someone should've said something. I should've said something. I knew you were into him and I wasn't sure if he was still with his girlfriend or whatever. But either way, I should've told you what I knew. I've been through the same thing and no one told me, and it feels horrible. I'm really sorry."

"Thank you, Adel. That means a lot," Sophie said, giving her a hug.

"I've got your back from here on out, though, I swear."

"Cool, thanks." Sophie laughed. She headed back over to the fridge and grabbed two drinks from the inside door.

"Anyone got a towel I can use to open these? My hands are too weak," Sophie said, trying to twist the cap off.

"Here," a voice said, grabbing the bottle from her hand.

"Devon," Sophie said, smiling at him.

"Glad you made it," he said, popping the second cap off the bottle with his shirt.

"Me, too. Uh, this is my friend, Julie," she said, grabbing Julie's arm and pulling her over.

"Hey, Julie, I'm Devon." he said, shaking her hand.

"Ah, you're Devon." She smiled.

"You've heard of me?" He laughed.

"Uh, no, it's just that Sophie said she had met this cute guy and he told her about a party and . . . "

"Just stop please . . . " Sophie said, totally embarrassed.

"Sorry," Julie said quietly.

He smiled back at Sophie. "Good to know that you think I'm cute. The feeling's mutual."

"Just a sec," he said, stepping away from them for a moment to grab a guy in the hallway.

"This is my roommate, Carter," he said, pushing his friend toward Julie.

"Hey, I'm Julie." She smiled at him.

"Hey beautiful," Carter said, shaking her hand. "And you must be Sophie, then, right?"

"Ya," she said, confused about how he knew her name.

"Looks like I talk, too," Devon teased her.

"Oh good, now we can both be embarrassed." Sophie laughed, feeling a bit better.

He handed the girls their drinks. "So how were classes at the school? We went there about a year and a half ago."

"They were good, mentally challenging, but a good learning experience," Sophie said, leaning back against the counter.

"Ya, the only class I hated was that one where we had to work on expressing different feelings. Talk about awkward." Carter laughed.

"Oh, ya, we did that. They really dug up some crap about you and drilled you on it. It felt like you left a therapy session when class was done," Julie said, taking a sip of her drink.

"I didn't get to see your monologue tonight, how'd it go?" Sophie asked.

"It went pretty well, but I forgot a section. So, I had to improvise. But other than that, good," Devon said, setting his drink down on the counter and leaning beside her.

"I think we need to do some shots," Carter suggested, pulling Julie over to the counter.

"Did someone say shots?" Mark yelled, running back to join them.

"Oh. Are you sure you can handle another, Mark?" Sophie said, looking him over. He wasn't totally plastered or anything, but definitely drunk.

"Na, I'm soooo good!" he said, dancing around them.

"Let the kid have one. He's a professional actor now!" Carter said, putting his arm around Mark's shoulders.

Carter mixed up some shots and poured five of them out.

"Ready? One, two, three!" he said, giving everyone a cheers, and then took the shot in one quick gulp.

"Ugh, nasty!" Sophie said, taking a sip of her drink to wash it down. "What was that?"

"A broken down golf cart!" Devon laughed.

"Ohh . . . Sophie, your favorite! Not!" Julie laughed.

"Well, it's my favorite!" Mark yelled, and then he danced away into the next room.

"That boy is in for a serious hangover tomorrow," Carter said, shaking his head.

Just then, Jake entered the room. He immediately spotted Sophie and walked over.

"Hey, you. You did well tonight," he said, smiling at her. "Have a drink with me?"

"I already have a drink, thanks," Sophie said, turning away from him.

Devon noticed the tension between them and stepped in. "She's good, buddy, no worries."

"Sorry, you are?" Jake asked, not amused.

"Devon," he answered confidently.

"Devon? I'm Jake." He grabbed Devon's hand and shook it tightly. "I was actually talking to Sophie, if you don't mind."

Julie looked at Sophie nervously, as Carter stepped a little closer to Devon.

"Well, I think she doesn't really want to talk to you, so it's probably best if you just leave her alone," Devon said, taking a step toward Jake.

Sophie was surprised by how Devon was helping her out. She didn't want this to get messy, so she'd have to make a quick fix.

"Look, I'm good, Jake, thank you. I'll talk with you later, okay?"

His eyes were still on Devon, staring him down. "Okay, Soph, later."

He kept his eyes on Devon, as he walked away.

"Wow, what was that about?" Carter laughed.

"Nothing," Sophie said, grabbing her drink and taking a sip.

"Well, it didn't look like nothing," Devon said, grabbing the drink from her hand and setting it down.

"He was a guy she used to like, but it turned out he had a girlfriend all long. He totally played her. Just like the last one. Guys are so immature," Julie said, shaking her head.

"Julie!" Sophie snapped at her. She didn't need anyone to know about her bad luck in dating. It was humiliating.

"Sorry, Soph, but it's nothing to be embarrassed about. There are a lot of shitty people out there. You can't help it that you've had a lot of bad picks."

"Oh god," Sophie said, covering her face.

Devon pulled her hands down from her face. "Don't be embarrassed. It happens to a lot of people. Julie's right. Want me to kick his ass?"

"What? No, it's fine." She laughed. He handed her drink back to her.

"Well, now that we got rid of the crazy ex, let's have some fun!" Devon said, leading Sophie into the other room where everyone was hanging out.

Mark had turned the coffee table into his own private dance podium. Adel and Elaina were cheering him on, and it was only a matter of time before he crashed. Just then, Natalie noticed them. She walked over toward Sophie.

"I see you've found a new guy. Thank god. Now, maybe you won't be so miserable." She smirked at Julie, and then shoved by.

"What are you talking about, Nat? I don't need any . . . " Sophie was interrupted by a loud crash. Mark had fallen off the table and was lying on the floor, laughing.

"Oh my god, Mark, are you okay?" Sophie said, running over to him.

"Oh, ya, I'm great. Guess my dance moves were way too fantastic for that table to handle," he said, trying to get up.

"They sure were." Sophie laughed, helping him to his feet. "Are you okay? Seriously, Mark."

"Awh . . . Look at you so worried about me. So cute!" he said, hugging her.

"Mark, of course, I'm worried about you," she said, holding him up as his legs gave in.

"Is he okay?" Elaina said, coming over to help. "I think you should lie down for a bit, Marky. Sophie, help me take him into the spare room."

The two of them dragged Mark to the spare room and shoved the door open.

"What the hell?" Natalie yelled from inside. She was making out with some short little guy.

"Nat, we need to lay Mark down. Can you move this to another place?" Sophie asked, as she and Elaina set Mark down on the bed.

"Um, no. He can just lie there. We're just talking," Natalie said, holding onto the guy's arm.

"Ah, man, I don't wanna watch them make out! Come on, let me go back to the party," Mark said, trying to get up.

"No, you lay down Mark! You're too drunk," Elaina said, pushing him back down on the bed.

"Whatever, Nat, be that way, then," Sophie said, brushing her off. "Just keep an eye on him, please." Sophie slammed the door behind them. She was getting sick of dealing with Natalie and her attitude.

A young girl met them just outside the spare room. She was a friend of Elaina.

"Hey, is everything all right?" she asked Elaina.

"Oh, ya, Mark's just hammered. We put him down." She laughed.

"Oh, Sophie, this is my good friend from high school, Charlotte. Charlotte, this is Sophie."

"Hey, nice to meet ya," Charlotte said happily.

"You, too, Charlotte."

The three of them headed back into the main room to join the party again. Sophie looked for her drink that she had set down on the table before grabbing Mark. There were a few of them there now, so she decided that the best choice, due to her recent experiences with leaving her drink, was to grab a new one.

"My drink's missing," Charlotte said, looking around. "Better get another one. Sophie, do you need one?" she asked.

"Ya, actually, I do. I'll come with you," Sophie said, following her to the kitchen.

"This is a really interesting party, eh?" Charlotte laughed.

"You're telling me."

"I was supposed to go to a movie tonight, but nobody wanted to go with me, so when Elaina asked me to come with her, I was definitely in."

"Oh, ya? What movie were you going to see?"

"Hell on Earth," she said embarrassed.

"Nice. I totally wanted to see that! I love horror movies!" Sophie said hysterically.

"Me. too! But my friends hate them, so I never have anyone to go with, and I always end up going alone."

"Really? Me, too. We should go together sometime if you still want to see it."

"Ya, that'd be awesome!"

They chatted some more after they grabbed their drinks from the fridge. Sophie found out that Charlotte had a lot more in common with her than they expected. She, too, had come from a family who wasn't really there for her and she was always on her own. She was in college, taking photography and working at the local tourist sites in Vancouver part-time for money.

She knew photography was a hard industry to do well in, but she was slowly working her way into it by taking photos for visitors when they arrived at the many Vancouver tourist sites. She told Sophie of her portfolio she was building in hopes of opening her own business someday. Sophie found Charlotte inspiring, and it was a lot like her own situation.

It was exactly how Gram had said, "If you love something, you should do it. You can have anything you want in life if you're willing to work for it." These words always ran through her mind whenever she felt like giving up.

Just then, Devon entered the room. "Hey, there you are!" he said, walking up to Sophie.

"Hey, Devon. Sorry, I had an emergency with Mark," she laughed.

"Oh, I know, I saw. He's a different one isn't he?"

"Mark's always entertaining," Sophie, said shaking her head.

"Sophie!!" Julie said, running into the room. She leaped at her just as Sophie was taking a sip of her drink, and the bottle cracked against her tooth.

"Ouch, Jules . . . " Sophie said, touching her lip. Her tooth had cut her lip and there was blood dripping down.

"Oh my god, Soph, I'm so sorry," Julie laughed. She clearly had had a few more drinks, while Sophie was gone. Carter came up and put his arm around Julie. "Okay, step away from the patient before you hurt her anymore," he teased.

"Come with me, Soph," Devon said, grabbing her hand and leading her to the bathroom.

"Here, Soph, give me your drink before you go," Charlotte said, holding out her hand.

Sophie handed her the drink and continued following Devon to the bathroom.

He knocked on the door to see if anyone was in there. When no one answered, he opened the door and flicked on the light. Sophie followed him inside and he closed the door behind her.

"Here, sit down."

"Man, that hurt," Sophie said, touching her lip softly.

"Don't touch it. Let me see. Did you chip your tooth?" He held her head up slightly, as she smiled at him. "Nope, no chip. You're lucky, but a beautiful smile is dangerous."

"Nice. Real slick." She laughed.

"I am, you just wait and see." He grabbed some tissue from the box off the back of the toilet and wet it a bit.

"Now, don't move for a sec." He carefully dabbed the blood from Sophie's lip, holding the side of her face. His hands were warm and he smelt good. Sophie looked up at him, as he cleaned her up. This was probably something she could do herself, but she wasn't going to deny a cute guy from taking care of her.

"It's official. You're going to live," he said quietly, moving closer to her face to examine her. "No more blood."

"Thank you, I was worried I wouldn't make it." She giggled.

"As long as you are with me, you will."

She didn't move, as he leaned in closer. He held his face close to hers, their lips barely touching. Finally, he pressed against her to kiss her. She found his confidence attracting. He kissed her softly, running his fingers through her hair. He then lifted her up and pulled her closer, continuing to kiss her. He ran his hands down to her lower back, holding her tightly.

She slowly pulled away after a few seconds and touched her lips softly. "They hurt."

"Sorry," he said, touching her face gently. He didn't remove his arm from around her.

"Um, this is a little . . . too fast," she said shyly.

"I know, sorry I couldn't help myself." He smiled at her.

They stood there for a moment, his arms still wrapped around her. She leaned back into him, kissing him softly on the lips. He pulled her in again. She couldn't figure out why she wanted to kiss him so badly. She wasn't one to make out with a person she just met.

"Okay, we have to stop," she said, still standing close.

"Okay," he said, kissing her again. She couldn't stop herself. He held her face with both hands, as he leaned against her more.

"Seriously." She slowly pulled his hands down from her face and stepped away.

"Sorry, guess we're both not good with this." He smiled at her.

Just then, Julie knocked at the door. "Hey Soppphhhiiee? You okay?" Her words slurred.

Sophie opened the door to Julie, leaning against the wall.

"I'm good, Jules. How are you doing?" She laughed.

"Oh boy, I think I may be done."

"I think you are, too," Sophie said, wrapping her arm around Julie's waist.

"Here, let me help you," Devon said, grabbing her other side. "Man, people tonight are just not holding out, are they?"

Carter met them halfway down the hall and grabbed Julie from them. "I got her," he said, lifting her up. "You girls need a cab?"

"Ya, I'm thinking it's about time to go. I just want to check on Mark before I leave, okay? I'll meet you at the door," she said, heading into the spare room.

The lights were off and Mark was fast asleep on the bed. She walked up to him and checked him over to make sure he was all right. Then, she quietly closed the door behind her on the way out. That's when she heard the yelling.

She ran to the front door to see Natalie and Julie screaming at the top of their lungs. Julie took a swing at Natalie, but she missed, cracking her fist on the wall. Natalie leaped at her, pulling her hair.

"Really? This is just pathetic!" Sophie said, running over to break it up. The boys found this quite entertaining and stepped back to watch the fight.

Natalie pulled Julie to the ground, which wasn't too hard to do, considering she was drunk. This was the perfect time for Natalie to attack Julie, because normally, Natalie could not take her, but drunk, maybe.

Sophie pulled at Natalie, trying to rip her from Julie. As she did, Julie took one big swing and cracked Natalie in the face. Natalie screamed, ripping out a piece of Julie's hair.

"Stop, guys, seriously!" Sophie screamed at them.

Finally, Devon stepped in, helping Sophie pull Natalie from Julie, and Carter quickly grabbed Julie before she had a chance to lunge again.

"Wow, this is truly the best party ever!" Carter laughed. "I got five bucks on Jules!"

"Shut up, Carter." Devon laughed, pulling Natalie into the kitchen.

"Just try me again, you little creep. I dare you to!" Julie screamed from the hallway.

"Oh. I will. You're nothing but a dumbass blonde!" Natalie screamed from Devon's arms.

"Will you shut up, Nat!" Sophie said, stepping in front of her, trying to bring her attention to herself.

"Oh, sure, take her side. She started it!"

"Actually, it was you, girlie. You made the remark about her picking up secondhand guys, and it was you who jumped Julie from behind," Devon said smugly.

181

"Really, Nat? This is just getting stupid. Grow the hell up!" Sophie said, walking away. Everyone was staring from the hallway, and this had now turned into another event by the two of them. Charlotte walked through the crowd into the kitchen.

"Sophie, what's going on in here?" She laughed.

"Oh nothing. Just more drama from my friends."

"Drama? Friends? Please, you creep!" Natalie yelled, breaking from Devon's hold, and running straight for Sophie. Charlotte stepped in front of her and pushed her back to Devon.

"Really?" Sophie said, giving Nat a pathetic look. "Thanks, Char. I'll text ya later about the movie, okay?"

"Sounds good! We got her, so just go," Charlotte said, blocking Natalie's view.

"Hey, wait!" Devon said, dropping Natalie and running over to her. "Can I see you again?"

She smiled at him. "Sure, I'm sorry. The fight distracted me. I didn't mean to just walk away."

"Hey, it's cool. Here, put your number in my phone and I'll do the same with yours." They passed each other their phones and entered their numbers.

"I'll talk to you later, then?" he said, walking her to the door. Carter had already taken Julie down to the entrance to wait for a cab.

"Definitely," she said, giving him a hug goodbye.

"That is so friggen rude, Soph! Help me up here!" Natalie yelled from the kitchen.

"Don't worry. I've got her. You go ahead and help Julie get home safe." He smiled at her, heading back to the kitchen to help Natalie.

"I don't even know you! Do you know how rude you are?" Natalie continued to bitch at him, while he helped her. Sophie laughed, as she walked out the door.

It took a very patient guy to be able to put up with Natalie. She wondered what had happened with that guy she was making out with in the spare room? She headed down the elevator to the entrance, where Julie and Carter were waiting.

"Is she okay?" Sophie asked, walking up to Carter.

"She's fine, no worries. Your cab is here, get in," he said, opening the door for her.

"Thanks for everything, Carter. It was nice to meet you."

"No prob, Soph." He was still holding Julie up with one arm, as she leaned against him.

"See ya, Jules. Text me when you wake up if you remember me, okay?" he teased.

"Oh, I'll remember you . . . " She leaned in and kissed him. Sophie turned away in the cab to give them a moment.

"Good night," Julie said, stepping away from him and falling into the cab.

"Hey, my friend!" she said, lying down on Sophie's lap.

"Hey, you," Sophie giggled.

"Did you see me kick that brat's ass tonight? Even drunk, I can still take her!"

"Ya, you did good, Jules." Sophie rolled her eyes. The two of them were becoming more drama than Sophie wanted in her life. Julie slept the entire way home. When the cab pulled up to the house, Sophie paid the driver and dragged her friend inside. She stopped at the front door, placing Julie down for a moment to unlock it.

"Hey. Need some help?" Nathan asked.

"Nate. Oh my gosh, yes, please. This is exhausting!" she said, trying to lift Julie back to her feet. She was like a dead weight. Nathan walked over and lifted her into his arms.

"Lead the way."

Sophie ran to grab a pillow and blanket from her room and met him back at the couch. She quickly made a bed for Julie, as Nathan placed her down gently.

Nathan then hit the lights and followed Sophie to her room. He stood in the doorway, as she took off her jacket and placed her purse on the floor.

"How was the party?"

"It was good."

"Good, eh? Anything interesting happen?"

"No, not really. Well, Natalie and Julie had it out. I mean, really had it out—fists flying and hair ripping—the whole nine yards. Oh, and Mark was, well . . . not good." She laughed.

"Mark, yes, I see. Meet any new friends?" he asked, walking in and sitting down on the edge of her bed.

"Nathan, why are you asking me these questions? Don't you see everything? You should know," she said nervously. She knew what he was really asking about. He wanted her to tell him about Devon.

"I'm just asking to make conversation. That's all." He smiled at her.

He suspected that she knew what he was getting at.

"Do you like him?" he asked quietly.

"Who, Devon? Well, I just met him. But, ya, he's nice."

"Just nice? I would've thought more than that by how you were kissing him," he said calmly.

She stopped and turned to him. She didn't know what to say. Obviously, she liked Nathan more than anything, but she may never get her shot with him. So, she didn't want to just ignore what was right in front of her. Isn't that what he wanted her to do? But she also never wanted to hurt Nathan, ever.

"I don't know what came over me," she said, sitting down beside him.

"I've never seen you act like that, Soph."

"Isn't this what you wanted me to do, Nathan? Didn't you want me to live the life that was right in front of me? Or are you changing your mind?"

"No, Soph."

"Because, if there's a chance for us, Nate, then tell me, and I'll take it with you. I don't understand what you want from me."

"No, Sophie, you're right. You're doing exactly what you're supposed to be doing. I'm just making sure you're being careful. That's all. I'm sorry. I don't mean to confuse you."

She looked at him, as he got up from the bed.

"Don't forget to call Gram tomorrow. She'll want to hear everything about today."

"I know," Sophie said, still studying him over.

"Well, I better be going. Good luck in your apartment search tomorrow."

"Thanks, Nate," she said, as he disappeared.

She didn't understand Nate recently. He was all over the place with his orders and emotions. After throwing on her pajamas, she brushed her teeth and jumped into bed. She leaned over and turned off the lamp on her nightstand, and stared into the darkness. It wasn't long before she fell asleep.

Her mind raced, as she fell deeper and deeper into slumber. It was cloudy everywhere and she could barely see where she was walking. It was cold and getting dark, as she walked through the forest. She could hear the trees rustling, as the wind blew through them. It was getting darker by the moment and harder to see.

Suddenly, the sound of branches breaking behind her stopped her dead in her tracks. She turned around and searched the darkness for someone or something. Nothing, there was nothing there. The branches began to break again. Someone or something was coming toward her. It sounded like it was speeding up! Sophie's eyes raced through the darkness, trying to catch a glimpse of what was coming at her!

"Run!" a woman's voice said.

Her breathing sped up, as she tried to decide what to do.

"I said run!" the voice said again.

This time, Sophie did, without a second thought. She turned and ran through the woods, slicing her skin on the sharp branches of trees and bushes. Whatever was behind her was catching up. She could feel its presence close. Her arms burned from the cuts, as she ran faster into the night.

She looked over her shoulder, as the horrific image of something tall with long arms and legs ran closely behind her. For a moment, she couldn't make out what it was. The image became clearer. It was definitely a man—at least she thought it was. He reached for her, but she pulled away, running faster. Panic started to kick in and Sophie's breath got shorter.

"Leave me alone!" she screamed into the night.

As she cut a corner, her feet stumbled beneath her. She fell to the ground, slamming herself into a tree. She covered her head in fear, knowing whatever was behind her had to have caught her. Her body trembled for what was about to grab her. She screamed, as a hand came down and touched her on the arm. She swung her arms wildly, striking whatever it was away. She opened her eyes with her arms still in defense position. Nothing.

There was nothing there. She looked around frantically for some form of life. She slowly peered around the tree, and saw a small meadow up ahead, filled with wild flowers. The moon seemed to shine a little brighter there. Slowly, she got up and headed toward it, keeping her eyes peeled for whatever had been following her.

The meadow was open and bright in the moonlight. There was a spot in the middle of the field where no flowers grew. She stared at it, as she walked closer. There was a gravestone. She knelt down beside it and brushed the dirt from the top. There was no name on it.

"It's not time, yet," a woman said from behind her.

She turned to see her grandmother behind her.

"Gram? What are you doing here?"

"I'm just checking in on you. Are you all right?"

"No, someone was chasing me, Gram! We have to get out of here, because it's still out there!" Sophie said, running to her, but Gram disappeared right in front of her.

"It will always be there 'til you deal with it, Sophie," Gram said, reappearing behind her. Sophie turned to face her. "What's going on, Gram? What's there?" she yelled frantically.

"You have to deal with it. No one else can help you. Not even me. I won't be here long enough to see it through."

"See what through? Where are you going? What's wrong?" she yelled, as the wind picked up around them.

"Please, try to hurry, my dear Sophie."

"Gram!" she yelled, watching her disappear. The wind knocked her to the ground on top of the gravestone. She stared down at it and read the words that were not there before.

"Here lies Vivian Reid, loving mother, grandmother, and dear friend."

Sophie's breath was taken away, as she glanced again at the words she read.

"No. No, this isn't real!" she said, rubbing her hands over the stone.

"Gram, you can't be. What the hell is going on?" she yelled.

"Gram . . . " she cried softly, lying down on the ground. "You can't leave me. I have no one."

"Please, let me wake up. This can't be real. Please . . . " she said to herself, as the wind blew stronger, making her body shiver. She wiped her eyes and tried to sit up.

"Nathan!" she screamed.

"Nathan! I need you, please! Nate!!" Her voice cracked in fear.

"I need you! Nathan, please!" She continued to scream until she exhausted herself and collapsed back to the ground. The wind blew around her, making the chill on her body worse with every moment.

"Nate . . . " she whispered, trembling in the cold.

"I'm here, Soph. I'm here." He touched her hand softly. She opened her eyes to see him beside her.

"Nate, I need you. I need you. Help me," she cried, sitting up in a panic to grab him.

"I know, sweetie. I'm right here." He hugged her tightly. Her hands gripped him, as if she were holding on for dear life.

"What is this? What's happening, Nate? This can't be real, right?" she said, trying to catch her breath. He sat down, as her arms wrapped around his neck tightly. She couldn't let go of him.

"Nate, tell me this isn't real," she begged him.

"It's not, Soph. It's not real," he said, trying to calm her. She slowly slid her arms from around his neck and down his chest. He kept his arms wrapped closely around her, as she leaned her head against his chest, taking a deep breath to calm herself down. Her hands gripped tightly to his shirt, as her breathing slowed.

"I need you, " she whispered.

"I know. I'm not going anywhere. Sophie. I'm right here," he said softly. "I've got you."

17

A Shiver of Sunlight

Morning came and Sophie awoke to the alarm on her phone. It felt as if she hadn't slept at all. The nightmares had come back and they were stronger and more real than ever. The previous night's dream had to be the worst she'd ever had. She sat up in bed, with her hands still shaking.

"It felt so real," she said to herself, checking her arms for scrapes from the trees. But there was nothing there.

"Gram!" she said, grabbing her phone from the table and dialing her number frantically. The phone rang twice, but there was no answer. She waited impatiently, as it rang another two times.

"Hello?" Gram's voice finally said.

"Oh my god. Hi, how are you?" Sophie said relieved.

"I'm good. What's wrong, Hun?" Gram asked worried.

"I just had the worst dream."

"Really? What was it about?"

Sophie thought for a moment, and she decided not to tell her gram about the gravestone. But she did tell her about the man chasing her and the fact that she couldn't see his face.

"Sophie. You know, they say that when you have dreams of running away, it means that you're not dealing with something in your own life."

"Ya, but Gram, this was different. I'm not running away, something is chasing me! I've had these for years and it's always the same thing. Maybe it's a warning that something or someone's coming for me."

"I don't think so, honey," Gram said with a giggle. "I really think it's something personal that you're not dealing with or are scared to deal with."

"But I'm not scared of anything."

"Maybe not exactly, but dreams can mean so much. You'll have to figure it out. You've been like this since you were a child, Sophie. You were always a light sleeper, worrying about everything. We used to put you down at night and I swear you'd sleep with one eye open." She laughed.

"And when you did sleep, you always seemed to have these nightmares, and we could never figure out why. Perhaps it was because you have such a creative mind."

"Ya, I guess so," Sophie said softly.

"But on a lighter note, how did the showcase go yesterday?"

"Oh, ya, it went great. You would've loved it! And an agent came up to me afterward and gave me her business card! She wants to meet with me this week about possibly signing me!"

"That's fantastic, Sophie! Congratulations!" Gram said happily. "I knew you could do it!"

"Ya, it was a nice end to the day. I'll send you some pictures from the event soon, all right?"

Sophie listened, as her grandmother's breathing grew louder.

"How are you feeling lately, Gram?" she asked nervously.

"Oh, so so. My chest is really bothering me today. I think I'll go see my doctor on Monday morning and get it checked out, just in case."

"I think that's a good idea, then let me know, okay?"

"Okay. But other than that, I've been playing cards with a new group of ladies every Monday night in my apartment lounge."

"Oh really? That's good. Any competition?" Sophie teased. She knew how her gram loved to play cards.

"Well, not from these old broads, but they do entertain me." She laughed.

"Well, that's all ya need, then. We all know I'm your only competition out there."

"Is that so? Well, we'll have to have a rematch when you come for a visit, because I seem to remember you losing pretty badly last time," Gram challenged.

"You're on! In fact, I may look into a flight soon, so that I can prove this to you!"

"You should do that. I'm not getting any younger," Gram teased.

"Hey, don't talk like that," Sophie said, thinking about her recent dream. She didn't want to think about not having her grandmother in her life. She had always been there, the one person who really knew her.

She would seriously have to think about looking into a flight soon to visit her. It was so expensive to live in Vancouver, let alone think about saving for a flight anywhere, but for Gram, she'd have to make it happen. Gram would do it for her if she could.

Her family had never come to visit her and she didn't care to visit them. But Gram was a whole different story. She would drop everything to be by her side if she needed her. The thought of going home only depressed her.

The people there only joked about her life and made her feel not worthy of anything. She never truly felt loved or even needed in the family. Everyone seemed to be doing such great things, and Sophie was nothing but a dream chaser to them.

They always talked about her and what ideas she would come up with next. They just couldn't accept that she was genuinely a creative person and needed to be part of something great in this world—and that she was only following her instincts on what to do with her life.

Sometimes, she was so confused and had mixed feelings, but she could never talk to them about it. No one understood her, no one but Gram. All Sophie knew was that she had a love for the entertainment industry and had to be part of it in some way or another. There was nothing else she had a passion for.

So, whatever she ended up doing would be somewhere in this field—acting, singing, or working behind the scenes. Anything that was in the arts would please her. She just had to find out which one it was. If she kept on this path, something was sure to come out of it.

"All right, Gram, don't forget to call me after your appointment Monday, okay?" Sophie said sternly.

"Of course, I won't forget. But it will be after my card game if you don't mind. You're three hours ahead of me, so you'll still be up."

"Ya, that's fine, Gram. I'll talk to you then."

"Sounds good. I love you."

"Love you, too. Bye."

Sophie hung up the phone and placed it back on the nightstand. She felt a little better, knowing her Gram was okay.

Sophie looked at her watch. It was 10:00 a.m. She needed to get up. She and Julie were to look at apartments. She wondered if Julie was awake. She hopped out of bed and got into the shower. The warm water was relaxing. Her body felt so tense from the night before.

After a long shower, she got out and headed to her room. It had been a while since she tidied it last, so she had to dig through her clothes to find the folded ones that were clean. She took her time doing her makeup and hair, with scenes from her dream playing through her mind. Nathan had saved her again. Where was he this morning? Usually, he would check up on her after an event like that.

There was a sudden soft knock at the door. Julie peaked her head in.

"Morning, friend," she said quietly.

"Morning, Jules! How ya feeling?" Sophie laughed.

"Shhh!!! Quiet voice day." Julie said, rubbing her head.

"Ahh . . . I see. Sorry," Sophie whispered. "We still on for looking at apartments?"

"Definitely! I won't leave you another moment in this horrible living situation," Julie teased.

"Great. I'm about ready. How long do you need?"

"Give me fifteen minutes. Can I borrow a face cloth?"

"Sure." Sophie handed her some towels and Julie headed into the bathroom to freshen up.

As she waited for Julie, she gathered her things and went out to the kitchen. Natalie's door to her room was open. She must've not come home last night.

Sophie still felt bad about sneaking out to look for apartments without Natalie knowing. She would have to give her enough of a notice, unless her landlords wouldn't mind renting out just Sophie's room. Then, she wouldn't have to worry about it.

That was it! She ran upstairs to ask her landlord if they would still allow Natalie to rent. She knew that it was easier to rent out two bedrooms than one and landlords preferred it. But maybe, just maybe, luck would be on her side for this.

Five minutes later, Sophie returned to the basement with a smile on her face. The landlords agreed to letting Natalie stay. They would only put the one bedroom up for rent. This made things even easier.

Julie finished getting ready and threw her stuff together in her bag. Sophie grabbed the addresses for the apartments they found online and shoved them in her pocket.

"Ready?" she said, as Julie tied her hair into a ponytail.

"Ready," Julie said, throwing her jacket on.

They headed out the door to the sky train, and stopped at a fast food restaurant for some breakfast to eat on the way. Julie was never going to last without it. For some reason, when you have a hangover, the taste of hash browns, apple juice, and a BLT bagel seems oh so delicious!

"These are the best hash browns I've ever had!!" Julie said, licking her fingers. "The best!"

"Good, I need you to have some energy today. We have a lot of places to look at," Sophie said, showing the list of apartments to her.

"Oh, man. I forgot we had that many. That's cool, more options!"

Sophie folded the list back up and put it in her purse. "We should make notes, so we remember which ones we liked."

"Good plan," Julie said, finishing off her apple juice.

The girls were just pulling up to their first stop when Sophie's phone went off.

"Hello?"

"Hey, you. How's the lip?"

"Devon. Hey, It's good. Just how you said, I lived. It's a miracle." Sophie laughed.

Julie smiled at her, leaning close to hear their conversation.

"Good to hear. So what are you up to today?"

"Well, actually, Julie and I are out looking at apartments," she said, getting up from her seat, as the train came to a stop.

"Really? So you mean you don't want to live with that crazy Natalie anymore? I can't imagine why," he teased.

"Ya, we're breaking free. I can't wait."

The girls headed off the train and down the street.

192

"Well, good luck with that. Listen, when you girls are finished, do you and Julie want to meet up with Carter and me for dinner?"

Julie slapped her arm with a huge smile on her face. "Yes! Say yes!"

"All right, Julie, geeze," Sophie whispered back to her. "Sure, that sounds good. Where should we meet you?"

"The Italian place on Broadway sound good?"

"Ya, sure. I've never been there, but I love Italian." Sophie gave Julie the thumbs up sign.

"Nice. We'll see you there at six, then."

"Great, see ya soon." Sophie hung up and slid her phone into her pocket.

"Yay, double date!" Julie laughed.

"Ya, should be interesting."

"Sophie, why do you do that? I know you like him. Every time a guy asks you out, you act like you're not that excited when I know you are."

"I know, Jules, it's just I don't like to get my hopes up. That's all."

"Really? I think it's because you have feelings for Nate and you're scared to admit it or do anything about it. Or maybe you're just waiting around for him to make a move?"

Sophie stared at Julie. She had forgotten about Nate meeting her, but what Julie said was true. She did have feelings for him, but she was trying to put them aside, so she didn't get him in trouble. She also knew that it would most likely never happen, so she had to follow Nate's advice and try to move on with her life—or at least, until they found out what would give him that second chance.

"Nothing is ever going to happen between me and Nate, Julie," Sophie said sadly.

"I think you're wrong. I think you should try, but if you're not going to, there is a second best choice right in front of you. He's also super cute if you hadn't noticed."

"It's hard to explain, but the Nate thing will never happen, so let's not talk about it. But, yes, Devon is really cute!" Sophie said, smiling at Julie.

"Oh, we're here! I think it's this one." Julie pointed to a tall apartment in front of them.

The girls walked up to the buzzer and pushed the one labeled "Landlord."

"Hallo?" a voice said.

"Hey, my name's Sophie. We called about viewing the apartment for rent."

"Ah, yes," the voice said. They waited for a response.

"So, is he letting us in?" Julie laughed.

"I'm not sure."

"He sounds Asian." Julie giggled.

"Julie . . . " Sophie laughed.

Soon enough a small Asian man came to the door. He opened it, signaling them to come in and follow him.

"You come. This way," he mumbled.

"I like him, he's funny." Julie giggled again.

They followed him up to the third floor and down the hall to apartment 308.

"Wait," he said, knocking on the door to see if anyone was home. "Okay."

The girls followed the man into the bright apartment. It was full of windows and open space. The kitchen was just off the entrance. It was small, but it had a stove, fridge, microwave, and dishwasher. Down the hall, there was a closet and inside was a washer with a dryer stacked on top. They were brand new. There were two bedrooms and two bathrooms. One of the bathrooms was connected to the master bedroom. The living room was a good size and it had an office just off of it.

"I like it," Sophie said, looking out the window. It overlooked a baseball diamond and basketball courts.

"Ya, and it's right across from the sky train pretty much. How much is it?" Julie asked the man.

"Twelve forty-five," he said.

"What?" Julie looked confused.

"I think he means twelve hundred and forty-five per month, correct?" Sophie asked him.

"Yes."

"Wow! That's a lot. That would be six hundred and twenty-two dollars a month for each of us, right?" Julie said, working it out in her head.

"Pretty much."

The man looked at them, waiting for an answer.

"Okay, well, thank you. We have a few more to look at today and we'll get back to you soon," Sophie said, heading toward the door.

"Okay," he said, following them out to the elevator and down to the front doors.

The girls thanked him again and left.

"Ah, man, was that place ever nice, eh, Soph?"

"Sure was. I wonder how the rest of the prices will compare."

"Plus, I like our little Asian landlord, he's silly." Julie giggled to herself.

"All right, Jules, the apartment wins an extra point for having a funny landlord." Sophie wrote down their opinions on the paper.

"Onto the next," she said, leading the way.

The girls went from apartment to apartment the entire afternoon. They all seemed to be around the same price. The only difference was what they had to offer. Some of them were so sketchy and run down.

The first apartment was still in the lead. It was the cleanest, safest, and had underground parking for their cars. Plus, it was in a great area. After the last apartment, they stopped for a slushie at the corner store.

"Well, my vote is in. I pick number one still."

"I think you're right, Jules. They were pretty much all the same moneywise, but this one was so nice. But I'm gonna have to get a part-time job, even if I'm acting, to get by."

"I think I'm good for now. But I may have to as well if my work slows in the fall."

It was agreed. They had chosen the first apartment, and now all they had to do was tell Natalie.

They called the landlord back and told him their decision. He informed them that the current renters would be out that weekend and they would be cleaning it the following week. The girls could pick up their keys and move in anytime after Friday. They were so excited about their new place.

"We so have to have a party to break the place in!" Julie said, choking on her slushie.

"Ah! Brain freeze!" she said, coughing it up and rubbing her head.

"Ah, geeze," Sophie said, patting her back. "Can't take you anywhere, can I?"

Julie wiped her mouth from the slushie and checked her watch.

"Hey, we gotta head downtown. It's five-thirty."

"Wow, is it really? We'd better go, then," Sophie said, getting up from the curb and brushing off her jeans. They headed back to the sky train, which was now full from the rush hour traffic. Broadway was only five stops from where they were, so it wouldn't take them long to get there.

18

Warnings

It was six o'clock on the dot when the girls arrived.

"Where are the guys?" Julie said, looking around the entrance.

Sophie opened the door for Julie and followed her inside. They looked around before spotting them at the bar.

"There they are," Sophie said, walking toward them. "Hey, guys."

Devon turned and stepped down from the stool at the bar. "Hey Soph," he said, hugging her. She was a little nervous touching him.

"Hey, you guys made it," Carter said, giving both of them a hug. "Let's grab a table." He motioned to the waitress who seated them close by in a booth.

"After you," Carter said, letting Julie slide in first, and then he followed.

"Guess we're on this side," Devon said, sliding in, as Sophie hung up her jacket on the hook by the booth.

"So, how did the apartment search go?" Carter asked.

"Total success," Sophie said, sitting down beside Devon.

"Yes it was! We found an amazing place close to the sky train. It's perfect and Sophie will be free of that witch by next weekend!"

"Julie." Sophie laughed. "But ya, it's true. We get to move in next weekend. I'm so excited, but not excited to have a talk with Natalie. She's gonna rip my head off, I know it."

"Want me to talk to her?" Devon said, nudging her. "I've tamed her before."

"No, but thank you. I've subjected you to her enough." Sophie laughed.

"No, I'm serious. I can come over and help you pack, and that's when you can tell her. That way, you have someone there if anything gets out of hand."

He was actually being serious about this. Did he really think that Sophie would get in a fight with Natalie? Or was he just saying this, because he didn't trust Natalie and was actually worried for her?

"It's actually a good idea, Soph. I'd help you, but we all know that would make things worse," Julie said, tapping her fists in a playful way.

"Easy there, killer," Carter said, putting his arm around her. "All I've done since I've met you is get you out of situations. Please tell me you're always this exciting."

She looked at him and winked. "Oh, I am."

"All right, you two, enough. I'm trying to be serious here," Devon said, shaking his head.

Just then, the waitress interrupted them to take their order. The conversation flowed through dinner and into desert. It was amazing how well the four of them got along. Sophie hadn't had this much fun since . . . her day with Nate. She suddenly felt herself missing him.

Devon was new and exciting, but Nate was something she couldn't have. What was she doing? Here she is with a great guy, having fun again, and getting ready to start a new path, and she was depressing herself at the thought of Nate.

"Whatcha thinking in that beautiful mind of yours?" Devon asked, bringing her back to reality.

Julie gave her a funny look, wondering where her mind had wondered off to. The three of them were silent for a moment.

"Sorry, guys. I was just thinking how nice this was to have a night with no drama." Sophie laughed.

"What are you talking about? Drama makes life interesting! I love drama," Carter said, finishing his drink.

"Me, too! Well, certain drama," Julie agreed.

After desert, the waitress came back to the table and asked how they'd like to pay.

"I got Julie and me," Carter said.

"Ya, and I'll take me and Sophie's," Devon said to the waitress.

"No, Devon, it's fine. I can pay for my own," Sophie said, grabbing her wallet.

"Sophie, don't be silly. I asked you out, so now let me pay."

Sophie wasn't used to having a guy pay for her dinner. The only other time someone paid for her was when Jake took her out on that dinner cruise. It felt awkward.

After paying the bill, they all headed out the front doors to the sidewalk.

"Where to now?" Carter asked.

"Wanna head back to our place? We can have some drinks and watch some television," Devon asked Sophie.

Sophie looked at Julie, who was shaking her head yes! "Sure, that sounds good."

"All right, then, let's go," Carter said, grabbing Julie's hand. The two of them walked ahead, as Sophie and Devon trailed behind.

"So, what are your plans now that school is finished?" he asked, walking slowly beside her.

"Well, I have a meeting with an agent at Vancouver Coast Talent this week, so there's that, and then move into my new apartment. And, hopefully, make it successfully as an actor? Oh, and look for a part-time job to be able to afford the new apartment," Sophie said, smiling.

"Good plan. It's hard to get by as an actor. I had to get a part-time job when I first got an agent, because it's always a slow start. But I wouldn't trade my lifestyle for anything in the world."

The boys didn't live too far from the restaurant. The four of them headed up the elevator to the second floor. It was an older apartment and had a few holes in the ceiling here and there. The elevator came to a halt, and they got off after a few seconds' wait for the doors to open.

"It always does that." Carter sighed. "Piece of crap."

The halls smelt of old wood and maybe some water damage, but when they entered the apartment, it wasn't as bad as what Sophie was expecting. It was smaller than the one Julie and she had just gotten, but it had a cozy appeal. There was only one bedroom, one bathroom, and a living room that had a small kitchen off it. In one corner of the living room was a bed.

"Who sleeps out here?" Sophie asked confused.

"I do. Carter and I flipped a coin to see who got the bedroom. He obviously won," Devon said, shaking his head.

"Yea. I did. Julie. Come check out my room. It's cool."

"We couldn't find a two-bedroom downtown that was affordable on an actor's wages. So, we went with a one-bedroom." Devon walked over and sat down on his bed.

"Ahh . . . the life of a starving actor, eh?" Sophie joked, sitting beside him.

"That it is."

They sat there for a moment in silence. They could hear Julie and Carter laughing in the other room. He was going on about all the famous people he wanted to meet and how he was going to do it. Julie found him very entertaining, and you could tell she really liked him. Both their personalities were so outgoing and energetic—just what she needed.

"So, I was wondering about something," Devon started to say.

"Last time we were together it was . . . interesting."

"Yes, it was." Sophie blushed.

"So, that guy, Jake is it? He really screwed you over, eh?"

"I guess. I mean we weren't officially dating, but I really thought that he liked me. It's kind of embarrassing, really."

"Why? You didn't do anything. He should be the one who's embarrassed."

"Ya, but I feel stupid. He told me he liked me and I fell for it. Everyone knew he had a girlfriend. The whole situation was just so messed up. And I've already gone through this once in my life, so it was really hard experiencing it again. It makes me mad."

"You should just move on. Don't waste your time worrying about him and being embarrassed. Life is way too short."

"I know."

"Plus, you did say that I was cute."

"Right . . . I do remember saying something about that. Damn Julie."

"And I told you that the feeling was mutual, if you remember?" he said, smiling at her slightly.

"Yes, I remember. It's just that I don't know if I . . . " He got up from the bed, interrupting her.

"Hey, no need to explain. Let's just go with the flow, all right. No worries."

She smiled at him. "Okay. Cool."

"Now, come have a drink with me." He grabbed her hand, pulling her off the bed. They headed into the kitchen, and he grabbed two beers from the fridge. Carter and Julie heard the fridge door close and came out to join them for a drink.

"Let's watch a movie," Julie suggested, noticing their stack of movies by the TV.

"Girls' pick!" she said, running over to scan through them.

"Just so you know, we don't have anything too mushy in this place—only action and horror!" Carter joked. "But it's cool. We can cuddle to horror."

Julie picked out an old one from the 80s. Carter hit the lights, and then joined Julie on the loveseat. Sophie sat down on the couch with a little distance between Devon and her.

The movie began and for a few moments, it was awkward for Sophie sitting there, while Julie and Carter snuggled. As the movie went on, it ended up being that only Devon and Sophie were awake for it. Julie and Carter had passed out. Sophie curled her legs up on the couch, as it was cold in their apartment.

"You know, I'm not going to bite or anything," Devon said quietly. "Plus, I have a blanket and I'm willing to share, but you have to move closer to me."

Sophie smiled at him and then slowly moved over beside him. He slid the blanket over the two of them. His arm touched hers, as they sat close.

"You know. I know I said we'll go with the flow, but I really want to kiss you again," He said, looking down at her.

She didn't answer him and her face blushed in embarrassment.

"Your emotions always show, Sophie, you know that?" he teased.

"I know," she said nervously. "I can't help it."

"I think it's cute and refreshing." He lifted his arm up and put it around her. "You warming up?"

"Ya. Thanks." For some reason, he really made her nervous, but in a good way. She liked him, but wasn't sure if she wanted to move on to another guy after going through the whole Jake thing.

Maybe she should just stay away from guys for a bit and concentrate on her career. Plus, there was the Nathan thing, too. So many thoughts were running through her mind.

"Hey, relax, Soph," he said, rubbing her arms. He could feel how tense she was. There was something comforting about him. He wasn't afraid to say what he was thinking, and he was confident in his words. She breathed deeply, trying to relax, but she just couldn't.

He lifted her chin up to look at her. "Can I kiss you, Soph?"

She didn't answer him, so he leaned in and kissed her gently on the lips.

She didn't fight it, She didn't do anything at all. He held her face securely, as he kissed her again. Sophie felt herself leaning back from him, but he kept coming forward. Soon, she was lying on the couch, and he was by her side, kissing her over and over again.

She felt her hand go up and hold his wrist, but she wasn't stopping him. She was enjoying it. He made her feel safe and wanted. His body moved over hers a little more, as he kissed her neck softly. She could stay like this the entire night. Her body was numb and this felt right.

"I don't wanna hurt you," he said, looking into her eyes.

"Then, don't." She didn't know what he meant by that, but on the other hand, she didn't care.

"I know. I mean, I won't." He smiled at her, kissing her again.

Suddenly, there was a firm knock at the door. Devon sat up. "Who could that be?"

Carter woke up to the second knock. It was much louder.

"Who the hell is at our door this late at night?" he said, looking at his watch. It was almost 1:00 a.m.

Devon got up from the couch to open the door. They couldn't see who it was from the living room.

"Yo, Devon, who is it?" Carter said, sliding up from beside Julie.

"What's going on?" she said, rubbing her eyes. She looked at Sophie who was leaning on the arm of the couch. They heard Devon's voice rise.

"Hey, who do you think you are?" he said, as a figure came in the room.

Sophie sat up instantly. It was Nate. She was in shock. What was he doing here in Devon's apartment?

"Nate?" Julie said confused. "What are you doing here?"

Sophie stared at him nervously.

"Come on, girls, we're going," he said, walking over to Sophie to help her up.

"Nate, what are you doing?" she said quietly to him.

"It's time to leave," he said, grabbing her arm and pulling her toward the door. Devon stood in front of it with his arms crossed.

"Get your hands off of her, buddy. Wanna tell me who you are? And why you're grabbing my friend like that?" he said sternly.

Carter stood by his side as back up.

"Move if you know what's good for you," Nathan said, with his hand still gripping Sophie's arm tightly. She never said a word.

"Oh, really?" Carter said, stepping toward him.

"No, guys, it's okay. Nathan is a family friend. He's our friend. It's all good," Julie said, stepping between them. She had no idea why Sophie wasn't saying anything, but someone had to fast.

"Sophie? Is he?" Devon asked her.

She shook her head, "Yes."

"Come here for a second," he said, holding out his hand for her to take. "I just wanna talk to you."

Nathan paused for a moment before letting her go. Devon led her into the kitchen.

"What's going on, Sophie? Is everything all right? You can tell me," he said, rubbing her arms.

"No, everything's okay. I promise," she said softly to him. She looked over at Nate.

"Who does this guy think he is barging in and taking you away? This seems weird, Soph. Are you sure you're okay?"

"No, he's okay. He just worries about me. We've been friends a long time."

"You can take care of yourself, Soph. Plus, you have me, okay? Now, if you want to stay, just say so, and you can stay. But if you want to go, then, that's fine, too. I'm just worried about you leaving with him."

"She doesn't feel well. She has to go," Nathan said from the hallway.

Devon looked into her eyes carefully. "Is that true?"

"Um, ya. I haven't been feeling well lately. That's why he's worried. It's fine. I'll just go."

"All right, then," he said, giving her a hug. He looked at Nathan, as he held her in his arms. Then, he kissed her on the forehead before letting her go.

"Thank you again for tonight, Devon. I'll talk to you soon," she said, as she walked out the door with Nathan close behind her.

"Soph, I'm gonna stay here if that's cool?" Julie said from the doorway. Sophie looked at Nathan, and he nodded to her that it was fine.

"Okay, I'll talk to you tomorrow, Julie. See ya, Carter."

"Night, Soph," he yelled from the doorway, as Sophie and Nathan entered the elevator.

The door closed behind them. The elevator moved slowly down to the bottom floor.

"Nathan, what's going on?" Sophie asked politely.

"You weren't in the right state of mind in there," he said, grabbing her hand and leading her out the front doors.

"Right state of mind? What does that mean?"

"You know when you feel that numbness in your body and you don't care about what you're doing? That's not the right state of mind. You didn't want to be in there doing what you were doing."

The night air was cold and damp from the rain that happened just an hour before. She shivered, as he led her down the street.

"How do you know what I want to be doing, Nate? I did so want to be in there," she said, pulling her hand from his.

"No, you didn't!" he said, turning to face her.

"Yes, I did! I like him, Nate. He's nice and I can do whatever I want. You can't just barge in and control my life!"

"I'm helping you, Sophie, trust me."

"No, Nate, you're not. I think you're just jealous and you stepped in because you felt like it."

"That's ridiculous, Sophie! I was just worried about you and I . . . " He paused, turning away from her. "I'm helping you. Can't you just trust me?" he said, yelling at her.

"This is really unfair, Nate. You're keeping me from being with someone else, but you tell me that I have to move on from you. What are you doing with me?" she said sadly.

He still didn't turn around. His fingers ran through his hair, as he took a deep breath.

"Nate?" she asked again.

"I don't know, Soph! Okay? I don't know!" he screamed at her.

"You can't do this to me," she said, wiping her eyes. "If you can't be with me, then what would you like me to do? Be alone forever, Nate?" Tears fell from her eyes.

He watched, as her emotions crumbled in front of him.

"I already feel like I'm alone, even with the few friends I do have here. I feel like no one loves me, Nate. Don't you understand? I need something more. I need someone to love me and I feel like it will never happen. So, you don't need to step in. I'm always going to be alone no matter who's around me."

She covered her face, as she broke down in front of him.

A feeling of guilt filled Nathan's soul. He didn't understand what he was doing, either. He didn't know what to say to her or how to fix it.

"Sophie," he said, walking over to her. He paused before touching her shoulders and pulling her in. At first, she pushed away, fighting against him with tears running down her face.

"I'm sorry, Sophie, I'm so sorry." He tightened his arms around her until she stopped and gave in, wrapping her arms around him.

"I don't know what to say. I don't want anyone else to have you. But I know . . . I know I can't, either," he said, placing his chin down on top of her head.

"Then, you have to let me go," she said softly.

"I know. I know that." He kissed her head, and then secretly wiped a tear from his eye.

"It's just, I lov . . . "

"Let her go, Nate," a voice said from behind them.

Sophie looked up from Nathan's chest to see a man in white, standing behind them.

"Gabriel," Nathan said, loosening his grip on Sophie.

"We warned you before, Nathan. You're overstepping your boundaries again. You have too much contact with this human," he said, walking closer to them.

Sophie stood there, staring at this man. He was beautiful, but intimidating at the same time.

He was tall and clean cut with perfect hair. Was he an angel, too, she wondered?

"I know. I'm sorry. I messed up, and it won't happen again," Nathan said, lowering his head to him.

"No, it won't," the man said, stopping before Sophie, examining her.

"You can never be with him," he said softly. His facial expression was calm and caring. "Do you understand?" he asked her.

"Yes," she said, looking into his eyes. They were almost enchanting.

"And I mean never. We will take him away from you if orders are not followed. I suggest you listen for your own sake."

Sophie's heart dropped at the thought of this, and she looked at Nate. His eyes were closed, as if he were wishing himself to not hear any of this.

"I apologize again, Gabriel. I was out of line."

"No, it was me. I'm making things hard for him," Sophie blurted out, surprising herself.

"Sophie," Nathan said, giving her a stern look.

Gabriel stared in her eyes once again. "I know about you. Do not take this warning lightly. You need an angel. . . do not try me again, young one." He glanced back to Nathan, and then, he was gone.

They stood there in the middle of the night at a loss for words.

"Nathan, I'm . . . "

"I should get you home," he said softly. "I'm sorry about this. It won't happen again."

"Was he an angel?" she asked.

"He's an archangel. I answer to him."

"An archangel?"

"A high-ranking angel. Gabriel is a messenger for God."

Sophie suddenly felt uneasy with all of this.

"Come on, let's get you home. We'll talk more there." He held out his hand for Sophie to take. She touched it gently, and in a second, they were gone.

She was clenching Nathan's arm with her eyes closed tightly when a familiar scent was in the air. It smelt like the perfume she always wore.

"Open your eyes," Nathan said quietly.

They were back in her bedroom. "Nate, how'd you? You've never done that before."

"I know. This was an emergency, though," he said, pulling his arm from her grip.

"Nathan, I'm really sorry. I didn't think of your feelings, I never thought . . . "

"You aren't supposed to think of my feelings, Sophie. This is my own issue, understand?"

"No, I don't understand."

"You're doing what you're supposed to be doing, and I could've changed fate right there by stepping in for you. It was so stupid of me."

"Changed fate? What do you mean?" she said nervously.

"You were meant to spend the night there, but I stepped in. I didn't think you were ready. I went against your choices. That's why Gabriel came. I really messed up, Soph."

"So what? What is that going to change? I don't get it."

"I don't know. We'll have to see. I only knew what you were deciding at that moment."

She was still confused on what he had done wrong.

"I've stepped into your real life too much, and we aren't allowed to do it at all."

"Then, why do you do it, Nate? Obviously your feelings are strong . . . isn't there anything we can do about this? There has to be some way we can be together. Can't you just stop being an angel or something?"

"Stop being an angel, Soph? That means I become one of the Fallen. It's not a life to live."

"The Fallen? What's that?"

"An angel who has defied the orders of God. I couldn't live a normal life if I tried. Your wings are clipped and eventually the higher powers will come for you."

"But I thought angels were good things, so why would anyone above come for the Fallen if they are only trying to live their lives?"

"Because their life is over. They've already had their time. You're supposedly blessed to be doing guardian work for the powers above. But sometimes, I think it's more of a curse.

"I enjoy the part where I get to help people, but it's hard to watch them live their lives and not feel jealous of it. I know it's selfish to say, and I get that my time has passed, but it's basically like dangling something we all desire right in front of us. It's torture at times."

Sophie stared at him, her heart breaking.

"Do I do that to you?" she asked quietly.

He looked at her for a moment. "I'm not jealous of your life, Sophie, but I am jealous that I can't be in it."

She walked away from him and sat down on her bed.

"This all seems so unfair. I don't want to hurt you, Nate. I want the same things. You know that. But if I can't have it, then, I have to move on or try to. But it seems cruel to have you here as I do. What are we going to do about this, Nate? This has just become too much."

"I don't know," he said, sitting beside her. "But please don't say that you don't want me here. I can handle it, I promise. And it will kill me more if I can't be your guardian. I'm the best one for this, Sophie. I know it. I know you better than anyone else."

"What if it gets you in trouble? What if you can't handle it one time? It seems cruel. Maybe I'll be okay without a guardian, maybe . . . "

"Sophie, please." He put his head in his hands.

She had never seen him like this—seriously upset and stressed out.

"Okay, then, I trust you, Nathan," she said slowly, rubbing his back.

For the first time, it was her turn to comfort him and she liked it.

"Come here," she said, pulling him back to lie down on the bed. She adjusted the pillows behind them, as they lay back against the headboard. They didn't speak, but they just lay there side by side, taking in everything that had happened. Sophie turned to face him.

His face was tense and his breathing was deep. She gently grabbed his hand, and he squeezed it tightly, not saying a word.

She didn't know what to say to him. Obviously, she didn't want to hurt him by keeping him there, but she also didn't want to let him go.

He finally turned to his side to face her, adjusting the pillow beneath his neck.

His eyes stared sadly into hers. "I'm sorry, crazy girl."

She smiled at him slightly, letting him know that all was forgiven. But forgiven wasn't even the word. Why would she need to forgive him for acting on his feelings for her. She loved that he cared for her so much, but it hurt at the same time, because it was never going to amount to anything. So, really, it was just stalling her life from moving forward.

She wondered about the life of a guardian angel. They were always known as these beautiful, kind, and loving spirits, but maybe no one took the time to see things from their perspective. Maybe it was like a heavenly sentence for those who were going to pass on into Heaven, like they needed to pass this before getting into the gates or something like that. It was almost like they were these tragic beings, left over from a life not lived—good hearts that were tested one last time before passing on.

This was everything that described Nathan. He has the best heart of anyone she had ever known. She wanted everything for him that he couldn't have. It was painful for her to watch him go through this. But he insisted on following it through, because it was the right thing to do and because he loved her so much that he couldn't live with himself if he didn't. Maybe this is why Nathan said that guardians watch over from a distance and step in only when needed. Spending too much time with the one you're guarding can become torture.

She pulled her hand from his and turned over in the bed. She choked back some tears, as she thought about everything he had gone through in his life up until now. It was too much for a person. He moved in close behind her, wrapping his arms around her. She could feel his body against hers and his breath on the back of her neck. She couldn't let him see her cry, not now.

"Sophie, I lov . . . "

"Don't say it, Nate. I know what you're going to say. But don't say it. Please. I won't be able to handle it," she said, gripping his hands that were close to her chest.

"You can't say something like that unless you're ready to take on everything that comes with it and you can't. So please. I'll want to say it back to you, and it will be too much for us to handle." She swallowed back her tears and cleared her throat.

"I want more than anything in the world to hear what I think you're going to say, but you can't. Let's just know what we know and try to move on."

He thought about her words before kissing her on the shoulder.

"Good night, Soph," he said quietly.

She wiped a tear from her face, and then closed her eyes and went to sleep.

That night, her mind raced. She was determined to put the thought of being with Nathan out of her head. She had accepted it now. He could be her friend, her guardian, but nothing more. No more staying over or lying around with him, talking. It had to be strictly business, or neither of them would make it through this.

19
Lost Without Each Other

The next morning, Sophie woke up alone in her bed. There was a note on the pillow beside her that read:

Dear Sophie,

I'm truly sorry about everything. I know you've gone through a lot and I know I can't tell you about what's to come. But know that I never mean to hurt you. The rules suck, but we can't do anything about it, so let's try from here on out to do things the right way.

We've said it before, but we really need to now more than ever. I let my feelings get in the way again and I'm sorry for that. I'll be watching from a little more distance from now on, but know this: I am your guardian angel, and more importantly, your friend. I won't let you down. I'm always here, even if you can't see me. I promise.

Nathan

The note made her feel relieved, but sad at the same time. She folded it up and put it in her nightstand drawer. It was late morning by the time she woke up, so she headed into the bathroom to freshen up. She washed her face and pulled her hair into a ponytail.

Today was a quiet day, a good day to clean up her room, so she could begin to pack. There were clothes all over the place. She grabbed the dirty ones off the floor and threw them in the hamper for the laundry. Then, she made her bed and vacuumed. On the way out to the laundry room with the hamper bag dragging behind her, she ran into Natalie.

They stopped and looked at each other for a moment, pondering over talking. Finally, Sophie broke the silence.

"Hey, Nat. How's it going?"

"It's going. What are you up to?" she asked smugly.

"Not much, just cleaning and laundry, you?"

"Nothing, kind of the same."

Sophie smiled at her, and then walked by her to start her laundry.

"Do you mind if I throw some in with yours?" Natalie asked, trying to keep the conversation going.

"Um, sure. I'm doing darks if you have any."

"I do. I'll be right back."

Natalie ran to her room and came back with a handful of clothes. Sophie loaded them in, poured the detergent, and closed the lid.

They stood there awkwardly. Sophie wondered if this would be a good time to tell Nat about their apartment.

"Hey, Nat, listen, I want to talk to you about . . . " But Natalie cut her off.

"I'm gonna make some lunch. Probably crap dinner if you want some," she said, walking into the kitchen. It was like she didn't want to hear what Sophie was going to say. Maybe she was trying to forget it all and move on. Maybe she felt badly or maybe she knew what was coming.

Sophie decided to not bring it up. Instead, she sat, acting like nothing had happened between Natalie and her. They talked and got caught up on what was happening in each other's lives. The day was drama-free.

The next few days went by quickly. Sophie had made a meeting with the agent from the showcase for Wednesday at noon. Her grandmother had called the night before to give her tips on how to talk to these "kinds" of people. Gram really didn't know much, but it was entertaining to hear what she thought.

She had also kept in touch with Devon. Their conversations became more regular and she looked forward to them each time. As for Nathan, she hadn't heard from him since the last time she saw him, which was hard, but better for her. It helped her with getting over him. Having fewer conversations meant less time to doubt herself and their possible relationship.

But even though she was getting ready to move in with Julie and things were going well with Devon, and even with the excitement of the agent meeting, Sophie still felt that something was missing. Something made her sad all the time.

She hadn't had many conversations with her family since being out in Vancouver. It was like she had become a stranger. She tried to stay confident and prove them wrong, but she wondered why she had to prove anything at all. The battles in her mind became more annoying. Sophie found herself getting stressed out easily, and her headaches were happening more often.

Why should she care so much about what they think? Why was she trying to prove herself to them? Shouldn't they be happy with whatever she was doing in her life and show some support? Everyday she tried to not think about her issues with her family, but they always came out at some point in her mind.

There was also the random thought of Lisa. She missed her friend. She also missed her friends from high school. The whole betrayal thing lingered in her mind everyday. She tried so hard to forget about these people, but once in a while, when things were quiet and no one was around, these thoughts would creep into her mind.

No one had been consistent in her life except for her gram. What was the point of getting so attached to people if they were just going to disappoint you and leave you some day?

On Wednesday morning, Sophie was up bright and early for her meeting with the Vancouver Coast Talent agent. She showered and dressed herself in a pair of black dress pants and a cute top. Her hair was straightened and her makeup was clean and minimal.

She placed two different headshots, her demo reel, and her acting resumé in a brown envelope. After having breakfast, she grabbed her jacket and placed her things by the door.

"Good luck today."

Sophie turned to see Nathan behind her.

"Thank you. I'm pretty nervous," she said, sliding her jacket on.

"You'll be fine," he said, crossing his arms and leaning against the wall. "But don't be scared, okay? It's like your gram says, 'Everything happens for a reason,' so go with it, all right?"

She looked at him funny. Every time Gram was brought into the subject, it made her worry. That dream was stuck in her mind, and everyday she tried to figure out what it was trying to tell her.

"Okay. Well, I'll see you later, then."

She smiled at him and headed out the door.

It was an overcast day and the streets seemed quiet for a Wednesday. Even the sky train wasn't as busy as usual. Sophie tried to stay concentrated on her interview. This was her chance and she couldn't afford to blow it.

Just then, her phone went off. She pulled it from her purse and saw Devon's name.

"Hey," she said relieved.

"Hi, where are you now?"

"On the train, just coming up to Chinatown exit. Why?"

"Oh, just wondering. Are you nervous?"

"Kind of," she said, smiling at the sound of his voice.

"Well, don't be. You're gonna be great."

"I hope so," she said, playing nervously with her hair.

"Well, just be confident and stop playing with your hair." He laughed.

"What? I'm not. Wait, how did you know that I was . . . " He then sat down beside her.

"Hi." He smiled at her.

She lowered her phone. "What are you doing here?"

"Just thought you could use a pep talk before going in."

She didn't know what to say. He was the perfect distraction she needed at that moment. She turned and hugged him. "Thank you."

"No worries," he said, holding her tightly.

They talked about random things the entire way to the Waterfront stop. It helped Sophie clear her mind and feel more relaxed. When the train came to a stop, they got up and headed out to the street. The sky had cleared up a bit and the sun was trying to come out.

"So, here it is, Soph. Be yourself and be energetic. That's what's going to sell you. Be open to her suggestions, but don't stray from what you believe in. You don't have to do anything you don't want to do." He stopped her for a moment.

"You got this. I know it."

She smiled at him and hugged him again. "Thank you."

"No worries, darling. Now, when you're done, come look for me. I'll be over in that café across the street there. See it?" he said, pointing across the road.

"Okay, I will." She turned and walked down a small sidewalk that led to a medium sized office building.

She buzzed the agency, and then headed inside and up to the third floor. The building was cold and old looking. She followed the hallway to the end where she came to a big door that read: VANCOUVER COAST TALENT.

She stopped to take a breath, and then went inside.

The receptionist at the desk was answering phone call after phone call. Finally, she stopped and turned to Sophie who waited patiently.

"Good afternoon, may I help you?" she asked politely.

"My name's Sophie Reid. I'm here to see Audrey Patell. My appointment's at noon."

The lady scanned her computer, "Yes, I see. Perfect. I'll let her know you're here."

"Thank you," Sophie said, sitting down to wait. She looked around the room. There were many headshots on the wall and lots of portfolios from local photographers around to look at.

Finally, Audrey came out and greeted her.

"Hi, Sophie, thanks for coming," she said, shaking her hand.

Sophie followed her into a small office.

"It's nice to see you again. How's life after school so far?"

"Oh, it's good, a little weird, but nice, because I can get started on what I really want to be doing. I also just got a new apartment, so I'm excited for that."

"That's great, a good start to your new path as an actor, eh?" Audrey said, clearing her desk.

"Did you bring me a headshot and resume?"

"Yes, I did," Sophie said, handing her the envelope. Audrey opened it and looked over her resume. "Ah, so you got a chance to do some voice-over, huh? It's such a great field and super fun, eh?" She then pulled out the headshots. "Very nice."

"Thank you," Sophie said, getting comfortable in her chair.

"So, what do you see yourself doing, Sophie?"

"Well, I really want to do film and television, but I also really like voice-over."

"How about commercials? Music videos? Anything like that interest you?"

"Sure, I mean I'm open for anything." They chatted a bit more, so that Audrey could get a better idea of what kind of person Sophie was. As confused as Sophie was in her personal life at that moment, she was good at putting on a face and acting fine.

"You're a very interesting one, Sophie. I must say and you also have a young face. I think I could pass you for anywhere between high school aged to late twenties—which is good, more variety."

Then, Audrey grabbed the demo reel and put it in her computer. Sophie found it awkward, sitting there, as she watched her scenes on the disc. After it was finished, Audrey placed the disc back in the case and closed her computer. Sophie waited nervously.

"All right, Sophie, here's what we're going to do. I'd like to offer myself as an agent to you if you're interested. I think you're a little raw, but nothing that a few auditions won't cure. Plus, I feel like you might surprise me. What do you think?"

A smile grew of Sophie's face. "Yes, thank you. I'm totally interested!"

"Great. Then, welcome to Vancouver Coast Talent! Let's get you started on your paperwork. Can I keep these headshots?"

"Yes, for sure."

"You may need new ones in a little while, so that I have a variety of looks for you to submit. But we'll worry about that later. Here's our contract. We'll go through it together, so you understand before signing."

Audrey carefully went through all the details of the contract, so Sophie understood what her obligations were to the agency. The agency would receive 15 percent of everything Sophie made. She also went through the rules of being on set on time, how to contact your agent or casting director if you can't make it, and so on.

After an hour, it was all over and Sophie had signed her acting career over to an agent. Now, there was nothing left to do but wait. She walked out the front doors into the sunlight, happy, but sad at the same time. That dark feeling inside her head was creeping around again. She decided to ignore it and head across the street to tell Devon the good news.

As she entered the café, the scent of freshly baked muffins filled the air along with the smell of coffee. She noticed Devon sitting in the corner at a small table. He looked up at her and smiled.

He instantly calmed the worries in her mind by just looking at her. She felt herself moving quickly toward him. He stood up, just as she reached him, and she jumped into his arms, hugging him tightly around the neck.

"Hey, you. How'd things go?" he said, holding onto her.

"Perfect. I got signed," she whispered to him happily.

"Really, that's great!" he said, pulling her back to look at him.

Without a second thought, she kissed him on the lips, holding him close to her.

"Soph, whoa . . . " he said, pulling back from her.

"Don't get me started or I won't be able to stop. Come here, tell me about the meeting." He laughed, pulling her to sit down beside him. She told him everything over lunch. They were there for nearly an hour and a half before the waiter started to give them dirty looks to hurry up.

"So, what are you up to now?" Devon asked.

"I think I'll head home and maybe start to pack up. That's about it."

"Want some help? We could just hang out, and then maybe make some dinner?" he said, smiling at her.

"Sure," she said. Why stop now, she thought. The day was going so well and she always enjoyed her time with Devon.

"Great, and you can tell Natalie if you get the chance. Break the news, ya know? Unless you already have?"

"Oh no. I haven't. I was about to yesterday, but she cut me off. We'll see about that one, as I don't want to ruin the day."

Sophie walked to the counter and paid for their lunches before Devon got a chance, and then they headed back to her place. She unlocked the door, nervous to see if Natalie was home and she was. Natalie's music played loudly from her room. As they walked into the apartment, Sophie waved to Natalie, as she walked past her room.

"Hey," Natalie yelled over the music, and then she noticed Devon. "Hey . . . You're that guy!" she said, running out to them.

"Nice to see you again, Natalie. We haven't actually met officially yet. I'm Devon," he said, holding out his hand for her to shake. But she didn't. She just stood there, staring at him, wondering if she should hate him or like him. It depended on whose side he was on, hers or Julie's.

"Nat, you remember Devon from the party," Sophie said nervously.

"Ya, you're the guy who held me back from Julie."

"Ya. Sorry about that. I was worried someone would get hurt," he said, lying.

"Yes, well, only one of us would've gotten hurt, and we know who that would've been," Natalie said confidently.

"Hey, Nat, since you're here, I wanted to talk to you about something," Sophie said, thinking it was now or never.

"I was signed with an agent today."

"Really? That's . . . uh, good," Natalie said surprised.

"Ya, so I was thinking that I want to move closer to downtown. Julie was looking at some apartments, and I asked to move in with her. It'll be better for what I want to do, but don't worry, I spoke to the landlords and they're fine with you staying. It won't affect you at all. But you'll get a new roommate." She waited, as Natalie processed what she had said.

"What? Why the hell would you move in with that whale?"

"Because, she's my friend, Nat."

"Friend? And what am I?"

"Nat, it's just that things have been weird between us lately. Don't you think? Maybe if we didn't live together, things would be better, and we could still stay friends. Then, you wouldn't be forced to hang with Julie."

"This is such bullshit, Sophie! You're choosing her side again, and you're nothing but a lying little bitch!" Natalie said, turning to walk away.

"Nat, I'm sorry. I didn't mean for it to hurt you. I just think things will be better this way. We're still friends. It's just that we won't live together," Sophie said, walking after her.

Natalie turned and slapped Sophie in the face.

"Hey, knock it off!" Devon said, grabbing Sophie to pull her away. Natalie walked into her room and slammed the door.

"You okay?" he said, turning Sophie toward him. She rubbed the side of her face where Natalie had hit her.

"I'm fine," she said, walking away from him toward her room. He followed her in and closed the door behind them.

"She won't be mad forever. She's looking at it in a whole other perspective. She sees it as you picking Julie over her."

"But I'm not picking anyone. They go at it every time we're together, so what am I supposed to do? Living with Julie is easier, because I won't have to deal with the mood swings or silent treatments. Plus, I have more fun with her. What the hell? I thought you were on my side."

"Sophie, relax. I am. I'm just telling you not to worry about it." He walked over and hugged her.

"I didn't mean to hurt her or anything. It's not what I'm trying to do."

"I know that. Don't worry about it," he said, stepping away. "Now let's start packing you up, okay?"

Sophie's mood had changed and she didn't feel like packing. She didn't feel like doing anything and just wanted to be left alone. Devon looked around for a box to start putting things in. He stopped when he noticed she wasn't helping.

"What, Soph? What's wrong?"

"Nothing," she said, sitting on her bed.

"No, it's not nothing. I can see your little mind turning in there. What's up?"

"Nothing, god, just let it go." She went to get up from the bed, but he grabbed her, pulling her back down to sit beside him.

"Whatever's going on in your mind, let it out. Holding that stuff in only makes you crazy. Are you mad at me?"

Sophie took a breath. She was annoyed. "No, I'm not mad at you." She really wasn't, but something had come over her. She felt mad and annoyed, plus a headache was starting to take over. "I just have a headache. I need to lie down."

Devon knew that wasn't what was going on, but he didn't push her anymore on the subject. He got up, letting Sophie lie back in the bed, and walked toward the door.

"Devon?"

"Ya?"

"Please don't leave. I just need a moment," she said quietly.

"I'm not going anywhere," he said, turning off the light.

She lay in the darkness, trying to relax. Why was she acting like that toward him? He didn't do anything wrong.

Her mind was just too full of things she had to deal with, and it seemed like adding one tiny thing more just filled it to the max. She rubbed the sides of her head, as the migraine pounded.

"Just breathe, Sophie. Breathe," Nathan whispered to her. She kept her eyes closed, trying to make the pain go away until finally she fell asleep.

As Sophie slept, Devon scrambled through the cupboards for something to make for dinner. He found some pasta and decided to make a big spaghetti dinner.

When Sophie woke up, her stomach grumbled to the smell that filled the air. She got out of bed and headed to the kitchen. Devon had set the table for them and dinner was ready.

"Natalie went out," he said, pulling the chair out for her.

She walked over to him slowly. "I'm sorry," she said, hugging him.

"It's forgotten. Let's eat," he said, holding the chair, as she sat down. He always seemed to make things comfortable no matter what the situation. They ate dinner and Devon kept the conversation flowing as usual. It was back to normal, and he was everything Sophie needed.

After dinner, they returned to her room and packed up a few boxes, leaving out only what she needed for the next two days until she moved.

"Ugh, so tired!" Devon said, flopping down on her bed, pulling the pillow up under his neck.

"Come here," he said, moving over for Sophie to join him.

She thought about it for a moment, and then walked over and got in the bed beside him. They lay there face to face quietly. He kissed her on the nose playfully, and then moved down to her lips. He was so careful with her, and she loved every moment by his side. His hands ran over her hips and up to her waist. She started to get nervous, as he began to unbutton her shirt. She stopped him halfway up.

"Sorry," he said, sliding his hands back around her bare waist.

She put her hands on his chest and moved in closer to kiss him. Her heart started to race, as she was pulled on top of him. His hands were warm on her back. She stopped just for a moment to look him in the eyes, as her lips hovered over his.

"I love you."

She froze for a moment and couldn't believe what she had just said. She had only known him for about a month. What was she doing? He looked at her and smiled.

"I mean, I think I might be falling in love with you," she corrected herself.

"No, no, don't go back on your words. Admit it, you love me," he teased.

She didn't know what to say. He pulled her back down and kissed her over and over again.

"I kind of think I might love you, too," he whispered in her ear, and then pulled her in to lie on his chest. She knew that she really liked him, but love? She thought she might. She must be in love with him if she said it, right? Holding him tightly, she pondered over the words she had just said. Maybe this was how things were to play out, she thought, as she quietly fell asleep against him.

Morning came once again and the sun was shining brightly through the window. Devon adjusted his eyes to the light. Sophie was still asleep, nestled against him closely. He ran his fingers through her long hair and kissed the top of her head, gently trying not to wake her. He could hear Natalie doing something in the kitchen, and then, minutes later, he heard the front door slam.

Sophie moved around against him. Her face was tense and her grip on him became stronger. He moved a bit to look at her. She seemed to be dreaming. Her eyes slowly started to water and her face began to get red. She was holding her breath.

"Sophie?" he said, giving her a little shake. "Sophie, wake up."

He sat up a little more, moving her off his chest and into his arms. "Breathe, Sophie, breathe." His hands shook, as he held her face. When she didn't respond, he started to panic.

"Sophie!" He yelled more loudly to her. This was too long to hold your breath. What was happening?

"Soph!" He yelled again. Her eyelids flickered at the sound, but didn't open.

There was water everywhere, and she held her breath, as it crashed against her. She struggled to keep a float, but the waves were too strong. As the water flowed over her once again, she was pushed too deep to pull herself up. She could barely hold her breath any longer when something grabbed her hand and pulled at her.

She woke up to the cold air blowing against her skin.

"Breathe," Nathan said, shaking her.

Sophie opened her eyes and gasped for air. Nathan held her in his arms for a moment, keeping her warm. "Crazy girl. What are you try-ing to do to me?"

"Nathan?"

"Sophie, it's Devon. Open your eyes." She looked around. She was back in her room, lying in Devon's arms.

"Sophie, what the hell was that?" he said, helping her sit up.

"I don't know. I was in the water one moment, and then I was . . . " She took a breath and started to get up.

"Whoa, maybe you should just sit here for a moment," he said, grab-bing her wrist.

"No, it's fine. I'm all right." She smiled at him and got up from her bed.

"Some nightmare, eh? You scared the hell out of me, Sophie."

"Sorry, I've been getting those a lot lately, but don't worry. It's noth-ing."

"Holding your breath is nothing?" He looked at her worried.

"I promise, Devon, it's nothing. Now let's go have some breakfast. You hungry?" she said, trying to change the subject. He decided not to say anything about her calling him Nathan. He shook his head, and then got up from the bed to follow her to the kitchen.

"Natalie must have gone out for the day?"

"Um, ya. I heard her this morning heading out," he said, walking up to her. He grabbed her arm to turn her toward him.

"What?" She giggled.

"Nothing," he said, giving her a hug. "Just want to make sure you're okay."

"I am. I promise," she said, hugging him tightly. "Sorry I worried you."

The rest of the day was spent hanging around the house in front of the television. It was quiet and relaxing. Around dinner, Sophie received a text from Adel. It read:

"HEY, SOPHIE, WHAT ARE YOU UP TO? I NEED SOMEONE TO TALK TO. ARE YOU FREE?"

"Who's that?" Devon asked, sitting up.

"It's Adel. She wants to talk."

"Oh, ya? Well, you can meet up with her if you want. I really gotta head out now anyway."

"You sure?"

"Ya, no worries. I promised Carter I'd hang with him tonight. So, I better get going."

He got up from the couch and headed into the bathroom to freshen up a bit. Sophie went into her bedroom to touch up her makeup and throw on some fresh clothes before texting Adel back. She was going to meet her at a close-by coffee shop.

Devon kissed her good-bye at the door, and then headed down the street toward the sky train. Sophie locked the door behind her and headed in the opposite direction to the coffee shop. She seldom heard from Adel, and the only time they really hung out was when the group went out for the night to party. Their texts consisted of fun plans and where to meet up for pre-parties. She wondered what could've happened?

It was almost seven by the time Sophie reached the coffee shop. Adel was waiting at the entrance.

"Hey!" she said, greeting Sophie with a hug.

"Hey, what's up? Are you all right?"

"Physically yes, mentally no. I need a good girl talk," she said, leading them into the shop. They each ordered a drink and took a seat in the back to talk privately.

"Sophie, my life is so messed up. I'm sorry to call you out like this, but I had no one else to talk to. You're a good person, and I knew of all people that you'd actually show up."

"It's no problem, Adel, but what happened?"

"Well, after we graduated last weekend, this friend of mine—well, more than a friend I guess you can say— and I decided that we were going to be together. You know, to officially be boyfriend/girlfriend," She smiled at the thought of it. "I've known him for only a few months, but he seemed like a really cool guy. But last night . . . " She stopped.

"What? What happened?" Sophie said worried.

"I caught him in a bar with another girl. I was out with my friends and I didn't know he was going to be there. He said he was gonna chill at home for the night. But he obviously didn't, and he was there making out with some chick!"

"What? I'm so sorry, Adel. That's horrible," Sophie said, touching her hand.

"When he saw me, he ran after me, trying to apologize. He said he was just drunk and that it was a mistake." She started to cry.

"I really like him and I want to forgive him. Maybe it was a mistake, but I've had this happen to me before. I don't want to go though it again. And I know you've been through it too, Sophie. So, what do you think I should do? Should I give him another chance?"

Sophie paused, thinking about what to say.

"I'm not sure, Adel. I don't know him like you do. But . . . if it were me, I don't think I could. When someone wrongs me like that, I have a hard time trusting him or her again, And trying to build a relationship with no trust usually doesn't work out, ya know?"

"But I know him, and he really feels badly about it. I can tell," Adel said, trying to convince herself. She wiped her eyes and cleared her throat.

Sophie knew how she felt. She had tried to do so herself at one time.

"Are you sure? Maybe you should just step away for a bit and think about it. You don't know how many times he's done this."

"I think this is the first time, Sophie. I really do."

"But what if it isn't? You said you only knew him for a few months and . . . "

Adel cut her off quickly. "I'll think about it tonight. So anyway, thanks, Sophie, for being here. How are things with you?"

Sophie looked at her sadly, as she knew Adel had finished with that topic. "I just got signed with an agent and Julie and I are moving into our new apartment this weekend."

"You and Julie? What about Natalie?"

"No, just Jules and me. I wanted to be closer to town and . . . "

"Say no more. I get it. I wouldn't want to live with her, either." Adel laughed.

"No, it's not like . . . "

Adel got up from the table. "Sophie, my dear, do what makes you happy. Listen, I gotta get going. I'm going out tonight. A few of us are going to The Dragon's nightclub next weekend. Wanna come? Tell Julie if you want, but just come."

"Sure, sounds good. You should actually come to our new place first to check it out. We can have pre-drinks before going out."

"Nice! Sounds like a plan. I'll see you next Friday. Text me your address. See ya then!" Adel leaned down to hug her, and then ran out the door.

Sophie finished her mocha, and then paid for her and Adel's bill. She conveniently forgot to pay it on the way out, but Sophie didn't mind. The conversation had left her thinking of her past relationships, if you could call them that. She would never go back to any of them ever, and she didn't understand how Adel could make excuses for that guy.

In Sophie's mind, there is no excuse that could explain cheating. It was so childish, she thought. Since her job was finished here, she decided not to rush home in case Natalie had returned. She got out her phone and texted Julie. "HELLO, FRIEND!"

"HI!!!!" Julie texted back.

"HOW'S IT GOING? ARE YOU GETTING EXCITED FOR OUR BIG MOVE THIS WEEKEND?"

"YES, I AM! I HEARD FROM DEVON ABOUT THE AGENT MEETING, CONGRATS!!"

"THANKS, BUDDY. ARE YOU WITH CARTER AND DEVON NOW?"

"I JUST LEFT THEM. THEY'RE HAVING A GUY'S NIGHT. I GOT CALLED TO WORK ON SET."

"OH, YA? NICE! COOL. WELL, I'LL LET YOU GO FOR NOW AND WE'LL CHAT LATER."

"FOR SURE! TTYL!"

"HAVE A GOOD NIGHT!" Sophie texted before putting her phone away.

On the walk home, Sophie thought long and hard about everything that had happened in her life. It seemed like it was a never-ending struggle. She pulled her phone out of her pocket and opened her contacts. Slowly, she scanned through them until she came to her father's cell number. Her finger paused over the number before pressing it. The phone rang a few times before he answered.

"Hello?"

"Hey dad. How's it going?"

"Hey, Soph, what's up?"

"Not much, just seeing how you are?"

"I'm good, just busy with work, ya know. How are things?"

"Good. I'm moving into a new place with my friend, Julie, and yesterday I was signed with an agent."

"Who's Julie?" he said, ignoring her words about the agent.

"Julie, Dad. She was in my class?" Sophie had only spoken to her parents here and there since being in Vancouver. She tried to fill them in on her life and who was in it, but they just didn't seem to care.

"What happened with that other girl?" For some reason, her dad never remembered the names of any of her friends. He could name pretty much all of her brother's friends, but never hers. This always bothered her.

"Natalie? Nothing. I'm just moving closer to downtown. It'll be easier for acting, ya know?" She knew he wouldn't want to hear about the fighting that went on between them, so she stuck with her story.

"You're always on the move. I don't know why you have to move at all. It costs money."

"I know, Dad. Anyway . . . " She felt her mood dropping. It was mentally exhausting talking to him, as he never saw things her way.

"So, have you found a job yet?" he asked.

"No, I just finished school. I'll be looking this weekend after my move."

"Well, you better get on it. That apartment's going to cost money, ya know?"

"I know, and I'm on it. I swear."

"All right, well, I have to go. I'm still at work. I'll talk with you later, okay?"

"All right. Bye." She hung up the phone and wondered why she had called him in the first place. He was worse than talking to her mother. At least her mom would fake to be interested until she started to make those "uh huh" sounds. That's when she was doing something, while on the phone and wasn't really listening at all.

Little raindrops started to fall from the sky, as Sophie continued to walk slowly home. As she got closer, the rain fell harder. She didn't care. She needed the quiet to calm her mind.

By the time she reached home, she was drenched. She went inside and threw on some flannel pants and a tank top. Her hair dripped wet over her shoulders. She was glad Natalie wasn't home yet, because tonight was going to be an early night. She crawled into bed and pulled the covers up around her. Sleep came fast and dragged her into another horrible nightmare.

20

The Famous Darkness

As Sophie walked through the streets of Vancouver, it was dark and misty. There was no one around, but she was heading somewhere. She felt the silence around her. The sound of footsteps behind her made her turn in fear. She breathed quietly, listening to every sound that the night carried.

She scanned the streets before seeing a man straight across from her. She couldn't make out his face, as he was wearing a black hoody that hung over his head, shadowing him from the street lights. He stood there facing her, but not moving.

Suddenly, there was the sound of more footsteps that stopped a few feet in front of her. There was another man dressed the same way. Sophie stepped back slowly, as a third man appeared behind the one in front of her. She knew this was her sign to run. She could hear them behind her, as she ran down the street, trying to scream, but nothing was coming out.

As she turned the corner, she saw a familiar house. It was her house back in Ontario. She ran up the front steps and banged on the door. She turned to see the men, running up the sidewalk behind her, screaming something. The barreling shrieks got louder, as they got closer, until she dropped to the ground, covering her ears in fear. A loud bang startled her, and then another one and another.

"Sophie!!" a voice yelled. It sounded angry, but it wasn't a man's voice. It was a female. It almost sounded like . . . Natalie?

Sophie awoke from her sleep to hear Natalie banging on her bedroom door. She reached over and checked the clock on her phone. It was 3:30 a.m. What the heck was she thinking?

Sophie got up from her bed and opened the door.

"What the hell, Nat?"

"You're such a little shit, Sophie. You know that?"

"Natalie, go to bed," Sophie said, closing the door. Natalie was clearly drunk and acting on her emotions. Nat shoved the door back open.

"No, you listen to me! That Julie is a piece of crap and you're becoming a stuck-up little snob just like her."

"No, I'm not, Nat. I haven't done anything to you. If you want the truth, then I'll tell you. I'm moving out because you're too much drama for me to handle! I have a lot going on in my life and when I go out with my friends, the last thing I need is more drama. You make me feel like I have to always choose, and I don't want to choose anyone. I want to be friends with both of you and I don't want to be embarrassed every time we go out, because you and Julie go at it. There, you happy?"

Natalie flicked on the lights and walked in after her.

"No, I'm not. That's bullshit because she starts it."

"Nat, I'm not even going to get into this tonight. I can't handle it, so please just go to bed. There's no point in talking, because we'll never agree, so let's just drop it, all right?" Sophie said, turning away from her. Natalie was furious and desperately needed to be right. She shoved Sophie from behind, knocking her to the ground.

"Really, Nat?" she said, getting up to face her. "Don't even start with me!"

"Why? Or what?" Natalie said, getting in Sophie's face, as she attempted to get up.

Sophie grabbed her and shoved her out of the room, closing the door behind her and locking it.

"That's it, Sophie! I hate you!"

"Fine, Nat, hate me," she said, hitting the lights and getting back into bed. She heard Natalie finally go into her room and close the door.

She didn't sleep at all that night. Around 6:00 a.m., she texted Julie:

"HEY, CAN WE PICK UP THE KEYS TODAY? I'M SO READY TO MOVE IN!"

It wasn't until 9:00 a.m. that Julie texted back. The girls were going to pick up the keys originally on Saturday, as they moved in, but Sophie needed to move in now. She couldn't spend another night there with Natalie.

Julie agreed to meet her at 11:00 a.m. at the apartment to get the keys, and then they would start their move. Sophie got up, showered, and packed the rest of her things, as quickly as she could. She was really tired from her lack of sleep. But this move had to happen now! Before she left to meet Julie, she texted Devon and told him what happened. He agreed to meet her at the apartment to help them move in.

She arrived at the apartment at 11 o'clock sharp. Julie was already there and had the keys in her hands. It wasn't long before Devon showed up with Carter.

"Hey, you," he said, walking up to her and giving her a hug. "You all right?"

"Ya, I'm good. I just need to get out of there."

"What a crazy bitch." Carter laughed.

"You're telling me. I'm ready to head over there and kick her ass," Julie said, making her fighting fists again.

"No, no one's going to fight. We're just going to go in there, get my stuff, and get out. Preferably with no words said," Sophie said, taking a breath to relax. The stress was getting to her.

"Right, sounds good, I guess. But if she says one word, it's on!" Julie said, walking over to her car that was parked just around the corner. The three of them headed over to the house.

When they arrived, Natalie was sitting in the kitchen eating breakfast. Sophie walked right by her into her room and started to hand boxes to Devon and Carter. Julie came in last and gave Natalie an ugly stare, as she walked by her into Sophie's room.

It only took thirty minutes to load everything into Julie's car. Sophie really didn't have that much to take—just a few boxes, suitcases, and bedding. She had to buy a new bed, because she was using the one that came with the rental. She had ordered one online from a furniture company and it was being delivered the next day.

As Julie grabbed the last suitcase from the room, she walked through the kitchen one last time.

"See ya, cow," Natalie said quietly.

"Excuse me?" Julie said, dropping the bag.

"Okay, let's go," Carter said, laughing and grabbing Julie around the waist and carrying her away.

"Excuse yourself. You're lucky you have him, because it's not over between us!" Nat yelled, walking after them.

"Natalie, stop!" Sophie said, coming back in the room. "This has to stop. It's getting ridiculous!"

"Careful, you don't want to drop the whale!" she yelled to Carter.

"Whale!! Now you're in for it, you little purple Grimis!!" Julie yelled, breaking free from Carter's arms.

She leaped at Natalie, toppling her to the ground.

"What the hell is a Grimis?" Carter laughed hysterically.

"Stop!" Sophie yelled, trying to get between them.

Julie threw one good punch to Natalie's face.

"Oh my god, you weigh a lot. You're gonna kill me by just sitting on me!!" Natalie knew just the right words to say to piss Julie off.

Natalie threw Julie over and climbed on top of her, pulling at her hair. She took one good second to look Julie in the eye, and then spit in her face.

"You little, I'm gonna . . . "

Devon grabbed Natalie and ripped her from Julie. "That's enough, you little shit," he said, pulling her into her room.

"Julie, come on. Let's go," Sophie said, helping her to her feet.

"Saved once again, Nat . . . I'll see you next time." Julie laughed, as Sophie and Carter pulled her out the front door.

After getting Julie in the car, Devon finally came out with the last suitcase and loaded it in. He closed the trunk and got in the back seat beside Sophie.

"Well, that went well," he said, smiling.

"Ah, man, Jules, that was fricken hilarious how you leaped on her. I almost peed myself." Carter laughed.

"I know, I have amazing skills, right?" Julie said proud of herself.

As they drove off, Sophie covered her face in relief that it was all over.

After loading Sophie's stuff into the apartment, they returned to Julie's old one to grab her stuff. It took the entire day to get everything in. Even that night was spent putting things away in their new apartment. Around 11:00 p.m., they stopped for the night. Since only Julie's bed was there, but not set up, the girls decided to have a sleepover in the living room. They grabbed some blankets and their pillows and set up for bed.

"Man, I so want to be part of this sleep over," Carter teased.

"Come on, let's let them get settled," Devon said, grabbing his jacket from the closet.

"Thanks so much, guys, for your help and everything else," Sophie said softly.

"No worries, anytime," he said, walking up to hug her. She kissed him good-bye a few times before Carter nudged Devon from behind.

"This is how you kiss my friend . . . " He grabbed Julie and bent her back to kiss her passionately.

"Oh god, please." Sophie laughed. Julie seemed to find his humor attracting.

"Now, that was a kiss!" Julie laughed, pushing him off of her and out the door.

"They are so much fun, eh, Soph?" Julie said, closing the door.

"Definitely!" Sophie walked in the living room and sighed.

"What's up?"

"Nothing, it's just exciting. Our new apartment. This is going to be fun, huh?"

"Oh, ya, it's like we're sisters now. We can do whatever we want!"

"Oh, Adel invited us out next Friday, and I told her she should come here beforehand and have some drinks—you know, have a housewarming pre-party," Sophie said excitedly.

"Really? Yay! Exciting! We need to invite other people, too! You know, let's make it an event!"

"Sure, whoever you want to invite, it's cool. Then, we'll go out to The Dragon's Club"

"Yay, fun times with no Natalie!!" Julie said, lying back on her pillow.

"Yes, it should be drama-free. I'm stoked!" Sophie said, lying down beside her.

They chatted some more about their party, and then finally fell asleep.

On Monday morning, Sophie went out to look for a job. She had a pile of resumes and was determined to hand them all out to anywhere she could. She completed the mall, movie stores, restaurants, and even local event companies.

Around 4:00 p.m., she received a phone call from Vancouver Coast Talent.

"Hey, Audrey, what's up?"

"You ready to go on set, Soph?" she asked excitedly.

"What? Really? Yes!"

"Okay, so I'll send you an email now with all the information, so you have it. It's tomorrow and you have to be there to check in with casting at 7:00 a.m. Make sure you're on time. I know this is your first time on set, so it's just extra work, but you can learn from it, all right? Everything you need to wear and bring will be listed in the email. So, have fun and take it all in, okay?"

"No problem, thanks so much, Audrey. What's the show?" Sophie asked nervously.

"It's the new show on TV called The Famous Darkness. Have you heard of it?"

"Oh my god, really? Yes, I have. I've watched it since it premiered last year and I love it! It's all about the supernatural," Sophie said hysterically.

"That's great. Then, you know what the vibe of the show is. But remember, you're an actor now, so don't get too excited on set, all right?" Audrey laughed.

"No, I won't. I understand. I can do this!"

"Great, well, check out the email and good luck tomorrow. Call me afterward and let me know how it went."

"Thanks, Audrey, bye." Sophie hung up the phone and danced around happily. One of her favorite actors ever was a lead on that show—Jared McQueen. She had had a crush on him from the day he starred in his first role, back when she was in high school. It was the whole reason that she had started to watch this show! Now, she was going to be on set with him. How much better news could she get today?

She quickly picked up her phone and called her mom to tell her the news. Unfortunately, her mom was busy, so she couldn't talk long. She didn't seem to understand how exciting this was. Sophie was not even going to bother with her father this time.

She hurried home to check her email, and on the way, her phone rang again.

"Hello?" Sophie said out of breath.

"Hi, is this Sophie Reid?" a man said.

"Yes."

"Hi, I'm Travis. I'm a manager at Jam Music. I have your resume here and I wanted to set up an interview with you."

"Hi, Travis, ya I just dropped one off to you guys today at the mall."

"Yes, so would you be free Wednesday at 10:00 a.m. to come in?"

"For sure, no problem," Sophie said, smiling.

"Great, then we'll see you then, thanks, Sophie."

She finally reached her apartment completely out of breath from running and excitement. She couldn't wait to tell Julie about her day. When she came in the front door, Julie had just finished making dinner.

"Good timing, friend. I made some yummy dinner," Julie said, setting the table.

"Oh my god, Julie, guess what?" Sophie said, running over to sit down.

"What?"

"Audrey called me today and I'm going on set tomorrow. It's for my favorite show, too! The Famous Darkness!" Sophie shrieked.

"Shut up! That's awesome, Sophie, congrats!"

"And! Wait, there's more. The manager from Jam Music—you know that big music store in the mall—asked me to come in for an interview Wednesday!"

"That's so great! Two jobs, way to go! This was a good day, eh, buddy?" Julie said, setting a plate of food down in front of Sophie.

"Totally, and I can't wait to celebrate this weekend!"

"Me, too!" Julie said, sitting down to eat.

"This is great, Jules, thanks," Sophie said, taking a bite of her dinner. "You are the best cook!"

After dinner, Sophie cleaned up the dishes in return for Julie cooking, and then checked her email to get all the info she needed for the next day. She then scrambled through her closet for the perfect outfits, especially if she was going to be on set with her favorite actor. She could barely sleep that night, tossing and turning. She nervously thought about her first day on set.

Finally, around 3:00 a.m., she fell asleep and woke up two hours later to get ready. She left the apartment right on time. The sun was just starting to come up when she reached the set.

There were people all over the place, running back and forth. Sophie found the casting check-in table and signed in. They directed her over to makeup where a lady looked over her clothes she had brought, picked an outfit, and then fixed up her makeup. It was very quick. People knew exactly what they were to be doing, so there was no time to waste.

The first two hours, Sophie sat around in a back room with a bunch of other people, waiting for their turn to go on set. There were a few of them who did extra work regularly and were great to chat with. Sophie tried hard to not act like a fan when talking about the show. She put on her acting face well. They had great food on set for all the actors and plenty of drinks to keep everyone hydrated. It was like a well-oil machine, and it ran perfectly.

Finally, a man came in and chose a few of the extras, including Sophie, and led them out to the set. They walked through many of the scenes Sophie recognized. She was amazed by everything she saw.

The scene she was in was located in a bar, and there were many people on set dressed to impress. She was led with two guys to the head bar. She was to act like a girl, who was trying to pick up any guy she could get.

This would play in perfectly to who the two lead actors were looking for in their scene. She was to confuse them about who they were looking for, making them choose the wrong girl just for a moment. They did one practice run with a stage guy, and then called in the lead actors.

Sophie set up for her scene, leaning against the bar in her cute little black dress, when Jared walked in. She felt her nerves kick in and her heart start to race. He was so much better looking in real life! He was six feet with dark eyes and wispy beautiful brown hair—complete perfection.

He stood directly across from her, and for a quick moment, he locked eyes with her, as the director informed him to look at Sophie when he thinks he has found the girl he's looking for. Sophie smiled slightly, trying to stay professional.

This was just too amazing, though! What were the chances of her scene being with Jared? She could hardly contain herself!

The other lead actor, playing his brother, was very good looking as well. It was amazing to be in the room with both of them, a dream come true.

The director then called, "Quiet on the set! Extras go!" Then, the extras started to do their thing. Sophie chatted with the guys at the bar, doing her best to show how she could flirt. Then, the director yelled, "Action!" That's when the two leads started their scene.

Jared said his lines with his on-screen brother, and then looked at Sophie. Then, he slowly started to walk toward her. Sophie glanced back at him, smiling in a seductive kind of way, like her character called for.

Her heart was racing, the closer he got to her. Inches before he reached her, his character received a vision, informing him that he had the wrong girl. The vision was strong, making him lose balance and fall against the bar for a quick second.

"Cut!" The director yelled, getting ready to start the scene again.

"Sorry, did I bump you?" Jared said to Sophie, who was in complete shock that he was standing right beside her.

"Uh, no. I'm fine, no worries," she stuttered out with a smile.

"Good. I'll try not to. Um . . . Good job there with your character. I'd definitely approach you at a bar," he teased.

Sophie blushed. He was so nice in person! She had always heard stories of actors who get on set and they act like they're better then everyone else, bossing people around and such. But Jared was totally not like that.

They set up once again for another take. This went on for a few hours before they set up for another scene. Sophie didn't care. It was all so much fun to her, and she knew instantly that this was the life for her. She loved performing and everything that came with it, even the nerves.

If you could last an entire day doing the same thing over and over again and not get sick of it, you know you love what you do. She had learned so much about filming a TV show from that one day on the set. It was perfect—the best day ever and something she'd remember for a lifetime!

From that day on, she continued to watch *The Famous Darkness* every Saturday night at 9:00 p.m. just for the fact that it inspired her. It was a reminder to her to never give up and to work hard for what she loved to do!

Close to 9:00 p.m., when the day was finished, she could barely keep her eyes open on the sky train ride home. It had been a long day, but worth every minute. Not only had she gained some experience on a real set, but she also got to spend the day with one of her favorite actors, even if she only got to say those few words to him. It was better than anything she could've wished for.

That night, after calling Audrey, she slipped into bed and fell asleep fast. Julie was out for the night with Carter, and Sophie had an interview to look forward to in the morning with the music store.

The next morning, after getting up and ready for her interview, Sophie sat down on the couch to eat a bowl of cereal before heading out. She flicked on the TV to watch her favorite music channel. She had a hard time sitting still when her favorite songs came on. Thankfully, Julie was used to seeing Sophie dance around and sing. So, there wasn't any other way she could embarrass herself anymore.

Just then, a commercial came on the television. It spoke of an audition happening for independent musicians to be part of a performance night at a local bar. Musical artist were to send in their submissions to be considered. Sophie quickly inputted the information in her phone in case by some miracle she had the guts to audition. She just couldn't shake those nerves she had when she sang. It was way worse than acting.

Julie was still asleep from coming in late the night before, when Sophie headed out the door to her interview. She arrived at quarter to ten with fifteen minutes to spare. Travis came out to greet her at the front. He was about 5' 6", Emo, and wore super skinny jeans, but a really nice guy! She followed him into his office in the back room.

The interview was different from any other she had ever had. Not only was he asking about her previous experience, but he also wanted to know lots about her personally—what kind of music and movies she liked, and of course, her knowledge about the entertainment industry.

She informed him of her being an aspiring actress and about her love for singing, even if she didn't have the guts to do it. He was impressed by her and offered her a job instantly. She was to start the next day!

After her interview, she headed to the bank to get a blank cheque for payroll. Heading into the bank, she ran into Charlotte, Elaina's friend from the house party.

"Hey, Soph!" she said cheerfully.

"Oh my gosh, hi!" Sophie said surprised.

"What are you up to?"

"Just came out of an interview with Jam Music."

"Oh, ya? Nice! I love that store, though it robs me of my money," Charlotte laughed.

"Me, too! But I got the job, so maybe it'll save me some."

"Cool, congrats! So, what are you doing now, then?" Charlotte asked, moving up in the line for the tellers.

"Nothing really, just grabbing a cheque for payroll to pay me. Why?"

"I was thinking of seeing that movie we talked about and I was actually gonna text you. Talk about perfect timing, eh?"

"Ya, I'm totally in!" Sophie said, stepping away from her for a moment to the teller.

The girls finished their banking and headed back across the street to the mall. Sophie filled Charlotte in on everything that had happened recently. Charlotte was always so easygoing to talk to, the way a friend should be. She was doing well with her photography, and she had finally started her own company. She still had to work at the tourist sites to get by, but at least her business was on its way.

After purchasing their movie tickets, the girls chose a seat in the back of the theatre to watch their gruesome movie! Before the lights went down, Sophie told Charlotte about Friday night and begged her to come out with them. She was definitely in and would head to Sophie and Julie's place first for pre-drinks!

The lights dimmed, while the surround sound filled the room, and the girls tensed up in excitement for the horror movie about to begin!

21

The Breaking Point

Sophie's first day at work was exciting, because she was surrounded by music, movies, and games. and her co-workers were really entertaining! She enjoyed informing customers of new bands and recommending movies, and she was quick at learning the computer system in the store.

One of the girls who was training her was at the university, majoring in English. Her name was Irely. She was from China and was not your classic Asian girl you'd meet in Vancouver. Even her name didn't make sense. Most Asians in Vancouver were very much still following the rules of their culture, and most were too shy to meet friends outside their group. But not Irely. She was outgoing and fun, and when her parents were not around, she was a hard-core partier!

She told Sophie of stories about her going out drinking at the bars, and then throwing some gum in her mouth, sobering herself up, and calling her mom for a ride. She acted like she was only out with her friends doing something quiet, like going to a movie or drinking bubble tea. It was like she had two sides to her, and her parents never found out. It was absolutely hilarious!

She was bold and confident, and you never knew what she was going to do next. Sophie got along so well with her that she invited her to go out with them Friday night. Even though she had only just met Sophie, Irely was up for the night of partying.

When work was finished, Devon met Sophie at the sky train. He had texted her earlier in the day. They were to hang out for the night and watch some movies. She jumped into his arms the moment she saw him.

"Hi!" She giggled.

He hugged her tightly, pulling back for a quick kiss. "How was work?"

"So good! I love it there already!" she said confidently.

"That's great, Soph. I'm happy for ya!"

"Me, too! So, what movie shall we watch tonight?"

"Anything but a chick flick, please," he begged.

"We'll see," she teased.

When they reached her apartment, Julie had conveniently gone out, so they had the place to themselves. Devon headed into the kitchen to throw some popcorn into the microwave, while Sophie went to change. She closed the bedroom door and threw her jacket and purse on the bed. She scrambled through her closet to find something to wear. When she turned around, Nathan was standing behind, startling her.

"You scared me," Sophie said, catching her breath.

"Hey, Soph, how are you?"

"I'm good, actually. Things have been slowly working themselves out, I guess."

"I see that. You were good on set the other day." He smiled at her. "Seems like I have some more competition, eh?"

She looked at him sadly, her emotions starting to come back.

"Nathan, you promised you'd . . . " She stopped, as he walked up and hugged her.

"I'm just teasing you, crazy girl," he whispered in her ear.

She instinctively wrapped her arms around him. His smell, his strength, and his warmth made her weak in the knees. She had to break away immediately, as this was not what they had promised to do.

"Nathan, I . . . "

"We can't, I know." He stepped away from her, sliding his hand through his hair.

"Is everything okay, Nathan?" she asked nervously.

He turned to face her again. "Ya, Soph, it's all good."

"You sure?" she asked again, confused about why he was there. She wondered if it was because Devon was there, too.

"Ya, I just wanted to check in, that's all. I really should go, but, Sophie, I want you to know that I'm here, okay? You always have me."

"I know, Nate," she said, as he disappeared.

What did he want? Was he trying to tell her something? He couldn't have just come to check in like that, and then leave. There was something he wasn't telling her. Sophie finished getting dressed and pushed the thought of Nate once again to the back of her mind before heading out to join Devon on the couch.

"Geeze, what were you doing in there?" he asked jokingly.

"Nothing, just tidying up a bit, that's all."

"I've already picked a movie out, so you've lost this battle," he teased, pulling her down beside him. He flicked on the movie, as she leaned back against him. Once again, it was an action movie. Her mind raced. As the movie went on, she couldn't get Nate out of her head.

Maybe this wasn't going to be as easy as she thought it would be. But Gabriel was watching closely now, and she couldn't afford to lose him. What had Gabriel meant by her needing an angel? Was she doomed for something? Too many thoughts started to fill her mind again. She felt that dark feeling taking over her body again.

"I need to get a pop," Sophie said, getting up from the couch.

Devon quickly grabbed her arm, pulling her back down beside him. He forced her back on the couch to lie down, and he then squeezed in beside her.

"What's going on?" he said, holding her hostage.

"Nothing, I'm just going to get a . . . "

"No, you're not. I can tell you have something on your mind. You're all tense and crap."

She took a deep breath, trying to relax, as she didn't know what to say.

"Come on, what's going on, Soph. There's no more Natalie, so what's wrong?"

"Nothing. I'm just not feeling too good." She didn't want to go into detail about her life and all the things she worried about at night. He didn't need to see that side of her, not if she was going to keep him around. No guy would want to deal with all that.

He held her face gently, looking into her eyes and waiting for some sort of answer that he would believe. She didn't want to ruin anything with him because or her issues. That was when her stupid emotions started to take over. Her eyes got glossy and she quickly looked away from him.

"Hey, Sweetie. I'm sorry. I'm not trying to pry or anything." He kissed her carefully, feeling bad for drilling her.

"No, it's fine," she said, wiping her eyes.

"No, it's not."

She wrapped her arms around him, hugging him tightly. He continued to kiss her, first on the shoulder and then on the neck, working his way up to her earlobe and finally back to her lips. His hands ran down her sides, making every hair on her body stand up. He knew exactly how to distract her. He stopped for just a moment to pull his shirt from over his head. Sophie caught her breath and then continued to kiss him over and over again.

She couldn't resist him, as he seemed to have some sort of spell over her that constantly pulled her in. He slowly started to push her tank top higher, as his hands ran up her stomach, around her ribs, and to her back, so that their skin touched slightly. Just then, her phone went off, and once again, they were interrupted from their moment.

Sophie pushed Devon to the side and reached over to the coffee table to grab her cell phone. "Hello?"

"Sophie? It's Adel! You won't believe this!" Adel yelled, out of breath. "I decided to give that guy another chance, and it just slapped me back in the face!" she cried out.

"What? Adel, slow down. What happened?"

"He cheated on me again! I was just out at a pub with my friends and he and a few of his friends were there in the back playing pool. I caught him making out with some chick!"

"What? You were there and he still made out with another girl?"

"No! He didn't know I was there. We just ran into him by accident. I can't take this, Sophie," Adel said, freaking out.

"I'm so sorry, Adel. Where are you now?"

"I left. I confronted him, slapped him, and then stormed out. My friends wouldn't leave! I need you, Sophie. Please meet me," she begged.

"All right, all right. Calm down. I'm coming. Where are you?" Sophie said, getting up from the couch. Devon sighed, as he watched her run into her room and come back out with her jacket and purse.

"Okay, I'll see you in a few minutes. Stay there." Sophie hung up the phone and looked at Devon. He knew what she was going to say and he wasn't pleased.

"Sophie, she'll be fine. She's just being dramatic. Tell her you'll talk tomorrow."

"She sounded really upset and even if it's not that big of a deal, it's important to her, so I'll just go. It's fine. I'm sorry, Devon. If you want, you can wait here, or come with . . . "

"No, I'm gonna go home. I'll just meet up with some friends who were going out tonight. I told them I couldn't go, because I was coming to see you," he said frustrated.

She felt badly about doing this to him, but she couldn't just ignore a friend in need. She watched, as Devon grabbed his jacket off the chair and headed toward the door.

"Devon wait . . . " she said, running up behind him.

He leaned against the door, as she ran up to him. "I'm really sorry," she said honestly.

"Whatever, Soph, it's fine." He quickly hugged her, and then turned to leave. She didn't believe him. She knew he was upset with her, but what could she do?

She turned to lock the door behind her, and then headed down the street. Since Adel wasn't that far, she decided to go on foot. It would give her time to think.

She eventually came to a local coffee shop where Adel had agreed to meet her. She waited out front for her until Adel came storming around the corner. Her face was red from either crying or screaming.

"Sophie!" she said, running and hugging her.

"Hey, are you all right?"

"No! This is so stupid, Soph. He's such a jerk! I hate him!"

Adel went on and on about her eventful night, as Sophie listened quietly. Eventually, she convinced Adel to grab a coffee and sit down. She was hysterical from this whole situation.

As much as Sophie didn't agree with her giving him another chance, she kept her mouth shut and let Adel talk until she was blue in the face. Suddenly, the sound of a text buzzed from Adel's phone.

"Oh my god," she said with a bit of a smile on her face. "It's him! Now what?" she said, reading his text.

"What does it say?" Sophie said, leaning over to see.

"He wants to talk, and he says he's really sorry."

"Adel, you can't be serious?"

"What?"

"You know what!" Sophie said confidently. She couldn't hold it in anymore. "He's just saying bullshit to you. Come on, Adel, this is all an act."

"Soph, I know. But he just wants to talk. Maybe I slapped some sense into him, literally!" she joked.

"I don't think . . . "

"Listen, I gotta run. Thanks, Sophie."

"Adel!" Sophie couldn't believe she was going to meet with him!

"I know, I know! I won't go easy on him, but just trust me, Soph. I know what I'm doing." Adel got up from the table and headed for the door. "I'll see you tomorrow for our night out! Text me your address, and don't forget!!"

"But, Adel, I really think . . . " But it was too late, as she was already gone. Sophie sat there in disbelief. She had come all this way and ditched Devon for only a few minutes with Adel. What a waste of time! She got up from the table and headed for home.

It was cold that night and the wind blew strong against her face. She pulled out her phone and texted Devon a few times to see if she could catch him. Maybe he'd still want to hang out. But he didn't answer her, not even after the third text. So, she gave up on him and decided to text Charlotte, Irely, and even Adel, while she was at it, with her new address for the next night. All three returned her text with thanks and confirmed that they were coming to her housewarming party.

That night, Sophie crawled into bed a little annoyed. She wanted Devon to text her back and to not be mad at her. She also worried about Adel, and on top of that, she hadn't checked in with her gram in a bit, so that was on her list, too. Julie was still out, so the apartment was pretty quiet.

There were faint sounds of people in the hallway and every once in a while, the walls creaked from the air conditioner. Even though the apartment was totally safe, Sophie was still nervous at night when she was by herself. Normally, Nate would come and be by her side if she was feeling like this, but they were trying to follow the rules and that meant no staying over.

As she lay there in bed, looking at the ceiling, her thoughts flooded her mind. She hoped she would get enough hours to survive out here in Vancouver, but the schedule at work only had her booked for two days the following week. Maybe Audrey would call with some work for her.

Once again, these were things she would normally talk to Nate about, but instead, she had to keep them to herself. On nights like these, she doubted herself and if she could actually make it out there. But things were okay, weren't they? She had a new job, she'd started acting professionally, she got a new stress-free place to live, and her relationship with Devon was going great. Time was flying by, yet she still felt like she had no control.

Her eyes gazed over at her clock, and it was now 1:30 a.m. She picked up her phone to see if Devon had texted her, but he hadn't. This went on the entire night, until finally, around 4:22 a.m., Sophie fell into a deep sleep from exhaustion.

It was around 10:15 a.m. that Sophie woke to the sound of the laundry machine. She rubbed her eyes, trying to adjust to the morning light. Julie must have come home early this morning, she thought.

She got out of bed and headed for the Kitchen. Sure enough, Julie was sitting in the living room, eating cereal and watching television.

"Good morning, friend!" she said cheerfully.

"Hey, did you just get in?" Sophie asked, grabbing a bowl of cereal to join her.

"Ya, I got in about an hour ago. I wanted to wash some clothes, so I'll have some options for tonight's festivities!"

"Nice. So, does that mean that you stayed at Carter's?" Sophie teased.

"Yes. He's very fun. I like him." Julie smiled back.

"I know you do." Sophie laughed.

"And how are things with you and Devon?"

"Good, but I think he may be mad at me. Last night, Adel called me all hysterical about some guys she's seeing and she asked me to meet her, because she was so upset. So, I said I would, and Devon just left. He didn't understand at all."

"I'm sure he'll get over it. He didn't come home last night to their apartment. He must have gone out with some buddies."

Sophie looked at her worried. "Do you think he's mad?"

"Na, don't worry about it. He was probably just mad at the moment, but not mad at you. Don't worry. You'll see him tonight and everything will be fine."

"Ya, I guess so," Sophie said, taking a big bite of cereal.

They finished their cereal and sat there for the rest of the morning and into the early afternoon watching television. Julie received a few texts from Kevin. He and his buddies were coming out that night along with Mark and Elaina. It was going to be a full house in their new apartment.

After eating an early dinner and tidying up the apartment, the girls took their turns to shower and started getting ready for the night. At seven o'clock on the dot, the doorbell rang. Julie ran to the door in excitement. She opened it to see Mark standing there with two big bags.

"Happy new house day!" He laughed.

"Mark! You're the best, thanks so much!" Julie said, giving him a hug and taking a bag from him.

"Ya, I know, check out what I brought!" He started pulling chips out of one bag and underneath them were fun glasses that lit up, straws with umbrellas, candies, and other random things only Mark could think of.

"Let's get this party started!" he said, grabbing some pop from the fridge, and then he started mixing some drinks.

"Mark! Yay, you're our first guest!" Sophie said, running out to hug him. Just then, there was a knock at the door and Adel peeked her head through.

"Hey, hey!" she said. Three girls followed her into the kitchen, followed by Elaina and Charlotte.

"Hey, Soph!" Charlotte said, hugging her.

"Hi!" Sophie said, hugging her two friends. It was so nice having all her friends together, and it was just what she needed to distract her from the thoughts swirling in her mind.

Sophie and Julie showed them around the apartment, and then everyone gathered back in the small kitchen to have some drinks and snacks.

"This place is great, Soph. You must be so happy, eh?" Charlotte said, filling her mouth with chips.

"I am. I really like it here."

"No Natalie drama either, eh? What a difference. Have you spoken with her lately?"

"Not really. I texted her a few times and we've have short conversations, but that's all. We don't hang out or anything."

"Well, maybe it's for the best. What about your other friend you told me about, the one from your job. Is she coming?"

"Oh, Irely? Ya, she says she is. You'll like her. She's hilarious!"

"This is so awesome. I love having people over in our new amazing apartment, Soph!" Julie said, jumping in the middle of their conversation. "I'm so glad you left that Grimis!"

"Grimis?" Charlotte laughed. She almost choked on her chips.

"Jules," Sophie said, shaking her head. As much as she didn't like how Natalie acted, she never liked to talk behind her friends' backs. Mark passed around more drinks that he created, and every one of them got stronger and stronger. Finally, Sophie took some water from the fridge. She wanted to pace herself, so she could last the night.

Just then, there was another knock at the door and Sophie ran to open it.

"Soph!" Kevin said, throwing his arms around her.

"Hey, Kev." She laughed. He was so much taller than her. He was such a large guy for a twenty-five year old. He had two guys with him who were just as big as he was. Kevin introduced them as they entered. Then, behind him was another person she could barely see past Kevin, until he finally showed his face.

"Hey, beautiful," Jake said politely.

"Jake," Sophie said surprised. "Hi."

"Kev suggested we get past our awkwardness and move on, so he said I should come."

Sophie thought about it for a moment. It was true that they really should get past this. They were all friends, and it only made things more awkward to avoid each other, so she went with it. There was nothing that was going to ruin her night.

"Sure, come in."

Julie's mouth dropped at the sight of Jake coming in the door. She ran to Sophie confused. "What's going on? Why is he here?"

"Kevin invited him, so let's just be cool. We all have to hang out, eventually."

"Wow, Soph, that's cool of you. I wouldn't be as forgiving as you, at least not that fast. But you're right."

"Who said I forgive him? I'm an actress," Sophie teased, trying to lighten the mood.

"That's better!" Julie said, leading her back to the kitchen.

Everyone was having fun drinking and hanging out. Mark started up some music and began to dance as usual.

"Oh god, I hope this isn't a repeat from the last party." Charlotte laughed.

"Me, too," Elaina said, as they watched him bust out his moves. Eventually, they decided to join him.

Sophie quickly ran to her room to grab her camera. Tonight would be a great night to take some memorable pictures, or at least some embarrassing ones. As she grabbed the camera from her drawer, she glanced at the photo of cherry blossoms on her nightstand.

For a moment, she missed Nate, She had begun to see him less and less. She wondered how much he watched over her. Was he around, but just not showing himself? Or was he just not there at all? She closed the drawer and turned to head back to the kitchen.

"Hey, you," Devon said, standing in the doorway.

"Devon. Hey." She stood there awkwardly, not sure if she should hug him and not sure if he was mad at her.

"Well? Do I get a hug?" he said, walking up to her.

She smiled slightly in relief and walked into his arms. She wrapped her arms around him tightly. "I'm sorry about last time."

"Moving on, no worries," he said, kissing her on the forehead.

"Sophie!" Carter said, coming down the hallway to hug her.

"What's up, girl?" He had already had a few drinks before coming over, so his energy was through the roof.

"Come on, guys! We're gonna do some shots before we have to go!" Julie yelled from the kitchen. The three of them headed back to join in, and when Sophie reached the kitchen, she ran into Irely.

"Hey! You made it!" Sophie said happily.

"Ya, of course I did! I love parties. You know me. Charlotte here has made me a nice drink!"

"That I did!" Charlotte said, feeling pretty pleased with herself.

"I told my parents I was going to a festival tonight with some friends. I'll call them later for a ride," Irely said, taking a big swallow of her drink.

"What? Your parents don't know where you are? Aren't you old enough to do what you want?" Charlotte said confused.

"Oh, ya, I know it sounds silly that a twenty-one year old should be hiding from her parents, but you don't have traditional Chinese parents. They are hard-core! So, until I move out, it's just easier to do it like this, and then they aren't disappointed in me." She laughed.

"Irely is very good at what she does," Sophie said, putting her arm around her proudly.

"Nice, but sounds like a lot of work." Charlotte laughed.

"Oh, you have no idea."

Elaina called to everyone to line up, as the shots were ready. She handed a shot to each person. Jake stood across from Sophie, eyeing her every move. Devon stepped beside her and gave him a nasty look.

"Everyone ready?" Elaina said, holding up her shot.

"Cheers to Sophie and Julie and their new apartment, and may we all be famous soon!" Everyone cheered to that, and as the shots poured quickly down the throats of the eager partiers, the door slammed open.

"I'm ready to party!" Natalie said, making her grand entrance!

Julie's shot spit out from her mouth. "What the f . . . " Carter quickly covered her mouth, holding her back.

"Natalie?" Sophie said, turning around.

"Hope you don't mind, but Mark told me he was coming, so thought I'd stop by to say hey and see the new place."

Sophie was surprised and didn't know how to handle this. Maybe Natalie was trying to make things right, but Julie was not ready for this yet.

"Nat!" Kevin yelled, walking over to hug her. "Now everyone's here, so let's party! It's so nice having everyone together!"

"What the hell is she doing here?" Julie said, breaking free from Carter's grip. Devon cut her off.

"Hey, Jules, I know you hate the life out of her, but maybe just for tonight, you should ignore her. Don't let her ruin your party. Let's just all pretend we get along for tonight. Please, it will only stress Sophie out. You girls waited so long to have this party. Let's just have fun, all right?"

She pondered his words for a moment, keeping her eyes on Natalie. "Fine. But only for Sophie's sake."

"Good girl," he said, giving her a pat on the shoulder, and then he let her pass. Sophie hurried over to Julie.

"Are you okay with this? Do you want me to make her leave?"

"No, Soph. It's fine. Let the little creep stay. There are so many other people here for me to distract myself."

"You sure?"

"I'm an actress." She winked at Sophie.

"Get out here and dance, everyone!" Mark yelled from the living room.

Surprisingly, Irely was already out dancing with Mark. She found him quite entertaining. Charlotte wasn't too far behind. Adel and her friends joined Kevin and his buddies on the floor. Everyone was having a good time, until they received a warning from the landlord to turn the music down.

Since the party was shut down, the cabs were called and everyone went down to the front entrance to wait. Natalie kept her distance from Julie, thanks to Mark, and, of course, Kevin and his friends were always a good distraction for her. Carter and Julie were all over each other, and Irely became an instant friend with Charlotte and Elaina. Adel seemed to be occupied with her phone. She was still texting that guy, and even her friends were getting a little annoyed with it.

Sophie tripped over her feet, as she walked to the front door, toppling to the ground.

"Soph!" Charlotte laughed. "Are you okay?"

"What are you doing, crazy girl?" Devon said, helping her to her feet. Sophie looked at him for a moment. Only Nathan called her crazy girl.

"What?" he said, pulling her up to him.

"Nothing . . . I don't know what happened there." She giggled covering herself up. He smiled at her, kissing her on the lips. "You better last tonight."

"I will, I didn't drink that much."

"Wanna come back to my place tonight? I think Carter said Julie was going to already."

Sophie thought for a moment. She wasn't too sure if she was ready to stay over yet. But she answered yes, and then kissed him back. Things were a lot more serious between them, and it made her nervous to go to his place, even though he had already stayed at hers once before.

"Someone had a few too many to start off, and we aren't even at the club yet. This is going to be a crazy night. I can feel it," Irely said. She quickly grabbed the camera from Sophie and took some pre-pictures. "These are the before pics!" she teased.

They continued out the door to find the cabs already waiting for them.

"Julie! Do you have the key to our place, because I think I forgot mine," Sophie yelled to her, as she got into a cab.

"Yup, no worries!" she yelled back. Four at a time they climbed into the cabs, ready for a night of fun!

The club was full that night, and the music vibrated off the walls. You could hear it from outside in the lineup. Since it was getting nicer out, they didn't need to bring any coats, so it was just a matter of paying the five-dollar entrance fee. Natalie was all over Kevin and his friends by the time they got into the club. Devon grabbed Sophie's hand and led her to the bar.

"A round of shots, please, surprise us!" he yelled to the bartender.

Everyone gathered around to take the shot. Sophie had a hard time taking it back, because it was so nasty and it reminded her of the shots she had on the cruise lines.

"Thanks, Devon! You're not that bad, even if you do like Julie." Natalie laughed, knowing that Julie could hear her from where she was standing. Julie stared her down, but didn't say anything. Devon shook his head and turned from her. He pulled Sophie close, as she stumbled in his arms. "You still with me, darling?"

She gazed up into his eyes. "Oh, ya, I'm good." She smiled at him. "Wanna dance?" she asked, pulling at his shirt.

"Not right now," he said, giving her a kiss on the nose. "I have some friends here I wanna say hi to. I'll be back."

Sophie frowned at him, but let him go. Charlotte, Irely, and Elaina quickly grabbed Sophie and dragged her to the dance floor. Adel and her famous guy, along with her friends, soon joined them, too. The girls danced close, and soon a group of guys surrounded them.

Sometimes, the guys at the clubs were so creepy. They scouted the dance floor for drunken girls to hook up with. Sophie and the girls were drunk, but not that drunk. They stuck close to each other, trying to give them the signal to back off.

Then, Kevin stepped in with his friends. They danced their way in between the girls, scaring off the rest of the guys with their size, Even Jake joined in, but kept his distance from Sophie. Mark pushed his way to the center of the circle, taking over the spotlight. The drinks continued and everyone was having a blast.

The only problem was that Sophie didn't see much of Devon as the night went on. Even Julie disappeared after a while to look for Carter. Sophie found it odd that they weren't around. Maybe Devon was still mad at her, but where was Carter? Julie eventually came back to find Sophie.

"Hey, have you seen the guys?" she yelled in Sophie's ear over the music.

"No, not at all," Sophie yelled back.

"Come with me to look for them," Julie said, pulling at her. The girls searched the club for the boys. After a few minutes, they found them at a small bar in the back of the club. They were there with four other guys and two girls. Julie ran up to Carter and jumped at him. He blocked her from wrapping her arms around him, but kissed her when she reached his face.

"Hey, you, here you are. When are you going to dance with me?" Sophie said, walking up to Devon.

"I will, just not right now. I'm talking with my friends," he said, ignoring her. Sophie looked at him, wondering if he was trying to punish her for what she had done to him the night that she left to see Adel.

"I haven't seen you the whole night. Can we talk for a sec?" she asked.

"No, Soph, not right now. I'm with my friends. I'll find you in a sec, I promise," he said, turning to order another drink from the bar. Sophie stood there, hurt from his words.

"Sophie!" a voice yelled from behind her. She turned to see Adel, running up to her.

"Sophie, come with me. That jerk met up with some chick here! Right in front of me!"

"What? Again? Adel, haven't you learned, yet?" Sophie said, frustrated with her and Devon's mean words.

"Don't be mad, Sophie, I need you. Just help me tell him off. I need you for support," Adel said, dragging her away from Devon. His back was still turned to her, as she walked away. Adel led Sophie all the way across the club to where that guy was dancing. It was true, as he was there dancing with some skinny blonde.

"Back me up, Soph!" she said, walking up to him.

"Adel, I think this is a bad . . . " but it was too late. Adel ripped him from the blonde. She was screaming at him, as the blonde pushed her away. Adel pushed back and it soon turned into a catfight. Sophie ran over to break it up, as arms were flying and nails were out. Sophie was slapped in the face by the blonde, making her lose her balance and fall to the ground. Adel continued to fight over top of her.

"It's on, bitches! Don't worry. I got this, Soph!" a girl yelled from behind. It was Irely. She pulled Sophie to her feet, and then ran and jumped on the back of the blonde. Sophie caught her breath and saw the masterpiece, building right before her. This was just getting stupid, she thought, standing there, watching these girls go at it.

"What the hell is going on?" Charlotte yelled over the music.

The two of them stood there, watching the fight unfold. It was actually quite entertaining. Irely was really skilled and quick, almost like a cat. Between Adel and her, that blonde didn't have a chance.

"Should we not stop this?" Charlotte laughed. Normally, they would, but they were too drunk to care anymore. So, they decided to dance.

Eventually, Irely joined them with a smile on her face. "Everything's good! That blonde got what she deserved and that guy . . . oh, man, you missed the best part. Adel punched him square between the eyes!" She laughed.

"That's hilarious! Good for her. It's about friggen time!" Sophie giggled. Then, Elaina danced over to them. "I'm so tired. I'm ready for bed. Can we go?" she asked Charlotte.

"Ya, actually, I have to go, too. I can't believe it's 2:00 a.m. already," Irely said, checking her phone. "My parents are coming to get me down the street. Anyone got any gum I can have?"

"I do," Sophie said, fumbling through her purse for the gum. Then, she handed a piece to Irely.

"We'll walk you to your parents' car, since we're going, too," Charlotte said. "Where is Julie, Soph? I don't wanna leave you here alone."

"Don't worry about me. I'll be fine. I'm going to Devon's place anyway."

Charlotte looked at her, not convinced, but trusted her words. "All right, girl. I'll text you tomorrow, okay? Be safe!" she said, hugging her. Elaina hugged her, too, and then the two of them headed for the door.

"Ya, this was so much fun, Soph. We really have to do this again. I'll see you at work next week, okay?" Irely said, waving good-bye.

"Sounds good! See ya!" Sophie said, sipping the last few drops of her drink. She headed over to the bar to set down her bottle, and then ordered a bottle of water.

She definitely had enough alcohol for the night. Her eyes scanned the club for anyone she knew. Where were Kevin, Natalie, and all those guys? Where was Adel? Where was anyone she recognized?

"Sophie, you all right?" Jake said from behind her.

"Ya, but where is everyone?"

"I'll take you home if you need a ride."

"No, Jake, it's fine. I'm here with Devon," she said, ignoring him.

What would Devon think if he found out that she went home with Jake? It was definitely not a good idea, even if he were just trying to help out. She would wait it out and find them. There was no way Julie would ditch her.

254

"Sophie, don't be dumb. No one's here, so just come with me," he said, grabbing her hand to pull her along."

"I said 'No!'" she said, pulling her hand away. Just then, she saw Carter hurry by, and Julie ran close behind.

"See, there are my friends now. I'm good, just go!" she said, leaving him to run after Julie. She tried to catch up, but Julie hurried out the door. Where was she going?

"Julie!" she yelled from the door. It looked like Carter and she were arguing outside.

"Give me a sec!" Julie yelled rudely back to her. Sophie backed off immediately. Something serious was happening. She decided to go look for Devon once again.

The club was slowing down and so was the music. Last call was announced over the speaker, and she still hadn't spent a second with Devon. She headed back toward the bar where she had seen him last. Sure enough, he was still there, talking with those same girls and the group of guys. She walked up to him slowly, not sure what was going on between them.

"Hey," she said softly to him.

"Hey, what's going on?" he said casually back to her.

"Well, I just saw Carter and Julie arguing out front. What's going on?"

"Oh, who knows." He laughed.

She stood there feeling uneasy with how he was interacting with her.

"So, are you going to dance with me at all before the night's over?" she asked again.

His friends were looking like they were getting ready to leave. He didn't even introduce her, and who were these people?

"Fine, Soph, look I'm gonna say goodbye to them and walk them out, and then I'll be right back, all right? Just wait here." He carefully stepped around her and followed his friends to the door.

Sophie stood by the bar, drinking her water. People were slowly starting to leave, but there was a good amount of people still on the dance floor. Only slow songs were playing over the speakers now, calming people before they left. She waited patiently for about ten minutes, and then another ten and another.

Her nerves kicked in, and her mind started to race, but she didn't dare think what was hidden in the back of her mind. Slowly, she walked through the club, looking for Devon, but he was nowhere in sight. She circled the dance floor, looking for him. "He wouldn't . . . no, he would never leave," she thought.

Her head started to feel faint, her breaths became short, and she started into panic mode at the thought of him ditching her. She refused to believe that he would act this way. He was supposed to be different. He was supposed to be . . .

Her feet froze at the side of the dance floor, as she gazed over the crowd of people dancing close. Gasp after gasp, she tried to hold back her emotions, but her body trembled, and she hurt all over. Her knees started to get weak, and she was going to collapse!

Her eyes started to tear up. She was breaking down, and nothing was going to stop it.

Suddenly, she felt a presence behind her.

"Don't cry over him. He's not worth it," Nathan said from behind her.

"Sophie, are you listening? You have to be strong here."

She still didn't answer or move from her frozen position on the side of the dance floor.

"Nathan, don't interfere," another voice said.

The base of the music filled the room, muffling their voices.

"Gabriel, I know what I'm doing, so don't worry."

"No, you don't. Let her be. She has to go through this," he warned.

Even though she could hear an argument happening behind her, Sophie still didn't move. She was too caught up in what was happening, and not even Nathan was getting through to her now. Their words faded away behind her.

"If you do this, there will be consequences, Nate!" Gabriel said, raising his voice.

"This is ridiculous, Gabriel. No one deserves this! She didn't do anything to have people treat her like this. I won't stand here and just watch her suffer alone. I can't. I won't do that to her!"

"Sophie," he said, taking a hold of her hand. She didn't respond, as tears fell from her eyes.

He led her to the middle of the dance floor, completely ignoring Gabriel's warning and leaving him behind.

"Come here," he said, pulling her into him.

His hands rubbed her back slowly, embracing her more tightly every moment.

"Listen to me, all right? I know this is horrible, but you have to get past it. He isn't worth you eating yourself up about this. I know you. You're probably thinking to yourself, 'What did I do?' right?" He kissed the top of her head, as her arms tucked in closely to his chest.

"You did nothing, okay? Absolutely nothing. He's just a shitty person who took advantage of a great girl. You're gonna be fine, all right, Soph? Do you trust me?" He leaned back to look down at her. She wouldn't raise her head to him, so he forced her to. Her face was flushed, and tears ran over his hands, as he held her face softly.

"Sophie . . . " he said quietly, leaning his face against hers. "Don't do this to yourself, please."

"I'm so stupid," she whispered.

"No, you're not, Soph! Don't ever say that!" He pulled her close again, and this time, she wrapped her arms around him, gripping him tightly. He breathed deep, trying to stay calm, and trying to not explode in anger about this piece of crap guy. He could feel her crying harder against his chest. She couldn't hold it in anymore. He held her close, letting her get it all out.

"I hate him for doing this to you, Soph. I hate seeing you like this. Tell me what to do, Sophie. What do you need? Please, I don't know how to help you."

Sophie wiped her face dry and pushed away from him slowly.

"You can't, Nate, you can't help me." She continued to step back until she was completely free from his grip.

"Soph?" he said confused, watching her walk away from him.

"I have to go . . . " she said, hurrying toward the door.

Outside, she signaled down a cab and jumped in. Without a second thought, she told him where to go. When the cab pulled up to the apartment, she took a deep breath to prepare herself before paying the driver the last bit of her money.

It was close to 4:00 a.m. by the time she arrived at Devon's place. An old man was just coming out the front entrance. Sophie hurried to grab the door before it shut. She entered the elevator and headed up to his floor. The door slowly opened and she stepped out to face her reality. Still shaken up, she walked up to his door and knocked on it.

No one answered, so she grabbed her cell phone from her purse and tried calling him. Still nothing, so she knocked again.

She could hear voices inside. Someone was in there, so she continued to knock. Finally, Carter opened the door, and he quickly hugged her, noticing the expression on her face.

"Sophie, come here," he said, squeezing her.

"What's going on, Carter? Where's Devon?"

"Sophie?" Julie's voice said from behind her. She had just arrived and quickly ran to Sophie's side.

"What the hell is going on, Carter?" Julie screamed at him. "Why did you run off like that? What's your problem?"

"Julie, relax," he said, brushing her off and heading inside.

Julie followed quickly behind him, not letting him out of her sight. Sophie walked in slowly behind them, keeping her eyes peeled for Devon. When she entered the living room, the same girl from the bar was sitting on the couch next to Devon. The other girl wasn't there.

"What's up, Soph?" he said casually.

"What's up? I don't know, I'm trying to figure that out. I thought you invited me back here tonight, but I guess that invitation was revoked, considering you left me at the club," she said calmly. She could hear Julie and Carter arguing in his bedroom.

"I told you I was trying to visit with my friends." He got up from the couch and headed into the kitchen for a drink. She stood there, as the young girl stared at her awkwardly.

Just then, the front door slammed open and three girls walked in.

"Carter! We're here!" the blonde teased. "Hey, Dev!" she said, passing him in the hallway. The three of them walked right past Sophie, and then noticed Carter in his room, arguing with Julie.

"Who the hell are you guys?" one girl asked rudely.

"Who the hell are you?" Julie yelled back, coming out to confront her.

Sophie quickly blocked her way.

"I think we should just go, Julie."

"Why? I wanna know who the hell these girls are and what the hell is going on here?" Julie said, staring them down.

"Look, Soph, you girls should go. I'm gonna hang with my friends tonight," Devon said, quietly trying to get her to leave.

"Your friends?" Sophie said unconvinced. She walked over to the girl on the couch and asked her quietly as the rest argued, "Are you Devon's friend?"

"I just met him at the bar. I don't really know him," she said confused.

Sophie's emotions raced through her body. She couldn't believe what was going on here. How could he treat her like this?

"Just go, Soph," he said again.

She was embarrassed to be there and didn't need him to tell her to go. She wanted to get out of there as quickly as possible. She walked up to Julie and grabbed her by the wrist.

"We're going!" she said, pulling her toward the door.

"No, Soph, stay! I'm not leaving him here with these bitches!" she said, pulling her arm away.

"Just listen to her, Julie, you idiot," Devon said, shaking his head. Sophie turned to him and stormed up to stare him in the face.

"You're a real jerk, you know that? I don't deserve this. How can you have the guts to treat someone like this?" Her pulse started to race. "Don't you dare call her an idiot. She has the right to be mad. You guys should be real men and tell us if you don't want to see us anymore. You don't have to act this way, Devon. Just break up with me, you coward!"

He stood there, quietly staring at her. She thought for a moment that he felt badly and that maybe he was realizing what he had done.

But then, he said, "We were never officially together in the first place, Soph. I don't owe you anything."

Her heart sank, as she stood there, keeping her eye contact strong with him. Her eyes started to water, so she turned to leave as quickly as possible. There was no way she was going to let him see her cry over him.

"I'm leaving, Julie, with or without you."

"Wait, Soph! How are you going to get home?" Julie said, running to her.

"I don't know. I'll walk probably, but I'm not staying here one more minute. It's degrading and stupid. Come with me, Jules. You deserve better then this," Sophie begged.

"I can't, Soph," she said sadly.

"Fine," Sophie said, heading out the door to the elevator.

"Wait!" Devon said, running to her. "Here, take a twenty. Don't walk, it's late."

"Are you kidding me?" She looked at him pathetically.

"I'd rather take my chances on the streets than ever take anything from you again." The elevator door closed and Sophie broke down.

Back in the apartment, Julie ran to the window to see if Sophie was actually going to walk. Devon joined her at the window, while Carter was still insisting on Julie leaving as well.

"She's walking. It's about a three-hour walk home," he said worried.

"What the hell is she thinking?" Julie said, pulling out her phone to call her.

Sophie stormed down the street, just as it started to rain. She wanted to get as far as she could from that place. Her phone lit up with calls from Julie and Devon, but she ignored every one of them. Eventually, she turned off the phone and put it in her purse.

The rain came down hard that night, and Sophie regretted using all her money up, because all she had on was a pair of jeans and a tube top. Her hands shivered, as she tucked them under her arms to keep warm. She tried to process what had happened, but her mind was a blank slate. Perhaps her subconscious wasn't ready to deal with this again, because it had completely closed off from her.

Vancouver wasn't really a place you wanted to be walking alone late at night, especially for a girl. There were random homeless people and sketchy parts of town that only could be seen in the late hours of the night. Every once in a while, she looked over her shoulder to make sure no one was following her.

A few young guys across the street hollered to her, as they walked past. Sophie kept her head down and continued walking. Eventually, one crossed the street and started walking up behind her. Sophie turned quickly to face him. "What do you want?" she said nervously.

"Where ya heading?" he asked.

"Home. I'm real close and my roommate knows I'm on the way."

"Oh, ya? Is your roommate hot like you? Cause I got a few friends over there." He pointed to the two guys crossing the street to join him.

"Look, I have to go. I'm in a hurry," Sophie said, walking a little faster, keeping her eyes on them, as they continued to follow her.

"Why don't you hang with us for a while. We could come over and meet your roommate," the guy smirked. "What's your name?"

Sophie didn't answer, as all she could think about was what her chances were of out running them? They were very slim, given the heals she was wearing.

"So, are you not going to tell me your name, then? That's pretty rude," the guy said, getting closer to her.

She couldn't do it anymore. She had to take her chances and run. With her purse tightly in her hand, she took off as fast as she could.

"Where ya going?" the guy yelled, running after her.

She didn't know if he was just teasing her and trying to scare her or if he was seriously trying to get her. But she wasn't planning on staying around to find out. She tried her best to keep up speed, as the footsteps behind started to gain on her with every second.

With a quick glance over her shoulder, a hand that grabbed her by the hair startled her. She felt herself jolt back in pain, as the guy wrapped his arms around her.

"Let me go!" she screamed in fear.

"Shhh . . . you're okay," he said, holding her tightly. The other two guys finally caught up to them. One of them took the place of the guy holding her, so he could come face-to-face with her.

"Sweetie, why are you running from me?" he asked politely. She could smell the alcohol on his breath, as he stood close to her.

His hand touched her face gently and tucked a few loose strands of hair behind her ear.

"Don't touch me!" She flinched from the cold touch of his fingertips.

"Listen to me carefully . . . Shut your face before I shut it for you."

Sophie stared him down, not losing eye contact with him. She wanted to show him that she wasn't scared, even though she was petrified inside. His hand gripped her chin tightly, as she tried to pull away from him.

"Quit fighting me. You're not going to win." The three of them laughed, as they found it sickly entertaining torturing her. A small tear came down her face, and she tried to hold it in, but fear was taking over.

"Oh, don't cry. It'll be over in a few minutes." He smiled at her, moving in closer. The guy behind her was holding her arms tightly, as the one in front of her leaned in to kiss her. His hands ran around her waist. She could taste the alcohol on him, as she tried to pull away.

"I think we should go find her roommate to have some fun," the third guy said, pushing him aside to look at Sophie.

"My turn . . . "

She quickly kneed him in the stomach and pulled away from the guy holding her.

"Help!" she yelled, breaking free and taking off down the street.

She didn't get far before the first guy grabbed her again. He toppled her to the ground and held her securely underneath him.

"Now, you've pissed me off." He struck her once across the face. She was finished, and she didn't know what to do or how she was going to get free from this. It was three against one. She had no chance!

He reached for the button on her jeans, trying to undo them. She tried again to scream, but he covered her mouth immediately. He looked around to see if anyone had heard them, and that's when he noticed that his buddies were lying on the ground down the street from where Sophie took off.

"What the hell?" he said, looking around nervously.

Suddenly, he was ripped from on top of her and thrown onto the grass beside her. Her heart raced, as she scrambled to button up her jeans and get to her feet.

"You're gonna wish you never touched her," Nathan said, pulling the guy to his feet.

He gripped the guy by the shirt and punched him straight between the eyes, knocking him back to the ground. The blood slowly ran down his face, and somehow he managed to get back to his feet. He charged at Nathan in rage, but Nathan stood there with no fear, raised his hand, and instantly the guy was thrown against the fence, knocking him unconscious. He was furious and wanted to finish him off, but his attention was turned to Sophie when he heard her cry.

"Sophie, come here," he said, walking quickly over to her. He reached for her hands that covered her face from where the guy had hit her. But she trembled for a moment, covering her ears, as she didn't want to hear what she thought he might say. She didn't want to talk about this, and after everything that had just happened that night, she didn't want to see Nate, not right now. She was completely humiliated from all of this.

"Sophie, stop, come here, Sweetie. Come on." He slowly touched her wrists, pulling her hands down from her ears.

"You're safe, come here." He carefully wrapped his arms around her, as she tried to push away. She was freaking out.

Eventually, she gave in to him. He could feel her tears start to dampen his shirt. She was so small in his arms. He never wanted to let her go, not if he could keep her safe.

The scary thing was the fact that Nathan saw nothing of this attack coming. Normally, he knew what was going to happen before it did, but this time, it caught him off guard. He was scared for what was happening and wondered if this was because of his stepping into her life. Had he brought this on her?

The night he barged in on Sophie and Devon had changed their fate. It had to have, because now, he had no idea what was happening to her. He was angry with himself for being so stupid. But now, more importantly, he feared for Sophie's life.

Would this event change fate again, because he stepped in? There were so many thoughts running through Nate's mind, and it was driving him crazy. He remembered that the last time he messed up, it had cost him his life and the girl he loved.

He kissed the top of Sophie's head, thinking of Serena. There was no way he was going to let anything happen to this one, even if it meant him staying there every second of the day. He would defy the orders of Gabriel and whoever else that challenged him. He was not going to make the same mistake twice. He gently lifted Sophie into his arms, and they disappeared into the night.

22

Truth Behind the Dreams

The night air was cold against her wet face. She opened her eyes to the distant stars in the sky. The steam from the water clouded the air around her.

She jolted up from the water in a panic, confused by her surroundings. There was nothing but trees around her. It felt warm and relaxing, though, as if she was in a hot tub. It was not like the last time when she was fighting for her life and gasping for air.

Her clouded mind was joined by the warmth of the water and quickly pulled her into a haze. Normally, she would try to figure out what was going on and what her dreams meant, but this time, she didn't care. Her mind was a blank slate and she liked it. She began to forget everyone and everything in her life for that moment.

Her body melted down into the water, floating ever so slightly at the top. She tried hard to see the stars in the sky, but had little success. Her breaths then became slower, as she closed her eyes to the night.

"Sophie . . . " a familiar voice whispered. "Open your eyes . . . "

She could hardly hear him from the water that muffled her ears.

"Sophie," he said again.

Suddenly, she felt a chill and wrapped her arms around herself, keeping her eyes closed. The air blew stronger against her skin, as she began to shake.

She adjusted her eyes, as they slowly opened, and found herself lying in the grass, still drenched from the water that was now nowhere in sight. Her body was freezing in the night air, as she sat up.

There was something there—she could feel it—a strange presence lingering around her. It was dark and made her feel like there was nothing but emptiness inside her. She had never felt this before. A feeling of sadness, pain, sickness, and loss rushed through her veins.

"Sophie," another voice whispered. This time it was a woman's.

"Gram," she whispered out loud. She didn't know why her grandmother came to her mind, but she did, and it was not a good feeling.

"Sophie," the same voice said again quietly, but this time it was joined by a second. It was a young girl's voice. She thought she saw a figure of a woman in the distance.

Her eyes went to a blank stare, and she suddenly knew the emotions that she was feeling. She knew what was coming, and she feared it with all of her heart.

"Not yet," she whispered to the air. "It can't happen, not now. Please I can't take it." Her eyes glanced to the sky to search for that one bright star to plead. But the sky had become dark, and Sophie's body collapsed, as her eyes rolled back into her head. Her body hit the ground lifelessly, as the air continued to chill her damp skin.

His warm hand against her cheek calmed her instantly. She then felt his lips against her forehead. Warmth instantly surrounded her, as she was lifted into his arms. Her hands gripped his shirt tightly, as she kept her eyes closed, not ready to face reality.

When she opened her eyes, she was resting against his chest and covered by blankets that warmed her entirely. His arms held her closely. She never felt safer in her entire life than in that moment, lying by Nathan's side. She could feel the warmth of his quiet breaths against the top of her head.

Her throat was beginning to feel a little sore, as she coughed quietly.

"Soph," Nathan whispered to her. "Are you okay?"

She didn't answer him.

He glanced down at her, waiting for an answer, but she kept her face from him and didn't move from his chest. Gently, he adjusted himself from under her and moved until her eyes slowly met his.

"Hey," he whispered, tucking the hair behind her ears, and then running his hand down her face.

"Nate . . . " she managed to get out from her strained voice. "I think I know what's coming."

He didn't know what she was talking about and definitely couldn't let her know that fate had changed and that he couldn't see her future anymore. It would only scare her, so he smiled at her slightly, trying to look confident.

Small tears made their way down Sophie's cheeks and across her nose. He pulled her in against him, again holding her tightly. There was nothing he could say.

His mind raced in fear of what he didn't know and what might happen to her.

He'd decided right there in that second that he wouldn't be leaving her side anytime soon. Who knew when the archangels would step in again and what they would do, but he couldn't worry about that now. Every second he spent with her was important now to what would become of her, especially if he couldn't see what was coming.

He had to make sure she was safe at all times, no matter what. This had now become more dangerous than he ever imagined, for himself and for Sophie. He pulled the covers up closely, keeping her warm. She coughed a few more times before settling in and falling asleep for what was left of the night.

In the morning, the sun didn't shine through the window as it normally did. The sky was overcast and hid any sort of light behind its clouds. Sophie woke with a chill still in her body from the night before. Nathan was still there, asleep with his arms around her.

She tried to remember the horrible things that had happened the night before. She worried about Julie.

Why would she want to stay there after what they pulled and how they spoke to her? Their change in personality was totally degrading and completely out of left field. They had missed something. Something about the two of them wasn't right, but she and Julie never saw it until it was too late.

Maybe they were too caught up in the perfect idea of the two of them being happy with these boys. Maybe it was too fast. Maybe it was the perfect illusion from the world right now. Whatever it was that happened, it blinded the girls completely from reality.

Her throat still burned that morning. The chill from being in the rain had caught her too quickly, even with Nathan's attempts to keep her warm. A confusing thought came to her mind, as she rubbed her throat in pain. Why did Nathan take so long to come for her? He almost didn't come at all. Why would he let her take that beating and let that guy handle her so much before stepping in? He could see her future, couldn't he?

Normally, he would start to act weird before something bad happened and usually was right there when it did, to take care of her and help her. Was he sticking to his rules of letting what was supposed to happen, happen? But if he cared for her as much as he said he did, how could he sit and watch something like that happen?

A fiery sensation trickled up her throat and made her cough again.

"Sophie?" Nathan said, waking up to her coughing attack.

She turned to face him. He placed his hand on her forehead, and then against her cheek to check her temperature. Her skin was warm and flushed looking, and she was slowly burning up.

"We're gonna have to do something about that. Stay here for a moment," he said, attempting to get up.

"Nathan wait," she said, taking a hard gulp. It hurt so badly to swallow. Her hand gripped his wrist from moving away. She had so many questions to ask him and didn't know where to start.

"We'll talk in a second, Soph. Let me get you some medicine. You're burning up," he said, pulling away from her.

As he disappeared out of the room, images from the past night's dream flashed through her mind, reminding her of the fear she felt and what was still coming her way. She sat up instantly and searched for her phone, but it was nowhere in sight. She had it the night before, didn't she? In a panic, she slid herself across the bed to check the floor for her purse. It was there just slightly under her bed. She pulled it out and managed to sit up on the edge of the bed to search through it.

It was there, just barely. The battery was about to die, and there were about fifty messages left from Julie from the night before right up until morning. There were a few from Devon and Carter, too. As much as she worried about Julie, she ignored them all for a moment and searched her contacts to dial her grandmother's number. She waited, as the phone took a moment to connect. It rang once, and then died.

"Damn it!" she said, throwing the phone down on the bed. Her head dropped to her hands, as she felt the blood rush through her body.

The room was spinning and she began to sweat. She took a moment to try to regain her focus before standing up, but instantly fell to the ground on her first attempt.

"Sophie! What are you doing?" Nathan said, dropping everything to run to her side. He carefully helped her back into bed, and then pulled the covers up around her once again.

"I told you to stay here, crazy girl."

She stared at him, confused by the dizziness that had taken over her body. She tried to swallow again, but only choked.

Nathan quickly returned to the doorway to grab the bottle of water, medicine, and the spoon he had dropped after retrieving it from their kitchen drawer. He ripped the cap from the bottle of water and held it up to Sophie's mouth.

"Take a sip. It will help cool your throat before taking the medicine." She attempted to swallow the water, but even that hurt her throat.

"It's all right. Let's try the medicine," he said, pouring it slowly, making sure not to spill any off the spoon.

It was just as hard to get down, but she did it. He gave her two spoonfuls before closing the lid of the medicine and placing it on her nightstand.

"Tell me what you know, Nate," she said softly.

"Soph, never mind that now. Just rest."

"No. Nate, tell me." Her voice was serious. He looked at her nervously, pondering what to say. He had no idea of what her future held now. The only thing left that he had complete control of was the emotional part. He could still feel her emotions just as strongly as ever. That was the only thing he could go off.

Guardian angels had the unique talent of feeling a person's emotions the very second that they happened, and sometimes even moments before. He wondered if that would be good enough. That was how he had stopped the guy from the night before. He had felt the fear inside her and responded instantly.

But Sophie's emotions were always all over the place, now more than ever. They only clouded his mind with confusion.

"You know I can't . . . "

"Don't give me that. Tell me now, and get it over with," she insisted.

"Calm down, Soph. You need to rest."

"No, I don't. There's something coming. I can feel it and I know you know what it is. Please, Nate, just tell me. It feels horrible inside."

"I can't. I'm sorry."

She stared at him, disappointed with his effort to calm her nerves.

"Can you please plug in my phone on your way out?" she said, turning over to face the wall.

"Sure. But I'm not going anywhere." He grabbed the cell phone from her bed and after searching through her nightstand for the charger, plugged it in. He hated lying to her, but he had no choice. What was he supposed to say to her? He quietly closed the door behind him and headed out into the kitchen to make her some tea.

As the kettle came to a boil, he turned to get some milk from the fridge, but a tall figure blocked his way.

"What are you doing, Nathan?" Gabriel said, not impressed by the recent events. Nathan stood nervously before him, as he waited for an answer.

"I can't do it," Nathan said sadly. "I can't let someone like her go through all this pain. She doesn't deserve it, Gabriel. Isn't there some sort of rule that exempts people like her from all the shitty things that happen in life? I don't mean to defy your orders, but I feel like I'm doing the right thing. Please try to understand."

Gabriel stepped around Nathan and picked up the kettle from the counter.

"I don't have to understand, Nate." He walked over to the sink and slowly poured out the water and watched it run down the drain. He was serious and Nathan suddenly felt uneasy with the situation.

"But how do you know? Maybe it could be the right thing? Maybe . . . "

"Enough!" Gabriel raised his voice, cutting Nate off.

"But what if . . . " Nathan urged back, but was instantly slammed against the fridge. Gabriel stood powerfully in front of him, his hand gripped tightly around Nathan's neck.

"Why do you insist on pushing this matter? Why do you insist on defying me over and over again? This is it! It's your last warning, Nathan!

If you push me one more time, I'll clip your wings and finish you as one of us."

Nathan struggled at the strength of his hand, trying to catch his breath that was being cut off.

"You know what becomes of the ones that defy his orders, don't you? Are you prepared to lose everything for a silly girl?" Gabriel stared into his eyes, knowing the hurt that he had just inflicted into his mind. "Choose wisely, your time's running out."

Then, he was gone.

Nathan gasped for air, gripping the counter for balance. The archangels were now all over him, watching his every move. Shaken up from his encounter with Gabriel, he reached for the kettle again to refill it, but was interrupted by the sound of keys that suddenly clicked and unlocked the front door.

The door crept open slowly, as Julie peered her head in to see if Sophie was around. She looked nervous, as she closed the door behind her. Nathan had already disappeared out of sight when she walked by the kitchen and headed for Sophie's room.

She knocked on the door and waited for Sophie to answer. After getting no response, Julie turned the knob quietly, in case Sophie was asleep, and peeked in the room.

"Soph?"

"What?" Sophie answered quietly from under the covers.

"Hey, I was worried about you. How come you never answered your messages?"

"My phone's dead," she said, giving her quick short answers. She wasn't in a talking mood right now.

"Okay, how did you get home? Are you okay?" Julie said, stepping closer to her.

"It doesn't matter, I'm here."

"Well, Devon was trying to get a hold of you all night. You should call him back."

"Why would I?"

"Because he cares."

"No, he doesn't and you're stupid for thinking they do. Don't be a dumb girl, Jules. They played us."

"I don't think they actually played us. I think the situation got a little confused."

"Look, can you please just leave me alone. I don't feel well."

Julie stood there feeling badly about the whole situation.

"Um, sure. I'll talk with you later, then. Get some sleep."

After Julie left the room, Nathan reappeared beside her. "She's only worried about you."

"I don't care," Sophie said sharply.

He didn't like the way she was responding. She had been upset before, but this time, something was totally different. She meant everything she said. He could feel it.

Between Jake, her family, Natalie, Devon, Carter, and now Julie, all of it was too much. This dark cloud that was now hovering over her every move had blocked every positive glimpse she had to turning herself around.

Nathan tried to think of some positive words to say to her, but nothing came to his mind. He himself had messed up, too, and couldn't bear to tell her what had happened. It would only add to everything that was already on her plate, especially what happened with Gabriel.

He spent the rest of the day watching her every move, which wasn't too hard because she never left the room or even got out of bed. He tried to carry on a conversation with her, but she continued to ignore him or gave him short answers.

Julie reattempted to talk to her, too, but Sophie pretended to sleep. She even turned her phone off while it was charging, so that she didn't have to hear those annoying phone calls from people she didn't care to talk to.

Nathan continued to bring her tea and medicine, using every remedy he could to try to heal her pain and make her feel better. It was the only contact she made with him.

Around 7:00 p.m., Sophie awoke to the sound of music playing softly on her stereo. Nathan sat comfortably on the floor against her bed, writing something in a small book.

"What are you writing?" she asked, leaning over to see.

"Just something I've been working on for a while now. How are you feeling?"

"A little better, thanks," she said, embarrassed of how she had been treating him.

He looked over at her for a moment, trying to choose the right words to say.

"Sophie, you can't stay like this," he said, taking her hand carefully.

"I know. Just let me figure things out, all right?" She squeezed his hand.

Just then, her phone went off.

"I thought I turned that off?" she said confused, as she reached for it.

"You did, but I turned it back on." He smiled at her sadly. "Answer it." He knew what this was about or was supposed to be about. He would soon find out if everything he once knew about her future had changed.

"Hello?"

"Dad? What's wrong?" Her voice became worried. "When did this happen? Is she okay? . . . No, I know. I'll pack right now. Just let me know, okay? Bye." Sophie hung up the phone and carefully placed it back on the nightstand. She looked at Nate sadly.

"It's Gram. She's in the hospital."

"I know, sweetie."

"My dad's buying me a ticket home, and he's gonna call me back with the details. I gotta pack now and be ready."

She pulled the covers back slowly and slid to the edge of the bed, and then sat there for a moment, as her dream once again haunted her mind. She looked at Nathan, trying to smile confidently, but the hurt was pushing through. She fell down to him, wrapping her arms around his neck tightly.

"You're not alone, Soph. Remember I'm here, okay?" He leaned back to let her go, but she pulled him back in.

"I'm scared, Nate."

"I know. Try not to think about it right now. I'll pack your things. You still need to rest." He leaned Sophie back against the bed and grabbed a blanket from the end of her bed to cover her with. Then, he proceeded to her closet to pull out her suitcase and began to pack for her. He had watched her so closely over the last few years that he felt comfortable choosing her wardrobe and knowing what she would need. He still knew her better than anyone else.

After her bag was packed, she headed to the bathroom to have a shower and get cleaned up. She didn't have all her strength back, but she had enough for a few moments to pull herself together. A hot shower was just what she needed.

Nathan stayed close by the door in case any of those depressing feelings came back to her mind. He didn't trust her enough to leave her alone. Although he gave her privacy in the shower and getting changed, he kept the conversation going through the door, making sure she was still there.

Her phone went off again just as she finished getting ready. She quickly ran to it and answered.

"Dad?" She said out of breath. "Ya, I'm ready. Okay, I'll head to the airport now." She continued to listen to the orders her dad gave her, as Nathan watched quietly. Before she said good-bye, she asked her dad one more question nervously.

"Dad? Am I going to make it in time?"

Nathan could feel her emotions taking over his body. He knew how this was supposed to end, but wasn't sure if it had been altered. She hung up the phone and grabbed her bag.

"Sophie," Nathan said, stopping her. "You'll make it," he said confidently to her. At least he hoped she would.

She smiled slightly at him, and then headed out to the front door.

"Sophie? What's going on? Where are you going?" Julie asked, as she passed her bedroom.

"It's my gram. She's in the hospital. I have to go now."

"Oh my god, Soph, I'm so sorry. Is she going to be okay?"

"I don't know. I'll call you later."

"Okay, no worries. Everything's going to be okay, don't worry," Julie said, trying to sound positive. "I'll let your agent know what's happened in case she's looking for you."

"Thanks," Sophie said, running to the front door. "Oh, and Julie?"

"Ya?"

"I'm sorry for getting mad at you. I'm angry at Devon and at Carter for how they treated us. I just don't want you to end up like me. I've been played by guys before and it's just . . . "

"It's fine, Soph, I get it. You were just looking out for me. I know. I was just trying to see the positive in it. But unfortunately, there isn't anything positive there at all. I get it now."

Sophie smiled at her, as Julie walked up and hugged her tightly.

"Now go!" she said, pushing her out the door.

Sophie quickly hurried to the sky train to head for the airport. The flight was fast only because she could barely keep her eyes open and practically slept the entire way. She woke up to the sound of the plane touching the runway. Her father was already at the airport, waiting to pick her up. After collecting her bag, they headed straight for the hospital.

The drive seemed to take forever and her dream from the night before still haunted her mind. It was a warning, wasn't it? Was her grandmother saying goodbye? She was sure that she heard her voice calling to her. She tried to remember the details of her dream some more, as she popped in a cough lozenge for her throat. It felt a little better, thanks to Nathan's persistence, but she still had a mean cough.

She grabbed her makeup compact from her purse, and then pulled down the mirror on the passenger side to fix herself up a bit. Her eyes had dark circles under them and looked tired from all her crying and lack of sleep. As she patted some foundation powder under her eyes, she noticed a figure behind her in the mirror. She dropped her makeup and stared in fear of the girl sitting behind her.

"Sophie, you all right?" her dad asked.

She didn't answer, and she couldn't move. Who was this girl in the mirror? She kept her eyes glued to hers, as the girl stared at her and smirked ever so slightly, and then disappeared.

Sophie instantly flung around to check the back seat.

"Sophie? What are you doing?" her dad asked again.

She looked at her dad, and then back again to the seat behind her.

"What the hell?" she said to herself.

"What's wrong?" her dad said, pulling into the hospital parking lot.

She glanced one more time into her mirror, but the girl was still gone.

"It's nothing, I'm fine," she managed to get out nervously.

"Pull yourself together, Sophie, and remember what I told you. She's in rough shape and I want you to be prepared."

"I know, Dad," she said, getting out of the car, while sliding her cardigan on.

They entered the hospital and headed down the long hallway to the elevators. It was a slow ride up to the sixth floor critical care unit. They made their way down another long hallway, and as they did, Sophie glanced into the rooms one by one as she passed. There was so much sadness on the faces of the people visiting their loved ones.

As they turned the corner, she saw her two brothers, standing in the hallway. She felt herself become sick to her stomach, as she reached the doorway. She glanced inside, but the curtain was pulled around the bed, as someone was in there with her already. Her younger brother hugged her tightly. "Glad you made it, Soph," he said sadly.

She turned to her older brother, and he smiled at her slightly. She hadn't seen him in a long time. She hugged him, trying not to cry.

A man and woman came out of the room and gestured for Sophie to enter.

"She's asking for you," her aunt said.

Sophie took a deep breath and slowly walked into the room. The lady in the bed beside her was very old and her breathing was short. Sophie quietly walked past her to the second bed and stepped through the curtain.

Her grandmother was lying there, breathing deeply and slowly. The sound of fluid in her lungs rippled through each of her breaths. Her eyes were closed, she looked pale, and her arms were bruised from the needles they tried to use on her very thin veins.

She didn't look like the grandmother she had always known. She was always so full of life, never missing out on anything that was happening around her or to any of her kids or grandchildren. Sophie walked up to the side of the bed and sat in the chair just to her right. She carefully touched her hand. It was so cold. She looked like a completely different person.

"Gram," she whispered, and then waited for a response. "Grandma."

Her grandmother's eyes flickered slowly and then opened. Those once bright green eyes were now a soft grey, as they had lost their colour completely.

"Hi, Hun," she said weakly.

"Hey, how are you?" Sophie said sadly. She knew that was a dumb question, but she didn't know what else to say.

"Oh, I've been better. How's Vancouver?"

"Gram, there's other things that are more important right now. Don't worry about me and my silly life."

"Your life isn't silly, Sophie. I'm so proud of you. You're so brave, and you always go after what you want in life, which is more than most people can say they've done. You're a survivor. You know that?"

Sophie smiled at her, listening to the words that warmed her heart. She shook her head "Yes" without answering.

"Keep doing what you're doing, Sophie. Promise me?"

"I need you, Gram, I really need you. You have to get better. What can I do?"

"Sophie, you're here. That's all I need."

"I should've been here sooner. I should've been helping you, but I've been all over the world, chasing crazy dreams instead of helping you."

"Sweetie, it's not your job to watch over me. I'm a grown woman, and it's your turn to live your life. You do more for me than you know."

"You always remember my birthday and take me places when you're here. We watch movies and play cards and even have adventures that no one will ever believe we've had. You remember all the fun times we've had together, don't you? We have a special connection, you and I, always."

"I still miss you all the time," Sophie said, wiping her eyes.

"I miss you, too, but you can't stop your life. You better keep going, doing what you're doing or I'll be so mad at you!"

"It's so hard, though."

"The best things in life aren't easy to get. Everything happens for a reason. Remember that."

"I know. I just wonder if I can actually do it."

"You can and you will. I know it."

Sophie stood up and leaned over to hug her gram carefully.

"I love you so much. You're the most important person in the world to me," she whispered in her ear.

"I love you, too," her gram answered back, gripping Sophie's shirt tightly.

Just then, the nurse came in.

"Hi, sweetie, I need to check your grandmother over. Can you give me a moment?"

"Sure." She stood up from her gram and smiled at her, still holding her hand.

"I'm fine, dear, I'll see you in a sec."

Sophie slowly released her hand and stepped away from the bed. As she left the room, she felt a chill run down her spine.

"Soph, have you eaten?" her younger brother asked.

"Um, no."

"Let's all go down to the café to eat something, while the nurse is doing her check-up. She'll need a few moments. Come on," he said, putting his arm around her and leading her down the hallway.

She hated the idea of leaving her for any amount of time just in case, but on the other hand, she couldn't go inside right now anyway and she was pretty hungry. She hadn't eaten since the night before. She walked with her brothers and father down to the café, and they each got something to eat. The smell of the hospital almost made her sick to her stomach. She hated everything about being there.

After eating, they made their way back up to her grandmother's floor. It was the most time any of them had spent together. It was nice having her father and brothers in the same place, especially at this moment, to be there for each other.

Hours went by and Gram's breathing got slower, and the sound of the fluid in her lungs became louder. Her heart was too weak to drain her lungs of the fluid, and she now needed assistance from a machine to breathe.

Her family filled the room, and just outside in the hallway, more friends and family waited. Everyone was staying close. They wanted her grandmother to know that they were all there and that she was loved and not alone.

As weak as Gram was, her face slightly lit up each time she saw a member of her family come in to see her. She always loved being surrounded by her family. She tried so hard to keep everyone in touch and stay in on what was happening in everyone's lives. It was a hard job with so many kids, grandchildren, and great grandchildren, but she always managed to do so.

They rotated in four at a time, trying to not overwhelm her. Sophie took a break and went to the end of the hall to sit down. She stared out the window. She couldn't believe the whole day had already passed and night had come once again. It seemed like only moments before that she had flown in on the redeye flight.

She felt her eyelids become heavy again. It was hard to fight the sleep that was so very badly needed, especially since she wasn't feeling well in the first place. She hadn't noticed that her coughing had become less and less, since arriving at the hospital. Still trying to fight exhaustion, she leaned her head back, getting as comfortable as she could in the wooden chair. Instantly, she dozed off.

The sun started to shine through the windows, as she walked out into the garden. It was warm and smelt like summer. Suddenly, she saw what looked like herself, walking a few feet ahead. At least she thought it was herself, but something was different. The little dog that had appeared before in her dreams was there walking alongside of her once again. But there was something wrong here. She studied closely from behind. She was taller and her clothes were different.

Sophie quickly tried to catch up to the person she thought was herself in front of her, when suddenly, just as she reached her, the girl spun around, staring her in the eyes. She was beautiful, but definitely not Sophie. The little dog jumped at Sophie, excited to see her, but Sophie's eyes were frozen on the girl in front of her.

The girl's face was calm and she didn't say a word. A small feeling of fear filled Sophie's body, as the girl moved closer to her, and then leaned in to whisper in her ear. She couldn't understand the words coming out of her mouth, as they were too quiet.

"Sophie," a familiar voice said. But Sophie didn't move, as the girl stood face to face with her.

"Sophie, wake up," the voice said again. This time, the girl leaned back from her with a smile on her face, and then disappeared.

"Wake up, Soph!" her brother said, shaking her once again. This time, Sophie's eyes shot open to the sound of his voice.

"What? I'm awake, what's happening?" she said startled.

"The nurse said we should go see Gram. She doesn't think it will be long now."

"Long now? Does she mean that she's . . . "

"Let's just go, Soph, come on," her brother said, helping her up.

"What time is it?" she asked, as they made their way to her room.

"It's 2:30 a.m."

"Really? I dozed off for longer than I thought," she said worried.

They entered the room. Everyone else was already in there. Family surrounded her grandmother's bed with tears in their eyes. The room was filled with love and Sophie could feel happiness and sadness, running through every inch of her body. She sat on the arm of her brother's chair next to her gram's bed and took her hand. No one spoke, as the same feelings were running through everyone's hearts.

It was amazing to Sophie how everyone came together for this one person. Even the people who hadn't spoken in what seemed like forever were together like nothing had happened. And it was all because of Gram. The minutes passed, as they watched Gram's breath become longer and less often until finally it was silent and the last breath had passed.

A numbness came over Sophie's body and a hard lump lodged in her throat, as she tried to swallow. She didn't cry at that moment. She couldn't. Her emotions had shut off. The night had become very silent and calm all in that one moment.

By the time they got home, it was close to 4:30 a.m. All of them climbed silently into bed with sadness in their hearts. A feeling of emptiness filled Sophie's soul, as her eyes stared at the ceiling. She could hear her breathing and wondered where Gram's soul had disappeared. Probably to Heaven, she thought. Her Gram believed so much that she was sure that was the only place she could be.

She thought of the many times that Gram had told her that she was praying for her and that she should do the same. But Sophie wasn't sure what she believed in yet, even after meeting Nathan. It was true that he was a guardian angel, but how come bad things still happened if there were angels here on Earth? She just couldn't understand it.

Angels were good, right? Weren't they supposed to keep bad things from happening to you? Sophie turned over in her bed and closed her eyes, but she couldn't sleep. So, she decided to text Julie and tell her what had happened. She didn't hear back from her, so she texted Charlotte. Instantly, she answered back.

It was nice to have someone to talk to about this, even if it was just a few words. A few minutes later, Sophie set her phone on the nightstand and tried once again to go back to sleep.

The next two days flew by, as Sophie was busy helping her family with her grandmother's wake and making arrangements for the funeral. When the day came for the funeral, it seemed surreal. Sophie got out of the shower and dressed herself in black pants and a black top, and then dried her hair. She took her time in the bathroom, doing her makeup and making herself look just right before heading back into her room to put on her usual perfume.

When she was ready, she headed down the stairs to meet up with her father and brothers at the front door. They were just about to leave when a figure stood on the porch in front of them. She couldn't see who it was past her brothers.

Finally, her dad turned to her and said, "Your friend is here, Soph. You guys can ride with your brothers. I'm going with your aunt."

As they headed down the steps, Sophie was left at the front door with Nathan, standing in front of her in a black suit. She felt her heart sink into her stomach. She smiled at him with relief, as he held out his hand for her to take.

She didn't ask him any questions and she didn't care how or why he was there. She was just grateful that he was. He opened the back door of the car for her to slide in, and then followed in behind. He held her hand tightly the entire way.

When everything was finished and Gram had been lowered into the ground, Sophie still lingered until she was the last person there. Her brothers went home with her aunt and father, but Sophie insisted on staying behind for just a little while longer. She stood by the gravestone still in disbelief of what had happened, with Nathan standing close behind.

In her hands were a couple of Spider Mums. She had always given her grandmother these flowers whenever she visited. They always lived for what seemed like forever. She placed them down on the grave perfectly against the stone. She had nothing to say, because there was nothing that was unsaid between them.

She thought about the promises she had made to her grandmother and about how quickly life had changed in these last few years. She wondered what would become of her and if she could keep the promises that she had made to Gram.

"She loved you very much, Sophie," Nathan said, walking up behind her.

"I know."

"You're going to be fine. I promise," he said, turning her to face him.

"Why haven't I cried, Nathan? It's like I'm so sad inside, but it's hidden behind this wall, and I feel nothing on the other side of it. What's wrong with me?"

"Nothing, Soph, it just hasn't sunk in yet. There's nothing wrong with you, crazy girl," he said, trying to lighten the mood. She stared at the ground, not really listening to what he said.

"Come here, sweetie," he said, pulling her in and wrapping his arms around her.

"Now what, Nate?" she whispered quietly against him.

"Now, you try to do what you've been trying to do all along. Follow your dreams and continue on with your life. Just as you promised Gram."

"But what if I can't? What if I just can't do it? Maybe I'm lying to myself and maybe I need to forget about all of this."

"You know that's not the answer, Soph. You're just confused right now. Give it some time. You'll see."

"But what if . . . "

"Sophie, stop. Just relax. You just had a lot happen here in a short amount of time, and you need to let it set in before moving on. Otherwise, you're fooling yourself."

She stopped at the thought of that and took a breath. "Did you mean what you said, Nate?"

"I mean everything I say, Soph," he said, laughing.

"Did you mean it when you said that you were going to be here for me? Always? You promise you're not going anywhere?"

He pulled back from her to look her in the eyes. "I'm right here. Always."

She smiled at him and then hugged him again.

"Come on, let's go home," he said, taking her hand and leading her to the car.

That night, Nathan stayed at her place and had dinner with her family. Sophie had planned to bring her car back to Vancouver and Nathan was going along for the ride. This sold her father on the idea of her driving back alone.

That evening, Sophie lay in bed next to Nathan, staring at the ceiling. She had a long drive ahead of her, but she just couldn't sleep. A buzzing sound went off under her pillow. She reached under and pulled out her phone. There was a text message from Julie. It read:

"SO SORRY ABOUT YOUR GRAM. I CAN'T WAIT FOR YOU TO GET BACK HERE. NATALIE'S DRIVING ME CRAZY! SHE HEARD ABOUT YOUR GRAM FROM CHARLOTTE AND FEELS LIKE SHE NEEDS TO BE HERE WHEN YOU COME BACK. BUT I KICKED HER OUT. SHE IS BUGGING THE CRAP OUT OF ME. I CAN'T STAND THAT GIRL!"

Sophie texted back with a sigh.

"NO WORRIES, JULES. I'M ON MY WAY BACK TOMORROW. I'LL BE DRIVING. SEE YOU SOON!"

She thought for sure that the roommate drama was over, but apparently not. Nathan moved his arm across Sophie's waist, holding her tightly. It was so weird to have him there again. She couldn't believe all that he had done to risk himself, just so he could be there for her through this whole thing.

She was afraid for him. What if Gabriel saw? He had already warned her. What would he say to Nathan now stepping into her life again and sleeping in her bed? Did Nate know what he was doing?

She slid her hand up to hold his against her waist. His face was so calm next to hers. She wondered if he dreamed, too.

His dark brown hair hung across his face and covered his eyes. She carefully reached over and brushed his hair to one side, so she could see his face completely. Quietly, she turned to face him, trying hard not to wake him. He was so beautiful to her. He had sharp features and a body that was all muscle.

His eyes were what caught her the most. They had this feeling of warmth in them and on most days were covered by his hair that hung just slightly over them. Their faces were close, as Sophie watched him sleep.

She wondered once again what it would be like to kiss Nathan. What was going to happen between them? She figured by now with all that had happened between them and with the warnings Gabriel had left them, that there was no way Nathan was getting his second chance. They had to have crossed the line.

This made her sad to think that she had ruined his one chance for happiness. If it weren't for her, he would've done his job normally and maybe would be one step closer to finding the answer he wanted. She moved slightly back from his face, and then closed her eyes and went to sleep.

23

Fallen Angels

A voice said softly, "Sophie." It seemed to echo in the air.

Sophie blinked her eyes a few times, trying to see through the darkness. She recognized the voice this time. It was the voice of that girl she kept seeing. Who was this girl who was suddenly appearing in her dreams?

"Sophie," she said again. Sophie looked around, but couldn't see anyone, as it was too dark.

"Who are you? What do you want?" Sophie yelled, starting to get nervous. She didn't know if she should fear this girl or what.

"Hello?" she said again, but the girl didn't answer. She could feel a presence around her and it moved quickly. Suddenly, the girl appeared behind her, gripping Sophie's arms tightly with her delicate hands. Sophie froze in fear, as she had never had contact with someone in her dreams other than Nate.

"What do you want?" she whispered.

The girl moved slowly around to face Sophie, not releasing her grip on her. She stared at the ground, not making eye contact. Her long hair covered her face, as she whispered to herself, "Sophie. Sophie. Sophie!" She then screamed, "Sophie!" But when she screamed her name that time, there was a duel voice. It was Nathan's. She instantly woke up to Nathan looking over her.

"Soph, are you all right? What was that dream you were having?"

Sophie lay there in shock for a moment. "I don't know."

"What do you mean? You don't know? Sophie, look at me! I couldn't see anything that you were dreaming! I mean nothing! I could feel your emotions and I knew there was something happening, but I couldn't get to you!" Nathan looked at her with fear in his eyes. He had always been able to see what Sophie dreamt. But this dream was different, and he couldn't get in. He had no control at all.

Sophie still didn't answer him, as she slowly sat up.

"Sophie, tell me what happened!" he insisted.

"I don't know, Nate, I can't remember," she lied. She really could remember, but she wasn't sure if she should tell Nate. It would only worry him.

"Try, Soph. Don't you understand? If I can't see what's happening, I can't protect you." He touched her face gently, making her bring her attention to him.

She raised her hand to hold his.

"I'm fine, Nate. It was just a silly dream. I promise. I'll tell you if something's wrong, okay?"

He looked at her unconvinced, but let it go for now. "You have to let me protect you."

"I know," she said.

He leaned in and hugged her tightly. As he pulled back, he stopped close to her face. His nose gently touched hers, as she closed her eyes. His scent made every nerve in her body tremble, as he hovered close to her lips.

"We should go. We have a long drive," he said, pulling away.

Sophie sighed and breathed again, as he stepped away and got out of bed. She wanted to kiss him so badly.

"I've already packed your car up, so you just need to get ready."

"Okay, I'll be ready in fifteen minutes," she said, sliding out of bed.

They packed their last few things in the car and said good-bye to her family. Her father was pretty impressed by Nathan and his charming skills. Even her brothers got along with him. She found it pretty entertaining that her family was interacting with someone who wasn't really there—if they only knew what was really happening in her life.

This only proved to her more that her family really didn't know her. It was like two different people living two different lives. One girl was the silly little daughter and sister who kept her head in the clouds. The other was this stranger whom no one had met—the girl that horrible things happened to and the girl who was surrounded by angels.

Then, she thought for a moment about Gram and how much she really knew her. No one in the world knew her better than Gram, except for Nate. Gram would've really liked him. She wondered if Nate could see her or knew how she was. Maybe at some point, she would ask him. But not now, as there was too much for them to deal with, and the reality of Gram's death hadn't sunk in yet. They waved good-bye and pulled out of the driveway.

Because ordinary people couldn't see Nate, Sophie had to do all the driving. Apparently, he could only make himself seen by those in Sophie's immediate life. But he kept her busy talking, making sure not to let her fall asleep. Around 9:00 p.m. on the first night, Sophie pulled into a truck stop to take a break and get some food. After getting her food and stocking the car up with munchies, she pulled to the side of the parking lot to take a rest.

"Get some sleep, Soph. You have another day of driving ahead of you."

He passed her a pillow and unfolded a blanket they had in the back seat, and covered her.

"Thank you for everything." She smiled at him. He leaned his seat back, getting comfortable and rested his hands behind his head. He stayed awake the entire time, as she quickly fell into a deep sleep.

What seemed like moments later, she awoke to Nathan driving. She leaned up in her seat to look around. It was raining pretty hard out, and there was a chill in the car.

"Nate? You're driving?" she asked.

"Ya, I decided to let you sleep more. It's fine, it's early enough that no one will notice and we're not near any city, so it's all good."

"Okay, thanks," she said confused. "Can you turn on the heat? It's so cold in here."

But he didn't, and he continued to drive. Sophie reached for the knob to turn on the heat, but Nathan's hand stopped her just as she touched it.

"Don't touch," he said.

She stared at him, thrown off by his cold words. "Nate, I'm cold," she said quietly.

"I said don't touch," he repeated, while shooting her a stern glance. His eyes were different. They weren't their normal colour. They had a more greenish tint to them. They weren't Nate's eyes. Sophie reached one more time for the heat, ignoring his words.

A hand grabbed Sophie's immediately, throwing it back against her.

"You!" Sophie screamed, seeing the girl from her dreams in the seat beside her.

The girl stepped on the pedal and the car sped up. Sophie grabbed the door, bracing herself, as the car made it's way up to one hundred, then one twenty. It was too rainy out to be driving at that speed, and on these country roads, it was a definite death trap.

"What are you doing? Stop the car!" she screamed.

"What do you think you're doing? You're messing everything up," the girl said calmly.

Sophie held tightly to the door, her body tensing up. "What are you talking about?"

The girl looked at her, shaking her head. "So naive. You're going to fall and you're taking him with you."

"Who?" Sophie said, shutting her eyes in fear, as the car swerved across the road.

She screamed in fear, as it flew off the road into the soggy grass and finally came to a screeching halt. Sophie was thrown against the dashboard, knocking herself out.

Seconds later, she felt a tight grip on the back of her head. The girl leaned in closely with her right hand tangled tightly in Sophie's hair. "I won't let you make him fall," she whispered in rage.

Sophie shook in fear, as her head stayed pinned to the dashboard. She closed her eyes, as the tears fell down. The grip loosened on the back of her head and soon felt like it was calmly stroking her hair.

"Wake up please, Sophie," Nathan said worried.

She opened her eyes and turned her head to Nathan.

"Soph, you scared me to death. I've been trying to wake you for the last half hour."

She rubbed her head where it had been smashed against the dashboard, or so she thought.

"Ouch," she said in pain.

"Sophie! You're bleeding!" he said, grabbing her face to examine her. He brushed her hair back to look her over completely.

"Sweetie, you have to tell me what's going on here. You're really starting to freak me out. All I saw was you sleeping, and then, the next moment, you threw yourself against the steering wheel like you were in an accident. I thought it knocked you unconscious!"

"I was, Nate. I was in an accident. My car went off the road into the grass and hit something!" she said trembling. "Someone was driving . . . a girl. I don't know who she is and this isn't the first time I've seen her."

Her hands shook, as she tried to calm herself down. She knew she had to tell Nathan everything now, because whoever that girl was, she was trying to kill her and she knew about Nate. She had to be one of the archangels coming for him.

"Nate, I'm so sorry I didn't tell you before. I think she's an angel. She's mad at me for making you defy Gabriel's orders. She has to be an archangel. Nate, they're coming for us. I know it."

"Sophie, angels don't normally attack humans. At least, I don't think so, but she did come in your dreams . . ."

He paused in thought for a moment. "I hate that I can't see into your dreams when this happens."

"She said I was going to fall and that I was taking you with me."

"What?" he said quietly.

"What am I doing to you, Nate?" she said worried.

"Nothing, Soph, I make my own choices. You're not doing anything to me all right?"

"Nathan, promise me."

"I promise. Everything's going to be fine. We're going to be fine," He said nervously, opening the glove box to grab some napkins to clean up her wound. When he turned back to face her, he froze, dropping the napkins from his hands.

"What?" Sophie said.

He carefully brushed her hair away from her face again to check her wound that wasn't bleeding any more. In fact, it wasn't there at all.

Sophie touched her forehead and felt no pain. She tilted the rearview mirror down to look at herself.

"What the . . . " She glanced back at Nathan. He was at a loss for words, just as she was.

"Come on, let's keep moving. We shouldn't linger," he said, sitting back in his seat and pulling it into an upright position.

Sophie did as he said and threw her pillow and blanket into the back seat, and then started up the car. They drove for a few hours, not speaking. They both were scared to ask any questions, because they feared the answers that might come out.

It was raining, just as it was in Sophie's dream that day. She drove with full concentration on the road, as Nathan gazed out the window in deep thought.

They stopped only once for an afternoon snack and to gas up. Sophie asked for the key to the bathroom, and then headed around back. She unlocked the door to the small bathroom that was decorated in a cottage-like theme. She looked at herself in the mirror. The bags under her eyes hadn't cleared. In fact, they looked worse.

She sighed, pulling out some makeup from her purse. She heard her phone go off, as she reached inside. It was a text message from Julie:

"HOW FAR ARE YOU? I JUST GOT INTO IT WITH NAT AGAIN! I CAN'T TAKE HER ANYMORE! I HAVE TOO MUCH TO DEAL WITH ALREADY. I DON'T KNOW IF I CAN MAKE IT UNTIL YOU GET HOME."

Sophie read the message again, confused by what it said. What did Julie mean by she might not make it until she got home? She quickly texted her back.

"I'LL BE THERE BY LATE AFTERNOON TOMORROW. JUST HANG IN THERE, PLEASE. WE'LL TALK ABOUT IT WHEN I GET THERE. I'M HURRYING."

This was all she needed to worry about right now—Julie and Natalie. There were bigger things happening, things that could kill her. They were more important than Julie and Natalie's stupid fight.

Sophie reached back into her bag to grab a comb. She ran it through her hair a few times, making herself a little more presentable before shoving it back into her purse. She rubbed the sides of her temples, messaging them, hoping to relieve the stress that filled her head. She closed her eyes, taking deeps breaths.

When she opened them, the room was dark. Her eyes shuffled around the room in fear. She reached for the wall, trying to find the light switch. Just as she did, it flicked on, and before her stood the girl from her dreams. Sophie jumped back in fear.

"You shouldn't have opened your mouth," she said quietly, and then lunged at her, knocking Sophie back against the bathroom doors. She struggled, as the girl pinned her back.

"Nate," she tried to scream, but the grip on her throat was too strong. The girl ripped her from the stall door and flung her to the ground, as if she were a rag doll. Sophie slid across the floor, hitting her head against the wall. She scrambled to her feet, trying to run for the door, but the girl cut her off. Sophie stopped just before her, trembling with fear.

"Please, just let me go," she begged. The girl stood there with a smirk on her face, as Sophie dropped to the ground. She knew she wasn't going to win this. There was nothing she could do. The girl walked over to her slowly, kneeled down in front of her, and grabbed her by the chin.

"I won't let him fall." The girl's nails dug into Sophie's skin, as she held her in place. Tears ran down her face, as she closed her eyes, thinking this was it.

Suddenly, there was a flash of light. She could hear loud horrifying sounds around her. She covered her ears in fear. "Nate," she whispered to herself, hoping he could feel her emotions.

Then, it happened. The lights went out and everything was silent. She breathed quietly, scared to make any sound.

"I warned you before, young one. Yet, you insist on defying me." The sound of Gabriel's voice made her nervous, but calmed her, all at the same time. She didn't know which would be worse, seeing Gabriel or that girl. A small light glowed beneath them, as he suddenly appeared from the darkness in front of her.

"Gabriel . . ."

"I'm going to take him from you."

"No please!" she begged, grabbing his hand desperately. "I'm sorry. I'm so sorry."

"There is something very dark following you," he said, glaring at her. "Tell me, why is it that Nathan cannot see it?"

"I don't know," she said, trembling. "What is it?"

His eyes stared into hers, as he understood now that Nathan and Sophie couldn't see what was right in front of them.

"You don't know? Interesting," he said with a smirk on his face. "This will be very interesting to see how this plays out."

Just then, Nathan flicked on the light and appeared behind them. "Gabriel!"

Gabriel glanced over his shoulder. "There you are," he said helping Sophie to her feet.

Nathan stood there, wanting to run to Sophie, but scared of how Gabriel would react. He could feel the horror she had just gone through.

"Nathan, why is it that you're just getting here now?" he asked politely. "Could it be that you cannot see into her future anymore?"

Sophie's eyes shot to Nathan in fear. "Is that true, Nate?"

He looked at her, and then back at Gabriel. He finally shook his head, "Yes. I'm so sorry, Soph."

"It's because you have stepped too much into her life. You have become a reality to her now."

Sophie's eyes froze on Nathan.

"I can still watch over her, I can still . . . "

"No, you can't. You didn't even see what was just happening to her until it was too late. It's fortunate for you that I stepped in. You almost lost her, Nathan."

"Thank you, Gabriel. I am grateful for your help," Nathan said, lowering his head.

"I'm not helping, and I will not stand for those who defy his orders and show themselves in this way. It is a disgrace to us and to him. The Fallen will be taken down one by one until they are all gone. It's only a matter of time before we end her."

"Who?" Nate asked confused.

Gabriel looked back at Sophie, as she trembled in fear of what he was about to say.

Nate's eyes shifted to Sophie's, as Gabriel walked over to him.

"This is very interesting," he said and then he was gone.

"Nate," Sophie cried. He quickly ran to her, pulling her into him.

"I'm sorry. I should've been here sooner," he said, holding her close, shaken by the thought of almost not making it there in time.

"Are you all right? Let me see you." He held her face gently, checking her over. There were a few bruises and scrapes, but nothing major. Her head hurt a lot from where she had hit it against the wall, and this time, the wounds were really there. He took her by the hand and led her out to the car.

The sun was just starting to set, as Nate took over the wheel. Sophie lay quietly in the passenger seat beside him. He couldn't figure out what had happened. Why had Gabriel let him go? Why was he there in the first place? The feelings he was getting from Sophie were horrifying.

Was Gabriel the one inflicting this upon Sophie? He couldn't be, because angels never attack humans. If anything, Gabriel would come for Nathan. He glanced over at Sophie, as she fought sleep.

"Keep your eyes open. Soph. Don't fall asleep," he said, touching her face gently, while keeping one hand on the wheel.

"I'm not," she said quietly.

"It's very important that you stay awake. I have to have you in my sight at all times. If you fall asleep, I can't protect you."

He continued to drive, glancing over at Sophie every few seconds. It was around 4:00 a.m. when Sophie's eyes started to give way.

"Stay awake, sweetie, come on." He shook her a few times, trying to keep his eyes on the road. She just couldn't do it, and her body was shutting down.

"Sophie!" he yelled to her, but she had already dozed off. He quickly grabbed her hand and squeezed it, but still nothing.

He watched her, as her eyes started to flinch, as a dream took over her mind once again. Her body jolted and her face became tense.

"Sophie, come on . . . wake up." He felt a quick rush of emotions flood his body. Fear had taken over again.

"Nate," she weakly cried out.

Then, her breaths became shorter and shorter until she couldn't breathe at all. She was gasping for air, as Nate drove the car off the road. He skidded across the grass and slammed on the brakes. He quickly reached over to rip the seatbelt from around her and lifted her up into a sitting position. His hands gripped her face in a panic.

"Breathe, Sophie! Breathe!!" he yelled at her. But she continued to choke.

"Sophie, open your eyes!"

"Whatever it is in there with you, Soph, you have to fight back!" he begged.

He quickly laid her back down and started to pump her chest, and then he leaned in and breathed into her mouth. His guardian powers couldn't help him now. Whatever it was that was taking Sophie from him was in her dreams, and he had been totally blocked from them. He continued to give her mouth-to-mouth, trying to open her airways.

"Please, Soph! Stay with me!" he screamed at her again. He felt himself slowly running out of energy, as he leaned down against her face. His hands were holding her soft, cold cheeks.

"Sophie, please. I need you," he whispered to her with his heart breaking into a million pieces, as he watched the girl he loved fade away. It was silent for what seemed like forever, until he felt her warm breath against his face.

"Nate . . . "

His heart began to race, as he leaned back from her, watching her eyes slowly open. A sigh of relief left his body, as he held her closely.

"Hey, crazy girl," he said, smiling. "You came back."

Her eyes filled with tears and she grabbed him quickly. "I heard you, Nate. I heard you this time. I tried. I tried to fight. I . . . "

"It's okay, you're all right," he said, calming her. She took a few deep breaths, trying to calm herself down, as her hands held tightly to his shirt.

"I fought back, Nate."

"Good girl," he said, not letting her go.

They stayed there on the side of the road, as the sun started to rise in the distance. She needed a moment to herself, so she opened the passenger door and stepped out into the crisp morning air, but Nathan followed close behind. She walked into the wooded area, breathing in the fresh air.

She was proud of herself for fighting back. That girl had come for her again, but this time, she could hear Nate in the distance, fighting to save her life. His strength had come through to her. With every second that he continued to fight for her, she felt strong emotions begin to fill her body.

It made her think. If he was willing to do whatever it took to fight for her and keep her safe, then she'd better do the same. She didn't want every second of her life to be controlled by someone or something that wasn't even there.

Then, she heard her phone go off. She grabbed it out of her pocket to see another text message from Julie. It read:

"I'VE HAD IT. I FINALLY TOOK HER DOWN! NATALIE AND I REALLY GOT INTO IT THIS TIME. SHE JUST WOULDN'T LEAVE. I'M SORRY, SOPH, BUT I'M OUT OF HERE! YOU DEAL WITH HER. I JUST SPENT THE LAST 48 HOURS FIGHTING HER AND LAST NIGHT WAS THE FINAL STRAW!

WE ACTUALLY GOT INTO IT, PHYSICALLY! I BEAT THE CRAP OUT OF HER. MY DAD'S ON HIS WAY DOWN WITH A TRAILER. I'LL BE GONE BY THE TIME YOU GET HERE. I'M SO SORRY, BUT I JUST CAN'T HANDLE HER ANYMORE. WE'LL TALK LATER."

Sophie couldn't believe what she was reading. Was Julie really going to leave her? Why couldn't she just wait 'til she got back? She was so close! She immediately tried phoning Julie to stop her. It rang three times before going to voice mail.

"Julie, come on, don't ditch me," Sophie said, dialing again. Again, it rang three times before going to voice mail. Emotions filled her body again. After everything she'd gone through, why throw another thing at her and now? If there was a God, he was definitely cruel.

She continued to dial Julie's number over and over again. Her fingers began to mess the numbers up and she started to get frustrated. She threw the phone to the ground and screamed.

"Soph," Nate said, walking up behind her. She quickly covered her face, dropped to the ground, and started to cry.

"That's everyone close to me now. Everyone. Even you. Gabriel says he's going to take you away, and then I'll be completely alone, Nate. Do you understand? Completely alone."

It was all rushing into her at that one moment. Her grandmother's death, Julie, and that girl almost killing her—it was all too much. Every time she got a glimpse of happiness, it was instantly taken away by something much worse.

"Why would Julie just leave me? Especially now when she knows what I just went through? I need her to be my friend right now."

Nathan knelt down beside her, watching her cry. "I don't know, Soph, but it was meant to happen."

"I'm sick of this meant to happen crap."

"I know," he said, pulling her to her feet. "Look, I know you don't want to listen to what I have to say right now, but please try. It seems like you're alone, but you're not.

"Yes, you've definitely had more things happen to you than any other normal person, and I know that I've added to that, and I apologize. I truly do. I never meant to make your life any more complicated. Sophie, please believe that.

"But I was drawn to you so much I couldn't help myself. You have the best heart of anyone I've ever met. And it's true, you reminded me of Serena, but it was you and your heart that kept me wanting more. I have this strong urge to be by your side every second of the day and not just as your guardian, but also as your friend.

"As much as you won't admit it, you know deep inside how I feel about you. I'd do anything for you, and I want more than anything to make you happy. Even if you're the last person I watch over, I'm still happy because it's you. You're everything to me, Soph. You're all I need."

She looked at him, as he tucked behind her ear the loose strands of hair that blew in the wind. His words were so full of love and warmed her soul, because he was right and she had to stop resisting it.

"Nate, you're so . . . " she stopped, infatuated and embarrassed by his charming words. "Perfect."

He smiled at her, finding her choice of words amusing as always. "Perfect, eh?"

"I . . . well . . . I mean . . . "

"No, no, perfect is good," he said, hugging her.

"So, now you have to go back and face reality. Things will still be hard, Soph, and you're still going to be really sad at times, but being sad here and there is healthy. You have to feel all the emotions to live a full life. But what's important is that you let yourself feel that for a moment and then pull yourself out of it and move on. You have to keep going, and you have to do what makes you happy. It starts by surrounding yourself with positive people.

"Now, you have to go back to Vancouver, into that empty apartment, and be sad for a moment, and then make a plan to move on. Your life still goes on. Remember, others don't have the same path as you and Julie isn't going to continue in Vancouver as you are. You just have to adjust to change."

"It's so hard doing things on your own though, Nate," she said sadly.

"But you've been doing it all along, Soph. You're surviving just as your grandmother said. She saw you for who you really are and what you can do. You just haven't let yourself see that person yet.

"Look at all the things you've managed to survive, and it's because you're strong. You have the heart of a lion and care more than most people. You have to embrace that, but not let people walk all over you. You're so strong, Soph, and I know you're going to be amazing. I've seen it, and I mean I've really seen it."

She looked at him, finally understanding it all.

"It's a clean slate, Soph, so start now and make your life better. Don't be scared of life."

"Nate, I feel like I haven't been as good of a friend to you as you've been to me. I feel like you're always giving me this strength and I have nothing to give back to you."

"Crazy girl, you've given me the only thing I've ever lacked in life—passion for living and wanting more in life. Serena was just starting to bring that out of me, but it got lost along the way, as I became a guardian. But you've made me feel something again.

"Soph, and I knew it the moment I met you. There was this fire inside of you that sparked me. No one but you could have done that, and I'll always be grateful to you."

"After Serena, it felt cold inside, and even as I helped others improve their lives, my own was so empty to me. I know we can never be together, but this was better than not having you at all. It made me feel like I had a second chance and it was good. So, thank you."

"Now come on, you can do this."

She smiled at him as he took her hand in his and led her back through the woods to the car. The sun was shining brightly now and continued to for the rest of their drive home.

24

Four Seasons of Love

When Sophie arrived back at the apartment, Nate let her go up alone to face her reality. The apartment was bare and no one was home. Julie had taken all her stuff, and it seemed so lonely in there now. She missed her best friend. She took a moment to let it sink in, and then did as Nate had suggested and moved on.

She took her suitcase into her room and started to unpack. Julie had left the last few months' rent on the counter in an envelope. This gave Sophie three months to find a roommate or move out.

Natalie never showed her face again, and she guessed that it was really just an act to fight with Julie. There was no way that Natalie was that concerned for Sophie's feelings. She had unfinished business with Julie which is why she provoked her.

Sophie spent the next few weeks getting back into her acting and filling her time with things to do. Nathan appeared everyday, checking in on her and spending some good quality time, and drinking slushies in the park as they had done before.

She looked forward to their talks and what crazy Asian food he would suggest to buy next. But she always remembered to keep her real life a priority. It was still hard because of the strong feelings she had for him that would never change, but she had accepted what she had with him.

In the second month, her acting had really picked up. She had been called back to her favorite TV show numerous times as a regular and filmed an independent on the side. She had even started to be an extra in music videos, which only made her miss her music more. So, she started going out to karaoke clubs with Charlotte, Irely, and Mark. This filled her musical soul for the moment, until she decided what else to do with it.

She didn't see too much of Adel anymore. She decided that late night calls from Adel to pour her heart out to her was not that much fun when Adel wasn't there in return for her. Friendship was a two-sided street, and she was not going to waste her time anymore on people like her!

As for Kevin and the others, she saw them once in a while at a few parties. Jake had even stopped bugging her and moved on. This was the same for Devon, too. Every once in a while, he would shoot her a text, but she learned to ignore it, and eventually, he got the picture.

Charlotte and Sophie also made weekly trips to the movie theatres to see the latest horror movie, which usually made them horrified to go to bed, so it always involved a sleepover, so no one would have to go home alone. Even Irely found a new love for horror movies—well kind of, as she wasn't sure yet.

Julie never did contact Sophie to explain herself. Sophie tried numerous times to call her to talk about the whole situation. She missed her so much, but she finally gave up and pushed on in life.

One night, Charlotte met with Sophie for a late night treat at the corner ice cream shop. The girls walked down the street, having their normal heart-to-heart talks.

"Hey, Soph?" Charlotte said, licking the drips of ice cream that fell from her cone.

"Ya?"

"So, I've been thinking of moving out of my place and I'm looking for a roommate. Would you be interested in having me as yours?"

Sophie stopped and looked at her with ice cream still around her lips.

"Or not, you don't have to. It was just a suggestion. Please don't throw your ice cream at me," she said, laughing.

"What? No, I mean, yes! Char! That would be amazing!! Yes, you totally can move in!" Sophie said, jumping to hug her.

"Soph! Great. I'm happy, too, but you're getting ice cream on me!"

"Oh, sorry. But get used to it if you wanna live with me. I throw my ice cream all over the place!" she teased.

The girls were through the roof with excitement for moving in together, so much so that Charlotte moved in that weekend. Irely and Elaina came over to help with the move. It was pretty quick and painless, as everything was with her new friends.

On the Saturday night after Charlotte moved in, Sophie was in her room, singing to music on her stereo, as she got ready for a night out at the karaoke club with her friends. Charlotte was still working and was running late. She still had to come home and get ready before going out, but Sophie didn't worry, because Charlotte was always fast.

Suddenly, there was a loud bang at the door! Sophie ran to it and peeked through the hole to see who it was, but a finger covering it blocked it.

"Open up, Soph!" Charlotte yelled.

Sophie wondered why Charlotte didn't just come in with her keys. Maybe she forgot them? She opened the door to Charlotte, standing there with a huge keyboard in her hands.

"Char! What's this?" she said, helping her carry it in.

"It's your new keyboard! Kind of a thank you for letting me move in and for being a great friend."

Sophie stared at it, as emotions flooded her quickly. It reminded her of how much she used to love to play and how much her grandmother loved to listen to her. Gram had never missed any of her piano recitals growing up.

"I don't know what to say," Sophie said, starting to cry.

"You're welcome!" Charlotte smiled, hugging her. "But play with it later. We need to get ready. Go fix your makeup, because your crying has messed it up!" she said, giggling.

Sophie wiped her eyes and followed Charlotte to the bathroom to finish getting ready. The night as usual was fun and drama-free. The karaoke nights were starting to give Sophie more confidence with her possible singing career.

When she went home that night, she pulled out the old piece of paper she had written on a while back about the music contest. Maybe she would enter it if she could get a song together in time. After all, what did she have to lose? She thought about it for a while, looking out the window from her bed.

By the third month, it was coming close to the end of summer. When Sophie wasn't acting or working, she spent the rest of her time playing on the keyboard and writing songs. She had forgotten how much she loved it, and she found herself in the late hours of the night still playing.

Charlotte didn't mind at all. In fact, she encouraged her. She also slept like a brick, so that always helped.

One evening while Charlotte was at work, Sophie sat down to work at the song she had prepared for the music contest. She had gone ahead and entered it without a second thought. The show was booked for the upcoming weekend, and she felt prepared for it. But even if she wasn't, it wouldn't matter, because she would do it, just to say that she did it.

She started playing the soft melody of the song she had written, when she felt a presence behind her. She stopped, as a chill ran up her spine.

"Sounds good, Soph," Nate said quietly.

She spun around to see him sitting behind her. "You scared me! You haven't done that in a while." She laughed.

"Ya, I thought it would be good for old time's sake," he said with a smirk.

"I'm excited to see you perform this weekend."

"You are? So, that means you're coming?" she said happily.

"Of course. I wouldn't miss it for the world. This is what I've been pushing you to do."

"I'm glad you did," she said, smiling. "I feel like things are good, Nate."

"Because they are. And I'm glad to see that even though I can't see into your future anymore, things still turned out the way I expected them to."

"Ya, I guess that's something we'll never get back, because of what we did, huh?"

"But it's okay, because I still feel you, and the emotions I get from you now are all good. Nothing's stopping you now, Soph."

She thought about that for a moment. "I wish Gram was here to see this."

He smiled and then slowly got up and walked over to join her on the keyboard bench.

"She says she's so proud of you."

Sophie's heart sank the second she heard him speak those words.

"You saw her?"

301

He smiled and then took her hand in his. "She says "Thank you" for not giving up. Oh, and something about if you do, she'll be mad at you? She was quite serious about that, and it actually frightened me."

Sophie laughed quietly, as she pictured Gram threatening Nathan.

"Thank you, Nate."

"No prob," he said, getting up from the bench. "I'll see you Saturday, then?"

"Right," she said, watching him disappear.

The weekend came fast and Sophie was prepared for her big show. Well, not really a big show, but an event at least. It was at a local bar, but big enough for her! Posters were up everywhere, displaying the names of the talent performing that night. On the way to the event, Charlotte ripped two down and rolled them up for souvenirs.

"One for you and one for me, for when you're famous!" she said, smiling.

Everyone had turned up for the event. Irely, Elaina, Kevin and his buddies, Mark, and many more from her workplace, even her agent, Audrey. Sophie felt her nerves kick in, as everyone wished her luck.

The place was small, but jam packed to the walls with people. This made things more up close and personal. They watched, as the show opened and many talented artists played their music. Sophie sat there nervously, cracking her knuckles, while waiting impatiently for her turn.

"You shouldn't do that. You'll ruin your joints," Nate said, pulling up a chair beside her.

"Nate! You made it!" She hugged him tightly.

"So, introduce me to your friends." He smiled.

Sophie looked at him happily and turned to her friends, who were already intrigued by his entrance.

"Hey, guys, this is Nate. He's one of my best friends from long ago."

"Hey, Nate! I'm Charlotte," she said, learning over Sophie to shake his hand.

"Ahh, yes, the photographer, right!" he said, smiling back.

Charlotte grinned at the thought of being called "The Photographer."

Suddenly, the host came to center stage to announce the next act.

"All right, let's keep this night going. Please help me welcome our next performer, Sophie Reid."

Charlotte and Irely leaped up, cheering loudly. Sophie stood up, embarrassed by the scene her friends were making and made her way to the stage. It was nice to have everyone there to support her. She sat down at the keyboard and adjusted her mic, taking a deep breath before she began.

Her fingers floated across the keyboard, and the sound filled the room. Everyone's attention was on her. She glanced through the crowd, as she sang the words she had only once thought. Her eyes met Nate's, and suddenly, she wasn't scared anymore. He smiled at her, leaning back in his chair.

This song was something she had written a while back. It had been rewritten many times, as she grew in life. But the one thing that didn't change was whom the song was written about. It was about the boy she had met in her dreams.

As the last note left her voice, she waited, as the crowd took a moment to respond. Nathan immediately started to clap, which then caused a ripple effect. They all loved it. Sophie couldn't believe the reaction she was getting. It was perfect.

At the end of the night, she was content with herself and what she had done. Nathan left just after her last note, but she didn't mind, because friends surrounded her. She didn't end up winning the contest, but she met many people in the industry, and hopefully, some day she would get the chance to make a real record.

Late that night, after celebrating with her friends, she found herself back at home, playing around on the keyboard again. She couldn't help herself. It's all she wanted to do. Charlotte had gone home with Elaina for a sleepover, so she was free to play to her heart's desire. She stumbled over a few notes before finding a new melody to work with. The apartment was quiet and echoed the sound she created.

"Hey, Soph," Nate said, appearing beside her.

"Hey, you," she said softly. "Did you like the show?"

"You were amazing, Soph," he answered quietly. "Can we talk?"

She looked at him funny, surprised by his question. They talked all the time, so what would he need to talk about that he would have to ask her? He held out his hand and waited for her. She suddenly felt nervous, but stood up from the bench and took his hand. He led her into her room and sat her down on the bed.

"I have to go," he said.

"Okay. Well, then, do you want to talk later?" she asked confused.

"No, I mean I have to go. It's time, Soph," he said, smiling at her sadly.

She stared at him, swallowing the lump in her throat that started to rise. She had feared this moment secretly for a long time. "Oh, that kind of go."

"But what if I still need you. I mean, I could . . . anything could happen, Nate. What if . . . "

"No, Soph. You're good. You're so good. You don't need me anymore."

She could feel the tears welling up in her eyes, as she looked at the ground.

"But you're my best friend. I'll always need you."

He closed his eyes, holding back the tears from her words that broke his heart.

"You'll always be my best friend, Soph."

She looked up at him, unable to contain herself. "I'm gonna miss you so much."

"Me, too, crazy girl. Now come here," he said, holding out his arms.

"But what about the rules?"

He shook his head. "The are no rules, anymore. It's over, Soph."

She slowly got up from the bed and wiped her eyes, as she walked over to him. He wrapped his arms around her one last time. Her hands gripped his shirt tightly, as the tears fell down her face.

"I'll miss you, Sophie...." he whispered to her.

She cried harder into his chest from his perfect words. He lifted her head up to face him. She stared into his eyes that now seemed brighter than usual. He smiled at her, brushing a strain of hair from her face.

"Nate, " she said quietly. "If this is it, then kiss me, please."

He looked into her eyes, holding her face gently. Slowly, he leaned in closer until their faces barely touched. She closed her eyes, preparing herself for the moment she had waited for since her very first dream of him. She could feel his warm breath on her face, as his hands ran down her arms to hold her hands. He gently kissed her on the forehead, as his soft lips pressed hard against her skin for what seemed like only a second, and then he was gone.

25

Two Years Later

The little dog howled in excitement, as Sophie grabbed the leash from the banister. She hooked it to his collar and grabbed her purse on the way out the door. She tried desperately to lock the door behind her, as the dog pulled at her.

"I'm hurrying, Bruce, geeze! You're so bossy." She giggled, following him down the steps of her new place. She loved the place so much. It was just the right size for her and her little dog.

They walked down the street with the sun shining brightly upon them. Bruce enjoyed his walks to the grocery store a little too much. Sophie held tightly, as he dragged her down the street. It was very important for her to get out with him when she could. She had become so busy lately, on the set everyday and in the studio at night, recording her new album. But Bruce was the perfect addition to her and the new home she had just purchased.

Bruce was a spur of the moment decision, made one day, as she and Irely walked through the pet store. He was there in a cage, wagging his little tail. His head was almost too big for his body, and the hair on him was uncontrollable! He was exactly how she remembered him from her dreams. And she had learned from experience that her dreams were a sign that shouldn't be ignored.

She had almost forgotten the world she once lived in. Her life had moved on rapidly and she never looked back. The darkness that once surrounded her had broken into clouds with a silver lining, until they were no more. She swore that she would forget the world she once knew, but would never forget about him.

He had changed her life forever and he would always hold a special place in her heart. Sometimes, she found herself at night, trying to create a dream in her mind about Nate, but he never came. She often wondered what life would be like if he were there with her.

She hurried inside the grocery store to grab a few things, while Bruce sat tied to the fence just outside where she could still see him. People were instantly drawn to him and his vibrant personality. Every time Sophie came outside, there were always people petting him, and she would need to steal him away.

On the way home, she stopped one more time to grab a slushie from the store that she and Nate once visited. The taste reminded her of their long talks and the fun they had together. She was never depressed about Nathan, because she was so happy in her life and what he had done for her. If it weren't for him, she would never be where she was right now. For that alone, she would always be happy when she thought of him.

As she turned the corner to her street, Bruce bolted from her hands and ran down the street toward her walkway.

"Bruce! Stop!" she screamed, running after him.

As she reached the steps that led to her front door, she noticed someone crouching down to pet Bruce. His hair hung over his face, as he scrubbed the dog playfully before looking up at her. Sophie froze at the image in front of her, dropping her slushie and grocery bags to the ground. She couldn't believe what she was looking at. Was he really there? She rubbed her eyes in disbelief, as her heart started to race.

""He got big fast, eh?" Nathan said, giving Bruce one more pat on the head before standing up. "Hey, Soph." He smiled at her.

She couldn't speak. Was he really there?

"Sophie? You in there, crazy girl?"

"Nate? Is that really you? I mean, are you really here?"

"Ya, Soph. Funny story. It turns out that if guardian angels follow their heart for the right reasons and never fall astray, they've then truly done all that they could do for the person they're watching. There's also another key to this. Guardian angels must do this as their part, but the other part falls on the one they're guarding," he said, walking down toward her.

"That person must truly understand his or her life for what is was and what it will become, facing all reality and truly accepting it in their heart. Most people are content with whatever they can get. That's why you always hear people say things like, 'Well, I'll just have to learn to deal with it. Or, it will do I guess.' They're just accepting what they got, instead of understanding what they can change. Very few of us end up truly happy in life, but you did, Soph. And because of you, I got another chance."

For the first time in a long time, Sophie's eyes teared up.

"You mean you're really here? For good?"

"I guess you were a better friend to me than you thought, eh?" He smiled at her. She covered her mouth, trying hard to hold in the cry that wanted to come out.

"I'm really here, Soph. For good," he said still waiting for a response from her.

"So, um . . . I was thinking I'd take you up on that offer you said to me long ago, that is if it still stands. Do you remember? You said that maybe I could be the one to make you happy and I wouldn't know until I tried. Or it was something along those lines . . . "

He stepped closer to her, as she trembled nervously at the feel of his touch as a human. His hands gently rubbed the sides of her arms.

"Sophie, I know you're doing great right now, and you have your happiness, but I'd still like that chance to be with you. I know I can make you happy. Let me prove it to you."

Her heart was still racing at the thought of him being there and everything he was saying.

She slowly shook her head, "No."

"Nathan, you have nothing to prove to me. I already know that you make me happy. Of course, I want to be with you. It's all I've ever wanted," she said, running her hands up his chest and around his neck. "I can't believe you're here."

"I know, Soph. I'm so happy," he whispered, pulling her in close against him. Their faces barely touched. "There's one more thing I should have done long ago, and it's been killing me."

"What?" she whispered back.

"This," he said, leaning down and kissing her gently on the lips. He took his time kissing her over and over again. It was exactly how Sophie had pictured it and more if possible.

"Nathan, I . . . "

"I love you, Sophie," he said, cutting her off.

She had waited for so long to hear those words from him, and only now could she say them back with more feeling than ever.

"I love you too, Nathan."

He leaned his head against hers, as Bruce howled behind them.

Nathan was so full of life now, but still the same old Nate who was always there and would always be there from here on out. He smiled at her, kissing her on the forehead one more time. "Looks like you need a new slushie."

"I think I do. Shall we?" She smiled back.

"Wait, one more," he said, pulling her back to kiss her again. Her hands gripped tightly again on his shirt, feeling everything she wanted to feel for so long. He slowly pulled back again, hovering close to her lips. "You might get sick of me wanting to do this all the time," he whispered.

"I don't think I ever will." She smiled back, feeling his heart race against hers.

"Good, because there's so much time we need to make up for. Let's go, Bruce!" Nate yelled, pulling at his leash. Bruce was more than excited to go for another walk. The two of them walked down the street just like they did in her dreams, with Bruce following alongside them happily.

When they reached the corner store, Nathan waited outside with Bruce, as Sophie went in to get the slushies. She grabbed two cups and looked over her selection of flavors before deciding on a mix of cola and berry mix from the order board above the counter.

"Can I help you?" The shop girl said at the counter.

"Cola and berry mix, please," they said in sync. Sophie glanced to the right, as a pretty young girl smiled at her with big sunglasses on. They were almost too big for her face.

"Oh, sorry, go ahead," the girl said politely, stepping back.

"No, you go, it's fine," Sophie insisted happily.

The girl smiled and ordered her cola berry mix. It took the shop girl only a second to blend that up and hand it to her. She took it and placed some change down on the counter. "Thanks, again," she said to Sophie, as she turned to leave.

Sophie noticed a small green bracelet with cherry blossoms on it left on the counter, where the girl had placed her change. After getting her two slushies, she hurried out to see if she could catch that girl, as it had to have been hers.

"Who ya looking for, Soph?" Nate asked, taking a slushie from her hand.

"Did you see a girl come out just now?"

"No, nobody but you, crazy girl," Nate teased.

"Really? She just disappeared? That's weird." She looked at the bracelet in her hand before tucking it in her pocket.

Nathan took a second glance at the bracelet before Sophie shoved it in her pocket. It looked familiar to him. Where had he seen it before? Then, a memory came to him . . . no, it was impossible. But it looked pretty close. He was thinking crazy. Perhaps Sophie's ways were rubbing off on him.

"Ready?" Sophie said, taking Bruce from him.

He shook the thought from his mind and smiled at her confidently. "Ready."

"So, what now?" she asked.

"Well . . . are you looking for a roommate?" He laughed. "I come with literally nothing, so I won't clog up your place. And I cook a mean breakfast."

"Hmm . . . I was really liking having the place to myself, but I guess I could be convinced otherwise in return for some cooking."

"Anything, sweetie," he said, kissing her hand. "I'm just looking forward to waking up next to you for the rest of my life."

She walked closely next to him down the street and wondered if her life could get any better than right now in this very moment. If this was it, it was perfect. She needed nothing more than what she had in front of her right now.

"That's all I need, Nate," she said happily to herself.

The End

Rebecca Carrigan
Author of
All I Need

Rebecca Carrigan was born in Hamilton, Ontario on March 29, 1981. Since she was young, she believed that she was meant for something more in this life. She studied classical piano for eighteen years, played travel baseball, draws, and watches a ridiculous amount of movies. She has worked around the world. You will never catch her without her iPhone on her, as music is the biggest influence in her life.

In 2005, she went to the Vancouver Academy of Dramatic Arts to pursue her acting career and then took voice-over lessons with actor Michael Dobson. Since high school, Rebecca has loved to write. Between her music and writing, her heart's secrets were shared with the world.

The story of *All I Need* has been an eight-year process and something that is very close to Rebecca's heart.

Rebecca writes:

Sometimes, things don't go your way in life and it seems like you'll never make it through. I used to wish for that one person who would come into my life and pull me out of the darkness. What I should have been doing is looking to myself for the answers, because they were always there deep inside. I was just too scared to listen or perhaps believe in them with all the craziness around me.

I had to learn to listen to my heart and not to those around me. Life is a challenge and you never know what cards you will be dealt next. But you can never give up, because even if a million doors close in your face, eventually, one will open and that will be the door that will lead to your heart's desire.

Special Thanks

They say you can count your real friends on one hand, and I believe that's true. We need to remember to treat others as we wish to be treated. Always take a moment in life to look at yourself and your surroundings.

So, with that in mind, I would like to give special thanks to my very dear friend, Sam, for being my partner in crime, even though you're always late! Nothing like a good trip to AE and some Bubble Tea to make the summer fun.

To Jason, for taking me in when I was new to Vancouver. You were the best roommate and I miss our hangouts! And to both of you for helping me finish that "game" that won't be mentioned that took me six years to play! I love you guys!

To my Uncle Cliff, I love you to death for taking interest in everything I do in my life, even though we are so far apart. I enjoy our visits and always wish for more! Thank you for making me believe that I can do anything and that the impossible is possible. xoxo!

To Dana, my friend whom I met years ago at a random concert, you are the best-hearted person I've met. You are a good friend whom I never saw coming and I wish we saw each other more. Thank you for all your help in designing the *All I Need* book cover and official website. You're so talented and deserve nothing but the best from life. I know we'll be friends always!

To Michael Dobson, a great actor and friend, thank you for teaching me and inspiring me as an actor. I remember our talks always. Everything has happened for a reason and I'm glad it did.

Lastly, I would like to thank the cast of *All I Need* —*The Independent Film*, coming soon. Look for it! Thank you for being the wonderful people you are and for believing in my book. You truly bring my characters to life and I love you all!

I hope everyone enjoys this story and wants more in life after reading it. —Rebecca Carrigan, Author of *All I Need*

To Order This Book

To order additional copies of this book, please:

E-mail: allineednovel@hotmail.com

Or go to: http://www.allineednovel.com

This book may also be ordered from 30,000
wholesalers, retailers, and booksellers in
the U. S., and in Canada and over
100 countries globally.

To contact Rebecca Carrigan
for an interview or a
speaking engagement, please:
E-mail: allineednovel@hotmail.com

CPSIA information can be obtained at www.ICGtesting.com
Printed in the USA
LVOW031948050112

262597LV00004B/4/P

9 780987 813206